Sons of Cain

CHRISTY KENNEALLY

HACHETTE
BOOKS
IRELAND

First published in 2013 by Hachette Books Ireland
First published in paperback in 2013 by Hachette Books Ireland

A CIP catalogue record for this title is available from the British Library

ISBN 978 1444 726 367

Typeset in Bembo by Bookends Publishing Services.
Printed and bound by CPI Group (UK) Ltd, Croydon, CR0 4YY.

Hachette Books Ireland policy is to use papers that are natural, renewable
and recyclable products and made from wood grown in sustainable forests.
The logging and manufacturing processes are expected to conform to the
environmental regulations of the country of origin.

Hachette Books Ireland
8 Castlecourt Centre
Castleknock
Dublin 15
Ireland

A division of Hachette UK Ltd.
338 Euston Road
London NW1 3BH

www.hachette.ie

Praise for Christy Kenneally

'With sparkling dialogue, deft characterisations and vivid sense of place Kenneally has the reader in the palm of his hand as the action speeds from continent to continent' *Irish Independent*

'A masterful debut' *Irish Times*

'Kenneally is a delight to read. Witty, dexterous, accessible, his prose elevates this novel from workaday thrillers' *Ireland on Sunday*

'An absolute pleasure to read' *Irish Examiner*

'A real page-turner' *Woman's Way*

'He manages to combine a fast-paced thriller with a gentle and affectionate portrait of a beautiful but remote and isolated community … It's a bit like reading Robert Ludlum crossed with John Millington Synge' *Irish Independent*

Christy Kenneally is a well-known Irish personality and author. He lives with his family in County Wicklow.

Also by Christy Kenneally and published by Hachette Books Ireland

Fiction
The Betrayed
Second Son
The Remnant
Tears of God

Non-fiction
Say Yes to Life: Discover Your Pathways to Happiness and Well-Being
(with Dr Linda Finnegan)

For Linda, Stephen and Shane

Acknowledgements

I would like to thank Breda Purdue and Ciara Doorley of Hachette Ireland for their continued support. I would also like to thank my literary agent Jonathan Williams.

Special thanks and love to my family, Linda, Stephen and Shane who keep me grounded in all matters.

HALLSTATT, AUSTRIA

Chalk-dust avalanched from the blackboard and Karl Hamner tried not to sneeze. His pupils, ranged in the desks behind him, chorused a perfunctory, 'Gesundheit.' They could be excruciatingly polite he thought and shook his head at his own prejudice. But they were different to the boys and girls who had sat with him in this very classroom when he had been a child among children who had answered politely and dreamed quietly. It wasn't that the present crop was disrespectful. They had survived a war – and that experience had tightened them, inside and out. Also, he concluded as he turned to face them, their eyes were different. They had seen too much of reality to dream, lost too much to be eager for connection. *Was this what Simon Tauber, our schoolmaster, had seen when he'd looked at us?* he wondered. *No. War, for us, was something that happened outside Hallstatt. Here in the bowl of the Dachstein Mountains, the Hallstätter See had been an innocent blue. Cradled by the massif and soothed by the lake, we'd dreamed.*

His recurring dream had been to inherit the chalk and the life of the schoolmaster. Elsa had dreamed of the University of Vienna and returning home to Hallstatt and ... He felt the old pain seep into his chest and looked for distraction among their faces. His eyes rested on Lisl and saw Elsa. The girl had the same hair, always one brush away from tidy, the same concentrated expression, even a similar well-worn book-bag, flopped like a sleeping dog at her feet. The pain in his chest intensified and he swept his gaze among the boys, looking for a match for Max, hoping to cauterise his anguish with anger. He sighed with relief. No Max. No boy dressed better than his peers, reflecting his mother's sense of superiority. He remembered how Max's mother had dominated her policeman husband and seen her son as the centre of the universe. Frau Steiger was dead now. It had taken the neighbours a week to discover her body, hunched over the kitchen table, the glass she'd used to mix the poison washed and dried and winking innocently among its fellows in the dresser. His eyes swept further along the line of boys, bent over their texts. No Max, to curl his lip at Simon Tauber's enthusiasm for learning or at his companions' zest for play; aping his father, the policeman, who'd hid his inadequacy behind his uniform – until the Russian Front had whittled him to the bone and he'd stood on blackened feet in the snow and confessed to the terrible thing his son had done in the mine above Hallstatt. Karl could see him now, his tears freezing on his lashes as he'd wept and screamed, the truth steaming from his cracked lips as if his insides were consumed by acid. He remembered him holding out a silver cross and chain, as a votive offering for forgiveness of a son's evil and a father's guilt.

And what a tsunami of evil that act had unleashed on the innocent. His own father Rudi had died in a snow-hole to delay the Cossack horsemen so that Tomas, their neighbour, could carry Karl to safety. Tomas, the miner, cut down by gunfire as he'd tumbled Karl on the last plane to escape the Red Army. And Herr Steiger himself, Max's father, sitting at the side of the road with the dull-eyed soldiers who had lost any reason to go on. That's what had winnowed the living from the dead, during those dreadful days, he concluded – a reason to go on. He had been his father's reason and Tomas the miner's reason. And his mother had become his reason to come back from the hospital, in his captain's uniform, with one hand, gnarled by frostbite, camouflaged in his father's Wehrmacht glove.

When his mother had died, only his sense of duty had brought him back to the war but, this time, in Rome as a captain in the German army. There had been a brief interlude of … what? Hope?

No – purpose. When he had helped to salvage a Jewish family from the SS during the *razzia* and, later, when he'd been entrusted with bringing that story to the Vatican. He'd crossed the line into the Vatican State, compelled by a cause greater than his duty, and branded himself a deserter. It hadn't saved over a thousand Roman Jews – the train had still rolled from Tiburtina Station to Auschwitz – and it hadn't saved him from Max. Max, in his madness, had dragged him into the cellars beneath Santa Maria della Concezione and, against a macabre backdrop of skeletons displayed for the edification of sinners, had offered him a share of his world. Elsa's killing, in the mine above Hallstatt, had been nothing to Max against his dream of his new religious order, the Fratres, who would evangelise and inherit the earth. When Karl had refused that poisoned chalice, Max had bartered his own safety against the silence of Cardinal Tisserant, and the Fratres had been recognised by Pope Pius XII. Afterwards, Karl found an oasis of normality in the International Capuchin College, adopting a dead man's name and identity to shield him from the Waffen-SS. For a brief period, there had been the sweet security of books, the measured round of lectures and study, while the city and the world beyond convulsed in the death throes of the war.

After the armistice, he'd put on his great coat, pinned his Operation Barbarossa medal to his lapel and begun the long trek home to Hallstatt. The Russians, at the checkpoints, had mocked his medal and, euphoric on victory and vodka, had shoved him on to the French, British and American checkpoints until, eventually, he'd found himself at the pier on the far side of the lake from Hallstatt, waiting for the ferry. Sitting on the warm timbers at the end of the dock, he'd looked into the lake and seen a stranger looking back. It wasn't the beard and the shaggy hair. It was the eyes and the absence in them. He had survived when millions had not, and he felt nothing. He was as the water, mountain and sky around him were – elemental and unfeeling. *Is this how Simon Tauber had felt?* he wondered. *Did the death of his wife and a policeman's questions* about his conversion from Judaism bleed him of the will to live until one day even the love of his students and his love for them wasn't enough to tether him to life? Was that why he put on his suit and closed the door and walked through the sleeping streets of Hallstatt to the lake and weighed his pockets with stones and—

'Herr Hamner!'

The voice brought him back to the tickle of chalk-dust; the peculiar tang of ink and the rows of faces. 'Yes, El— Lisl?'

'The question, sir, it isn't complete.'

He turned to the blackboard and read what he had chalked there. 'Russia was Napoleon's …'

'Bête noire,' he added.

'What does "bête noire" mean, sir?' Jurgen asked.

'Black beast,' he answered. Then added, 'A bugbear, something or someone who will not let you rest.'

The Fratres Schloss, Switzerland

His suite of rooms was on the top floor of the Schloss, as befitted the founder and Father General of the Fratres. An ornate desk was placed strategically before the floor-to-ceiling windows set in the western wall so that important guests at his morning audiences would be impressed by the mountain vista behind him. Supplicants and those due chastisement were scheduled for the evening and forced to endure the harsh glare of the dying sun. The view was pixelated, now, with a million flakes of snow, so that the window reflected the room and its sole occupant; who stood close to the glass, seemingly absorbed in the whitened world. An observer might have been struck by the simplicity of his robe or by his tall, thin frame and shock of raven-black hair. An observer might have wondered at the pallor of his face and the twin scars, furrowing from the edge of his left eye to the corner of his bloodless mouth. But no observer would ever get that close to Max Steiger unless he wished them to do so, in which case he would ensure they saw what he wanted them to see. He didn't want anyone to observe him now and the icy anger that shook his frame. Yet another reply had come from the Vatican, another embossed and wax-sealed letter containing careful Latin phrases that translated into … nothing.

'The Holy See wishes to acknowledge the correspondence received from Father Max Steiger. It will convey the contents to the appropriate authority.'

It was a facsimile of the reply that had come to his previous letter, and to the one before that, and to all the others he had sent. It was almost a decade since the pope had granted papal recognition of the Fratres. *A qualified recognition*, he remembered bitterly. Thanks to that meddlesome Cardinal Tisserant, the Fratres had to be chaperoned by Cardinal Maglione, who had been the powerful Secretary of State, and they would have to prove themselves worthy of full acceptance by the Roman Catholic Church. He placed his palms against the window and welcomed the cold sting, willing it up his arms and through his body to his brain. What more proof could he provide? He had multiplied his first band of followers with hundreds of young men and women soured by war and searching for meaning and purpose in a broken world. Priests and monks had flocked to him from the major religious orders, disaffected by their irrelevance during the war and their torpor in its wake. Who else offered them a vision of a new Europe – a Europe re-evangelised and influenced by the Church as had never been seen since Constantine recognised Christianity and unleashed it on his empire? He pushed away from the window to pace the room. The Fratres, he fumed, were already rich in resources and equipped for the campaign. He had almost twenty million dollars lodged in the Vatican Bank. There were cardinals and other high-ranking clerics in the Vatican and elsewhere who were sympathetic to their cause. An army of Fratres had already infiltrated some of the most prestigious educational institutions in Europe and stood ready to extend that influence into the sphere of politics. Europe hung within touching distance of their fingertips, and Rome …? His pacing brought him back to the desk and he crushed the letter in his frustration.

It was 1953 and though Maglione had been dead these seven years, he hadn't been replaced by a Secretary of State or by a new mentor to the Fratres. Pius XII, Eugenio Pacelli, had absorbed the power of that office into his own august personage and had become – purposeless; circling in an ever-narrowing gyre of paranoia, seeing enemies everywhere within the Church. If Pacelli wanted to cleanse the Church of deviants and dissenters, what better than to have the Fratres as inquisitors? If he wanted to build on his wartime reputation for moral probity and spiritual leadership, the Fratres, with their special vow of obedience to the pope, were ready to proclaim him. Instead, Pacelli had become a recluse in the Vatican while the great powers had divided the world without him. Perhaps Stalin was right, Max mused, when he'd asked sarcastically at Yalta, 'How many divisions has the pope?' He, Max Steiger, could have answered him. 'The pope has millions under his direct command and religious shock-troops who would willingly give their lives to a new crusade.' But Pius had proved to be a wartime pope, who found peace too problematic, and he had retrenched rather than advanced. 'The centre cannot hold,' he'd muttered, quoting an Irish poet. Enthusiasm, Max knew, was a jolt of adrenaline that leached away quickly. On the cusp of the first millennium, the religious houses of Europe had been inundated with vocations, people terrified before the impending Armageddon. It hadn't happened. When 1 January 1000 had dawned and the Horsemen of the Apocalypse failed to appear, the trickle of defections had begun. We need someone to break the log-jam, Max fumed, someone like Archimedes with a lever and a firm place to stand to move the world.

He slumped at the desk and a second letter caught his eye. The New York cardinal, Francis Spellman, had invited Father Max Steiger of the Fratres to address guests at an important function in New York City. Another time, he might have laughed at the little man's hubris. Spellman was a cleric who had toured the front so many times during the war that a general had greeted him with, 'We'd never know we were in a war unless you showed up.' He'd blessed the troops and blessed the guns and advised Eisenhower to 'go the whole hog' after Berlin.

Max Steiger lifted the letter from the desk and read it again. The second reading didn't improve the quality of the prose or his opinion of the bumptious Spellman, but he held it in his hand long after he'd finished reading. The world had divided into East and West. He knew from his sources that it was only a matter of time until everything east of Berlin would secede from Europe and become *terra incognita*, an unknown country, to the Church. Europe was already beholden to America for Marshall Aid and military protection, but the Western giant was tiring of its 'poor relations' and was leaning back to isolationism. 'If you cannot change the kingdom, change the king,' Max whispered, quoting the old Indian proverb. If the Fratres could ride the coat-tails of the American giant before it was too late, then … He snatched a pen from the desk and slid a fresh page to the blotter.

THE CEMETERY, HALLSTATT, AUSTRIA

Winter leaves reluctantly this year, he thought. Snow still crusted the angles of the graves, as if the wan sunlight was a housemaid who dusted indifferently. Even the surface of the lake was as opaque as a dusty mirror. His eyes climbed the surrounding peaks, still slumbering under snow, and dropped to the village that hugged the lakeshore. People moved slowly between the houses, awkward beneath their winter clothing.

His parents' grave was as tidy as only an Austrian grave could be; a rectangle, curbed with local stone. The headstone was understated. There was no gothic cross superimposed on the stone, like the others that crowded the cemetery. There were no cameo photographs of the dead; the kind that studded the other monuments, pictures of young men in military uniform fading behind crazed glass. There was no inscription that included 'der Reich' or 'der Vaterland'. Karl placed a small bunch of blue flowers on the meagre grass and straightened. 'Rest in peace, Mama,' he said quietly. 'You too, Papa,' he added, even though his father didn't lie there.

He had left his father lying in a snow-hole during the retreat from Moscow. Death had already marked Rudi Hamner's hands and face with frostbite and he'd chosen to make a stand against the pursuing Cossacks to buy time, so that his son could return to Hallstatt. Karl had dreamed of that return almost every night on the long march with the Fourth Army. While his comrades had talked of Moscow and glory and had plodded along with purpose, his thoughts and dreams had been strong counter-currents, tugging his heart towards home. When the great wave of Hitler's army had broken within sight of the Russian capital and retreated, those who'd survived had retraced their steps across the white wilderness.

Who could have thought that hell would be so cold? he mused and, instinctively, put his left hand in his coat pocket. His hand throbbed even in the warmth of the much-mended Wehrmacht glove. 'Summer issue,' he muttered and felt the old bitterness rise like bile in his throat. He turned abruptly and walked towards the gates of the cemetery, his thoughts punctuated by the crunch of gravel under his boots. They had worn summer uniforms, gloves and shoes because the generals had insisted that it would all be over in a few weeks. Even when the rain had come and mud had sucked the Panzers to a standstill. Even when the snow had come and frozen the oil in the lorries and the carbines and the big guns, and had frozen the coffee soldiers carried in their canteens. Even when men had become disoriented in the white wilderness and frozen to death or huddled forty to a hut to share a little warmth and a plague of lice. Even— He stopped on the path and took a deep, ragged breath. *Almost a decade has passed,* he reminded himself. *The war is over. The boundaries of Europe have been redrawn. Many cities* and towns have been rebuilt; even the land itself has healed over with a new skin of fields. He wondered if the pain he felt would last forever. Other men from Hallstatt had fought on various fronts. Many of those who had survived seemed to adjust to post-war life with gusto, as if they'd woken up from some horrific dream, taken a deep breath of relief and gone on with a normal life. Some told war stories in Gert's bar or compared wounds and souvenirs. Some even laughed and slapped each other on the shoulder in recognition of their camaraderie. But Karl Hamner could not remember the last time he'd laughed.

THE VATICAN, ROME

'The zucchetto! Where is the abominable thing? I had it in my hand a—'

'It's on my head, Emil.'

'Oh!'

Emil Dupont, secretary to Cardinal Tisserant, dusted the prelate's shoulders with his palm.

'Ribbons for my beard?' Tisserant suggested slyly.

'No, you look suitably Mosaic, very Old Testament. Now remember, Eugène, no shouting.'

'I do not sh—'

'I rest my case. Let me look at you. *Très bon*. This is the first meeting Pius has called in – oh, I can't remember how long.'

He centred the pectoral cross on the prelate's chest.

'For God's sake, E—'

'Silence?'

'Wha—'

'Allow a silence before you speak. It focuses the attention of the others and adds gravitas to what you say.'

'Gravitas,' Tisserant grumbled. 'A Latin word meaning heavy, an apt description of the Vatican since the war. It's like wading through mud.'

'Sarcastic!'

'I was simply say—'

'No, no. At the meeting, don't be sarcastic. Sarcasm is the sign of a small mind, Eugène. It will only make you enemies.'

Cardinal Tisserant stared until Emil stopped his fussing and caught his eye.

'Have it your own way,' the secretary smiled, 'more enemies.'

THE FRATRES SCHLOSS, SWITZERLAND

The snow had stopped falling and the white peaks flared behind him as he read and re-read his letter of acceptance to Cardinal Spellman's invitation.

The style and content of the prelate's letter smacked of someone accustomed to communicating with Vatican departments. The opening paragraph groaned under the weight of flowery greetings and fraternal good wishes. The actual request was nestled in the second paragraph, sandwiched between praise for 'your immense contribution to Mother Church' and apologies for 'adding the weight of our humble request to Father General's already onerous workload'.

The 'sweetener', as Max Steiger identified it, beckoned from the third paragraph. 'The function will be attended by illustrious Catholic laymen from the highest echelons of commerce and politics.' 'Money and power,' he murmured.

The final paragraph was a literary version of a Great Amen sung by the Sistine Choir. A single sentiment, swooping and looping through slightly different versions of itself until it built to a crescendo 'In Christ Jesus, Our Lord' and collapsed into a sprawling signature.

He put the letter aside and blew out a pent-up breath. Perhaps Churchill was wrong when he wrote that Britain and the United States were divided by a common language, Max thought. That may be true of the language of the 'governed' but Spellman's letter was a template of the lingua franca used by the powerful, it could be read and interpreted with ease by the denizens of the Court of Saint

James and the White House.

'Enter,' he called, in response to an almost imperceptible knock.

His secretary eased inside the door and closed it noiselessly behind him. He bowed to Father General and then seemed to just hang there. Max Steiger remembered that Brother Cyprian had joined the Fratres from one of those pallid little religious communities one sometimes encountered in Switzerland. They seemed content to keep bees and minister to a largely contented congregation of villagers and alpine farmers. He wondered if they'd noticed Brother Cyprian's defection from their ranks, the man was so self-effacing as to be almost invisible. He might have refused his services except that Brother Cyprian had also been a confidant to the lady of the local Schloss, a widowed and extremely wealthy dowager who had been influenced by Brother Cyprian to bequeath the Schloss to the Fratres. He understood she had another outside Bern and one near Lausanne. Before she is called to her eternal reward, she might decide to thwart her heirs in favour of the Fratres. He was careful to allow Brother Cyprian the opportunity to minister to the good lady. The monk was also the perfect secretary, devoted to detail and singularly without ideas or opinions. Max Steiger peeled his reply to Spellman from the blotter and floated it into the out tray. Slowly, he took another document from the pile and began to read. He liked to keep people waiting, it could be instructive. His father – stepfather – had been a policeman in the Austrian village of Hallstatt. He remembered him boasting of how he'd make an appointment to interview some local suspect and then turn up three hours late. 'Imagine the tension,' his stepfather would enthuse. 'By the time I show up he's admitting everything and shopping everyone else.'

His previous secretary had confessed to a minor infringement of the rules after just ten minutes of silence; which was why he was the 'previous secretary'. He suspected Cyprian had more of the glacier in him and could outwait God.

'Yes?' he asked, without looking up from his work.

'A Sister Rosa is waiting to see you again, Father General.'

Max signed a document and capped his pen with an audible click, just to see if the Brother would blink. He didn't.

He swivelled his chair so that the secretary wouldn't see his face as he parsed that message. 'A Sister Rosa' is so deliciously Swiss, he mused, so wonderfully detached. 'Again' was something to consider. Did it suggest impatience or annoyance on the part of his secretary? No, he concluded, it was simply Cyprian at his informational best. A person has been here before and is here again.

'And you said?'

'You are busy.'

'And she said?'

'She will wait.'

And she would wait, he had no doubt about that. The girl was too naïve to see things for what they were. It had been no more than a sudden urge that needed to be satisfied. He didn't regard their coupling as a 'liaison' or an 'encounter' – both words implied a relationship of sorts, and there'd been none and never would be. She had been a *remedium concupiscentiae*, a 'remedy for lust', as a former professor of his had defined marriage. He had not forced her, although he could have done and had done with others. She had been obviously infatuated and, although initially resisting him, had responded with passion. And that was an emotion he could never tolerate in any sexual encounter. Rejection, submission, even defiance were all acceptable – but not passion. Passion implied intimacy and that was what was bringing her back when she hadn't been sent for.

'You will inform the Mistress of Novices that I do not wish to see this novice again and I rely on her to ensure it.'

'Yes, Father General.'

'See that this letter goes in the evening post. I will be travelling to New York in the United States on the twenty-second of this month. Make the necessary travel arrangements. Brother Cyprian—' He looked away and counted to twenty before turning back to his secretary, 'that will be all.'

For a moment, he thought he'd caught a spark of defiance in his secretary's eyes and it cheered him.

THE VATICAN, ROME

Cardinal Eugène Tisserant bustled along in the latticed shadows of the great columns that curved from the basilica to embrace St Peter's Square. He remembered the fascist trucks that had hovered like ravens on the Via della Conciliazione, just beyond the white line that marked the Vatican State. As the war had moved to its close, they'd been replaced by grey troop-carriers, ugly with swastikas. 'Fascist or Nazi, they never crossed the line,' he muttered with satisfaction. Except, he reminded himself, Captain Karl Hamner who came to tell me of the *razzia*. Even now, the memory of that terrible night when the Waffen-SS had trucked over a thousand Jews from their quarter in Trastevere via the Collegio Militare to the railway station at Tiburtina and to Auschwitz. He stood, head bowed, and placed his palm against a pillar for support. *Whoever said that time heals all wounds was a fool*, he thought bitterly. *Some wounds should never be allowed to heal so that we will be reminded of our failures forever.*

He entered by the bronze door and began to climb the Scala Regia, puffing with exertion. *And where is Captain Karl Hamner now?* he wondered, and then prayed that Karl had found some peace. At the first landing, he stopped and raised his skull cap to wipe the top of his head. *They're adding steps to this damn stairs.* By the time he reached the top landing, he was wheezing. The Swiss Guard on duty at a small table moved to help him. 'Eminence?' the guard enquired anxiously. *God, he's so young*, Tisserant thought as he fought to control his breathing. Finally, he managed to straighten, square his shoulders and fix the guard with an imperious eye.

'It's the Visigoths,' he informed the startled guard. 'Hold them off until I return.'

KARL'S HOUSE, HALLSTATT

He had a visitor. The little house looked exactly as he had left it but—

War teaches men to differentiate between what seems and what is. Or maybe it reverses evolution and we rely on more feral instincts. And there is someone in the world who does not wish me well.

'It's me. Johann,' a voice yelled from inside and Karl replaced the cord of timber in the neat pile. 'Saw you coming from the window,' Johann added as Karl pushed through the door. 'If you're expecting trouble,' he said, fingering two glasses from the shelf, 'you should prepare for it.'

Karl sat on the other side of the table and accepted a glass of his own schnapps. They toasted and drank. Johann bobbed and weaved on the stool as if he was still riding the lake. Karl wondered if the one-armed ferryman ever got used to the stability of dry land. He waited. Something in the other man's expression suggested this wasn't a courtesy call. Silence had never been one of Johann's strengths.

'If you ask me, I'll tell you,' he blurted.

'Ask you what?'

'If you're stupid enough to ask that question then you're too stupid to understand the answer.'

Karl felt a throbbing in his temples and massaged them with his fingertips. Schnapps at midday was never a good idea – in retrospect. He'd have to do it the hard way.

'I'm asking.'

Given his opening, Johann seemed uncertain how to begin. Karl saw him measure his empty glass against the bottle and shake his head. He steeled himself.

'Look, boy,' Johann said, gruffly, 'no one comes back from a war – well, not the same anyway.'

'Someone told me that a long time ago.'

'You should have listened to him.'

'Her.'

'Then you should have listened bloody harder. Women know about that kind of thing.'

Johann nodded at his own insight before continuing.

'Marta set me straight, after the first war. "You say you left your arm in Verdun," she says to me one evening. "That's right," I says, wondering where the hell this was going. "Go back for it," she says. "You know I can't do that, Marta," I says. "I know that, Johann," she says, "but do you? You act like you lost yourself over there. It was just an arm, Johann," she says, and she's crying. "I – we need the rest of you." "How do I do that, Marta," I ask her? And I mean it. She blows her nose and I know she has it all worked out. "I can look after the girls," she says, "but you've got a son that needs a father. Erich is how God made him," she says, "and maybe God hadn't much to work with. I don't understand things like that. But Erich rows that ferry boat better than any man in Hallstatt – better than you did when you had two arms." It's the truth. I was a carpenter before Verdun, better in the boat now with one arm than I ever was with two. Not better than Erich, mind. "Go in the boat with him," she says. "I'll be no damned good to him with one arm," I says. "Erich doesn't need a one-armed man to spell him at the oars," she says, "he needs to have his father in the boat."

So, I went in the boat. Wasn't easy, oh no. Sometimes, I can get a bit het up – get a bit short with Erich, sometimes. Doesn't bother Erich. He just smiles and rows. And when we beach her in the evening, he takes my hand, like a little boy, and we walk home together.'

His voice had been creaking for a while and now strengthened suddenly as he leaned across the table. 'I never told that to nobody,' he said.

'Why are you telling me, Johann?'

'Because – because you're Rudi's boy, dammit. Rudi didn't come back but you did, Karl. You came back with a piece of you missing and you'll lose what's left of you if you don't get into some damn boat.'

He took a deep breath and looked longingly at the bottle. Karl took pity on his irascible neighbour and poured a generous measure for both of them.

'I've seen them,' Johann said quietly, 'and you've seen them. Men like you and me. Men who came back and never left where they'd been. At the start it's all "welcome home" and hugs and kisses. Then, the house gets too small and the kids are too noisy. So, they go to the bar and the beer lets them say the things they can't say at home. Nobody listens, Karl. Not after the first time. They go walking, trying to stay one step ahead of the nightmares – walking and walking because if they stop, all that shit they saw comes up behind them like a wave.'

Another long sip warned Karl that there was more to come. Johann's voice sank to little more than a whisper.

'I've cut them down in the forest and barns, Karl,' he said. 'Maybe five since the war ended. You remember Dietrich?'

Karl nodded.

'Bastard brought his gun back – as a souvenir.' He spat out all three syllables of the word like bitter tobacco shreds. 'Cleaned and oiled the fucking thing every day. Then, one day, blew his brains out.'

'I don't have a gun.'

It was the wrong thing to say. He meant it to sound reassuring but it came out sounding callow and smart-arsed, even to his own ears, and it fired Johann like a match to touch-paper.

'Plenty of stones in Hallstatt,' he roared. 'Put them in your pocket like Tauber, and walk into the fucking lake.'

He waited until Johann's breathing had calmed.

'Sorry, Johann,' he said, 'I didn't mean to—'

'Forget it,' the older man snapped, rising abruptly. 'Mail train's due. Erich will be waiting. Oh,' he said, at the door, 'Frau Bertha asked me to give you this.'

He dropped a small, blue envelope on the table. Karl caught

Johann's calloused hand in his own and held it. Johann matched his grip and then left.

As he opened the envelope, Karl wondered if this was the only message Bertha had asked Johann to deliver and if Johann knew how lucky he was to have someone waiting for him.

'News,' the note read, 'come to dinner.'

THE PAPAL ANTECHAMBER, THE VATICAN

'You work too hard, Father Leiber.'

The pope's secretary started and a sheaf of papers seesawed to the floor. He began to scrabble after them, breathing heavily.

'Sit,' Tisserant barked and the sweating Jesuit slumped obediently in his chair. The cardinal bent and began to retrieve the truant documents.

'Eminence, you must not,' Leiber wheezed, struggling to rise.

'I believe I must,' Tisserant said firmly. 'And you must find someone to ease your burden, Robert,' he added, more gently. The use of his first name by the great Cardinal Tisserant wasn't lost on Robert Leiber, and he looked like he might cry. Instead, he leaned back in his chair and mopped his forehead with an enormous white handkerchief.

'So kind,' he gasped. 'Since Kaas died … just me. Busy … so busy. Lecture Angelicum … buses … three.'

Tisserant realised the man was speaking in staccato bursts in an effort to regulate his breathing and felt a mixture of pity and shame. Pity, because Father Leiber was not a young man and, despite his chronic asthma, was required to use public transport to get from his teaching job in the seminary to the Vatican – the pope considered taxis for his secretary a needless expense. He felt an equal stab of shame. The late Monsignor Kaas and the wheezing Father Leiber had never merited more than a glare from the powerful cardinal. Well, he countered, they had been Pius' secretaries all through the war and had raised obsequiousness to an art form, always falling on their knees and getting underfoot. 'Obsequious' meant 'compliant', Tisserant the linguist reminded himself and the Vatican reeked of compliance. Still, his better nature asserted, Leiber did his best, according to his lights, and a prince of the Church shouldn't harbour petty grudges.

'Why don't you let Montini handle the meeting?' he suggested, putting the papers on Leiber's desk.

The secretary rolled his eyes.

'Now, now, Father,' Tisserant chided gently. 'Montini is a young man and the young need experience. And the pope needs a healthy secretary.'

Father Leiber looked at him suspiciously, and Tisserant wondered if his unction had been a trifle extreme. Unexpectedly, the secretary flapped a hand in surrender.

'The others will be here shortly,' Tisserant continued smoothly. 'Why don't you retire for coffee? No, don't worry,' he added quickly, when Leiber looked as if he might resist, 'at the stroke of eight, I will see to it that Montini knocks and ushers us inside.'

'Thank you, Eminence,' the secretary managed to say before he levered himself from the chair and tottered away.

'Forgive me my mixed motives, O Lord,' Tisserant whispered as he leafed through the papers on the secretary's desk.

'Shall I call the Swiss Guard?'

Tisserant started and the papers encored their recent flight. 'Damn it, Domenico,' he growled. 'I thought Leiber had caught me red-handed.'

'He wouldn't have dared,' Father Domenico Tardini laughed as he bent to help. 'Everyone knows Your Eminence is "red in tooth and claw". It's a quality that seems to come with the red hat.'

'Your day for the red hat will come too,' Tisserant growled. 'Why do you keep refusing?'

'Misery loves company, eh?' Tardini teased. 'Why do I refuse? It must be the Augustine in me, Eminence. Every time the pope asks to make me a cardinal, I say yes, but not yet.'

'Why does he accept your refusal? No one says no to Pius.'

'I pray it's because he thinks I'm humble. Also, I think he gets an odd pleasure out of meeting someone who says no. Humility is served either way.'

'And the real reason?'

'Oh, Eminence, I have my orphans to look after in the Villa Nazareth. And, as one half of the Secretary of State – happily the external part – I pop in and out of the Vatican whenever I please. Imagine being here all the time. What would become of me?'

'I'm here all the time,' Tisserant objected.

'Exactly,' Tardini said and smiled beatifically.

Tisserant fidgeted with his skull cap and checked his watch.

'Isn't Pizzardo coming?' he asked.

'He's probably polishing the instruments of torture in the Holy Office,' Tardini said grimly. '*Pace*, Eminence,' he continued, when Tisserant glared. 'He'll come. Who would miss such an unusual event?'

They were interrupted by the arrival of Montini, the other half of the Secretariat of State – the internal half. Another one who looks like a child, Tisserant thought. He'd remarked to Emil once that Montini looked like an altar boy who'd been plucked from his peers and ordered to sing a High Mass. Emil had replied that Montini had the permanently anxious face of the eldest child in a large family. Montini's thin shoulders sagged with relief when he saw them and then resumed their normal elevation as a hint of panic tightened his boy-face.

'Cardinal Pizzardo?' he whispered.

'Here,' a voice boomed at his shoulder and Montini jumped.

Tisserant thought that whenever he saw Montini and Pizzardo together, it was like seeing a very timid rabbit in the presence of a very large dog. He'd shared that insight with Emil, who'd sniffed, 'One shouldn't compare Cardinal Pizzardo to a blessed animal.'

Pizzardo hugged Montini with one huge arm and nodded perfunctorily to Tardini. 'Father Tardini.'

The greeting was an unsubtle statement of the gulf that existed between the prince and the priest. He released the dishevelled, but not displeased, Montini and bowed formally to his brother cardinal. Tisserant schooled his features to conceal his visceral dislike of the man. He inclined his head fractionally, and locked stares with this modern Torquemada. Pizzardo, he knew, was a son of Davona, a centre for the iron industry. He wondered if some of the iron had seeped into the soul of the man, he was so reluctant to bend. *Here we are*, he mused sadly, *like two gladiators measuring each other before the arena*. At least the original gladiators stood toe to toe and stabbed each other in the front. Pizzardo, he knew, preferred to use the net and trident, tripping and then pricking from afar. *Old men like us should be playing dominos under an olive tree*.

'It is time,' Montini whispered.

Tisserant nodded at the man he considered to be his opponent. Let the games begin, he thought. He saw Tardini step aside in deference to Pizzardo.

'Still playing the humble priest?' he whispered as they paired to enter.

'Would you have Pizzardo at your back?'

Montini has, Tisserant thought but didn't say.

KURT AND BERTHA'S HOME, HALLSTATT

He felt guilty he hadn't visited more often. It had been Kurt who'd lured him back to the classroom after they'd finished General von Kluge's memoirs. It had been a long wooing, spiced with schnapps. Kurt's irrefutable argument had been von Kluge's reason for granting Karl a seat on the aircraft to freedom while refusing Kurt's offer to give up his own seat. 'Germany will need teachers more than she needs generals.'

Teaching had given him a reason to get up in the morning and correcting assignments had distracted him during his solitary evenings. His students, he knew, admired him but they didn't love him the way he had loved Simon Tauber. Perhaps it was because Simon Tauber brought his whole being to the classroom, while he brought only his skills as a teacher and historian. The rest of him, he locked away inside himself. He knew, at a cerebral level, that his reticence was a loss to his students and to him but, as yet, he'd found no key to loosen that lock.

Smells of cooking, the warmth of the little house and Bertha's welcome seemed to thaw that ice-bound place inside him and he felt … regret? Longing? He didn't know. He knew it was good to be among friends and simply to feel. There was a comfort, albeit a cold one, in the Spartan house that he rented and a part of him felt vulnerable and exposed by the warmth of Bertha's welcome.

She kissed him soundly on both cheeks. 'It's like kissing a bear,' she laughed. 'Come in, come in. The Herr Professor is doing an archaeological dig at a small tell of papers in his office. We mere mortals get to open the schnapps.'

'It's good news, then?' he said, as he followed her into the kitchen.

'All will be revealed,' she said, as she poured the fiery spirit. 'To the future,' she toasted.

He tilted his glass and sipped.

'You don't think very much of the future, do you, Karl?' she said gently. It was a question he could have fudged with anyone else except Bertha.

'No, not if the past is anything to go by.'

She nodded and took a moment to assimilate what he'd said and order her thoughts.

'I think war absorbs us so completely that, when it's over, we … we find it hard to come back to the ordinary. It's like we're caught between two worlds: one that is horrific, beyond words and the other horrifically mundane by comparison. In the beginning, Kurt couldn't talk about where he'd been and hadn't any patience with talk of here. He talks more often now about … things.'

'I hoped he would.'

'You said he would, remember?'

He nodded and they sat in silence for a while.

'Why didn't I die, Bertha?' he asked.

She came to sit beside him so that she could take his mangled hand in hers. She was the only one who did that, the only one he would allow. 'Did you want to?'

'Yes, at the beginning.'

'And then?'

'And then, I felt an obligation to people – a duty to make a difference. That sounds very hollow now but it made some sense then.'

'But you did make a difference in Rome.'

'Yes, in a very small way.'

'And now?'

'My thoughts keep going back, Bertha, as if everyone who mattered – who still matters – is back there.'

'When you're old enough to love, you're old enough to grieve, Karl. When my father … took his life, I had Kurt. And then Kurt went to war. I grieved him as if he were dead, Karl, it was the only way I could deal with the separation. My reason for living became the school and the other women I knew in Hallstatt – your mother, Eloise, Frau Mende and her son. There was so much to be done. It was reason enough to keep going but I'm not sure if I would have survived the peace if Kurt hadn't come back.'

'But he did come back, Bertha.'

'And your father and Tomas the miner didn't, Karl. And Elsa isn't coming back. I'm sorry if that sounds harsh but survivors must speak the truth to each other.'

He nodded.

'Perhaps you need to find someone or something to be your reason. Call it duty or obligation or whatever, it doesn't matter. It may grow into something else because you want it to.'

Her hand tightened painfully on his, and he schooled his face to remain impassive.

'If you … if you were to … well, we would miss you terribly,' she said brokenly. 'I suppose that's very selfish,' she continued, blotting her eyes with a handkerchief, 'but it might be enough – for now.'

He leaned across and kissed the top of her head.

'Bertha, where are you?' Kurt called from the sitting room.

'Where am I?' she laughed tremulously. 'He asks the same question at least once a day. Why does he do that?'

'To hear you answer, Bertha,' Karl said wistfully.

Kurt sat as close to the stove as was possible without singeing his clothes. He was crowned with a knitted cap that folded over the tops of his ears. A knotted scarf crouched under his chin, peeking through the greatcoat that swallowed him all the way down to his boots. Fur-lined, Karl noted. The Russian Front has left its mark on all of us, he mused.

'Kurt, if you're in there,' he said, 'I want to propose that hibernation is not a human occupation.'

'I am evidence to the contrary,' Kurt said happily, closing his book in the ultimate sign of hospitality. 'Our ancestors stored up for the winter and only stepped outside the cave to—'

'Charming,' Bertha interjected dryly, 'and, since none of us are competent in ancient history, hardly debatable. Shall we eat?'

The meal was punctuated with the companionable silences savoured by old friends. Over coffee, Bertha was encouraged to retell stories of how the women and children of Hallstatt had hidden in the mines during the last days of the war.

'Then,' she concluded, smiling, 'the Americans arrived – lots of sunny young men with lots of gleaming white teeth. Suddenly, everyone wanted to go back to the village.'

'So,' Kurt needled, 'all that squirreling away of supplies was for nothing. The Cossacks didn't come.'

Karl flinched involuntarily, but the others didn't seem to notice.

'No,' Bertha conceded, 'the Russians didn't come. We can be thankful for that; other places weren't so fortunate.'

For a few moments, they sipped their coffee in silence. It was scalding hot. The only way Kurt would drink it. Karl suspected they were each remembering the stories of rape and brutality the vengeful Soviet army had inflicted on the people of the areas they'd occupied.

'Of course, the Germans came,' Bertha continued quickly, as if aware she'd cast a pall over their happy evening.

So now we call them 'The Germans', Karl, the historian, noted. He considered writing an article entitled 'Austrian Amnesia', and put the thought from his mind as Bertha continued.

'We watched them moving on the far side of the lake. Johann said they were throwing stuff into the lake as they passed. I remember he said that he saw hundreds of small splashes, as if a shoal of fish was breaking the surface, parallel to the road. Sometimes, there were big splashes. He thought they were mortars.' She gestured with the coffee pot and the two men shook their heads, not wanting to stem her flow. 'Johann brings up all sorts of stuff in the net – campaign medals, pistols, ammunition. Oh, that's a secret, by the way.'

'To everyone outside Hallstatt,' Kurt growled.

'They were moving so fast,' Bertha said, ignoring him. 'It was more a rout than a retreat. I expect they were hoping that if anyone caught up with them it would be the Americans.'

She began to gather the dishes, then added as an afterthought, 'Thankfully, they stayed on the other side of the lake, except the group who came to the mine that time.'

'What?' the men chorused.

'You never mentioned that before,' Kurt accused.

'Because the evidence is based on hearsay, Herr Professor,' she flashed back, poking his arm 'And you would have driven me insane, looking for details I couldn't supply.'

'We'll forfeit the history for the story,' Karl said.

'Obviously, I slept through the whole thing,' Bertha began. 'In the morning, someone, maybe Eloise, said she'd heard German voices in the mouth of the mine during the night. She said they were men's voices and she heard a lot of clattering, as if they were moving something heavy. She thought they'd gone and then … then she heard a kind of booming sound that seemed to come from somewhere deep in the mountain. Sound plays funny tricks in the mines,' she concluded.

'And in the mind,' Kurt said dismissively. 'Eloise. I ask you, Bertha, is Eloise a dependable primary source? I remember having Eloise in class, such a dreamer. She always seemed to be listening to something else because she never listened to me.'

'Perhaps that's why she became such a good teacher,' Bertha riposted.

Karl hadn't realised how much he'd missed the verbal fencing of his friends. They pressed him for stories from the classroom and the essay title popped out of his mouth.

'My God!' Kurt said, '"Russia was Napoleon's bête noire". That's exactly the essay title I set for your class.'

'Imitation is the homage mediocrity gives to genius,' Karl said, smiling. 'And only Jurgen asked what "bête noire" meant.'

'Good for Jurgen,' Bertha said. 'I'll bet the others were glad he asked.'

'I remember,' Kurt continued, 'you and Elsa didn't ask. You two already knew, of course, as did Max.'

Bertha stole an anxious look at Karl. He smiled back and she relaxed. They both knew there wasn't an ounce of malice in Kurt Brandt though, Karl remembered, Kurt's runaway tongue had almost got him killed during the war, by his own side.

'Eloise is growing into such a fine teacher,' Bertha said. 'The young ones really love her.'

'Someone else might have loved her,' Kurt ploughed on, 'if he'd given her even the slightest encouragement.' He looked anxiously at Bertha. 'I've said the wrong thing, haven't I, dear?'

The others burst out laughing.

'I'm really sorry,' Kurt continued weakly. 'I seem to—'

'No, dear,' Bertha said, when she'd recovered her breath. 'The important thing is that you realise you're doing it – eventually. That's progression, wouldn't you agree, Karl?'

'Definitely, a huge improvement.'

'Anyway,' Bertha announced, 'Eloise is getting all the encouragement she needs from that young archaeologist who's working on the Celtic site. And now, Kurt,' she said, 'it's time you shared your news.'

'What news?' Kurt asked, looking genuinely perplexed.

'The letter, Kurt.'

'Oh.'

Kurt went through his ritual rummaging through layers of clothing until he unearthed a letter which he passed to Karl.

'*Tolle lege*,' he said grandly. 'Take and read.'

Karl read the letter and handed it back to his friend. 'Congratulations, Kurt,' he said warmly, 'but it's no great surprise that the university would offer you the Chair of Modern History. The only surprise is that it's taken them so long. Your edition of General von Kluge's memoirs was very fine.'

'*Our* edition,' Kurt said generously.

Karl waved a deprecatory hand. 'I was merely the sorcerer's apprentice. Will you accept it?'

'I think I will. Remember the Chinese curse, Karl? May you live in interesting times.'

'Exactly,' Karl said enthusiastically. 'History doesn't stop with the armistice. Austria, we're supposed to believe, was the first victim of the Nazis, and it seems the Allies have bought us from the Soviets.'

'More bartered than bought,' Kurt corrected. 'The West gets Austria, the East gets any country bordering the Soviet Union – except Finland, of course. Stalin would never risk having another Barbarossa launched from the Soviet borders. This way, he gets to keep his buffer zone.'

'And we get Marshall Aid from the Americans to save our economy and persuade us to be good Europeans.'

'Or good Americans,' Kurt murmured. '*Timeo Danaos ac dona ferentes* ... I fear the Greeks, bearing gifts.'

'I hate to interrupt your seminar, Professor,' Bertha said, 'but isn't it time you asked him?'

This time, Kurt didn't engage in his usual game-playing.

'I want you to join me as a lecturer on the faculty.'

'Is it in your gift?'

'It's not offered as a gift to a friend, Karl, it's an invitation to a colleague and fellow historian.'

'I ... I don't know what to say.'

'Perhaps Karl would like to sleep on it,' Bertha said, coming to his rescue.

'Very well,' Kurt agreed.

'So,' Karl said, relieved that the need to make a decision had been deferred, 'how do you feel about going back to Vienna?'

'Apprehensive, elated – I'm not sure,' Kurt laughed. 'I mean the position is more than I ever dreamed of; even when I thought I knew everything and had married the Chancellor's daughter. I think,' he continued more soberly, 'I will find life in a city less – challenging. Hallstatt is beautiful, but it's colder and the sky is very wide. Do you understand, Karl?' he asked, almost timidly.

Karl thought. 'Yes,' he said, 'I understand.'

Kurt's reference to the Russian sky had reminded him of the endless plains they had traversed during Operation Barbarossa and the complete absence of mountains or other landmarks to relieve the encircling openness. He remembered wondering if it was possible to live in a landscape that was all horizon, and of lying on his back one day, thinking that he was stretched on the outer skin of the world, afraid that if he moved he would fall forever into that huge sky. Those wide skies had bred 'steppe fever' among many of the soldiers, men who favoured small spaces and cramped quarters. He came back to the conversation to find Kurt looking at him. He looked as if he understood where Karl's thoughts had been.

'And you, Bertha?' Karl asked.

'I have friends in Hallstatt,' she said quietly, 'and I have made my home here.'

'Oh, it isn't as if Vienna is on the far side of the moon, Bertha,' Kurt protested.

'To the Hallstatters, anywhere beyond the Dachstein Mountains might as well be on the far side of the moon,' she said ruefully. 'I know Vienna. I was born there and we lived there after our marriage, but going back is never easy; especially if you think you're going back to what you knew before. I'll see to the stove,' she added and left.

'Did I say something wrong?' Kurt asked.

'No, Kurt, but I think you may have missed the chance to say something right.'

'Oh, it's easy for you single fellows to ... I was about to do it again, wasn't I?'

'Yes.'

'Forgive me, Karl.'

'For what? For being my friend and the teacher who made everything possible? Even for a lad from Hallstatt to be offered a post at the university.'

'I merely polished the stone I found, Karl, it was always a diamond.'

Kurt stood and spread his arms. They embraced with the careful tenderness of two old friends made fragile by a shared experience.

'Dancing is in the drawing room,' Bertha said from the door. They loosed an arm each to include her.

THE OFFICE OF POPE PIUS XII, THE VATICAN

Eugenio Pacelli, Pope Pius XII, Vicar of Christ, Successor of St Peter and Supreme Pontiff of the Holy Roman Catholic Church, didn't look up from his papers when the group entered. They fanned out to stand behind their chairs. He nodded absently and they sat.

The world has burned around us, Tisserant thought angrily, *and we still insist on playing feudal games.*

As Pius scratched his initials on documents, Tisserant took the opportunity to assess him. *I never liked him*, he confessed inwardly. *He was groomed for this from childhood and favoured by his predecessor. Envy?* his conscience queried. *No! What mortal man could carry that burden? Was Pius more than mortal?*

Tisserant knew many people in the Vatican already whispered of sainthood. He thought it a bit premature. Pius himself had admitted to seeing Jesus in his bedroom. 'One trembles to consider their mutual embarrassment,' Emil had remarked dryly. Tisserant held a handkerchief to his mouth and pretended to cough until the urge to laugh had eased. Pius had also claimed to have seen the sun spinning in the sky, like those children at Fatima. Happily, his driver, Giovanni Stefanori, had seen nothing – and Vatican drivers saw everything. Pilgrims, granted an audience, regularly spoke of the odour of sanctity emanating from the pope. Tisserant knew, for a fact, that the papal housekeeper, the German nun, Sister Pascalina, regularly sprayed his hands with antiseptic to protect him from the handshakes of the unwashed. *What kind of pope needs to see visions?* he wondered. *What kind of nuncio goes to Germany and sells out the Catholic party to Hitler? And for what? Control of the Catholic schools and the appointment of German bishops? Do you offer a lion a lamb and expect him not to devour it?*

The schools had been subsumed into the Reich and many of the German bishops had proved all too eager to goosestep to the Führer's tune. During the war, Pius had refused to criticise the Nazis publicly in order to preserve the Church in Germany. *Even when we had evidence of atrocities and the Nazis took the Jews of Rome from beneath his window. Maybe Tardini is right*, Tisserant admitted. *I've been here too long. I'm as much a prisoner of the Vatican as Pius is. In all my years here, I've probably met the pope, oh, too many times to count. Pacelli, the man? Maybe twice – when the mask slipped and the man was revealed.*

He'd never forgotten those epiphanies. He'd seen the utter aloneness of the man who carried the weight of the triple tiara and his heart would never let him forget or allow him to be so coldly critical again. God knew he'd worked hard at some semblance of a friendship and he'd been largely content with the little Pius seemed capable of offering in return. No, Eugenio Pacelli was the pope and the pope would always supersede the man.

'The war had been over for eight years, long enough for him to evaluate how the pope had handled the peace. He concluded that Pius had become even more remote. Positions, like Maglione's as Secretary of State, had been left vacant or split between Montini and Tardini – neither of whom was even a bishop. *They say war can soften even the hardest heart,* he thought, *but Pius seems to have grown more rigid.*

Tisserant tried to distract himself from this train of thought by looking at the dome of St Peter's, bisected by the window. *Even the basilica softens with age,* he mused. *When you stand close to the statues of Peter and Paul, they seem almost avuncular; weathered to something less awe-inspiring than Bernini had intended.* He brought his attention back to the white-clad figure behind the desk. *Pius looks like that damned Egyptian obelisk in St Peter's Square,* he thought, *still shiny and hard after centuries. We stole it, capped it with a cross and stuck it in the square as a trophy. It didn't unmake what it was and what it meant.* He refocused on the pope – on the pale face, the black stains under his eyes and the too-bright eyes behind the steel-rimmed spectacles. *He looks consumptive,* he thought, *as if he is being sucked from inside.*

As if on cue, the pope hiccupped. His eyes widened as if he was mortified at such an ordinary occurrence. He hiccupped again and his right hand moved to press his chest under his pectoral cross. Tisserant rose abruptly and left the room. He returned with a glass of water and placed it on the desk.

'Sip it, Holiness,' he said, 'that always works for me.'

The waxen face eased fractionally as Pius reached for the glass. 'Thank you, Eminence,' he said in a thready voice.

Tisserant bustled back to his chair, ignoring Tardini's quizzical look. He didn't need to look at Pizzardo to know he disapproved of the breach of protocol. Montini looked as if he was going to melt. The pope has simple hiccups, Tisserant thought angrily and the most powerful men in the Vatican act like they are paralysed. He hoped it was simple. Pius was still massaging his chest between sips of water. Another attack racked his thin frame and he set the glass aside. He smiled wanly at Tisserant. 'You must show me how to do this properly, Eugène,' he said, and the cardinal could only nod.

He knew what would happen now. Pacelli would retreat behind Pius and the meeting would proceed. The metamorphosis occurred as he'd predicted. '*Procedamus*,' the pope said, tonelessly. 'Let us proceed.'

Montini immediately scrambled to put a document before the pope. Pius scanned it carefully and inclined his head towards Pizzardo.

'This document refers to the so-called 'worker priests' in France, Holiness,' the big man rumbled. Pius nodded fractionally and the cardinal continued. 'It has come to the attention of the Holy Office that their religious life is irregular.'

'Well, it would be irregular, Eminence,' Tisserant interjected coolly. 'If they had remained regular and confined to their religious houses, they wouldn't have been able to witness to Christ and His Church among the disaffected factory workers. War is, by its very nature, irregular. Those priests are simply adapting their ministry to the reality of our times. It's not an insurmountable difficulty for the Church to regularise their irregular religious life. We do have historical precedents. Ignatius and the Jesuits adapted to the court and customs of Japan in the sixteenth century. Francis and his followers were extremely irregular when they danced before the pontiff of their day. Happily, the Church in the thirteenth century was wise enough to recognise a group of humble men dedicated to bringing the simplicity of the gospel message to the people – despite their irregular lifestyle and practices.'

Tisserant sat back and watched the pope.

'There are also reports of socialist groups in those factories influencing the worker priests,' Pizzardo added.

Tisserant knew he had lost the argument. Socialism was the pope's blind spot. Ever since his nunciature in Germany had been invaded by socialists, he'd harboured a mortal fear of them. Stalin had become the personification of his worst nightmare. While he'd detested Hitler and Nazism, he considered Stalin and socialism a greater threat to the Church. For a pope who had been so careful in his public utterances never to alienate Hitler, Pius took every opportunity to lambast Stalin and godless socialism.

'What does your department recommend, Eminence?' he asked Pizzardo.

'That those priests be ordered to leave the factories and return to the regular life of their religious houses.'

Pius uncapped his pen and signed the document. He sat with his hands folded on the desk until Montini presented the next document.

For the next two hours, Tisserant argued against the silencing of various theologians, condemnations of leading philosophers and the addition of even more writings to the *Index of Forbidden Books*. It was to no avail. Pizzardo presented the case, Pius asked for a recommendation and signed the documents. *Stalin has his gulags*, Tisserant reflected, *and we have ours. We don't condemn our intellectuals and dissenters to hard labour in the salt mines of Siberia. We silence them and remove them from their teaching posts. In effect, we take away their gift and their opportunity to use it, and we separate them from their peers and students.* He had to force himself to stay in the room. He was torn between an image of himself as John the Apostle, standing in solidarity at the foot of the cross, as good men were crucified by diktat, and as Paul, holding the coats of those who stoned Stephen, the first martyr. Finally it was over. They bowed. The pope was already reaching for another document as they left. He would work at his desk until after midnight writing letters and speeches in pen before tapping them out on his little white typewriter. He would then place each document in its proper file, return each book to its proper place on the shelves and turn off the lights to avoid wasting electricity. The pope would retire to his quarters and rise again at five to resume the burden of his office.

Tisserant nodded a curt farewell to his companions and exited the antechamber. In the corridor outside and on the stairs, his pounding steps alerted staff to detour out of his way as Swiss Guards snapped to attention in his wake. When he arrived at his apartments, his face was brick-red and running with sweat.

'Sit down before you explode,' Emil Dupont ordered. The cardinal scraped his skull cap from his head and flung it across the room.

'That bad?' his secretary observed, and went immediately to the liquor cabinet. He returned with a bottle of French cognac and three large balloon glasses. Tisserant was sprawled in his chair, rubbing his face with a handkerchief.

'Calm down, Eugène,' Emil said gently. 'Apoplexy is not the answer.'

Tisserant accepted the generous measure and held it under his nose with both hands, as if the fragrance might soothe his mind.

'Why three glasses?' he muttered

'I'm expecting a visitor.'

'Who?'

'I have no idea – yet. Tell me the fate of our countrymen who had the temerity to write. Did Chenus survive Pizzardo?'

'Gone – not to teach or publish.'

'Congar?'

'Gone! Same sentence.'

'De Chardin?'

'Offered a choice of gulag,' Tisserant said dejectedly. 'He can retire to a rustic retreat house under close supervision or—'

'Or?'

'America. He's going to New York.'

'Picked the hard option, eh?' Emil jested, but neither man smiled. 'Speaking of hard options,' he continued, 'what of the worker priests? Surely they can't—'

'Out of work,' Tisserant snarled and began to pace. 'Safely withdrawn behind the ramparts of their religious houses. *Mon Dieu*, Emil, how can we conquer the post-war world for Christ when we fire our best generals and keep our crack troops confined to barracks?'

He stopped pacing at his desk, picked up a book and slammed it down again.

'Not more books?' Emil asked, appalled.

'Of course, more books are added to the *Index of Forbidden Books* every day. Anything that questions the world, as the Church perceives it, is anathema. If Columbus arrived at the Vatican today with maps of the New World, they would be erased as heretical.'

He slumped into his chair and cupped his chin in his hands.

'Shall I tell you an amusing story?' Emil asked.

'No!'

'I'll tell you anyway,' Emil said blithely. 'A French priest writes a book entitled *The Problem of Sin and the Catholic Church*.'

'Père Oraison,' Tisserant muttered.

'You are such a show-off, Eugène,' Emil said tartly. 'Now, *écoutez*! This Père Oraison is summoned to Rome by the Holy Office where he meets Pizzardo and Ottaviani for lunch. Which is like being invited to dinner by cannibals – it's difficult to enjoy the main course when you might be dessert. After much pounding between the Hammer and the Anvil, they ask if he has a question. "Only one," the bruised Père replies. "How should one avoid sexual sin?" "Easy," Ottaviani says. "Sexual sin is best avoided through fear and a healthy diet." Our Père is perplexed. Then Pizzardo pinches his cheek affectionately and explains. "His Eminence means fear of sin, and a diet of spaghetti and pizza.'"

'You made that up.'

'I wish I had. I will never look at pizza—'

He was interrupted by a gentle tap on the door. Emil opened it to reveal Father Montini hovering outside nervously.

'Please excuse me,' he whispered, 'I ... I felt I had to speak to His Eminence – after this morning.'

'Please, Giovanni, come and sit,' Emil said warmly. 'The bear has eaten, you are quite safe.'

'Who sent you?' Tisserant asked bluntly, as Montini eased into an armchair. A little colour flushed the priest's pallid cheeks and Tisserant thought he saw a flash of fire in his hooded eyes.

'I was not sent, Eminence,' Montini said in a firmer voice.

Good, Tisserant thought. *The boy has managed to salvage some degree of independence from this wrecking yard.*

'Why did you come, then?'

'Because I shared the opinions expressed by Your Eminence at the meeting.'

'But not the courage to express them yourself,' Tisserant pressed cruelly.

Montini flinched but didn't rise to leave.

'Your Eminence is a historian,' he said stiffly. 'You must know the foolishness of winning a battle and losing a war.'

Tisserant turned his head to glare at his secretary, who stared back in wide-eyed innocence. 'I said nothing,' Emil protested.

'I heard it anyway,' Tisserant growled and turned back to Montini. 'And which particular war are you fighting, Giovanni Montini?' he asked.

'Not – not the one I volunteered for,' Montini said, 'not any longer.' He leaned forward, animation flooding his soft, boyish face. 'The war changed everything, Eminence,' he whispered. 'Before the war, I had a career.' His mouth quirked on the word and he pressed on. 'The pope approved of me and I was favoured by Cardinal

Pizzardo. That's what I think is called common knowledge,' he added with a sad smile.

Tisserant nodded encouragingly.

'I worked in the Refugee Office for the last year of the war and two years after,' Montini continued.

'Not easy,' Tisserant allowed.

'No, it was not. In the three years, we had more than 10 million letters begging us to find a father, a mother, brothers ...' His voice trailed off. 'People were desperately searching for information – any information.' His lower lip trembled and he paused to compose himself. 'My father was a member of parliament,' he continued. 'My mother was of the nobility. I have two brothers. I have never known anything like that.' He sighed and sat back. 'Many things have appeared inconsequential since then.'

'Like the Church?' Tisserant offered.

'No!' He was sitting forward again, his hands seeming to weave the words as they tumbled from his mouth. 'The Church is of great consequence, Eminence,' he insisted, 'now more than ever. Or rather, its mission is.'

'And what is that?'

'I know what it's not, Eminence,' he said slowly. 'It's not exclusion. In the war, we were open to everybody. We helped Jews and partisans – even socialists. Our office provided papers for British pilots and escaped prisoners of war. And, after the war, we ... we provided the same service to those in need. No,' he repeated more quietly, 'the Church cannot be about excluding people or ideas or books because they are – different.'

He seemed to have exhausted his passion and sank into the armchair.

'Is the pope sick?' Tisserant demanded.

'Yes!'

Montini's mouth remained open for a few moments as if he'd shocked himself with his own candour. 'Yes,' he said again. 'He doesn't want anyone to know.'

'Anyone else, you mean.'

'Yes, obviously, I know – and Sister Pascalina.'

Tisserant snorted and Montini seemed to sink a little further in the cushions.

'Doctors?'

'Doctor,' Montini corrected. 'Professor Galeazzi-Lisi was appointed *archiatra* by His Holiness.'

Tisserant cocked a quizzical eyebrow at Emil.

'Doctor Galeazzi-Lisi is an eye-doctor,' Emil supplied from his encyclopaedic memory.

'And who recommended this … eye-doctor to His Holiness?'

'His brother, Count Galeazzi – and Sister Pascalina.'

'This is the Count Galeazzi who went to America with His Holiness in 1939?'

'He was an architect before he became a diplomat,' Emil offered.

'So,' Tisserant mused with heavy sarcasm, 'an eye-doctor is appointed the papal doctor on the recommendation of an architect and a housekeeper. And the treatment?'

'Actually,' Montini whispered, 'His Holiness was worried that his teeth were getting loose. He was afraid that he wouldn't be able to deliver his, eh, allocutions.'

Oh, yes, Tisserant thought, *his speeches to gynaecologists, newscasters, psychiatrists and central-heating engineers.* He'd culled that information from one of the papers on Father Leiber's desk.

'Doctor Galeazzi-Lisi suggested a Roman dentist, who prescribed for His Holiness,' Montini concluded.

'Prescribed what?'

'Chromic acid,' Montini said almost inaudibly.

Again Tisserant turned to Emil.

'Used for tanning leather,' Emil said. They stared at each other in mutual disbelief until Tisserant swivelled towards Montini, like a gun-turret swivelling in search of a target. 'And then,' he said, 'the hiccups began?'

Montini nodded.

'And the treatment for hiccups?' Tisserant asked, relentlessly.

'In–Injections,' Montini stammered, his face even more miserable and pallid than before. He cleared his throat and continued. 'Galeazzi-Lisi recommended a Swiss specialist, an expert in cellular therapy.'

Tisserant's eyebrows rose menacingly and Montini rushed to elaborate.

'I–I understand he injects cells from the foetuses of sheep and monkeys under the skin. The cells from the front part of the brain are, eh, favoured.'

'And the pope has had this – treatment?'

'Yes. His Holiness seemed to improve but, lately—'

To the surprise of Tisserant and his secretary, Montini's eyes welled with tears.

Tisserant leaned back in his chair and released a long sigh. 'You are close to him, Giovanni,' he said gently.

Montini nodded. 'He has been kind to me,' he said in a strangled voice.

Tisserant waited for him to compose himself.

'Has anyone tried to dissuade His Holiness from this—' He searched his prodigious vocabulary in the twelve languages he spoke without finding an adequate word to describe what he'd just heard. Montini was looking at him as if genuinely astonished that anyone would consider dissuading the pope.

'No,' Montini managed. 'Also, Sister Pascalina favours Galeazzi-Lisi, Eminence,' he added urgently. 'If anyone should suspect I—'

'No,' Tisserant assured him, 'what is said here stays here.'

The frail man wilted with relief.

'I will do everything in my power,' the cardinal said, 'to discover what I can – without arousing suspicion. Our mutual and overriding concern is the wellbeing of the pope.'

'Thank you, Eminence,' Montini said fervently. He made to rise until Emil's voice restrained him.

'You have carried a heavy and lonely burden, Giovanni,' he said. 'Perhaps, there is something else you would like His Eminence to help with?'

Tisserant masked his surprise and relaxed in his chair. He respected his old friend too much to doubt his intuition. Montini's face tightened and then relaxed.

'Yes,' he said, 'I would like … there is something else.'

Tisserant watched the young man place his glass on the occasional table and straighten his posture. He looked directly at the cardinal and spoke firmly.

'Your Eminence knows that I was appointed as Secretary of State for Internal Affairs.'

'Yes,' Tisserant answered, 'Tardini has the external portfolio.'

'My duties are varied,' Montini continued. 'I come into contact with many Vatican departments and, eh, institutions.'

The slight hesitation piqued Tisserant's interest and he gave the man his full attention. He thought he could almost hear the gears grinding in Montini's head as he attempted a balance between revelation and concealment.

'It has been brought to my attention,' Montini began, slowly enough for Tisserant to admire the careful phrasing, 'that there may be some … irregularities of a financial nature.' He took a deep, steadying breath. 'And that these irregularities could be interpreted as favouring a particular Church body.'

Tisserant was tempted to shake his head in admiration at the masterclass in Vatican-speak he'd just heard. *He feels he's actually told me something*, he marvelled. *If I press him for facts, figures and names, he will startle and dig deeper into his comfort zone. He could, of course, demand and be damned or—*

'Your prudence is what one would expect from a secretary of state,' he said smoothly. Montini's shoulders lowered a fraction, and Tisserant knew it was a gesture of acceptance. Montini knew the rules of the game and Tisserant had agreed to play by those rules. 'My own sources,' he said carefully, 'suggest that there is a bank account that contains a considerable sum in the name of a very new religious order.'

Montini made no response.

'Furthermore,' Tisserant continued, aware that he was now treading on the most delicate of diplomatic eggshells, 'the representative of that particular institution is aware of this account and complicit' – he saw the tiniest frown pucker between Montini's eyes and rushed to correct himself – 'or has been constrained to waive the normal requirements of such institutions to report unusual deposits or withdrawals.'

He became aware of a single drop of sweat that had welled at the nape of his neck and was cooling rapidly as it trickled down his spine. It took every ounce of his energy to remain impassive and maintain an expressionless face. In the ensuing silence, he thought he heard a squeak of shoe leather, as if the Swiss Guard patrolling the corridor had come to the limit of his beat and turned to retrace his steps. *Would Montini realise that he'd reached the limits of his courage and now retreat?* Tisserant wondered. *How difficult it was for a man who had been immersed in the almost pathological secrecy of the Vatican to break the omertà and—*

Montini rose from the chair.

'Your Eminence has been most kind,' he whispered. 'I agree that the internal branch of the secretariat and Your Eminence's department should work closely together in all matters pertaining to the wellbeing of Holy Mother Church.'

He stepped forwards, dropped to one knee and kissed the cardinal's ring. Emil hastened to open the door and Giovanni Montini departed.

Emil resumed his seat and waited for Tisserant to break the silence. He could see that the cardinal was agitated by Montini's revelations. He was hunched over in his chair, elbow anchored to his knee and hand clamped under his chin as if trapping his tongue while his brain processed the interview.

Typically, the tongue spoke before the process was completed.

'They're killing the pope,' Tisserant whispered fiercely.

Emil sighed with a mixture of exasperation and affection.

'That's precisely the kind of emotional reaction I had to beat out of you when you were a student, Eugène,' he said patiently. 'Please recall my old mantra – breathe, think and rephrase.'

The cardinal took a deep breath and released it in a long sigh.

'This Galeazzi-Lisi,' he asked, 'what do you know of him?'

'The facts about the papal physician are straightforward if bizarre,' Emil replied promptly. 'He's an eye-doctor who charmed Pacelli with his medical omniscience and got himself appointed *archiatra* and, as such, he exerts a huge influence over the pope. Galeazzi-Lisi favours, shall we say, an unorthodox approach to medicine – hence the mumbo-jumbo about injections of sheep glands and visits from a Swiss specialist. It reminds me of Pope Clement sitting between two raging fires to avoid the plague.'

'Clement didn't get the plague,' Tisserant said.

'So, he didn't have the plague before he sat between two fires and he didn't have it after. Logic, Eugène, was never your strong subject. I put a mouse in St Peter's Square to deter elephants. There are no elephants in St Peter's Square, ergo, the mouse is effective.'

'But, Pacelli is an intelligent man, he—'

'The pope is a hypochondriac, Eugène. He has been a hypochondriac since he was a boy – a boy with a delicate constitution and an over-protective mother. They are not killing the pope. Where do you get such fanciful ideas?'

'From the fanciful, romantic novels you leave strewn about the apartment.'

'Sometimes, I despair of you, Eugène.'

'You're a historian,' Tisserant persisted. 'You know that popes have been poisoned and strangled. Pope Clement I was tied to an anchor and drowned. Formosus—'

'Not Formosus, please,' Emil begged.

'Formosus, after his death, was dug up and tried before a

court by his successor. They found him guilty, cut off his right hand and dumped the corpse in the Tiber. That's history, Emil, not fantasy.'

'But surely you don't think—'

'I think this pope could die of neglect,' Tisserant interrupted. 'He is surrounded by people who have a vested interest in playing along with his delusions.'

'What do you propose to do?'

'I propose to rescue him from this witch doctor and from that smothering Mother Pascalina.'

'Oh for heaven's sake, Eugène, you are not Roland. Put your lance back in its socket and apply your mind to more immediate matters. Think carefully. What did Montini actually say?'

Tisserant huffed angrily, before reciting tonelessly. 'You heard him. There are financial irregularities in the accounts of Vatican departments and institutions.'

'And you suggested?'

'And I suggested a new religious order was making huge deposits in the Vatican Bank. What has—'

'Did he deny it?'

'No!'

'Montini is a bureaucrat to the marrow of his bones, Eugène,' Emil said earnestly. 'His silence on that matter confirms what we already know. Steiger set up the Fratres with the millions he brought in gold from Croatia. We know it was blood money, robbed from the corpses of Serbs slaughtered by the Croatian militia. Steiger was the courier for powerful men who were investing in their future as the war swung against them. He did invest some of it towards its intended purpose and some of the leaders were spirited out of Europe to South America, Egypt, Syria – mostly to dictatorships who were willing to waive their past for bribes or because they had skills useful to a dictator.'

'And the rest of the money?'

'Steiger has complete control of it. The original investors are unlikely to claim it, are they? Montini suggests he's been adding to the original lodgement. Again, he didn't deny it when you suggested it was done without the usual checks and balances. When you started to suggest it was done with the compliance of the director of the Vatican Bank, I was sure you'd lose him. But you avoided that crevasse masterfully. Most unusual for you.'

'Thank you.'

'You said the director has been "constrained". That single word saved the day. Montini would never swallow the fact that the man appointed as Director of the Vatican Bank by Pacelli had been bought by Steiger.'

'I tried to bring it to Pacelli's attention before, Emil,' the cardinal reminded him. 'I think it influenced his decision not to grant full approval to the Fratres. But,' he sighed, 'time goes by and Steiger is building up a powerful organisation. If only we could persuade Montini to dig a little deeper, or if we could find a stick sharp enough to poke Steiger into the open, we might produce the kind of evidence the pope couldn't ignore. What about your contacts in the Vatican?'

'I could ask around, I suppose,' Emil said slowly. 'It's no secret within these walls that I'm your man and that makes people wary of me. Also,' he sighed, 'I'm not a young man, Eugène. I tire more easily and I've become absent-minded.'

'You were always absent-minded,' Tisserant teased.

'I'll try to forget you said that,' Emil said dryly. 'No, Eugène, the truth is we need a younger man we can trust absolutely – someone who's from outside the Vatican and who has no love for Steiger and his Fratres.'

'That job description fits only one man we both know, Emil.'

'Yes,' his secretary agreed reluctantly. 'I always hoped he could put the past behind him. He has suffered so much already, he deserves to just get on with his life.'

'That's not a luxury afforded to any of us,' the cardinal said decisively. 'I think it's time we sent for Karl Hamner.'

'I agree,' Emil said without enthusiasm. 'You will tell him everything, Eugène?'

'Of course.'

'No, don't agree so readily,' Emil said seriously, 'it makes me suspicious. If you bring him back to Rome, you will be putting him in harm's way. You must tell him that, Eugène, and he must be free to refuse.'

'What do you take me for?'

'I regard you as a good man who has a powerful commitment to the truth,' Emil said slowly. 'But you insist on reminding me that I'm a historian and history is littered with the dreams of innocent men who were sacrificed to the visions of the powerful. I'd better write that letter,' he added, pushing himself out of the chair, 'before I forget.'

THE MINE, HALLSTATT

Coffee, flask, chocolate, spare socks, sandwiches wrapped in muslin – the haversack swallowed them all. At the door, he took a walking staff from the corner, automatically checking his height against it. 'It's six feet tall,' his father, Rudi, had said the day he'd brought it from the workshop. Karl remembered that it had smelled of sap. He held it to his nose, trying to recapture the fresh, resin smell. 'Let's measure you, lad,' his father had said. He'd placed his hand flat on the crown of Karl's head and notched the shaft with his whittling knife. 'When you're both the same size, it's yours,' he'd promised. It was his now, a bittersweet reminder of Rudi.

The sky was a blue oval in the cup of the mountains, but the air still held the sting of winter. The climb was so familiar that he could risk looking around as he ascended. Above the tree line, at the mouth of the mine, he leaned on the staff to rest and gather himself for what lay within. Over his head, a pair of ravens sported in a thermal. He thought they looked carefree and watched them until they glided to roost in the trees lower down.

The candle flame led him between salt-sparkled walls until the tunnel yawned into a familiar chamber. He could have doused the candle and still found his way by memory. Every fold and crevice was painfully familiar. Elsa had sat right there, spilling the light on where she had chosen to sketch. He conjured up the last words they'd exchanged.

'Karl. Thanks for coming with me,' she'd said.

'I wanted to come.'

'Why?'

'Because – you asked me.'

'And if I'd asked you to jump in the lake would you have done that also?'

'Probably.'

'Are you still here, Karl?'

'No, Fraulein Drucker,' he'd said and walked away.

He burrowed farther into the mountain to where he'd found the Celtic staircase that day. The candle danced shadows on the wall of slim timbers transformed and preserved by over a thousand years of exposure to salt. *Like Lot's wife in the Bible*, he thought and shivered. He was convinced he'd heard a sound, as he'd done on that terrible day. Quickly, he retraced his steps to the empty chamber – to where Max had assaulted Elsa. She'd died in this place because of Max's insane lust. The only time he and Max had spoken of it had been in the cellars beneath the Santa della Concezione Church in Rome and the only witnesses had been hundreds of Franciscan skeletons, all arranged in a macabre *memento mori*. *All except one*, he recalled. A freshly murdered man in a Franciscan cassock who had betrayed Max and died for it. *It's all in the past*, he decided, shaking his head to dispel the memories. On the flank of the mountain, he'd made up his mind to accept Kurt's offer. He would leave Hallstatt. That part of his history was behind him. It was time to say goodbye.

He placed his jacket on the spot where he had laid it for Elsa and sat on it. One-handed, he dug in the rucksack for the pad and pencil, and began to draw. The candle stood sentry against the dark as he traced a tree; a tree that grew from the base of the page and branched so that its crown filled the space above. It was identical to the tree he'd drawn for Elsa before, a lifetime before, when he, Elsa and Max had gone to the Celtic site at the head of the lake. Max had drawn a sword with such intensity that his pencil had gouged the paper and the sword had stood up in relief from the page. Elsa, he remembered sadly, had drawn an amulet. 'A ward against evil,' she'd said. And he had drawn a tree. He knew she'd liked it. There had been tension between Elsa and Max that day, and she'd stayed close to Karl on the path home, as if for protection. *Like a bird might find sanctuary in a tree from a hunting hawk*, he thought. He tore the page from the pad with unnecessary force. The sound ripped out and back through the labyrinth. He took a steadying breath before placing the page on the floor and smoothing the jagged edges with gentle strokes. 'Sorry, Elsa,' he whispered. *It's not enough*, he thought. The apology reduced both of them to victims and they'd been more – so much more. He bent forwards over the drawing and whispered the words he wished he'd said on that day. 'I love you, Elsa.' When he lifted the candle, he saw salt-stars twinkling in the firmament of rock over his head.

Karl's home, Hallstatt

'Hello, Johann,' he called, kicking snow from his boots outside the door.

'More like a real soldier,' Johann nodded approvingly as Karl entered the kitchen. 'This came for you on the early train,' he said, sliding an envelope across the table. 'It must be important,' he added innocently, 'what with the fancy crest and all.'

Karl stacked his staff in the corner and freed himself from the straps of the rucksack. He sat at the table and opened the envelope, holding it steady with his left elbow and slitting it with his right thumb.

'Well?' Johann demanded.

'Rome.'

'Again! Didn't they get enough of you the last time?'

'It seems Rome wants some more of me,' Karl said quietly. 'You should be happy, Johann,' he added with a small smile. 'I'm being offered a berth in that boat you mentioned.'

'I didn't mean the barque of bloody St Peter,' Johann growled.

Karl read and re-read the letter before lifting his pen and some paper from the table drawer. There was nothing else in the drawer. He'd sorted the tangle of old spectacles, spools of thread and all the small items his parents thought 'might come in useful, some day'. When it was all piled on the table, he'd invited Bertha for coffee. She'd gone through the little pile, separating the spectacles and spools from stubs of pencils, a thimble and keys to doors that had never been locked.

'Is there anything you'd like to keep, Karl?'

'No.'

She'd held the coffee cup under her chin for a long time before speaking.

'The hardest thing about coming to Hallstatt was that I couldn't visit my father's grave every day. Whenever we went back to Vienna for a visit, it was always my first port of call. I think being in Hallstatt gave me time to accept that he wasn't really in the cemetery. Some days, he just pops into my head – something he said or the way he held his coffee cup with both hands under his chin.' She'd smiled. 'I think they grow deeper inside us as time passes, until the things we associate with them become less important.'

'Like spectacles and thimbles?'

'Yes. I know some older men in the village who would be grateful for the spectacles. They'd appreciate the fact that they were Rudi's. I'd like to keep the thimble, your mother was a true and dear friend. Do you mind?'

'No, I think she'd like that. Thank you, Bertha.'

Kurt and Bertha will be disappointed, he thought, as he drafted a reply. He sealed the envelope and pushed it across the table. 'Will you put that in the mailbag when you cross?'

'Are you sure, Karl?'

'No.'

The Fratres Schloss, Switzerland

'Wait!'

The secretary nodded at a bench. It was, Laura thought as she sat down, just far enough away from the man who used words like a miser composing a telegram.

My name is Laura Morton, she repeated in her head like a comforting mantra, nodding to push it into the forefront of her brain. *When I entered the Fratres Novitiate, I took the name Sister Rosa, in memory of my mother, Rosa Morton.* She risked a look at the severe man sitting at the small desk nearby, straightened her back and added, *I'm from Chicago.*

The bench was varnished and cold. She felt it was like everything else in this forbidding building, spare and comfortless. Sister Pilar, their Spanish Novice Mistress, went on and on about how Father General had ordered the Schloss to be stripped back to the bare essentials. According to Sister Pilar, the Fratres were 'cutting back on all the excrescences that had polluted religious life'. Laura wasn't sure what 'excrescences' meant. She figured it must be the opposite of rock-hard beds, paper-thin towels, scratchy robes and ... She chided herself for complaining. It wasn't as if she'd expected the comforts of home. 'Home' conjured images and textures of fluffy slippers and pink dressing gowns. She stretched her legs at the memory, bending her toes back with pleasure and abruptly tucked her feet beneath the bench at an admonitory sniff from the secretary. *Well*, she reasoned, *he shouldn't be watching, should he?* She found him ... unsettling. Not because he had a bland face but because of a kind of fierceness that the mask of his face seemed to hold in check. She felt like hugging herself for warmth and resisted. Sister Pilar said that when they were distracted by the devil, they should imagine themselves in some edifying place, like before the altar or in the presence of Father General.

Maybe the latter is Sister Pilar's particular distraction, she thought wickedly and struggled not to smile. Instead, she let memory guide her back to Chicago, to the comfortable chaos of Father Reilly's sitting room. 'See, in your mind's eye, the space around you,' Sister Pilar had counselled. The sitting room was stacked and strewn with books and newspapers, mercifully hiding what passed for a carpet. The next step in the meditation was to visualise the objects in that space. She saw two tired armchairs and a table with one gimpy leg balancing on a thick book. 'And finally,' Sister Pilar would say in an awed whisper, 'behold the presence of the other.'

The 'other' Laura saw was Father Reilly. He was sitting in an armchair that seemed to have moulded itself to his thin frame. Unlike some of the other priests from Irish stock, he lacked a round and reddened face. His face was long and angular, topped off with sharp, blue eyes behind dusty spectacles. His cassock looked as if he'd inherited it from a broader man. It bore the ash stains from his pipe, a flecked bib extending from under his collar to the third button on his chest. It was like a grey river flowing into a black sea. She felt warmed by the tickly comfort of the throw that camouflaged the armchair she sat in. Father Reilly held the pipe before his spectacles, tapped the ash into submission with a brown forefinger and smiled. 'Hardly an adornment to our parish,' her poppa had said from behind his newspaper, a newspaper he read religiously and used as a shield against any ordinary intimacy with his wife and daughter. 'Well read,' he'd continued, 'I'll grant him that, but hardly a priest who will climb the ecclesiastical ladder. Do fine in a rural parish, I guess – that folksy style would suit the rustics. Now, the Jesuits—'

She'd reached for a mental switch and turned Poppa off. It was a well-practised gesture. Laura Morton, sitting on a cold bench thousands of miles from Chicago, turned up the volume of memory and relived her last conversation with Father Reilly.

'The Fratres,' he mumbled around the pipe stem, 'well, they're kinda the new kids on the block ... Churchwise. Bit soon to tell which way they'll blow. Some of the fellas say they're a bit to the right of Genghis Khan, not that I'm being critical, mind.' He released a stream of smoke and continued from inside the cloud. Laura had worked out, from previous conversations, that 'fellas' were priests. 'Goodfellas', she knew, were not. 'Never thought of joinin' the Mercy Sisters, have ye, Laura? No! How's about the Sisters of Charity?' She'd shaken her head. He'd given a half-cough, half-chuckle. 'Mercy without Charity and Charity without Mercy. Least, that's what my sisters always said. Let me ask around and see what I come up with. There's a young fella over in Jude's seems very taken with the Fratres. Wouldn't surprise me if he ups sticks and joins them. Bright enough young fella but perpetually newly ordained, if you get my drift?'

'No, Father.'

Father Reilly took a long draw from the pipe for inspiration. 'He's what you might call enthusiastic.'

'Isn't that a good thing, Father?'

'Ah, yes, of course. There's a long history of enthusiasm in religion,' he went on, 'all the way back to the Essenes with the Jews. The Turks had their dervishes and the Greeks had the Oracle at Delphi, who was a young girl, like yourself. She sat on a tripod stool over a volcanic vent and prophesised. Probably the smoke, ye know. Never worked for me,' he smiled. 'Ah yes, *entheos* from the Greek. It means 'having the spirit of God come inside you and take over'. Trouble is, it can be manipulated kinda easily. The priests did it in Delphi. Set themselves up as go-betweens, explaining the Oracle to the ordinary people – for a price, of course. Same in all the religious traditions, a good idea gets into the wrong hands and there's crusades, pogroms, jihads and all that sort of malarkey. Ach,' he said and shook brown, bitter juice from the pipe-stem into the grate. 'Sure you won't have coffee?'

'No ... no thank you, Father. I had breakfast just a while back.' She knew Father Reilly 'did' for himself. It didn't include doing the dishes. He tapped his pipe in the ashtray and she took it as a signal to go.

'Sit down, girl,' he said. 'What hurry is on you?'

He dipped the pipe bowl in a mouldering leather pouch and teased tobacco with his forefinger. Satisfied, he flashed a match with his thumbnail and held it while it flared. He brought the flame to hover over the pipe, sucking it down in small puffs. With a twist of his wrist, the dead match flew and landed in a cut-forest of companions in the grate.

'I was very sorry about your father and mother,' he said, so gently that she swallowed a few times before replying.

'I know that, Father. Thank you.'

'I'm not going to tell you it was God's holy will,' he pressed on,' it was an accident – a tragic accident. Don't want you thinking your poppa and momma were taken by God to make you a better person, or any of that ould nonsense. D'ye hear me now?'

'Yes, Father.'

'Your father was ... a good man, according to his lights,' he pronounced from inside a fresh cloud that haloed him.

'Yes, Father, he—'

'Fine teacher,' he interrupted. 'Always taught the A-students, top marks every time. Lots of kids around here would never have seen college but for your poppa. Helluva teacher. Sometimes,' he said, tilting his chin back to inspect the ceiling, 'it must be hard, for a man like that, not to have, eh, expectations of his own child. D'ye follow me?'

'Yes, Father.'

'Sometimes, people who are what you might call book-bright want their child to be that way too.'

'Yes, Father.' For no reason she could fathom, she was crying.

'Some fathers get a child whose gift is different and they spend their lives pushin' and pullin' to change it, to make them more like themselves, ye know? Others, the lucky ones, live long enough to know different. If your poppa had lived a bit longer I think he might have been one of the lucky ones.'

He let the silence settle while she dabbed her eyes.

'Now, your mother,' he said, laughing wheezily, 'was a piece of work. I remember I had the bishop here, for Confirmation I suppose. Well, I asked your momma to give a hand, he was coming with all the usual hangers-on and they expected to be fed. Feudal, of course, but that's the way. You never in your life saw such a spread. She had a tablecloth that would make you snow-blind and napkins rolled up in fancy rings. Everything's going just dandy until the bishop taps his empty glass and asks your mother for a refill. God in heaven, the bottle is sitting right there on the table. He was that kind of fella, liked being a bishop.'

'What happened, Father?' she prompted.

'"What did your last slave die of, Bishop?"' she asked him. After much coughing, he resumed. 'She was her own woman, your mother. Will you pass me the matches, Laura?' he asked suddenly.

It was out of her mouth before her brain could engage. 'What did your last slave die of, Father Reilly?' she asked.

Father Reilly nodded approvingly. 'Oh yes, girl,' he smiled, 'you're the livin' image of her. Are you all right for money?'

It was such an abrupt change of tack that her mouth opened and nothing came out.

'Nod or shake your head,' he suggested helpfully.

She nodded. She considered her generous inheritance and nodded again.

'Good. Don't say another word, 'tis no one's business but your own. These days,' he continued, in a more measured way, 'if a girl wants to join a religious order, money changes hands. They call it a dowry.' He plucked the pipe from his lips, as if it had left a bitter aftertaste. 'As if they were doing you a favour,' he muttered. 'Not tellin' you your business, now,' he said slowly, 'but I suggest you put the bulk of it in the bank – before you sign on. That way, you'll always have something to come back to – if it doesn't work out. Anyways, from what the fellas tell me, them Fratres aren't short a few dollars.'

Father Reilly's kindly face faded and the hard bench and the hovering secretary came into sharp focus. *I should have listened to Father Reilly*, she thought. It was the first thing they'd asked for when she'd arrived in Zurich. She remembered the trip to the bank. It had all been very Swiss.

'The Fraulein will please sign here and here. Just so. Danke, auf Wiedersehen.'

She'd come home for an audience with Father General and … he'd been mesmerising. It sounded like a word from some shabby fairground poster but he had been so persuasive, sharing his vision of the Fratres and their crusade to re-evangelise Europe with little Laura Morton from Chicago. And she could barely breathe when he stood close to her and she saw the twin scars that ran from his eye to the corner of his mouth. He'd hugged her and called her his little rose and when his hands moved to her breasts she'd been frightened and exhilarated. She blushed and shook her head to dislodge the memory of what had followed. And now? Now, she needed to see him so very badly and she was stuck here on a hard bench in a cold corridor. She felt a sudden urge to get up and leave. Slowly, she relaxed on the bench and composed herself. *I am Laura Morton, Rosa Morton's daughter*, she reminded herself. *I am my own woman*. She felt the disapproving stare of the secretary and turned her head to stare back at him until he dropped his eyes. *And I'm from Chicago*, she thought fiercely.

CIA OFFICE, THE ROCKEFELLER BUILDING, NEW YORK

'On his second drink, Mister Director,' the waiter whispered as he relieved the director of his coat.

'*Gracias*, Joaquin,' the director murmured and pushed through

the double doors to his office. Out of habit, he stopped inside
the door and scanned the room. There were two armchairs,
facing off, in the circle of light from a standard lamp, a low table
crouched between them. A silver head flashed briefly in the light
as Bill Donovan reached for the bottle on the table. *That's three
drinks and counting*, the director thought. Wild Bill Donovan,
his predecessor as Director of the CIA, would be mellow rather
than maudlin.

'Bill,' he greeted the older man, who rose from the armchair.

The rugged features relaxed into a grin. 'Hey, boy, good to see
you.'

The director knew that 'boy' was a sign of affection and a measure
of authority all rolled into one. He felt no annoyance and showed
none as he exchanged a firm handclasp. Wild Bill, as he was known
to the older staffers, had founded the agency out of the wartime
OSS – despite Truman's reluctance and the territorial howls of both
the army and navy intelligence services. Senator Joe McCarthy
hadn't helped either and J. Edgar Hoover had tried to smother the
fledgling agency at birth. They exchanged the usual white lies that
pass for small talk when one generation meets another.

'Looking good, Bill.'

'Nah, knees are shot.'

He'd noticed the time-lapse between Donovan's surge from the
chair and becoming upright and nodded sympathetically.

'Too many jumps, Bill,' he said lightly, offering a chance for
denial, which duly arrived.

'Too many tackles more like,' Donovan laughed. 'Playing ball for
Columbia was a helluva lot scarier than the damn war.'

The director smiled dutifully and sat in the armchair facing the
door. *No*, he thought, as he aligned his back with the chair, *what
Bill Donovan did during the war was a whole lot scarier, mostly for
the enemy*. He may have gained his nickname for his style of play on
the football field but he'd earned it behind enemy lines.

'Jeez, I really hate Spellman's parties,' Donovan groused. 'I'm getting too old for climbing into a tux and having my back slapped by the Knights of Columbus.'

'Slaps beat stabs, Bill,' the director suggested wryly. 'Anyway, the knights like to venerate their icons.'

'Icons!' Donovan snorted. 'That's just a fancy word for old and you know it.'

'Still,' the director persisted, 'it must be nice to pin on the medals every now and then?'

'Yeah, you're right,' Donovan grudged, 'gets me out of the house as well. Ye know the hardest thing after you've been away for so long is being back. Mrs Donovan says she married me for better or for worse, but not for lunch.' He barked a short laugh. 'And the kids?' he continued. 'Well, the kids are all grown up and living their own lives. You never get that time back again, do you?'

His face tightened suddenly and the awkward silence lengthened.

'Lots of old friends to catch up with, Bill,' the director said and saw the relief flood the other man's face. He fished a pipe from his pocket and began the ritual of loading and lighting, taking time to marshal his thoughts. When he had a good head of smoke going, he said, 'D'you think our cardinal could become our pope?'

Donovan sipped his drink and leaned back. 'You know damn well, Mister Director,' he said evenly, 'that his altar boy could be pope, once he's ours.'

The director waved his pipe in acknowledgement. 'Point taken, Bill.'

Donovan shifted in his chair and sipped again.

'There is, of course, the problem of his, eh, proclivities,' he said.

What is it with Irish Catholics, the director wondered, *that makes them so antsy around someone's sexual preferences?* Donovan and the other members of the Knights of Columbus could be cold-blooded in war and ruthless in business and yet—

'We keep an eye, Bill,' he said cryptically.

Donovan might guess that Spellman's driver was on the agency payroll or that someone higher up the pecking order at the Chancery was more than he seemed, but he'd never ask. *And God knows*, the director thought, *the old man fought tooth and nail to naturalise and employ people who should have been hanged at Nuremberg. It's what we do for the greater good*, he concluded tiredly.

Donovan kept shifting in his chair and the director knew he wouldn't let this go.

'Wasn't there some talk about some stuff appearing in the newspapers? Yeah, and there was this guy Connolly or Cooney, I dunno which, writing some damn book about this?'

Donovan, the director knew, was simulating vagueness. It was the prerogative of the man who had vacated the chair the director now sat in, and who didn't want to appear too enquiring or critical.

'Not a problem, Bill,' he said easily. 'Word went round the print shops that they could kiss goodbye to the Catholic advertisers. Oh, and the writer is Cooney, by the way. I understand the book is a few pages lighter than planned.'

'What will it take to put Spellman in the Vatican?'

'A truckload of dollars in the Vatican Bank.'

'Along with all the other truckloads we sent them to win the election for the Christian Democrat Union after the war.'

'Money well spent, Bill,' the director said, tapping the ash flat in his pipe with a firm finger. 'In return,' he added, 'we get a pope and … other benefits.'

Donovan nodded. He knew the rules; once you're out of the loop, it's strictly 'need to know'.

'We haven't had much interest from the army or navy recently,' the director continued, as if he was discussing some neglectful relatives. 'And,' he added, 'the senator and the Feds haven't dropped by in a while.'

Donovan couldn't resist a feral grin. Both men relished the fact that the creation of the agency had put the noses of the forces' intelligence departments seriously out of joint. Hoover of the FBI and McCarthy, the commie-hating senator, had joined forces with the baying pack to bring the agency down whichever way they could.

'Ike isn't Truman,' Donovan said sagely. 'He knows which way the wind is blowing.'

The director knew that Donovan still had the president's ear.

'Thanks for that, Bill,' he said.

Donovan raised his glass in a half-toast and emptied the contents.

'Anytime,' Bill said equably. He started to protest as the director brandished the bottle and then relented. 'Why not? Maybe it'll kill the pain of listening to another priest looking for money. Know anything about this Steiger fella?'

The director reached into his jacket pocket and offered a single, densely typed page.

Donovan held the page at arm's length. Another prerogative of old men, the director thought, as he attended to his pipe, to pretend that they don't need spectacles.

'Some priest,' Donovan said finally, and both men smiled. It was an Americanism and could be interpreted as a commendation or as a condemnation.

A tap at the door interrupted their conversation. A young staffer pushed inside and closed the door noiselessly behind her. 'Sorry, Mister Director,' she said, holding a printout before her like a votive offering. 'You said if anything came in from—'

'It's okay, Elizabeth,' he said quickly. 'Thank you.'

She blushed and backed to the door. Elizabeth was new and stuck with the night shift. He'd have to speak with her supervisor later. The girl had been one word away from naming an asset, probably the most important asset the agency had in the field. Maybe she thought it was okay with just Donovan in the room, but it wasn't. *Dammit*, he argued with himself, *she's just a kid. She doesn't even know the code so what's the big deal?* But it *was* a big deal. Anything that came from this asset was. He'd wait until her supervisor had chewed her out and then ask her to his office. She'd be nervous and penitent, already working on her resumé.

'I was a staffer in our Bern office. I was young – well, younger anyways,' he'd begin, 'and I was stuck with the weekend shift. On Saturday afternoon, a guy calls up and says his name is Lenin and he wants to negotiate something important with the US government. I knew he hung around with the local group of émigrés. I also knew I had a doubles tennis match lined up with a friend and two lovely ladies. "Call back Monday," I said. "Pity," he said, "by then it will be too late." Nobody starts good, Elizabeth,' he'd continue. 'Everything is learned and part of that learning is to make mistakes. The secret is not to make the same mistake twice, okay?' She'd say, 'Yes, sir', and he'd say, 'You have the makings of a fine staffer', and usher her out of his office.

'Can you give me a minute, Bill?'

'Sure. Glad to. Bathroom where it always was?'

'Yes, some things never change.'

Alone, he moved to the desk, drawing a key chain from his pants pocket – Yale key, top drawer, to frustrate the spooks who despised the obvious. He laid the code book flat on the desk and parsed with his forefinger as he read the code, rubbing back and forward, picking letters from words and committing them to memory.

'Never use a pen or pencil to underline,' the instructor in Virginia had insisted, 'makes it easy reading for the next guy.'

'So, rub it out after reading,' some wise-ass had offered.

'How you gonna rub out the impression on the page beneath?' the instructor had cracked back and they'd laughed.

He wasn't laughing now. He read the message again and remembered the tremor of excitement and fear when he'd let go of the rope, as a kid, and the river had risen up to smack him.

'Read twice, act once,' the instructor had cautioned. 'Dammit, read twenty times before you get up and go.' The instructor had usually followed this with another story. 'Old bull, young bull! Young bull spies a herd of cows and says, "Let's gallop down there and get us a cow." Old bull says, "Let's stroll down there and get the whole herd."'

The director folded the printout and put it in his pocket, locked the code book in its lair and tapped on the bathroom door.

'You need some help in there, Bill?'

'Niagara drips not falls when you get to my age,' Donovan shot back.

Everything's coded in our world, the director thought tiredly as he sat in his chair. *We can't just say leave the room while I read a message and then come back, I've read it.* Would he ever get used to ordinary conversation when he retired? Could he ever read a letter without a code book? Most likely, he'd spend an hour trying to decipher a shopping list.

The message had been simple – the work of two minutes with the code book. It read:

'It is necessary for one man to die for the people.' As a Presbyterian, he knew his Bible better than most. His stomach reprised its flip and churn. It meant they were committed. It also meant the asset would be terminated. If so, he accepted, the quote was doubly apt.

'I'm having some folks over after the party,' the director said, rising from his armchair as Donovan came back inside. 'Figure we'd have a, eh, heads-up on the, eh, wider picture. Appreciate it if you could sit in.'

Donovan waved a deprecatory hand.

'Shouldn't queer your pitch, Mister Director,' he protested. 'Best that the new broom sweeps clean.'

'It's been said,' the director conceded, 'but the old broom knows where the dirt is. You got a driver?'

'Sure, I got a driver.'

'I'll catch you later.'

'Duty calls,' Donovan replied, waving his glass in farewell.

THE FRATRES SCHLOSS, SWITZERLAND

Laura woke at four in the morning and checked her underwear. Nothing. How many days – weeks? she wondered frantically, and then sat on the bed and took a deep breath to steady herself. After dressing the bed army-style, she knelt beside it to pray. When she attempted to picture God's face, she saw Fr Reilly and smiled sadly. The slap, slap of the discipline echoed from the other rooms on the corridor and she flinched. She had buried the little whip under her spare habit in the bottom of the wardrobe. It was against the rules, but so was the journal she kept in the pocket of the habit. Sister Pilar had said it was against Holy Poverty for any of them to own anything other than what the Fratres gave them. But her momma had given her the journal and there were lots of entries about Momma. There were entries about Father General also. She had no one to confide in and writing it in the journal helped her to sleep. The sting of the cold water in the basin helped her focus. She would go and see him today after mass. She'd walk right by that darned secretary-bird and—

The great doors of the chapel opened and Laura watched the celebrant and his assistants process to the altar. She felt a queasy sensation and prayed it was hunger. The celebrant had a sonorous voice and droned through the Latin. Oh, God, she prayed silently and fervently, let there not be incense. The dull clanking of the thurible chain reverberated through her as the heady incense wafted over the congregation. To the surprise of her companions on either side, she rose from her knees and keeled over. The last words she heard were, '*Ad Deum, qui laetificat juventutem meam* – To God, who brings joy to my youth.' Then the light had faded.

She dreamed of the day Poppa had taken her to the lake. She was ten years old and Momma had disappeared to a cousin's wedding. Poppa didn't go. Laura was sorry he hadn't gone, she could have gone to the Trentons' and played with a whole houseful of kids. The Trenton girls had a brother they called a jerk but he always held the back of the saddle when she rode their bike. Poppa held her hand firmly as they walked the path by the shoreline. 'I'm ten now, Poppa,' she'd said, 'you can let go my hand.'

'Ten! Are you sure?'

'Sure I'm sure.'

'The first "sure" is unnecessary, Laura,' he'd said in his teacher's voice. 'One sure is sufficient. The first is slang or tautology and we can't have that, can we?'

'No, Poppa.'

'Can you tell me the name of this lake?'

'It's Lake Michigan, Poppa.'

'Are you sure?'

'Su— I'm sure.'

Behind them, she saw kids riding bikes, throwing footballs and flying kites with their poppas.

'Can you name any of the other Great Lakes?'

'Superior and Huron, Poppa.' The Trenton boy said 'whoreon'. He thought that was funny.

'And which country is on the other side of the Great Lakes?'

It felt just like school, she thought, only worse. She knew he'd go on and on until he found a question she couldn't answer.

'Canada, Poppa,' she said.

'And what would you find in Canada?'

'They got bears and lots of trees and—'

'And what language do they speak in Canada?'

'They speak English, just like us, Poppa. And some people speak French.'

'Malcolm,' a man passing them said, 'good to see ya.' The man was taller than Poppa. He shook Poppa's hand and held a girl of her own age with his other hand. 'And this is Suze,' he said, in that drawly kind of voice adults used when they talked about kids. 'Suze is a straight A student. Wins the spelling bee every darn time. Guess your girl got her daddy's brains also, Malcolm?'

Poppa didn't answer. He started talking about school and stuff. Another teacher. Laura gave the other girl a sympathetic smile but she just stared right through her. 'Well,' the man said, 'you must come visit, little girl, so you and Suze can get better acquainted.' He patted her on the head. Momma said patting on the head was for dogs.

'I'm not a dog,' she said, 'and I'm ten.'

The man removed his hand as if she were on fire.

'Gotta scoot,' he said. 'Let's do lunch sometime, huh?'

Poppa waited until they were out of sight. He bent down and looked at her with hot angry eyes. 'Don't you ever shame me like that again.'

'Sorry, Poppa,' she said – but the man she was looking at wasn't Poppa. He had a bald head and disinterested eyes. He plucked a stethoscope from his chest and placed it on her belly. It was cold and made her flinch. *Our family doctor always warms the stethoscope,* she thought. He straightened and pulled her habit down, roughly.

'Ja,' he said.

He disappeared from view and Sister Pilar's face replaced his. Her face was a white mask. When the door closed, she leaned forward and spat, '*Puta. Hija del diablo.*'

The door slammed and Laura was alone. 'Momma,' she whispered. 'Momma.'

THE VETERANS' HOSPITAL, NEW YORK

The driver held the door as the director climbed into the rear of the black car, then he slid behind the wheel. There was no talk of destinations or directions. Though the car was warm, the director hunched into the black cashmere coat he wore over his tuxedo. He'd brought Harry, the driver, with him when he'd left the law practice for the agency – that had been a good call. As Harry edged into traffic, the director thought about how Harry never exceeded the speed limit, never looked in the rear-view mirror and never missed a target with the Smith and Wesson he kept camouflaged under his jacket.

Outside the Veterans' Hospital, he slewed the car into an ambulance bay and gazed stoically forward while the director exited from the rear. The director took a stethoscope from his coat pocket and draped it around his neck. He took a nametag from the top pocket of his jacket and stuck it on his lapel. He'd learned years ago to inhabit the character he needed to play in any situation.

Feet slapping rhythmically on the marble floor, he made his unhurried way through the reception area. To look for eye contact would be to invite it and, inevitably, questions. He kept his eyes fixed firmly ahead, like a man who did this every day. His badge read Major General John Cornwell MD, if anyone had come close enough to read it. Most of the people he encountered dropped their eyes or hurried about their business. A huddle of anxious relatives tensed at his approach and then nodded respectfully as the tall, slightly stooped gentleman with salt-and-pepper hair and moustache entered the elevator.

The sixth floor was not one the public could access easily. It had its own receptionist, who sat at a gunmetal-grey desk opposite the elevator. The doors whooshed open and the male receptionist looked up enquiringly.

'Evening,' the director said, making a perfunctory salute.

Instinctively, the receptionist rose to his feet and snapped off a smart salute in return.

The young man lying in the bed seemed oblivious to the hum, chirp and wheeze of the machinery that was keeping him alive. A tangle of tubes snaked in and out beneath the covers, looping back to monitors and bags that hung suspended like rotten fruit. The director could see only one side of the man's face and the slender tube that sucked his mouth awry. Slow bubbles ebbed up the transparent tube. It reminded the director of a distiller's coil and he tensed to think of the man's essence being extracted in this sterile place. His hands gripped the bed rail until his knuckles bled white. He had predicted that Korea would give them the experience they'd need for the next war. How sage he'd sounded and how approvingly his acolytes had nodded. His lips stretched into a straight line as he remembered. *Who could have predicted this experience?* he wondered. They must have heard it coming and scrambled for shelter. They must have jumped to their feet again after the shrapnel had scythed harmlessly over their heads, except for the guy with the piece of iron in his brain, except for him – his son. The rising crescendo of approaching footsteps peeled his fingers from the rail.

The young medic was unshaven and bleary-eyed. 'Sir?' he enquired.

Without taking his eyes from the form in the bed, the director tapped the badge in his lapel. 'Surgeon Cornwell,' he said. 'And you, soldier?'

'Lieutenant Speers, sir. James Speers.'

'Your evaluation of this patient, Lieutenant?'

'Hard to say with a brain injury, sir,' the lieutenant said slowly. 'Vital signs are steady, no other trauma. I guess time will tell, sir,' he added lamely.

No other trauma, the director thought and fought to keep his face impassive. He had a sudden vision of his wife waiting up for him tonight, as she always did. She was the only human being who saw inside his mask and his chest tightened in anticipation of the hope that would flicker and die in her eyes.

'Thank you, Lieutenant Speers,' he said gruffly. 'Carry on.'

He stood erect and snapped off a smart salute before exiting the room. The lieutenant had already raised his hand to return the salute of a senior officer and dropped it as the door closed, convinced that it had not been intended for him.

THE TRAIN TO ROME

Sister Pilar had brought her clothes at six and dumped them on the bed. Laura had been surprised to see they were the clothes she had arrived in from Chicago. The Fratres had cast her out. She'd fingered the overcoat while she let that reality form and settle inside her. The coat had been Momma's and just wrapping it around her gave her a sense of warmth and strength. 'Take a standing count of eight,' Momma had said whenever someone was all het up. She was always coming up with boxing aphorisms like 'rub off the blood and box on'. She'd thought that one was particularly apt. Only there wasn't any blood and that was the problem.

'¡*Vamos!*'

Laura had trailed the striding Pilar through the echoing building to the door. Outside, a car was crouched at the foot of the steps. There were seven steps – she remembered counting them on the day she'd arrived. Sister Pilar had sat up front with the driver. Laura had sat alone in the back.

When the train jerked, she clutched at the seat and then sat back. The platform slid backwards so that people looked like they were hurrying in the opposite direction. The train gathered speed and settled into a rhythmic clicking. The sound seemed to come up through her feet. It felt so much like a heartbeat that she bent to the window, fastening her eyes on the countryside to try and regulate her breathing. The countryside was beautiful but somehow remote beyond the window pane. Scenes passed like slightly different versions of the same postcard. There were valleys with villages sloping neatly down to green lakes and roofs that looked like conical caps on brooding farmhouses. She saw no rusty tractors in farmyards or coils of weary car tyres, even the wood piles were perfect. The postcards flipped across the lower part of the window; the view through the upper part was of an unfolding graph of mountains. Their lower slopes were studded with trees while the upper reaches shone with snow, like polished silver. She shivered and drew Momma's coat a little tighter. The train angled higher and higher until flanks and peaks crowded the window. She held her breath as they were sucked into tunnels and she guessed that they were leaving Switzerland.

THE BASEMENT, THE VETERANS' HOSPITAL, NEW YORK

Like all nurses, she was in a hurry to somewhere else. 'Lobby?' she asked and pushed the button when he nodded. He stood at the back, resting his back against the wall of the elevator. She crossed her arms, eyes on the floor as if willing it to drop faster. They descended in the silence of strangers who share a confined space for a short time.

'After you,' she said as the door slid open.

'I insist,' he smiled, and watched as she clattered across the concourse. She looked back as the doors closed, surprised to see him still inside the elevator.

He pressed a sub-basement button and inhaled deeply as if diving under water. The air was a cocktail of fuggy elevator, medicines, cleaning products and the mouldy breath of old buildings. The nurse had left a citrus note of perfume and he clung to it as the floor dropped under him.

The light shone directly in his face as he stepped outside.

'Please stand still, sir, and hold your arms away from your sides.'

Blinded and disoriented, he did as he was bid.

'Password,' the voice challenged.

'Dante,' he replied, wondering who the classicist was on the security detail and whether the irony was deliberate.

'Visiting?'

'Doctor Gottlieb.'

He heard the telephone rattle from its cradle and a single spin of the dial. The light winked out, leaving a purple after-image on his vision.

'This way, Mister Director.'

He felt both piqued and pleased that his status hadn't exempted him from the usual precautions. Gottlieb ran a tight ship. Automatically, he matched his step to that of the man 'on point', his head scanning left and right as he had been trained to do a lifetime ago. *Phantom pains*, he thought, immediately regretting his choice of words.

The metal doors that studded either side of the corridor were relieved by spy-holes. Apart from the synchronised tread of footsteps, he heard the occasional whimper. A male voice rose and fell in an incontinent and unceasing babble. Near the end of the corridor, a single voice soared to proclaim, '*De profundis clamavi ad te, Domine*' – 'Out of the depths I cry unto thee, O Lord.' *Are we Dante or Oppenheimer?* he wondered, to distract himself from the voices. *Have we recreated purgatory or become the destroyer of worlds?* Running the gauntlet of the cries and whispers of those who had, wittingly or not, offered themselves to the service of their country as participants in Project MKUltra, he grunted, 'Needs must.'

'Sir?'

'Nothing.'

Never explain, he reminded himself. The politicians liked to say that explaining was losing. Inevitably, the day would come when 'the secret thoughts of many would be laid bare', probably before a committee of investigation comprised of politicians. In the meantime, there was a war to be won and sacrifices to be made. At the last moment, he became aware that the man in front had halted and he only barely avoided slamming into his broad back. They had arrived.

Sidney Gottlieb remained focused on his papers as the director took his seat. There were reams of paper, climbing from a single page directly before him to a mound on either side that teetered precariously over the edge of the desk. At least, the director presumed, there was a desk under the twin glaciers of paper. He liked to keep a clean desk himself, operating on a read-and-file basis, partly because, as a lawyer, he'd been trained that way. As Director of the CIA, any piece of paper that crossed his desk was strictly your-eyes-only. If he'd had a degree from Caltech, like Sidney, he might have been able to glean some information, while the saturnine chemist tilted his head down the single page. As it was, the material might have been written in Sumerian for all he understood. He sat and waited. He might be the Director of the CIA, but Sidney was the top man in this alchemical neck of the woods – even if it had been the director who had asked for the meeting. But this was Gottlieb's ball park, so they would play by his rules, the director mused and waited. Eventually, Gottlieb signed the paper, recapped his pen and consigned the paper to the pile on his left. The mound tilted and settled.

'You know, one of these days, that's gonna come tumbling down,' the director smiled. 'What then?'

'I've read them,' Gottlieb said dryly. A lifelong stutterer, he favoured short responses. 'Welcome,' he added, extending a hand through the gap in the paper valley. He didn't get up – wouldn't, unless he had to, conscious of his club foot.

'Thank you,' the director said and leaned back in the uncomfortable, aluminium chair.

'Like a-a-a drink?' Gottlieb offered.

The director had a thick file locked in his office cabinet, detailing Gottlieb's history of offering spiked drinks to the unwary and the consequences when they accepted. Some of the consequences featured in autopsy reports. 'I'll pass,' he said.

Gottlieb allowed himself the hint of a smile.

'I've been reading the Korean material,' the director continued, although that wasn't what he'd come to talk about. Gottlieb nodded in a way that suggested he knew this and was willing to play the conversational game, according to the director's rules – for now. 'Everything locked down tight on that?' the director asked. Like any good lawyer, he only asked a question if he already knew the answer.

'Yes.'

'If …' the director paused and let the word hang between them. 'If some inquisitive reporter was to get a sniff of that story …?' Again, he left the pause before continuing. 'Our contingency plan, in that event, is to build a firewall around the agency.'

Gottlieb was a bright man, he knew. He would know that 'our contingency plan' was the director's plan and, in the event of a leak, Gottlieb would be outside the firewall.

'If,' Gottlieb began, 'any reporter got a sniff of anthrax, he would die slowly and painfully. It can be arranged. Also,' he added, 'the p-p-personnel in the loop are all P-Paperclip personnel.'

The director nodded in capitulation. He knew that Gottlieb's Korean team had been hand-picked from the pool of Nazi biochemists and scientists that the agency had recruited after the war. By using the code name Operation Paperclip, he was signalling his knowledge of the fact that the director had sanitised the records of war criminals. Despite President Truman's suspicions, the falsified records had ensured American visas for those on the list. *The Bronx boy still knows how to throw a curve ball*, he thought. *He's also certain the bases are stacked in his favour*. After all, the Germans are unlikely to play footsie with the Fourth Estate or the enemy. The agency provided lots of perks to keep those experts on side and lots of information concerning former colleagues in the employ of the opposition to keep them in line. The agency was the only game in town and Gottlieb's Germans were bright enough to know that. The leak wouldn't come from there. He decided it was time to up his game.

'I read your report on the LSD trials,' he said easily. 'Seemed to go well.'

'Yes. We aerosoli–aero-a … we sprayed at Pont-Saint-Esprit in France, a small rural p-population. The stats are thirty-seven admissions to m-m-mental institutions and seven fatalities. P-proves it could be e-e-effective against cities or large m-military groups. And the beauty of it is that the drug is totally legal in the United States.' He sat back and cocked an eyebrow at the director. 'If any reporter got a sniff of that story, Mister Director, he'd live but he'd be much too happy to file it.'

Gottlieb was obviously enjoying himself in the witness box, the former lawyer concluded. It was time to spring the trap.

'But not Paperclip personnel on this one, Doctor?' he said quietly, and watched the flicker of unease ruffle the bland face.

'N-no, well, y-yes. In f-fact, m-m-most of the bio-bio-biochemists were P-Paperc-c-clip.'

It was a long sentence for a man with his affliction, cruelly long because it contained so many consonants he would usually avoid, if he wasn't rattled.

'Most of the biochemists, you say,' the director said, pressing his advantage, 'but not all of them. My information is that a biochemist called Olson is American-born, one of ours, Doctor. And he's been expressing … reservations. You know him, of course,' he added innocently.

'Ols— y-yes of c—'

'Of course you do,' the director continued, finishing the sentence for a man who detested that kind of patronisation. 'I'd really appreciate it if you could look into that,' he said offhandedly as he stood.

It is all a game, the director thought. He'd never been much of a ball player as a kid and the Little League baseball coach had consigned him to the dugout. 'You think too much,' he'd said. The kindly old guy with the crocked knees had been right, the kids who played by instinct scored the bases. By the time he'd figured the trajectory and velocity of the pitch, the catcher was already polishing the ball in his mitt. Still, he'd had plenty of time among the substitutes to become a hotshot on the theory of the game. So far, in the game with Gottlieb, his first pitch had been far enough away for the Black Sorcerer to ignore it. The second had been fast and dangerously close, making him wince a little. Gottlieb would be all cranked up now, waiting for the one in the zone – the one that would clear all the bases. Time for the lob. He'd seen it work its magic on the best batsmen, the look of surprise, the awkward realignment of the body and the snatched swing that curled it up and down into the glove. Out!

'Had a query from one of our guys,' he said from the door, as if it had just occurred to him. 'Seemed right up your street, Sidney,' he added, turning back to the desk. The familiar use of his first name was already registering in the face and body of the chemist as the director continued. 'The target is an elderly male – all the usual medical problems plus bouts of rage and a taste for hard liquor. You get the picture.'

He pulled a folded page from his pocket and dropped it on the desk.

'That's a précis of his most recent medical report,' he said.

Gottlieb read it through and looked up when he'd finished.

'This m-man shouldn't b-be alive,' he said dismissively.

The director nodded. 'A lot of people share that opinion.'

'Transmission?' Gottlieb snapped.

'Probably liquid, something to add to his usual medicine.'

'Diagnosis?'

'Stroke. Yeah, that wouldn't be unexpected.'

'Incapacitation or—'

'Terminal.'

'And if it's traced?'

'I gather the Chinese are getting up to speed on that sort of thing.'

'I'll have one of my g-g—'

The director raised an eyebrow.

'One of my P-P-Paperclip guys,' Gottlieb said grudgingly.

'I'd be a whole lot happier if this one came from you, Doctor.'

He waited until the other man dropped his eyes.

'This evening would be fine,' the director said and turned away. 'I've often meant to ask you, Sidney,' he said suddenly as he buttoned his coat, 'what happens to people who press the wrong button on the elevator?'

'They volunteer to serve their country, Mister Director – as I did,' Sidney Gottlieb snapped tightly without a trace of a stammer.

I never liked Gottlieb, the director admitted to himself as he waited for security to collect him. *I needed to rattle his cage about Olson, if only to wipe the smugness from his face.* But he felt no sense of victory, only the burden of the decisions he made every day and the consequences he accumulated. He'd tried to broach that subject with his father one time. 'Consequences,' the old man had propounded, 'are the result of decisions. Real men know that and get on with it. A real general sends soldiers into situations where they will almost certainly die. A real squadron leader orders bombs to be dropped on civilians. Why? For the greater good. The downside of being real is that you must live with the consequences.' *This is the downside*, he thought as he looked along the corridor.

Behind those cyclop doors, men are being fed barbiturates through one I/V and amphetamines through another so that they swim in a stream of consciousness and babble incoherently. There were men here on LSD who thought the doctor was their daddy and men soaring on mescaline wings who cried like babies at the loss of paradise, every time they fell to earth. *We have created a pharmacological Bedlam in this basement in the hope of what? Have we bypassed the thumb-screws and the testicle-crushers for a tiny tincture of some mind-altering drug so that a hardened enemy agent will become a fount of information at the slight sting of a hypodermic? Yes. And is it part of the plan that John and Mary Doe, the ordinary US citizen, will be able to recall every detail of a document, blueprint or formula? Yes to that also. We turn them into someone else, for a time, listen to the revelations of that 'someone else' and then bring them back. Except that, sometimes, we can't bring them back. And sometimes we don't bring them back because they have nothing more to give, or because we can't hope to rehabilitate them, so they go all the way to the terminus. Sometimes, just sometimes, some of our own people go rogue or grow a conscience or, by some lethal irony, know too much and so fall prey to the pharmacological honey-traps of the other side.*

Like this time. Like Olson.

He heard footsteps approaching and braced himself. She'll be waiting up, he reminded himself. She'll lean up and peck my cheek and say, 'How's the world, honey?' Of course, she'll smile to take the sting from the question; they both accepted he'd have a separate life when he took the job. It was a life that she could never be part of and he couldn't talk about. He knew she went to the hospital every day – just sat there, stroking their son's hair and whispering. *Did she tell him about the guys he'd grown up with who'd been promoted by the military? Did she tell him about their wives and babies? How could she do that and not—* He should take her to Europe for a vacation. They should go to the opera and walk in the Forum – walk somewhere, anywhere, where they could be just folks on tour. Folks on tour, he thought bitterly, with their very own bullet-proof car and a back-up team of agents as part of their luggage.

'Ready, sir?'

'Ready.'

She'll unbutton my coat and toss it over a chair and push me into an armchair by the fire. 'Bourbon?' she'll ask. It had been bourbon for over thirty years but she'll still ask. It was one of their rituals, one of the rituals that propped up the illusion of normality.

'Good night, Mister Director.'

His thoughts had carried him through to the Gates of Hades, as they always did. Maybe he should resign and go back to the law practice, he thought as the elevator began to rise. He'd said that to his wife when … when the boy had been brought back from Korea. 'Would you really leave the agency?' she'd asked.

'Yes.' He'd been certain, no hesitation in his voice.

'But would the agency leave you, honey?' she'd said, sadly. The lawyer had no answer to that question, and they'd never spoken of it again.

THE TRAIN TO ROME

She must have dozed. She woke to a different landscape that was untidy and bright. They stopped at stations with lots of syllables on the signs and people rushed from feeder trains or tore themselves from embraces to board. Stoic Swiss faces were replaced by expressive Italian ones and she wondered if the rise in temperature was because they were travelling south. For most of the journey, they were alone in the compartment. Occasionally, people would peer hopefully inside and then hurry on. She thought it must be the stiff pose of Sister Pilar that discouraged them. Perhaps it was the copy of the *Dark Night of the Soul* she held open before her like a shield. At Civitavecchia, a woman backed through the door lugging a large suitcase and carrying a baby in a sling. Laura helped her stow the case and the woman smiled and patted her cheek. When the train was moving again, she moved her blouse aside and brought the baby to her breast. Sister Pilar stiffened and turned to the window; Laura couldn't tear her eyes away. The baby was so small, just a tiny face in a bundle of blankets. It fastened on the brown nipple and sucked furiously. The woman shrugged the baby a little higher and looked up, her eyes catching Laura's. She smiled and nodded. Despite Sister Pilar's disapproving presence, Laura smiled back.

When she woke again, the mother and baby had disappeared. She wondered if she had imagined them.

St Patrick's Cathedral, New York

He was careful to be deferential. In the first few seconds of meeting Cardinal Spellman, he'd become aware that his superior height somehow threatened the other man and so dropped to his knees to kiss his ring.

'No need for that,' the cardinal said affably, but he didn't withdraw his hand and held Steiger's for a little longer than was necessary.

Americans, Steiger decided, practised an aggressive informality but delighted in titles and gestures of respect. They also had an unquenchable urge to display their possessions. He knew it was stereotyping on his part, but Spellman acted like the stereotypical archetype and Spellman held the key to the power Max Steiger wanted to access.

'C'mon, Father Steiger,' the cardinal said in his high, nasal voice, 'let me show you our beautiful cathedral. The land was bought at auction in the eighteen hundreds. Trustees figured they'd make it a cemetery. Well, I guess it was outside the city at the time. Problem with trustees is they got no vision, Father. One of the first things I did when I got here was wrap up the trustees and make my own decisions about what should be built and where.'

Steiger nodded appreciatively and the cardinal continued.

'Jesuits set up a church and school here a few years later. Did I tell you I'm a Jesuit boy myself? Sure, did my schooling in Fordham before I entered seminary.'

According to Spellman, Steiger thought, history would have lots of footnotes on Spellman.

Steiger found the cathedral drab and uninteresting. Spellman was prattling on about the eighteenth and nineteenth centuries as if he was talking about antiquity. He smiled inwardly, thinking of Chartres and Santa Maria Maggiore. Like the Romans, he thought, Americans are cultural plagiarists, copying the treasures of truly ancient cultures to lend gravitas to their new buildings.

'That window came from Chartres,' Spellman said proudly, as if reading Steiger's mind. Steiger knew it was from an artist in Chartres rather than from the famous cathedral. He stood in the wash of coloured light from the window and nodded appreciatively.

'Trappists came next – from France,' the cardinal added. 'Went back home after Napoleon died.'

Steiger thought Spellman sounded disappointed. He tried to block out the insistent voice that whined slowly through the completion of the cathedral, the addition of the two towers and the slates on the roof that 'came all the way from Boston'. He wondered why Americans had such a fixation with statistics and dimensions. Spellman had been eager to point out that the towers were three hundred and thirty feet high. *Why does everything have to be higher, longer and bigger than in Europe? Does the émigré soothe his loss with disparaging comparisons?*

'Our Pietà, here, is three times bigger than Michelangelo's,' the cardinal exulted.

As Steiger trailed Spellman gratefully to his adjoining living quarters, he thought the cardinal walked like a Hallstatt farmer in his Sunday suit, holding himself a little too stiffly and self-consciously lifting the hem of his cassock or touching the skull cap on his round head. He was dismayed to learn that they would now tour the cardinal's apartments – even the bathroom. His dismay curdled to contempt at the gold-plated bath taps and he felt liberated when Spellman suggested he 'might freshen up before going to the party'.

In the sanctuary of the guest room, Steiger reflected that the cathedral was a statement. It said, we Irish built this with labourers fresh from the coffin ships, when we were the lowest rung on the immigrant ladder. Today, our cathedral takes up a whole block on Fifth Avenue. Sure, it's shadowed by other buildings but it says we've arrived – the rich and powerful heirs of impoverished immigrants. He wondered if he could work some of that into his speech.

ON THE TRAIN TO ROME

The book remained in the bag. Karl looked out the window with the intensity of a man who hadn't seen the world for a very long time. Houses were built like beads along the strings of road, always presenting their faces to the passing traffic. The railroad had been a brash, new invention that disdained propriety. The train ran where it willed and as directly as the contours of the land allowed. Sometimes they were hurrying furtively between embankments; sometimes climbing on a raised railbed to view the backs of the houses. Clotheslines waved at him as they passed and a woman, toiling under a bucket, paused from her labours to look. Once, he saw a group of children turn from their play. He lifted his hand in greeting, but only the littlest one waved back. Too young to remember, he thought. Too young to remember trains full of soldiers going east – or trains with a different cargo. They nosed into a loop line at a country station, and waited for an express to go by. It flickered past like a film come loose from a spool. His stomach clenched at the prospect of what it might reveal. Would there be cattle-wagons skulking at the other side of the railyard? Would a little window on a wagon sprout fingers like butterflies from behind the bars until a soldier banged his carbine against the door and they disappeared inside their chrysalis? It was an image he'd seen from a different train, a different journey. The express whooshed by and in the rocking silence after its passing he saw bare tracks knitting and perling their way into the dimness of rusting sheds. Just memories, he assured himself. But his stomach stayed tight with disbelief and the next time they entered a tunnel, he saw his father and the others reflected in the black window.

South of Civitavecchia, he hurried from his feeder train and didn't look back. He let the cadence of the placename breathe through him until his breathing settled. The connecting train sweated steam at the other side of the platform, gulping water from a hanging pipe for the journey south. He was relieved to find a compartment already occupied by a sister and a young woman and placed his bag on the overhead rack. The nun was reading but never seemed to turn the page. A sideways glance confirmed the book was *Dark Night of the Soul*, by St John of the Cross. If it hadn't been for the warmth of Kurt and Bertha and the occasional, rough companionship of Johann, he might have given himself to the Dark Night. He felt a pang of pity for the solitary nun who was thin to the point of emaciation. She sat opposite, her body angled away from her forbidding companion. She was petite and her small, oval face was dappled with childish freckles. Attracted by his gaze, her eyes turned to his. He smiled and nodded. Her face brightened and then became wary and withdrawn. He wondered why her hand quested now and then to stroke her overcoat and why her face lightened when she did so.

The Al Smith fundraiser, New York

'Maybe you'd like to collect your thoughts, Father?'

Steiger knew he was being dismissed. The cardinal's eyes had already strayed to the men in gleaming white shirts and black tuxedos who filed through the doors. He would get his moment in the sun, but the limelight belonged to Spellman for now. He found a quiet corner and settled into an armchair.

'You the speaker?'

He was startled by the man who materialised at his elbow. 'Y-Yes,' he stammered.

'Tough,' the man said, lowering his long frame into an armchair. 'Manny Bernstein,' he said. 'Call me Manny.'

'Call me Manny', Steiger saw, was long-limbed and skeletal. His face looked like pictures Steiger had seen of unwrapped mummies, translucent skin shining over prominent cheekbones and puddling into shadows around his eyes. In his left hand, he dangled an ivory cigarette holder. 'Padre,' Manny said, in a smoke-roughened voice, extending his hand.

In the gap between the cuff and hand, Steiger saw the tattoo. He shook the hand and released it.

'You were in the camps,' he said.

'One of them,' Manny corrected easily, fitting a cigarette in the holder. The flame reflected in brown, sharp eyes and he dragged the smoke into his lungs like a parched man drinks water. 'Good of you to mention it,' he added through a cloud, 'most people try not to. And you are?'

'Father Max Steiger.'

The drooping eyelids flickered.

'Austrian,' Steiger added.

Manny nodded and angled his chair so that they were both surveying the room.

'And what is it you do?' Steiger asked. He'd noticed it was almost always the first question Americans asked of each other.

'Just now, I'm reading the room, Father Steiger.'

'And you see?'

'I see the ones who came late to the war. They're ravens, Father, always the last to come to the party. See how sleek and shiny they are and so full of energy. Boy, I tell ya, if they all smiled together the lights would dim in Jersey.' He gave a gruff laugh and coughed. 'So, tell me,' he said, smiling, 'what do *you* see?'

Steiger let his gaze wander among the groups.

'I see men who look angry,' he said thoughtfully. 'They stand so … openly, as if their bodies would intimidate. Also, they speak loudly, using their voices like levers to shift the discussion. A European would greet or agree by bowing slightly from the waist. Americans are so … inflexible. They just nod.'

'Good,' Manny crowed, 'pretty damn good. Now, to claim the brass ring, you gotta pick out the one man in the room the cardinal really hates.'

'Only one?'

'You're stallin', Father.'

Again, Steiger let his eyes roam over the boisterous men with perfect teeth and bright, red faces.

'The bishop?'

'Bravo,' Manny breathed. 'And you know this, how?'

'He never looks at him.'

'Yep,' Manny confirmed, 'Sheen dazzles him every time.' In response to Steiger's quizzical look, he elaborated. 'Bishop Fulton Sheen is his nemesis. Poor Spellman claws his way up from nothing and then inherits a bishop who's always had everything. Sheen ages beautifully, doncha think? Just enough grey in the black hair to give him gravitas. Note the sculpted features and the sallow complexion – straight out of Central Casting. And his voice! I gotta tell ya, he has the voice of an angel, well, an American angel, cos God don't allow perfection.'

He sighed and waved the cigarette holder before his face as if dispelling a vision. 'Now, Francis J. Spellman,' he continued, 'talks like a very large lady is standing on his larynx. And his shape?' he sighed. 'Time and gravity have ganged up to create a pear. Course, he wears that god-awful bellyband to hold it in, makes him look like an egg-timer.' He raised his shoulders and let them fall in a 'what can you do?' gesture. 'So, tell me, Father Max Steiger,' he said, smiling, 'what brings you to the rich man's table?'

'I haven't come for crumbs,' Steiger said coldly. 'I don't want their charity.'

Manny widened his eyes in mock horror. 'Only two currencies are legal tender in this room, Father,' he said slowly. 'If dollars ain't on the table, I guess we're just dealin' for power. Have another look,' he invited, waving his cigarette at the gathering. 'Pick me a power person.'

'The older gentleman, speaking with the cardinal,' Steiger said without hesitation.

Manny grunted and coughed a little more. 'Can you do that with horses?' he asked hopefully. 'Take too long to explain,' he added, when Steiger looked confused. He held the cigarette holder between his teeth and swung it in the direction Steiger had indicated. 'That, Father Steiger, is Joseph Kennedy Senior,' he whispered. 'And that,' he said, angling it to centre on a young man sitting alone at the top table, 'is his son, Jack. Old Joe's got other sons but, these days, he only talks about Jack.'

'He's the heir?'

'No, the spare.'

'Pardon?'

Manny tilted his head back to brood behind his eyelids. 'The heir didn't make it back from the war,' he said tonelessly. 'Jack's been elevated to fulfil the dreams of his father.'

'How high is that particular elevation?'

'As high as any American can ascend.'

Steiger sat up straighter and locked his eyes on the young man.

'Why does he sit so … still?' he whispered.

'Addison's disease,' Manny said. 'It attacks the immune system. Guy can hardly walk.'

'Won't that—'

'No, Father,' Manny cut in, smiling humourlessly. 'This is America. His daddy can buy him the White House and carry him through the door – wouldn't be the first time that happened.'

'So, this Joseph Kennedy is the power in the room?' Steiger pressed.

'Hold your horses,' Manny protested. 'Slowly, slowly catchy monkey, Father. You gotta look for the power broker,' he said seriously. 'He's the guy in the room who harnesses all the power. Get that man on your side and—' He raised his hand, palm upwards and Steiger was distracted by the blue numbers on the pale skin.

'Can I ask you a question, Manny?'

'You just did.'

'How did you survive Auschwitz?' he asked.

Manny turned his head to look at him. Steiger could see no trace of light in his eyes.

'You a survivor, Father?'

For a gut-wrenching moment, Steiger saw a hill of bodies and felt the yield of dead flesh as his feet began to climb. He saw a man with innocent blue eyes slit an old man's throat with a shiny arc of sharpened steel and walked on to the summit. A girl with a perfect black spot in her forehead opened her eyes and stared at him.

Manny Bernstein's solemn eyes surfaced through his vision. He nodded slowly. 'I'll tell you how I survived. You know what a pawnbroker is?'

Steiger overcame frozen lips and surprise to stammer a reply. 'Y–Yes,' he said. 'He's a person who evaluates objects and, based on their value, lends a certain amount of money to the owner. If the owner comes to reclaim, he pays the pawnbroker the amount borrowed, with interest. If he does not, the pawnbroker may keep or sell them.'

'That's the gist of it,' Manny conceded, with a nod. 'I was the pawnbroker in Auschwitz.'

Steiger felt himself drawn into those brown eyes until the raucous chatter in the room became muted.

'The Nazis got a two-for-one deal when they got me,' Manny recited tonelessly. 'I got two badges – one a yellow star; the other a pink patch. Jew and deviant – *Untermensch* squared, you might say. That's two strikes already and Commandant Baer is a demon pitcher. What they don't have is a pawnbroker, a guy who knows the value of stuff and boy did they have stuff – jewels, furs, icons, the whole nine yards. So, Manny Bernstein, the pawnbroker, kept the books – item in the left-hand column, value in the right hand column. Ledgers with hard cardboard covers stacked right up to the ceiling, evaluating every item in Auschwitz-Birkenau and the other camps that made up the complex. No one ever came back to claim. Did I mention hair? We had tons of it.'

His eyes seemed to dull and grow distant and Steiger spoke into the silence.

'Will you come to work for me, Manny?'

Manny's eyes hardened into a stare.

'I already survived men who wanted to own the world, Father Steiger,' he said. 'I gave them everything I had so I could survive. I put my soul in hock in Auschwitz. Every day of my life, I pay the interest on it. One day, I may even redeem it. No, Father Steiger, I will not work for you. I would never pawn my soul again. Now, if you'll excuse me.'

Manny Bernstein tried to control his trembling as he walked to the door. A tall, stooped man with salt-and-pepper hair and moustache was handing a black cashmere coat to an attendant.

'Hi, Manny,' the man said quietly. 'Any winners you'd like to share with a punter?'

'Only one, sir,' Manny said as he passed. 'Coming up in the next race.'

Manny sat in the vestibule and blotted his face with a purple handkerchief. He wondered if there was a difference between working as a valuer for Commandant Baer or for Father Max Steiger or for the Central Intelligence Agency. They were all wolves in wolves' clothing. He'd known scientists, doctors and commandants who could talk Schubert and Heine. He'd known men given to old-fashioned courtesy and delicate kindness who could turn into monsters at the slightest irritation, whose skin of refinement sloughed off as they prepared instruments that blinded or opened babies for no other reason than to see what happened next. Narcissists, he nodded, who saw no one in any mirror but themselves. The eyes were always the clue. No one was revealed in those eyes. No one looked through the windows of those souls. Their sight was limited to the inner surface of the retina where they saw no reflection other than their own. Father Max Steiger had such eyes, Manny had seen them change when he'd asked if he was a survivor. When the director asked for his evaluation, his reply had been as oblique as the question. He could have said more – so much more, but he'd been afraid he'd start to babble and become incoherent and be unable to stop. It's why survivors preferred the quick quip or the sardonic laugh or silence. He could have said there for the grace of God goes God. As an evaluation, it was neither original nor comprehensive, and he might have been asked to elaborate. He found he was shaking all over again.

'You sick, sir?' a waiter asked in a broad brogue.

Nein, he almost shouted, taken unawares. *The sick are taken away and don't come back*, he might have added, if he hadn't ground his teeth together until they hurt. 'No, thank you,' he managed in a whispery voice.

'You're really shaking, sir,' the young man said sympathetically. 'Someone walk over your grave?'

'Yes,' Manny Bernstein said, 'all the time.'

On the train to Rome

Laura wondered why the bearded young man had exploded from the train at the other side of the platform. He strode between embracing couples and milling families as if fleeing something. She smiled at her imaginings but was pleased when he entered their compartment and slung his bag on the rack. Maybe twenty-five, maybe older, she thought, though his beard made him look older. That, and the eyes, she decided. 'The eyes are the window of the soul,' Momma had always said. *How can a young man have such an old soul?* Suddenly aware of Sister Pilar's disapproving presence, she averted her eyes. '*Custos oculorum*' – 'Custody of the eyes.' It was a favourite saying of Sister Pilar. Momma had said it was important to look people in the eye. During her stay with the Fratres, Laura could hardly remember a time when anyone had done that. Except for … him – and Sister Pilar when she'd called her a 'whore' and the 'daughter of the Devil'.

The Al Smith fundraiser, New York

God, how Spellman loves the microphone. The director sipped a glass of iced water as the little man drizzled charm over the assembly. There was the annual lap of honour as he detailed the number of new schools and churches built under his stewardship. There was also the inevitable name-dropping, the 'as I said to' moments. The director counted four cardinals and the pope in that egotistical flurry. He thought Spellman looked like a bird of paradise in his cardinal's plumage compared to the young priest who brooded at the top table in crow-black.

He tuned out the cardinal and focused on Father Max Steiger. He wondered where the twin scars that furrowed from his left eye to the corner of his mouth had come from and made a mental note to quiz the staffer who'd prepared the brief he'd given Donovan. *Every scar has a story*, he mused. Francis Spellman was still on his favourite schtick, phrases that began with 'me and the pope' twanged nasally around the restive room. An informant had painted a different picture of Spellman's politicking in Rome. Catholic prelates were expected to visit Rome every four years to present a report on their diocese to the various Vatican departments. Spellman went every year and sometimes holidayed with the pope in Castel Gandolfo. 'Francis,' his informant had said wickedly, 'does so much bowing and scraping in Rome that he's two inches shorter when he comes back.'

Reluctantly but to relieved applause, Spellman turned from the microphone and sat. For a slow count of ten, the priest made no move to replace him at the podium. He timed the pause to perfection so that the hum of chatter that had preceded the cardinal's departure had faded to silence and hadn't yet edged into unease. If he was nervous, the director saw no sign of it as Max Steiger placed a single page on the podium.

'You Irish-Americans are the envy of the Christian world,' he said.

The director was struck by the economy of that opening phrase. Priests who came cap-in-hand to this monied gathering usually spent the first few minutes smooching Spellman or gushing at the great honour afforded them. The director sensed the frisson of interest that sparked around the room at this departure from protocol. *You've hit the first ball to the boundary line, Father Steiger*, he thought admiringly. *The fans have stopped chewing their hotdogs and drinking their beer. Now let's see you whack it into the bleachers while bringing the cardinal back onside. Even miffed cardinals love a winner.*

Father Steiger didn't disappoint.

'When Europe was threatened with paganism, it was Ireland that kept the flame of faith alive. When Rome was overrun and the popes decamped to Constantinople, Ireland – a tiny island on the threshold of Europe – hoarded that flame and reflected it in manuscripts that conserved the gospels. It was the Irish who formed the First Crusade – long before popes and European emperors combined to free the holy places in the east. The Irish Crusade was to re-Christianise Europe. Did they accomplish this by force of arms? No, they were bookmen not swordsmen. Was it achieved through divine intervention like the miraculous *chi rho* Constantine saw in the sky before the great battle for Rome? No! Columbanus, Aidan, Killian and the others were intelligent men who knew the political realities of their time. *Cuius regio, eius religio* – whoever reigns, that will be the religion. And so they converted the clan leaders, local princes and crowned heads of the European mainland and the people flocked to the faith of their leaders. When Columbus brought the cross to the Americas, it was borrowed for the journey from the Irish. When your ancestors crossed the Atlantic in search of refuge from famine, and political and religious persecution, they sailed over a highway of the bones of those who didn't make it. But your ancestors did make it and you, the heirs of immigrants, have made your mark in the new world and retained your faith in spite of the intolerance you experienced.'

The director's attention was split between the message and the medium. As a speaker, Steiger had a physical stillness that sucked the chatter from the room and concentrated the audience on his message. Only his head moved, to scan his audience; sometimes settling on individuals, so that those at the surrounding tables would feel included in his gaze. His English might be a little archaic but, coupled with a deliberate delivery, it enhanced rather than distracted from his message. The priest had teased the room with his references to Ireland – that was a sure-fire lure for this particular audience – but this was a generation of Americans who had been to war. It was time to hook them with allusions closer to their reality.

'You have won the war,' Max Steiger declared and, before the applause could gather volume, he overrode it. 'But the peace is not yet a reality. Yes, you have pumped millions of dollars into Europe to revitalise its ruined economies and industries. You could have left them to their own devices – to make something of the freedom paid for in American blood. You could have retired behind your borders, as many in America think you should have.'

There were heads still nodding at this when he continued.

'Why not? Because you had won the battle but not the war. China built a wall to keep the Western world at bay. Did that stop the Portuguese or the opium trade? Russia has spread its borders to include the neighbouring states all the way across Europe to divided Berlin. Is Stalin ensuring that another Operation Barbarossa will not be launched at the borders of Mother Russia? Yes! But he's doing more. He now has a launchpad for communism and this is an enemy that cannot be fought with Sherman tanks or aircraft or Marines or atomic bombs. No! Conventional warfare, under the shadow of the mushroom cloud, is obsolete. The new war – some call it the Cold War – is being fought with an idea. That idea runs counter to everything you stand for and no ring of steel or barbed-wire borders are effective against it.'

'Gee, he's really pissed on our parade,' the director heard someone remark in the silence and he saw shoulders heave with repressed laughter. He figured it was relieved laughter. That could turn to resentment and ridicule if Steiger didn't win them back.

'When Rome fell, it could have spelled the end of Christianity, except that Constantine, a wise Emperor, had already enlisted the Christian Church in the war on paganism. The Christian peace was carried to the corners of the empire, not by centurions or foot soldiers but by Christian missionaries. Patrick went from Roman Britain to Celtic Ireland and you are the living proof of his success. Cyril and Methodius went to the east and the Christian peace endured long after the fall of Rome. In the aftermath of a victory, who wants to go back to war? Most soldiers want to forget the horror and celebrate the peace. Today, you are admired by the world. How long will it be before admiration turns to envy and envy sours to antipathy and antipathy to bitter aggression? This process has already begun in Europe and South America where the disillusioned and the disaffected are being sold an idea – an idea bought and paid for by the Kremlin. You may console yourselves with the thought that none of those disaffected states are your equal in arms. But how do you fight an idea? You can cut the head from a Hydra but it will then grow two heads. An idea can only be countered with a better idea. You Americans already have a better idea. Do you think the Russians are happy to forfeit personal freedom, freedom of speech and the freedom to enjoy the fruits of their labour for gulags, political murder and collectivisation at the whim of a dictator in the Kremlin? Do you think that Hungary, Poland, Romania and the other Soviet-occupied states celebrate swapping their freedom from Hitler for oppression by Stalin?

'Right here on your doorstep, will the people of South America welcome the cold ideology of the steppes as an alternative to corrupt dictators and grinding poverty? Yes, they will, if there is no alternative. The *Pax Americana* is the alternative. But how will they know this if you put up the shutters on the store? Did you make your fortunes by minding the store or by selling the goods? I have founded a new religious order in the Church with the pope's blessing. It was Pius XII who prophesied that communism would be a greater threat to the world than Nazism. The Fratres is a new order that has already brought thousands of men and women to its standard from every part of the Christian world. Our eyes and efforts are not bent on the recapture of the Holy Places of antiquity but on the re-Christianisation of Europe and the re-evangelising of Asia, Africa and South America and all those places which will shake off the ancient empires and construct new national identities. Which model will they choose, democracy or totalitarianism? Which handbook will they read from to construct their national ideology? Will it be Marx or Mark – the communist or the evangelist?

'I have called a crusade for the evangelisation of the world. I carry the twin banners of freedom of faith and freedom of democracy. I have come to the new world in search of knights. I have come to you because faith and democracy have flourished in your light. You have among you men who enjoy the respect and confidences of leaders in your own country, as Cardinal Spellman enjoys the confidence and respect of the pope in Rome. But, above all, I have come to you because you are a young country, a young people – still young enough to dream. Are you worthy of the dream that an Irish-American Catholic could one day sit in the Oval Office?'

As one, the director saw the eyes of the audience sweep from the speaker to the young man who sat more erect in his chair.

'Are you worthy of the dream that an Irish-American Catholic could one day sit on the throne of Saint Peter?' he thundered, and all eyes turned to Spellman who seemed dazed by this benediction.

'By such dreams are the world and its peoples restored and redeemed,' he concluded.

Max Steiger bowed his head as a tidal wave of applause washed over him. They rose to their feet and clapped their hands over their heads as those at the back climbed on chairs. The cardinal moved quickly to the young man's side, raising his hand like that of a victorious boxer. *Good old Francis*, the director thought cynically, *always first into the ring at the bell, always to the front of the photograph*.

The director sat and pondered the speech as men climbed over each other to swamp the speaker. Sure, he had played the Irish card like a croupier in Atlantic City, pulling all the toora loora heartstrings of the ould country. He'd segued into the American dream and warned of the seduction of isolationism, waving the red flag at an angry bull, before holding out the possibility of future glory to a crowd of young post-war Alexanders who might be tempted to weep because they had no more worlds to conquer. Steiger had struck all the right notes. Dammit, he admitted, he'd struck them hard enough to put a new crack in the Liberty Bell but, apart from an avalanche of cheques, what did he want? He raised his head to find Max Steiger looking directly at him, seemingly oblivious to the circle of back-slapping admirers. 'Oh, you bastard,' he whispered admiringly, and nodded.

THE TRAIN TO ROME

The intriguing couple were getting off at a station that wore the Dome of St Peter's like a giant tiara. The older nun had been anticipating their destination, closing her book and hiding it in the folds of her brown robe.

'Which order do you belong to, Sister?' Karl asked.

She stared at him as if trying to remember his presence. 'The Fratres,' she snapped. 'Are you familiar with our order?'

He nodded, not trusting himself to reply. The nun brushed aside his offer of help and tugged her bag from the rack overhead. She nodded for the girl to do the same. He saw the look of consternation that tightened the younger woman's face and the way her palm moved to rest protectively on her belly. '*Permette?*' he said and brought the bag to the seat beside her.

'Thank you,' she said.

'You are American?'

'Yes. From Chicago,' she added. Her face seemed conflicted between her eagerness to make contact and her temerity at doing so.

'Is this your first visit to Rome?'

'Yes,' she said wistfully, and he regretted asking.

'*Vamos*,' the older nun urged.

He was still mulling over the strange encounter when the Stazione Tiburtina drew the train into its massive shadow.

CIA OFFICES, NEW YORK

The director ate just enough at Spellman's dinner to avoid attracting attention. He was already assessing Max Steiger's speech and those who might have spoken to him were dissuaded by his abstracted expression. The cardinal paused his tour of the room long enough to shake his hand.

'Helluva speech, Your Eminence,' he remarked, and Spellman glowed as if he'd delivered the speech and not the speaker.

Spellman didn't tarry – there were chequebooks to be lightened and an auxiliary bishop to be upstaged. 'Glad you could make it, Mister Director,' Spellman said. He was already sighting on his next target and the director didn't delay him. Bishop Sheen had wisely moved to the back of the room, leaving the field clear for his nemesis.

'I'd appreciate your counsel, Bishop,' the director said, as he paused on his way to the exit. 'My driver will be outside in, say, thirty minutes.' It sounded peremptory and he lingered to add, on a lighter note, 'Think you can last that long?'

'If passing the basket were ever to become an Olympic event,' the bishop said in his perfectly modulated voice, 'Francis J. Spellman would be odds-on for gold.'

'Well, I guess there's a time to "render unto Caesar",' the director said softly, and the bishop's handsome face tightened.

'See you later,' he said.

The director moved like a wraith through the loud room. Sheen, he thought, was a paradox. He was a Roman Catholic auxiliary bishop in the shadow of a cardinal who loathed him and did everything in his power to ensure that he would never be more than an auxiliary bishop. He was a sublime preacher and writer who carried his learning lightly, whose sermons and articles were accessible to the laity. But it was his mastery of radio that had spread his fame and following beyond the borders of New York's boroughs and earned him the title of the 'Radio Bishop'. Hitler had recognised the power of that medium and used it to broadcast his massed rallies, choreographed by Speer. Even now, eight years after the discovery of the burned bodies in the bunker, he got goosebumps listening to recordings of the Führer in full flow. Mussolini had opted for opera, trying to mimic his master's voice and sounding like some third-rate tenor impersonating Caruso. Churchill had been rousing and quotable, but had always sounded like he was addressing the House of Lords. For the director's money, Roosevelt had been the radio genius. With his high, fluty voice, he could never hope to excite the passions like Adolf. Dammit, the President of the United States couldn't even stand upright at a microphone unless someone first locked his leg calipers. Even then, he couldn't stay upright long enough to build up the kind of verbal electricity that had crackled through the radio from the Brandenburg Gate. The wily old fox had brought the mountain to Mohammed in his 'Fireside Chats', doing his own, inimitable take of the folksy, down-home politician from the comfort of an armchair in the White House. He'd managed to stand long enough before Congress to talk them into the war but the 'Fireside Chats' had talked the New Deal into every home in the union. Unlike many of the great radio 'voices', Sheen had moved seamlessly to television. Of course, a programme needed sponsors and Sheen had a big corporation picking up the tab, but it had taken a nudge from the director to make that happen. Sheen knew about that little arrangement, and if the bishop had reservations about their Faustian pact, he'd never aired them. He was a clever guy, clever enough to know that the day would come when the agency would come to collect. That day had arrived, the director concluded. It was time to 'render unto Caesar'.

In the lobby, he passed on the canapés laid out on a small table manned by Joaquin. As a practising Presbyterian, he had reservations about the national urge to eat at every opportunity. That immigrant instinct had been further suppressed at home where three solid meals appeared at set times and there were no snacks or nibbles. He did accept a glass of Chardonnay. He might even take a sip or two to ease his guests into believing this was a social occasion. Donovan was already holding court with Medusa and the Clipboard Kid. The young man in the Sears suit, buttoned-down white shirt and navy knitted tie, was one of the new breed in the agency. Cy Tucker had come with a first-class degree in politics from Harvard. He also had the physique of a seventeen-year-old kid, with sloping shoulders hanging from his lanky frame. The 'Clipboard Kid' was the tag the field agents had given him when he'd introduced accountability to men accustomed to spending someone else's dollar. Cy was impervious to the snide and dedicated to detail. He was the future.

'Maybe we could get a few things talked through before the others arrive?' the director suggested to the little group.

'Where'd you get the girl?' Donovan whispered as they arranged the chairs.

'Long story,' the director said.

'Gives me the creeps,' Donovan confided.

'Imagine what she does to the opposition,' the director countered. 'What's on the agenda, Cy?' he asked when they were settled.

'British ambassador in Iran suggests bilateral action—'

'Cut to the chase, Cy, and keep it in English,' the director interrupted, letting his smile soften the rebuke.

'Sorry, sir. The British ambassador says the Iranian government are planning to nationalise their oil fields. He wants our help to get them back in line.'

'Thanks, Cy. Did he mention communism?'

'Yes, sir. Six times, exactly.'

'Communism is getting to be a mantra with our friends,' the director said ruefully. 'It's like some Pavlovian thing. They think all they gotta do is holler "red" and we'll bark.'

'Where's the shah these days?' Donovan asked.

'Cooling his heels in exile, waiting to be restored,' the director replied.

'And are we in restorative mood?' Donovan asked with a raised eyebrow.

'Yes. We have three good reasons – oil, oil and oil,' the director replied and the others smiled dutifully. 'Actually,' he continued, 'we have two other reasons. One is we get to sweat the British for a bigger cut of the oil revenues and the other is that we put our guy back on the throne. Get a team working on that, Cy. Draw up a budget for rent-a-mob and all the usual kick-backs.'

Cy nodded without taking his head from his notepad.

'Spell out the quid pro quo to the shah,' the director added. 'Let him know we have other options. Next.'

'Stradivarius' report from the DDR, Sir,' Cy read from his notepad. 'East Germany. I guess that's your field, Medusa.'

'We've read the report, Medusa,' the director interjected, 'so let's have your take.'

'Lots of dissident groups, spread across the major urban areas,' she began, 'mostly, armchair revolutionaries. Strad says the one in East Berlin is an exception. If they call it, it's a go.'

'What do they want?'

'Money,' she stated flatly. 'Strad says it's for the cause – they're genuine patriots.'

'That's an old tune,' Donovan snorted.

'According to the man on the ground,' Medusa said icily, 'these guys are genuine *Meistersingers*. I say we go with Strad on this one.'

'I agree,' the director said and saw Donovan shake his head. He's not in the loop, the director reminded himself. Best throw him a bone on this one, for form's sake.

'You on that, Medusa?' he asked.

'On it.'

'You got somebody who can cross over?'

'Yes.'

'Yours?'

'Mine,' she said.

The director was the only one present who saw the cruel smile that played on Donovan's lips. But Medusa knew the score – her man, her op, her responsibility. It was always good to have that degree of buy-in. Time to up the ante.

'Firewall?'

It was the question the handlers hated and he saw the tension in Medusa. The agency couldn't afford the fallout if things went wrong.

There were enough left-leaning press people in the US who would rejoice in revealing the agency's hand, particularly if it got burned behind the wire. Their coverage would fuel the militarists who objected to every dollar that was diverted from armaments to agents.

'We clean as we cook,' she said, and Donovan smiled openly at the homely phrase from such an unlikely source.

He probably doesn't understand its true meaning, the director thought. In the shorthand of the agency under his directorship, it meant that those who were used by Medusa to put an operation in place would not survive to enjoy the fruits of their labour. Donovan and his ilk would find it hard to stomach the realpolitik of the war the agency was waging. Men who cut throats behind enemy lines in the last war tended to think we should play by some set of rules in this one. The expected tap on the door arrived on cue.

'Your guest has arrived, Mister Director,' Joaquin whispered from the door.

'Good of you to drop by, Bill,' the director said, offering his hand to his predecessor.

Donovan's smile was tight but his handshake was as firm as ever. He was enough of a pro to know he was being dismissed and to handle it gracefully. 'Any time, Mister Director,' he said and shrugged into his coat.

The bishop sat in an armchair beside an empty fireplace. He was still in his formal garb and the director thought he looked like an extra in a costume drama who'd wandered on stage in the wrong play.

'Good of you to come, Bishop,' he said easily, and the bishop smiled.

'Thanks for inviting me, Mister Director,' he said, in the mellifluous voice that drew people, even those not of his faith, to hush the kids and turn up the volume on their radios.

Now that the courtesies had been observed, they could get down to business. The director passed across a sheaf of papers. 'I'd like you to read this,' he said and settled into the chair on the other side of the cold hearth.

He tried to read the bishop's face as the bishop read the document.

'I take it you want me to read this script on the programme,' he said finally.

'I do.'

'What can I say?' the bishop smiled. 'I could say I wish I'd written it. It's uncannily close to my own style. You know how it is when someone mimics your voice and they get you down pat? This,' he said, waving the script, 'is like someone mimicking your voice and doing it a little better than you'd do it yourself. A little scary and very humbling, Mister Director.'

'Take it as a compliment, Bishop. We've had a team of linguists and scriptwriters working on this for some time.'

Sheen bowed his head fractionally to accept the compliment.

'When will this be broadcast?'

'I can't tell you that until you're in the studio. Sorry. Security is watertight on this one. For the same reason, you can't take it with you. My driver will figure out times and places that are convenient for you to study it.'

'Can I change it in any way?'

'No. It has to be what's on the script. I know it's not ideal, but needs must.'

'Well,' the bishop said, rising, 'I hope it's worth all the trouble you're taking.'

'From your mouth to the ear of God, Bishop.'

Medusa and Cy seemed relieved when the director returned. He figured the reason for that was that neither had mastered the art of small talk – and for the same reason.

'Moscow?' he asked, resuming his seat.

'Our man in the embassy is ready to go,' Cy said. 'The ambassador isn't part of our plan, but won't be obstructive.'

'Well, bully for him,' the director said laconically. 'Medusa?'

'After the DDR is done and dusted, I'll liaise with our Moscow asset and deliver the package. After it's delivered, I'll debrief and cut the contact.'

Cy looked up in surprise and then dropped his eyes again to his papers. *Obviously, we've stepped outside the Harvard syllabus,* the director thought grimly. The agency was proving to be a steep learning curve for the Phi-Beta-Kappa Cy, but he figured he'd be able to handle it – especially when he considered the alternative. 'Any other business?' the director asked, shuffling his papers into a neat pile.

'The bomb,' Cy blurted.

'Oh, that,' Medusa said dismissively, and the director chuckled.

'We have reports coming in from well-placed assets in Kazakh Mister Director,' Cy said doggedly. 'They claim that military activity at the—'

'Cy.'

'Sir?'

'We have a store room on Rikers Island stacked to the ceiling with reports like those. Leave them on my desk and I'll add them to the pile.'

'But—'

'Cy.'

'Yes, sir.'

'Well, I think that about concludes our business here. Medusa, can you stay a while?'

When the door closed behind Cy, the director breathed a long sigh.

'Think he's a risk?' she asked.

'No,' he said, slowly. 'No,' he added more emphatically. 'Cy's a good man at getting the information and laying it out. It takes a different kind of brain to join up the dots.'

'And to take the steps necessary when a dot won't join,' she murmured.

'Yes,' he said quietly, 'that too.'

'Why are we doing Moscow a favour?' she asked.

It was the kind of question staffers never asked of their boss and yet the fact that she *did* ask was another reason why he valued Medusa. At the same time, he had no illusions about her. The file marked 'Medusa' was not for the faint-hearted. He wondered if she'd been born without the ability to relate to others or if it had been excised by her nightmare childhood. The psych people he'd consulted said that most kids endured or even placated their abusers to survive. Medusa's parents had burned in a house fire. 'Faulty electrics', the investigating officers reported and moved on. She'd been taken into care and a care worker had drowned in the bath. There had been another fatality at another state institution and then another until an FBI agent had joined the dots. The director had headhunted that FBI agent for the CIA and – bingo! Serendipity, discovering something you weren't looking for in the first place.

Through and after the war, the agency had been manned mostly by military personnel. Donovan had been comfortable with that model. As one old-timer had put it, 'If the mules held a beauty contest, which animal was likely to win?' He'd seen the need for a different kind of agent for a different kind of war – hence Claus Fischer, Cy Tucker and Medusa. Fischer was a chameleon who could blend behind the wire. Tucker was the brain that kept the brawn focused and within budget. Medusa had all of their attributes and then some. He had been hard on her earlier. He felt she deserved an answer to her question. And yet the psychologists said that to train an animal, you starved it. When it was ravenous, you rewarded every command obeyed with a titbit – not the whole reward at once, just enough to keep it interested and hungry for more.

'If Ivan accepts a gift from us, he has to be sure it's in neither of our interests to talk about it.'

'What do we get out of that?'

'In this case, it's to our mutual benefit. I can't be more specific right now. What I can say is that we'll be sending him a Trojan horse – a gift that carries inside it the seeds of his own destruction.'

'I know the story of the Trojan horse,' she said.

'Yes, but I haven't finished my story,' he replied. 'We send the gift and we send news of it to someone within the besieged city.'

'Who?'

He wrote on a slip of paper and passed it to her. She read it and he handed her his box of matches. When she returned from the bathroom, a faint scent of smoke came with her.

'Burned and flushed down the pan,' she said.

'I have your old friend Father Max Steiger in the other room,' he said, rising and stretching. 'I want you to come in, maybe five minutes after me, and take a seat behind him.'

Medusa grinned and the director hoped to God his name never merited that grin.

TIBURTINA STATION, ROME

Emil was unmissable. He stood, as self-possessed as a river rock, oblivious to the flow of people around him. As Karl approached, he saw Emil's eyes focus and then crease with pleasure. The old priest straightened from his stoop to embrace him. Emil felt fragile – so very fragile. Karl was trying not to hug him too tightly, aware of the emotion that tightened his throat.

'Let me look at you.' Emil held him at arm's length. 'You are a man, Karl,' he declared delightedly. 'And the beard, Eugène will be so jealous. Take my arm,' he commanded, 'my legs are sometimes uncooperative.'

They strolled companionably, arm in arm, to the pavement outside the station. The car was a surprise.

'Pacelli wasn't using it,' Emil confided with a wicked grin, 'and you, my boy, are a guest of honour. We can speak freely,' he added as the driver started the engine. 'I have known Alfredo since he was a boy and he's totally deaf,' he said, switching to Italian. 'Isn't that so, Fredo?'

'Si, Monsignor,' the driver laughed, waving his thanks to the policeman who halted the traffic to give them precedence.

'And how is His Eminence?' Karl enquired.

'Older but no wiser,' Emil said happily. 'You'll see.'

As they passed the inevitable monuments, Emil kept up a lively commentary. At an intersection on the Via Cavour, he pointed to the Santa Maria Maggiore Church. 'It's even got its own Sistine Chapel,' he confided. 'It was built for … for …' He looked perplexed for a moment.

'And was Sixtus the Fifth worthy of such grandeur?' Karl asked quickly.

'No,' Emil said emphatically. 'A little grandiose for someone who spent a mere five years on the throne.' He leaned across and squeezed Karl's arm gratefully. 'History happens every moment, Karl,' he said quietly. 'Savour the moment.'

SANTA MAGDALENA CONVENT, ROME

Rome, Laura thought, was like a huge, open-air museum. Her neck ached from looking out the cab window as monuments, churches and fountains flew past. She wished the driver would ease up a little on the gas so she could savour the sights. 'Savour', that was one of Momma's favourite words, one of her favourite clean words. 'Savour the moment, honey,' she'd say. The driver was a big guy, wedged into the tiny cab-front and he drove with just one delicate finger on the wheel. They raced through a brick-built arch and a pyramid loomed on their left. 'Wow,' she breathed. *What was a pyramid doing in Rome?* The driver must have seen her reaction in his mirror.

'Pyramid of Cestius,' he said, turning his head right around to explain. 'Crazy, no?'

'Yes,' she agreed, willing his attention back to the road. 'Crazy.'

Sister Pilar sniffed. *She's reading that darn book again. How long did it take to read a thin book?* The cab shot across an ornate bridge and Laura smiled at the thought that the statues had jumped on the balustrade to escape it. At the other side of the bridge, it bullied its way through a solid stream of traffic and burrowed into the shadows of narrow streets. Kids played on the sidewalks, arguing with expressive hand movements, and washing hung like bunting from one balcony to another. She craned for a glimpse of the sky but the buildings stretched all the way to the top of the window. The building they stopped at looked used but not lived in, like some frowsy municipal building in Chicago. A place where things were stored, she thought, and her good mood drained away.

The big guy opened her door and offered his hand to help her to the sidewalk. '*Un momento, signorina,*' he said and dragged the bags from the trunk.

'Leave them,' Sister Pilar snapped as she turned away to rummage in her purse. The driver looked at Laura with such a comical expression that she had to fake a cough. Sister Pilar counted the fare into his palm and strode to the door, leaving the bags for Laura.

'Come,' she said over her shoulder.

Laura went to lift the bags and, immediately, the big man picked them up. 'No, *bella signorina,*' he said and lugged the bags to the door.

'*Grazie,*' she managed and he beamed.

'Crazy,' he confided, shifting his eyes in Sister Pilar's direction. '*Ciao, cara.*'

She watched him 'play chicken' with a truck and heard him honk the horn in triumph when the truck pulled over. Some of the warmth of the day seemed to go with him. He'd been kind and considerate in an old-fashioned way, like the young guy on the train. *Savour the moment*, she reminded herself.

The door opened, revealing a tiny Italian nun with timid eyes magnified behind huge spectacles. '*Buongiorno*', she quavered and shrank back as Sister Pilar strode past. Laura stood in a hallway, bracketed on both sides with religious portraits. Her eyes followed the converging lines of frames to a bright atrium and a marble staircase that swept up and out of sight.

The nun appeared at her side and touched her hand. 'A butterfly's kiss' was how her momma described such a light touch. 'Eat,' she said and led Laura into a dining room off the atrium. The room was long and high and painted an industrial green that made the marble statues at either end look poorly. It was spotless and cheerless. Two tables huddled marooned in the centre of the flagstoned floor, their varnish long scrubbed away so that the knots in the pale timber tops looked like fossils she'd seen in a museum. 'Sit,' the little nun insisted, and pressed Laura's shoulder with her palm.

The soup was thick and the bread smelled heavenly. The nun sat opposite, smiling and nodding encouragement as Laura ate. Sister Pilar sat at the other end of the table and sipped a glass of water. Overhead, someone laughed. Laura looked at Sister Pilar, who was staring disapprovingly at the ceiling. Laura wondered who had something to laugh about in this place.

'Up,' gestured the little nun and they climbed. Laura stopped on the first landing to catch her breath. She sensed she was being watched and looked up to where a young woman was leaning over the banister on the second landing. Her blonde hair was tied back in a ponytail. She had a face that was angular, rather than pretty, and her two steady blue eyes were fixed on Laura.

'Hi,' Laura said shyly, and was amazed to see the change that rippled over that face. The transformation started in a delighted look that creased her eyes. Then the hard planes of her face softened as she smiled.

'Hi, yourself,' she called. 'You're not Italian.'

'No, I'm Laura Morton, from the US – Chicago.'

'Don't move,' the young woman ordered and then disappeared.

Laura heard the clattering of sandals on the stone stairs and braced herself as a figure rounded the banister and hurtled on to the landing.

'Am I glad to see you,' she said, and grabbed her in a fierce hug. Lord, but she had strong arms and Laura felt breathless by the time she was released.

'I'm Sarah, Sarah Walker, from New York City. C'mon, let me see you up to the "pigeon loft".' She linked Laura companionably and they began to climb. The Italian nun called plaintively from above and Sarah Walker yelled back in fluent Italian. 'Dorothea is a doll,' she confided, 'but she gets antsy. She give you lunch?'

'Yes.'

'Soup and bread, right?'

'Right.'

'Soup and bread,' Sarah laughed as she bumped a door open with her hip. 'It's her antidote to everything – headaches, toothaches, cholera, for God's sake. Soup and bread.'

She did such a perfect imitation of Sister Dorothea that Laura laughed. Immediately, she put her hand to her mouth and looked up guiltily.

'Who told you to do that, Laura?' Sarah asked casually as she ushered her into the bedroom under the eaves.

'Do what?'

'Gag your laugh.'

'The Fratres don't approve of laughing,' Laura said, stopping to fold back the covers on the bed. She felt as if the temperature in the room had dropped. Sister Pilar stood in the doorway.

'*Basta!*' she snapped. '*Per favore,*' she added, holding the door for Sarah with exaggerated courtesy. Sarah Walker straightened slowly from where she was putting shoes at the bottom of the wardrobe. Laura's heart sank as she walked to the door.

'Laura must be examined,' she said calmly.

'When the dottore comes—'

Sarah stepped closer to Sister Pilar and Laura imagined she had grown a few inches taller.

'*I* am the dottore,' she said. 'Now, if you'll excuse us – *per favore.*'

Sister Pilar opened and closed her mouth twice, and then retreated before the young woman's hard stare. Sarah closed the door. She extended her thumb and pinky finger from her fist and forked it at the door. 'My mother was Sicilian,' she explained, as she came to sit demurely on the bed. She swung her blonde ponytail with a flick of the head. 'Blonde hair and blue eyes, my mother blamed the Normans.'

'You're the doctor?' Laura asked.

'Yep! "The Dottore", as the sisters call him, and I guess you picked up on the capital *D*, is a retired guy who calls by every now and then. Looks like Mussolini and smells of Chianti but he's a sweetheart. He's a general practitioner, knows what to do when the baby pops out if he has plenty of hot water and carbolic.' She took a deep breath and raised her arms like a victorious boxer. 'Me,' she declared, 'I'm a qualified obstetrician, the genuine article, real McCoy, whole nine yards. Impressed?'

Laura nodded.

'Good. That sister, she one of the Fratres?'

Laura nodded again.

'Hardly joy unconfined,' Sarah muttered darkly. 'Okay,' she continued brightly, 'here's the drill. I call you Laura, you call me Sarah, *capisce?*' She tugged a stethoscope from somewhere and huffed on the disc. It was all too much for Laura. She began to cry. She'd been kicked out of the Fratres, brought, in disgrace, to a strange place and she'd really tried to 'hold tough' as Momma had taught her to do. But Momma was gone and— Sarah Walker sat up close and held her. When the weeping had reduced to a sniffle, Sarah wet a towel at the basin and wiped Laura's face. She did it just as gently as Momma would have done.

'Better out than in, honey,' she said, patting her face with a dry corner of the towel. 'I'm going to examine you, Laura,' she said. 'Have you been examined before?'

Laura nodded and her apprehension wasn't lost on Sarah Walker. 'When I'm done, if you have any questions, just shoot.'

It was so different to the examination she'd endured at the Schloss. The doctor there had handled her like meat. And all the time, he'd looked as if he'd wanted to be somewhere else. Like Father Steiger had looked, after they'd— She turned her attention to Sarah, pushing those hurtful memories out of her head. The wisecracks were over, she thought, the doctor is back in the building. Sarah Walker's mobile face had focused, like the face of a kid doing a school assignment. She checked Laura's heart and lungs with the stethoscope and held her hand in her lap to take her pulse. Time seemed to slow. Every separate action was done at a measured pace, as if they were moving together through a sacred ritual. There were small, thoughtful touches that brought Laura to the edge of tears. Sarah re-buttoned her blouse after the stethoscope and squeezed her hand after taking her pulse. She moved the stethoscope again and placed it on her abdomen, sliding it gently and deliberately, her eyes unfocused. Finally, she hung the stethoscope around her neck and exhaled.

'Everything's fine, Laura,' she said, 'but Professor Burns in Columbia always said the tool is only as good as the hand that holds it. "Trust your hands" was his great mantra. Gonna do the hands-on bit now, Laura. You just lie back and think of— What do you like to think of?'

'Momma,' she blurted.

Sarah nodded. 'Think of the way Momma rubbed your tummy when you had an ache,' she said. She rubbed her palms together and stroked them over Laura's belly, pressing gently and kneading, like she was shaping clay. At the end, she massaged gently, again until Laura felt sleepy. 'Everything's fine, Laura,' she confirmed. She looked tired and rubbed the heels of her hands in her eye sockets. 'Think you'll sleep?'

'Yes.'

'We have two other guests, Carla and Lucia,' Sarah said, rising from the bedside. 'You'll meet them at breakfast. I'll drop by a little later. If you're sleeping, I won't bother you. Sleep is good medicine,' she added, yawning. 'My room is right across the hallway. If you need anything, sing out.'

Laura didn't sleep and she didn't 'sing out' for Sarah Walker. There were too many things bouncing around inside her head for her to ease into the quiet and let go. Poppa insisted on pragmatism. That was *his* favourite word. Whenever he was on bedtime duty and she had fears, he'd get her to line them up for inspection. 'Use your brain,' he'd say. 'Every question has an answer. There's a reason for everything that happens.'

'The moon is looking in my bedroom window, Poppa.'

'The moon is a hunk of rock, Laura. It orbi— moves around the earth regulating the tides – ebb and flow, out and in. What it does not do is look inside your bedroom. When you have a problem, you have to be pragmatic. Ask yourself, can I do something about this problem right now? If the answer is yes, go right ahead and do it. If the answer is no, file it under 'review' or 'forget'.'

She was certain he'd said a lot more but she was usually asleep by then. So maybe pragmatism really worked. She'd told Momma, who rolled her eyes and said, 'Men.'

Father Max Steiger had wronged her, she knew that. She felt wronged because he hadn't stopped when she'd asked him to. And afterwards, he couldn't wait for her to be gone. He'd also left her sitting outside on a hard bench. *Why didn't I just pack my bags and go home?* she asked herself. She felt tears coming and shook her head. No, she reprimanded herself, Poppa was right, 'use your brain'. The reason is I have no home to go to. That thought hurt like hell but she'd put it out there. She couldn't blame the Fratres for not wanting her, things being the way they were, but she had felt shunted, like a misaddressed package. She wondered what would happen after the baby was born. Would the Fratres take the baby? No, she'd never agree to that. She was willing to defy Sister Pilar and— That name snagged her to a halt. Why was Sister Pilar still here? Okay, she'd come to see her settled but why had she stayed? Suddenly, Laura felt cold and burrowed deeper in the bed. What if they knew about the journal and Sister Pilar was waiting to take it? Maybe I'm being irrational, she thought. She turned her head to face the window. A sickle moon, angled in to the top right-hand corner. 'It's just a hunk of rock,' she reminded herself. But it shone with a cold light and looked sharp as a blade.

The door eased open and Laura breathed a sigh of relief as Sarah Walker stepped inside.

'Did I wake you?'

'No, I was just lying here.'

Sarah pulled a chair to the bed and leaned on the coverlet so that Laura didn't need to change position to see her.

'How come you're here, Sarah?' Laura whispered.

Sarah cocked her head and seemed to take a long time to consider the question.

'Columbus sailed for India and found America,' she said. 'I volunteered for Ethiopia and landed in Rome. It's complicated,' she added. 'The ships to Ethiopia leave from here but the papers must come from there. It takes time. I decided I might as well work while I'm waiting.'

'Why Ethiopia?'

'Blame it on Salk and Sweitzer,' Laura laughed. 'We've got all the super drugs and Ethiopia is still in the Stone Age, medically speaking. That was really bugging me and then this Ethiopian doctor came to Columbia to do some further training, I guess. Professor Burns got him to give a lecture on how things were in his country and Sarah Walker had her Eureka moment.' She laughed. 'Being appalled is a luxury if you're not prepared to do something about it, right? I volunteered. And, oh boy,' she said, and slapped her palm to her forehead. 'Even Professor Burns tried to talk me out of it.' She winked and added innocently, 'Some folks think I'm kinda stubborn, Laura.'

'What about your family? Laura asked and regretted it as Sarah's good humour dimmed. 'Sorry,' she added, 'it was really none of my b—'

'No, it's okay. No family,' she said cryptically. She stood abruptly and walked to look out of the window. 'My mother passed away some years back. I guess that's why I decided to become a doctor. There must be more to medicine when there's nothing more to be done.' She blew out a long breath and continued in a softer voice. 'My dad passed. He passed on being our dad when I was four years old. I hear he's living in Boston with a secretary from his company. I guess they deserve each other.'

Laura wondered if the wisecracks were Sarah's way of dealing with pain. Sarah Walker seemed fascinated by the curved moon that had eased to the centre of the window and hung there, like a Halloween decoration.

'I had a brother,' Sarah continued. 'Jack went to Korea.' She wheeled from the window. 'Gee,' she said, 'bedtime stories sure have changed since I was a kid.'

Laura patted the bed beside her. 'Come, sit,' she said. 'You know we got something in common, me and you,' she said awkwardly when Sarah accepted the invitation.

'We do? You mean apart from being from the US and our stunning good looks?'

'My parents died in an automobile accident,' Laura said and had to clear her throat before continuing. 'I heard about the Fratres and thought I might be, you know, useful.' She tried to smile and abandoned the effort. 'It didn't work out,' she said, 'not the way I thought it would anyways.'

Their eyes met and locked, and then dropped to Laura's swollen belly before rising to meet again. The import of what she'd said came to them simultaneously and they began to laugh. It began as a wheeze and developed into the roll-around laughter of people who haven't laughed for a long time. Why is it that the funniest things always happen in the most inappropriate places? Laura thought as she fought for breath. It's after midnight in a Roman convent and we're—

'Oh,' Sarah gasped, 'that was unexpected.' And they were off again. Sarah dragged the coverlet over her head to contain her shrieks. Laura hadn't the same mobility and just rocked backwards and forwards. 'If I – if I keep laughing like this,' she panted, 'I – I'm going to have the baby.'

'That's no laughing matter,' Sarah groaned from under the coverlet. Finally, they were spent and used the coverlet to wipe their streaming eyes. 'I'd tell you to sleep but you might find that funny,' Sarah breathed. 'See you in the morning, Laura Morton.'

'G'night, Doctor Sarah Walker.'

In the hallway, Sarah stood still and listened. There was no sound from any of the other rooms and she tiptoed to her own door. She wondered what had happened in Switzerland. How come a young religious novice winds up pregnant and what kind of religious order produces a Pilar?

CIA HEADQUARTERS, NEW YORK

Max Steiger had been waiting for two hours and it showed. He sat stiffly in the chair and two bright spots glowed, like beacons, on the cheekbones of his sallow face. Joaquin had offered refreshment at regular intervals and had been dismissed with increasing annoyance as the time wore on. The director had been apprised of this in the corridor. Steiger was someone he preferred to keep off-balance.

'Thank you for your patience, Father Steiger,' the director said, easing himself into the chair recently vacated by Bishop Sheen. 'You've had a long, tiring day. I appreciate that and won't delay you too long.'

He saw the annoyance replaced by concern in the young priest's eyes. Steiger was the supplicant in this scenario, he wasn't likely to blow his chances with a fit of pique.

'Great speech,' the direstor said and Steiger relaxed. 'Susceptible to flattery,' the brief had said. Susceptible to a lot of other more serious failings, the director thought. The researchers had pulled out all the stops on this one; to the point of having an asset visit his hometown in Austria. That section of the report had piqued his interest and amused him, in equal measure. He scanned the summary sheets on his lap until he found the relevant section:

Observation:

The people of Hallstatt are as forthcoming to strangers as New Englanders are to the Inland Revenue.

Excerpt from interview with Johann (Ferry man):

Q. Do you remember a Max Steiger?

A. Yes.

Q. Did you know that he became a priest?

A. Well, (expletive). [Laughs (not humorously)].

Q. The scar on his face, how did that happen?

A. Ask his parents.

Q. Where would I find his father?

A. Somewhere in Russia, under the snow.

Q. His mother?

A. In the cemetery – just.

NB The addition of 'just' to the final answer may indicate that she was a suicide.

Yes, he knew a lot about the founder of the Fratres but he decided to start with the unknown.

'How did you get that scar?' he asked.

Steiger paled so that the scar appeared more livid.

'A childhood accident,' he said.

'Childhood is certainly a time for accidents,' the director mused aloud as he filled his pipe, 'same all over the world. I guess in

Hallstatt kids were always falling out of trees.' He struck the match and held it over the bowl of his pipe, watching Steiger through the flame. 'Falling down mineshafts as well, from what I hear,' he said and watched the priest wince and look away. *Rumours*, the former lawyer reminded himself, *are not evidence. In his defence, Steiger's father had been the local policeman and particularly unloved by the locals.* He quenched the match and placed it in the ashtray.

'What is it you want, Father Steiger?' he asked and sat back, crossing one knee over the other.

'It is the mission of the Fratres to re-evangelise Europe and—'

'Yes,' the director interrupted, 'I was aware of that. You said all of that in your speech. So, let me pose the question again and please note the emphasis, Father Steiger. What do *you* want?'

Medusa opened the door and stepped inside. Silently, she took a seat behind the priest.

'I take it you know the lady?' the director said.

'We've met.'

'Yes, so you have,' the director said, thumbing through his notes. 'You met in Rome in the presence of Father Krunoslav Draganović?'

'Yes.'

'Strange company for a priest who wants to re-evangelise Europe,' the director said mildly.

'Father Draganović is—'

'Is, or at any rate was, a lead player in the systematic murder of Serbs. After the war, he oversaw ratlines that spirited Pavelić and other Croatian mass-murderers to South America.'

'I never—'

'Don't waste my time here, Father,' the director growled. He leaned forward and waited for Steiger's eyes to lock on his. 'Let me be crystal clear,' he said. 'We are not a war crimes tribunal. We are the Central Intelligence Agency. Our brief is to protect the US against any and all threats from outside our borders. What happened in Croatia and your part in it is not on our agenda.' He softened his voice. "The enemy of my enemy is my friend," he quoted. 'Are you familiar with that saying, Father?'

'Yes.'

'Good. Regard this as a business meeting between parties who share a common purpose. Business means that both sides prosper; you get what you want and so do we. I'm asking, for the last time, what do you want?'

Max Steiger sat forward, mirroring the body language of the older man. 'I want recognition of the Fratres by the Vatican,' he said evenly. 'I want a cardinal appointed as a mentor. Since Maglione died, the pope hasn't nominated another in his place. And I want the co-operation and resources of the Central Intelligence Agency in the re-evangelisation of Europe.'

The director nodded and placed his pipe in the ashtray.

'How much money did you collect tonight?' he asked.

Steiger looked perplexed at the question. 'Six million dollars,' he said finally.

'Impressive,' the director said. 'Actually, it was ten million.'

'I swear to—'

'No, Father,' the director said, 'I'm not suggesting you're lying. The fact is that ten million dollars was donated to the Fratres at the dinner. Cardinal Spellman took a cut of four million.'

Steiger looked as if he'd been pole-axed.

'Your naivety is touching, Father,' the director continued. 'The agency is willing to make up the, eh, shortfall. We're prepared to top that up with a further ten million dollars. You will lodge that ten million at the Vatican Bank – in a separate account from the Croatian money. Out of that, you will gift the pope five million. That should buy you an audience at least. The cardinal brings ten million every year to the papal coffers and has unlimited access to the papal chambers as well as invitations to holiday with the pope in Castel Gandalfo. We buy your entrance ticket, Father Steiger. You must take it from there. If the pope asks who you'd wish to have as a mentor to the Fratres, you will nominate Cardinal Francis J. Spellman. Agreed?'

'Agreed.'

'You will also agree to promote Cardinal Spellman through your contacts in the Vatican. Agreed?'

Steiger was an apt pupil. The sudden gleam of realisation in his eyes proved he wasn't unaware of what he was being asked to do and why.

'Let's turn to your third point,' the director said. 'The agency will fund you to the tune of ten million dollars per annum. You will use that money to place your Fratres and lay associates in positions of influence throughout Europe. Whatever intelligence they supply, you'll share with us. You'll liaise with ...' He paused and looked over Steiger's shoulder at Medusa.

'Maria Donati,' she said.

'Maria Donati will be your contact with the agency, Father. In particular, she will receive whatever intelligence you glean from the East. In effect, your assets will be ours and ours will be yours. As a token of good faith, I'm offering a series of interviews with journalists from the major European newspapers to publicise the Fratres and promote your work. Miss Donati will draw up the list and make the contacts. She will do the same for the various broadcast corporations in Europe and the United States.'

He sat back and smiled. 'If you have any reservations or questions, speak now or forever hold your peace.'

Max Steiger became utterly still, absorbing what he'd been offered. 'How long will this, eh, arrangement last?' he asked finally.

'As long as it's of benefit to the agency,' the director replied. 'In the event that we are dissatisfied with your performance, we will terminate the agreement and seek compensation.'

Medusa spoke into the silence.

'I think that means I get to kill you,' she offered helpfully.

Max Steiger swung right around to face her.

'I am not that easy to kill, Miss Donati,' he said.

'Then I won't make it easy,' she assured him.

He turned back to the director.

'Is there anything else?'

'Yes,' the director said, 'there is. We will do all in our power to protect your past, Father Steiger. If a scandal should surface, the agency will not be tainted by the, eh, shall we say contagion. Do you understand the implications for you?'

'Yes.'

'Then we are agreed?'

'We are agreed.'

'My driver will take you back to the cardinal's residence,' the director said and held the door for Medusa.

Max Steiger sat and stared, unseeing. He'd achieved the breakthrough he'd hungered for and was tempted to savour his triumph. This was the first step on the path he'd envisioned. He had no doubt that the director would honour the promises he'd made. And he didn't doubt that there would be a price to be paid if he failed to fulfil his side of the pact. If the great scheme ended in ashes, he would die. His destiny was to survive and be glorious, and no one could come in the way of that destiny and live. No one! The driver stuck his head inside the door.

'You ready, Father?'

'Ready and willing,' Max Steiger said.

Cardinal Tisserant's apartments, the Vatican

'So,' Tisserant boomed, rising from behind his desk, 'I send you forth to fetch Karl Hamner and you return with Rasputin.'

The cardinal was as Karl remembered him. He had retained the granite presence, long beard and unflinching eyes. Instinctively, he bent to kiss his ring and found himself hauled into a hug. 'We'll have none of that mediaeval nonsense,' Tisserant said gruffly. 'Now, young man,' he said, steering him by the elbow to a low table, 'you've been travelling and you must be famished.'

'*Voilà!*' Emil whisked a cloth from a tray like a magician.

Karl sat at the table as the two clerics moved up their armchairs to flank him. Karl tried not to gobble but it had been a long and hungry journey.

'I remember a time when I could eat like that,' Tisserant said wistfully.

'And so you should,' Emil quipped, 'it was at breakfast this morning.'

When the pace of Karl's eating had slowed to mere chewing, they peppered him with questions.

'Tell us of your adventures,' Emil said eagerly.

Karl felt at a loss. He'd gone home to Hallstatt, taught in the school, made his daily pilgrimage to the cemetery and mine, and visited with Kurt and Bertha. 'I was a teacher,' he said lamely.

'Oh, to be a teacher,' Emil said.

'You were my teacher,' Tisserant said impatiently.

'Ah, yes. And my failure is always before me, I suppose,' Emil added. 'The adventures of young men would strain our hearts. Karl is here now and that's what matters. *Carpe diem* – seize the day.' He nodded at the cardinal, like a teacher ceding the floor to his student. Karl's head reeled from the fast-paced banter between the two old friends. He and Kurt had often talked into the night, dissecting the history they had lived through during Operation Barbarossa. He was now in the presence of men who sat at the centre of a global web that attracted and analysed news from all over the world. The Catholic Church had representatives in almost every country on earth, except in the Soviet Union and its satellites and China, and Tisserant spoke to all of them. He remembered from the discussions they'd had before how the cardinal could draw disparate strands together and make that tangled web accessible. As a fledgling historian, it had made a deep impression on him. Tisserant was also prone to switching into any of the twelve languages he spoke fluently, assuming his audience was composed of polyglots like himself. Karl was relieved when

Emil positioned himself at his shoulder, offering translations and witty asides as the mood took him.

'After most wars,' Tisserant began, 'there are winners and losers. After this war, Italy was neither. Certainly, Mussolini and the fascists were finished, but Italy was left without a government. There were two main contenders. On the left, we had the communists – Stalin worshippers – and on the right, we had those who longed for the American Way. Italy was still an occupied country – flooded with American GIs.'

'And American clothes,' interjected Emil. 'And movies, chewing gum and Coca-Cola.' He elongated the last word and the cardinal smiled.

'He loved every minute of it,' he said to Karl. 'Especially Coca-Cola,' he added, mimicking his secretary perfectly. 'There were cultural benefits, Emil,' he insisted.

'Oh, yes. I'd forgotten,' Emil said. 'The US government sponsored the distribution of the *Reader's Digest* to half a million Italian families.'

'The pope was caught between communism and consumerism,' Tisserant continued. 'Typically, he chose a third way – Franco's Spanish model, the perfect marriage of Church and state.'

'Hardly perfect,' Emil interjected. 'El Caudillo is, after all, a man – a Spanish man. He would want to be the dominant partner in any marriage.'

'Yes, but Mother Church is a wily old lady, Emil, much-married to a series of powerful partners, right back to the time of Constantine. Pius made the first overture. He honoured Franco with the highest title the Church can award, The Supreme Order of Christ. And so, the mating dance began.'

'To continue the marriage analogy,' Emil said, 'Franco financed Spanish pilgrimages to Rome. Consider them suitors from a lord to his lady. They stood in St Peter's Square and shouted, "Spain for the Pope."'

'I stood on the balcony with Pius,' Tisserant said, 'and he shouted back, "And the pope for Spain." It was, as the Americans say, a done deal.'

'You see, Karl,' Emil said in an audible whisper, 'even Eugène is not immune to the American infection.'

'Pius saw democracy as the lesser of two evils,' Tisserant continued, 'so he damned it with faint praise.'

'*Merde*,' Emil exploded. 'Hark to the historian hiding behind the linguist. What he actually said was that democracy was the mindless rule of the masses.'

'Nevertheless,' Tisserant countered, 'history will say he rode the crest of a wave that was sweeping Europe. Schuman in France and Adenauer in Germany were already pushing the idea of Christian Democracy in the New Europe. The battlelines were drawn for the Italian election. On the one side, we had the communists, who claimed credit for defeating the fascists. Ranged on the other side were the Allies – America, the Italian Christian Democrats and the pope. As the slogan put it: "To prevent the Cossacks and Stalin camping in St Peter's Square." If you believed my eminent colleagues, it was the Battle of Lepanto all over again. Again, the first shots were fired long before election day. Tell him, Emil.'

'Pius gave one hundred million lira to the cause from his personal fund,' Emil said tonelessly.

'Where does a pope get that kind of money?' Karl blurted.

'You have a choice of two rumours,' Emil offered. 'The first is that the US sold war materiel and gave the money to Pius.'

'And their swords shall be beaten into bucks,' Tisserant murmured. 'We know it was lodged to the Vatican Bank for Pius to spend on anti-communist activities.'

'And the second?' Karl prompted when Emil didn't pick up the narrative.

'What? Oh, forgive me. I was—'

'Daydreaming?' Tisserant offered.

'The second story is that Cardinal Spellman of New York went, or was sent, to General George Marshall with a Vatican begging bowl and the US government released large sums in what they call "black currency" to the Catholic Church in Italy.'

'How much?' Karl asked.

'Twelve billion.'

'*Billion*?'

'Twelve! Spellman told Pius about this,' Tisserant said. 'He's not the kind to hide his light under a bucket.'

'Bushel,' Emil corrected.

'The pedant is back,' Tisserant smiled. 'Yes, Francis of New York likes to make an impression. Happily for us, he made that impression on the pope in the presence of a very startled monsignor of Emil's acquaintance. Spellman's American friends, the Knights of Columbus, raised 'truth dollars' for Radio Free Europe. Bing Crosby, Frank Sinatra and Gary Cooper broadcast to the Italian public. They said the outcome to the election spelled the difference between freedom and slavery.'

'Not very subtle,' Karl remarked dryly.

'Why be subtle when you're a superpower?' Emil said. 'Oh, and in case it was being too subtle,' he continued, 'they diverted a whole consignment of tanks bound for Greece and landed them in Naples.'

'Even with that kind of firepower,' Tisserant said, 'the pope was in a funk.'

'Another Americanism,' Emil sighed. 'He's a linguist and can't help himself. It means they were fearful, Karl.'

'Fearful enough to mention it to the Irish ambassador,' Tisserant said. "How will I rule the Church if we lose?" the pope asked him. The ambassador assured him he'd be welcome in Ireland. In a remarkable way, that offer of refuge brought out the Roman in the pope. "My post is in Rome," he said. "I am ready to be martyred for Him in Rome."

'Rather unfair to Ireland, I thought,' Emil said.

'Just to be on the safe side,' Tisserant said, 'he ordered a salvo from the big guns on the ecclesiastical front. Cardinal Schuster in

Milan preached that the election was the struggle between Satan and Christ. Siri in Genoa said it was a mortal sin not to vote and one couldn't vote communist and be a Catholic. The Christian Democrats won the vote and Pius lost a fortune, even though he'd backed the winner.'

'What of Yugoslavia?' Karl asked.

'A lighter shade of red under Tito,' Emil said dismissively.

'And the German Democratic Republic?'

'A poor copy of Mother Russia,' Tisserant said tiredly. 'They have all the freedoms of collectivisation – investment in heavy industry, poor wages and food shortages. They have, of course, an abundance of political prisoners. Our sources are certain there will be an uprising. They're equally certain that it will be smashed with Soviet armour.'

'Poland, Romania and Hungary labour under the illusion of autonomy,' Emil said. 'When Stalin wants them, he'll take them and the West will protest, like Britain did when Hitler took Czechoslovakia.'

'Like we failed to do when the Nazis took the Roman Jews,' Tisserant said. 'Stalin can't afford to fail,' he added, 'not again. He made a mistake with Hitler and men like Stalin tend to purge their guilt with the blood of others.'

'I understand he has the largest standing army in the world,' Karl said.

'He can't afford to send them home,' Emil replied.

'And he has the bomb,' Tisserant said. 'The wherewithal to start the beginning of the end of all of us.'

They sat in silence for a long time.

'What will the West do?' Karl asked eventually.

'The West is America,' Tisserant muttered. 'America already grows weary of propping up its poor relations in Europe. It has its Senator McCarthy and his communist witch-hunts and a lot of military people who feel they missed their chance at the end of the war and should have rolled 'good old Uncle Joe', as Roosevelt called him, all the way home to Moscow.'

'And the Vatican?' Karl pressed.

'*Uno Duce una voce*,' Emil said morosely. 'And to think we laughed at Mussolini.'

Tisserant roused himself.

'Taking no sides during the war meant Pius became irrelevant to all sides after it. He's like a man who has looked into a strong light for four years. When the light is switched off, he can see nothing except its after-image. Communism is his after-image and everything he sees is tainted with that shadow. It paralyses him. He's become even more aloof than he was before. The Secretary of State, Maglione, died and Pius didn't replace him. He had to be pushed by the Americans to appoint cardinals who were more representative of the Church worldwide. The one who pays the piper names the tune. With the latest appointments, he's reverted to type. They're top-heavy with Italians and most of them will work here, more bureaucracy in the service of autocracy. Like Narcissus, Karl, the Vatican has become fascinated by its own reflection. Europe is being renewed and we have nothing new to say. Those who do speak are silenced. All those wonderful, challenging voices silenced.'

He looked away for a moment before resuming.

'And the extraordinary thing is that now that the war is over and the peace has been made without him, the pope can't stop speaking. He lectures gynaecologists and engineers and movie makers. Father Leiber, his secretary, has a small army of monsignori who do his research. He has a library of fifty thousand volumes. Which subjects are being researched? History? Theology? No! Everything from obstetrics to anaesthetics. Speaking of which, I need a drink.'

'No, you don't,' Emil said sharply. 'You'd like one,' he relented, 'and so would we.'

When Karl demurred, Emil pressed a glass into his hand. 'You'll need it,' he said, 'he's just coming to the best part. Karl didn't come all the way from Hallstatt to hear you ramble, Eugène,' he chided. 'Get to the point.'

Tisserant took a long draught to fortify himself.

'Before you returned to Hallstatt,' he said, 'you began a thesis – 'The Jews of Rome in the Reign of Pius the Twelfth'. We'd like you to take it up again.'

Before Karl could respond, he continued.

'We can arrange access for you to the Vatican Library, even the Secret Archives. I believe your friends in the ghetto will be happy to help. There is one person in particular – but Emil will tell you about him later. We've also arranged for the Dominican Fathers in the San Clemente to employ you as a part-time tour guide. That, as the intelligence people say, will be your cover.'

'Eugène,' Emil said warningly.

'I'm coming to it,' Tisserant growled. He took a deep breath and looked keenly at Karl. 'I must tell you about Max Steiger,' he said, almost apologetically.

A tremor ran through Karl's body. 'To name your demon is to tame your demon,' someone had told him a long time ago, before adding, 'Some fear or horror, concealed inside, becomes formless. It feeds on your imagination and grows monstrous.' If the cardinal was aware of the effect of his words, he showed no sign of it.

'Max Steiger has been bombarding the Vatican with petitions. He wants Pius to formally recognise his new order. He also asks – demands – the appointment of a cardinal-mentor to the Fratres. Maglione wasn't replaced in that capacity either. Steiger hasn't been idle otherwise. He has been extending the Fratres' reach and influence throughout the Vatican. He's also inserting lay affiliates of the Fratres into prominent positions in education and government in a number of European countries. Why is he so successful? Because nature abhors a vacuum, Karl. In the absence of leadership, people can be seduced by the unlikeliest voice. The Austrian corporal taught us that bitter lesson. The money is the key,' he said fiercely. 'We know Steiger brought a fortune from Croatia and lodged it in the Vatican Bank. But we can't prove it. Not without exposing someone the pope would not wish to be exposed – and not without risking your life. I fear the Fratres are trying to create a church within the Church, which would be as intolerant of thought and freedom of expression within the Church as it is implacably against those of other faiths. We need to trace the money that finances the people they've placed inside and outside the Vatican.'

'Surely someone within the Vatican would—'

'No,' Tisserant said firmly. 'Outside of the people in this room, there is no one we can trust without reservation. Steiger knows I have no love for him or his Fratres. They will be suspicious of Emil because they know we are of one mind. It's possible that your research will reveal something we can use for leverage.'

Karl sat back in his chair and steepled his fingers under his chin. 'If I understand you correctly, Eminence, you want me to produce a book that will, more than likely, be critical of the Church?'

'Yes,' Tisserant said, 'I want you to shame us.'

Santa Magdalena Convent, Rome

Sister Pilar disapproved of her room. Compared to her cell in the Schloss, it was decadent. The mattress was too yielding, and the bed linen and blankets too smooth and soft. She decided to sleep on the bare boards. A portrait of a blowsy Madonna and one of a simpering St Francis whispered inanities until she silenced them by turning their faces to the wall. She hated that fat Sister Dorothea, loathed those young sluts with round bellies and the American dottore. In the privacy of her room, she stripped to her skin and threw her itchy habit in a corner. Reverently, she opened her Bible and placed it, together with the *Dark Night of the Soul*, on the floor before her. From childhood, she'd been attracted to the writings of St John of the Cross and contemptuous of the comfortable religion practised by her parents. They were people of the earth, given to earthly pleasures. Of course, they attended the processions of the saints during the fiestas, but that, she concluded, was superstition cloaked under a patina of religiosity. The stark suffering of the cross was what she hungered for, the one true icon of her fallen state. She was nothing, less than nothing, a base creature condemned to suffer in the flesh of a putrid body. Her parents had taken her to the local priest. She barked a laugh at the memory. Padre Ignacio was a man with soft hands. She'd seen him dance at weddings and take wine with her parents. He suggested they take her to the Sagrada Familia in Barcelona and she'd run screaming as Gaudi's fantastical pillars writhed before her eyes. The great monstrosity of Montserrat was another nightmare. While others listened in awe to the chanting monks, she'd heard only the susurration of evil in her skull. Finally, there were pilgrimages to doctors who prodded and poked and asked intimate questions until she'd retreated into her silence.

Her parents had been relieved when she expressed an interest in the Fratres, an interest ignited when she read an article by Father Max Steiger. They arranged a trip for her to hear him speak and even though it was in the hateful Sagrada Familia, his voice had cowed the pagan interior and captivated Maria Garces – her name before he'd renamed her Pilar. Only Father Steiger had ever truly listened. Only he had applied a poultice to her suppurating soul and drawn parallels between her sufferings and those of the great mystics. 'Hadn't Thérèse of Lisieux suffered for championing reform among her sisters?' he'd said. 'Hadn't she enlisted John of the Cross to refine her order in the furnace of true spirituality?' It was Father Steiger who had set her on the path to true mysticism, explaining the two-step process. She must purify her senses and purify her spirit. To purify her senses, he said, she must give herself totally to her carnal nature and find it wanting. Only out of the ashes of her lust would she rise, phoenix-like, as his soul-companion; as Thérèse had been to John of the Cross.

A shiver rippled from the base of her belly as she recalled their coupling. He'd encouraged her to lose her inhibitions, loose the bonds that held her suspended between human passion and spiritual ecstasy. Even now, kneeling naked on the bare floor, her body thrummed and ached at the memory. Feverishly, she applied the little whip to her back and buttocks. He had raised her up, appointed her Mistress of Novices. It was she, Pilar, who would mould the next generation of sisters. It was she who would select from among the novices those most susceptible to the temptations of the flesh so that he might liberate them from their carnal confinement.

She had felt the sting of jealousy and confessed it. Attachment, he'd assured her, was the lure of the world. She applied the whip even more rigorously, letting the pain cleanse her of her fault. And then she'd sent him a devil clothed in flesh. She abased herself on the floor. '*Ego autem sum vermis*,' she whispered, 'I am a worm.' She reared up on her knees and spread her arms in imitation of Christ crucified. The devil had conceived. Her palms pressed either side of her skull as if she could squeeze that reality from her brain like pus from a wound. But the agony would not leave her. It was another, the American *puta*, who would bear the child of the chosen one, and not her. Laura Morton was a witch. She was a succubus who had attached herself to Father General, not for the attainment of perfection but for her own foul pleasure. Sister Pilar raised her Bible and searched the heavily scored pages for comfort.

'And, in my name, you shall cast out devils,' she read and was comforted.

THE PUBLISHER'S OFFICE, ROME

The shingle on the door announced 'Mario Schwartz', and, in smaller print beneath, 'Publisher'. The nameplate was appropriately faded to suggest a long-established firm. Or, Emil Dupont surmised, the firm was too famous to require legibility. To the side, there was a metal bell-pull cast in the shape of Janus. It was connected to a bell that was only audible to those within. Callers, who knew this, pulled once and waited. Those who didn't pulled repeatedly. That distinction had saved many Romans from the Waffen-SS during the occupation. Monsignor Dupont was well acquainted with the firm. He pulled once and awaited the appearance of Tilda. Tilda Forsyth was the Cerberus who guarded the inner sanctum of the firm. Many years before, her aristocratic English family had encouraged her to 'take the tour' and, like many of her contemporaries, she'd come to Rome. Unlike most of the others, she'd stayed. Tilda took apartments near the Spanish Steps, where she established a literary salon. She'd served scented, English tea to Mussolini, von Kesselring and most of the principal players in the drama that ended with the armistice. They were unaware that the gloriously eccentric English lady encoded their confidences which were then secreted between the pages of the devotional literature the English ambassador to the Vatican favoured. Emil Dupont knew this because, as the eyes and ears of the powerful Cardinal Tisserant, it was his business to know such things.

The door opened and Tilda filled the available space. 'Tilda,' a portrait painter from Verona once remarked, 'possessed a figure that would have had Rubens screaming for more canvas.' To which a normally humourless American diplomat had replied, 'If there was a Nobel Prize for architecture, Tilda's mom and dad would be a shoo-in.'

It was common knowledge among the Roman literati that Mussolini had foundered between the Scylla and Charybdis of Tilda's bosoms, before she'd been replaced by Clara Petacci. A liaison that had proved fatal for Carla had added a frisson to Tilda's reputation. *C'est la guerre*, Emil thought, as Tilda's chins assembled themselves into a smile.

'Ah, Monsignor,' she boomed, 'sent by the inquisition to burn that heretic Schwartz.'

'Torquemada is long dead, Tilda,' he said mildly.

'Not while Pacelli lives,' she snorted. 'They tell me Tardini is haring among the Vatican statuary, covering up the naughty bits. They also say that the number of banned books exceeds the number of books published.'

'You have impeccable sources, Tilda.'

'The very least you can do is to excommunicate Schwartz, you know, the bell, book and candle thingummy.'

'Ah, *je suis désolé*, Tilda,' Emil said. 'I fear I'm much too old to carry the instruments of excommunication or torture. Anyway, Schwartz is Jewish.'

'You have a point,' she conceded, kissing him noisily on both cheeks. 'Do come in. Beelzebub is torturing a new author,' she added in a whisper as a bellow echoed around the building. 'We will take refuge and refreshment in Alexandria.'

Emil followed her through a catacomb of books. Alexandria was Tilda's lair, a high-ceilinged room, furnished with uncomfortable armchairs and dedicated to books. Not just any books, he knew, as he picked his careful way through a minefield of volumes to the armchair that seemed least likely to swallow him. The original Alexandria was the site of the famous, lost library of Egypt. Tilda's version was a treasure-trove of books the Church had banned from the bookshelves of Europe. On his way to the armchair, he was heartened to observe a volume of Graham Greene's standing spine to spine in solidarity with an Yves Congar. He took a deep satisfying breath as he sank into the cushions. Emil Dupont was a scholar-priest. He preferred the incense of Alexandria's dusty air to the odour of sanctity.

Tilda fetched a bottle from a book-barnacled table and brought it and two glasses to the coffee table. 'Against the chill,' she said, as she poured the wine. 'Fires and books, *mon cher ami*, are intellectually and materially incompatible. Heine says when one burns books, one will, in the end, burn people.'

'Heine was a prophet unwelcome in his own country, Tilda,' Emil agreed, accepting his glass.

'And how is your lord and master?' she enquired coyly.

'Cardinal Tisserant is quite well.'

'Ever the diplomat, Emil,' she said and smiled. 'I saw him in Saint Peter's recently. He's still sporting that frightful beard and still trying to walk like the Patriarch of Constantinople. Place not your trust in princes, Emil.'

'It's been said.'

'Oh, *touché*, you old pedant,' she laughed. 'But, keep in mind that cardinals are created.'

'And?'

'And, by definition, it is something that is made out of nothing. Should one expect something from nothing?'

'You're much too young to be so cynical, Tilda.'

'And you're much too … mature, to be so naïve.'

Their jousting was interrupted by another bellow from afar.

'I take it the new author is now the ex-author,' Emil said dryly.

'Not at all, my dear,' she said confidently, 'Mario is the Caruso of shouters, tone and timbre mean everything. That particular bellow means a rewrite is required.'

'How is Mario?'

'Only as well as he should be,' she said dismissively. 'He missed the translation rights to Churchill's *Stemming the Tide*. Much tearing of hair, darling. 'Though, in Mario's case, that was a very singular pursuit.'

'Are you well, Tilda?'

'Sweet of you to ask, Emil. I am … as you find me,' she said slowly, 'a rather overweight, and frequently overwrought, English lady, needing opera glasses to look back at youth. In the real world,' she grimaced, 'I imagine I would be cosseted to within an inch of madness and confined to conversations with a cat. Here,' she added, raising her glass to toast the room and the visitor, 'I have my books and my friends. One does need some small sense of purpose, don't you think, particularly as the years glide by. And you, *cher ami*?'

'Sometimes … I forget things.'

He hadn't intended the revelation and his eyes misted before he could change the subject.

'Surely, that's one of the blessings of old age,' she said gently.

'Considering all we have experienced, how could we bear to remember everything? Think of it as a spring-cleaning of the mind – throwing out the old furniture to make room for the new.'

'I said something like that to a young man.'

'So, physician, heal thyself,' she crowed. 'I hope he listened,' she added. 'I find the young have the ability to hear everything and listen to—'

'Tilda.' The imperious roar jerked them both upright.

'Anon, anon, sir,' Tilda shouted in reply. As Emil freed himself from the armchair, she clutched his elbow. 'A word to the wise,' she said, and he was struck by her serious tone. 'Those dreadful Fratres are absolutely everywhere; like duckweed in a pond. Word among the print houses is that they are placing their own people on various editorial boards. A friend at *L'Osservatore Romano* tells me—'

'Tilda!'

'He'll smell the wine on your breath and believe he has the upper hand,' she whispered, as she led him to the publisher's office. 'Poor Mario,' she said, wickedly, 'snacking on Christians all morning and now a real lion enters the arena.' He could hear her laughing in the corridor as he closed the door behind him.

Mario Schwartz was a tiny man, elevated to eye level by three plump cushions. Three more cushions rested under the desk to spare his feet the embarrassment of dangling. He wore a well-cut black suit over a gleaming open-necked white shirt. A bulbous, bald head occupied the space where his neck should have been and his brown eyes regarded the monsignor dolefully.

'Just give me my penance,' he said, 'you've already heard my sins.'

'And a good morning to you too, Mario,' Emil said airily. 'Thank you for seeing me. I gather you're busy.'

'Busy does not make business,' Mario said, waving his guest to a chair. 'It's that damned war,' he continued, as if the entire event had been waged against him personally. 'Why do the survivors write?' he wondered plaintively.

'Presumably, because the victims can't, Mario.'

'You know what I'm talking about, Monsignor. The Allies write about what they did and the Axis about what they didn't do. They share a fetish for facts, maps, ordinance and strategies and are uniformly dull.' He plucked a cigar from the desk and rolled it longingly between his thumb and forefinger before replacing it. 'Generals are the worst,' he confided. 'The victorious ones write for Hollywood, casting themselves in the leading role. The plot is always the same – junior officer works his way up the ranks and languishes in the shadow of lesser men until the critical moment of the ultimate battle. Then, *mirabile*, he makes an intervention and wins the day.'

'I didn't realise generals could write for a popular audience,' Emil said. 'Everything written in the Vatican is edited to within an inch of its margin – to the point where it can mean one thing or the other or neither.'

'Ghostwriters,' Mario whispered.

'Pardon?'

'An amanuensis, *caro Monsignor*,' Mario insisted.

'You mean—'

'Someone else does the writing. It's usually a journalist who translates them into simple language, someone who turns the base metal of tedious facts into readable nuggets. Someone,' he continued, warming to his theme, 'who can defuse hyperbole, camouflage ambition and lay down a smokescreen of sympathy when the poor sods at the sharp end follow orders and die for the privilege.'

'You should have been a writer, Mario.'

'I was. I starved.'

'And what of the vanquished generals?'

'They write apologias for a lost war replete with suggestions about the incompetence of other generals and claims that they were somewhere else when the nasty stuff happened.' He sighed and shook his massive head. 'The possibility of hanging enhances creativity, Monsignor,' he said.

'Except for von Kluge, of course.'

'Well, yes,' Mario allowed, 'but he had the benefit of two ghostwriters – neither credited, of course. Does that surprise you?'

'No, I happen to know one of them,' Emil replied. 'He's a historian.'

'Historians,' Mario snorted, 'are just upmarket literary whores – eh, your pardon, Monsignor.'

'Granted, Mario. But not every historian writes a defeated general's memoirs and makes it readable and a financial success, Mario.'

'It's a one-book wonder,' Mario said dismissively, 'unless, of course, von Kluge is planning a third war.' He was laughing at his own joke when he realised he laughed alone.

'Imagine, Mario,' Emil said softly, 'a conscript plucked from his idyllic Austrian village and sent to the Russian Front with his father, teacher, neighbour – even the local policeman.'

'Unusual but not unique,' Mario countered. 'The Nazis were taking fourteen-year-old boys and their granddads at the end. Anyway,' he continued, 'a conscript's view of war is usually the rear end of the conscript ahead of him, too narrow a viewpoint on such an epic experience, Monsignor. No, most old soldiers tell stories of trench foot and weevils in the bread.'

'Except,' Emil said, raising a hand to stem the other man's flow, 'that this particular conscript served at von Kluge's table. He observed Guderian, von Bock and all the other brass – before and after the decisive battles.'

'The table talk of generals is of some interest,' Mario grudged, 'but it's a sidebar to the real story.'

'You come directly to the meat of the matter,' Emil declared admiringly.

'The real story is of a boy who sees boxcars in sidings on his train journey to Russia. This boy becomes a horse-wrangler in the most mechanised army in the world. He becomes a stretcher-bearer at Borodino and feeds a machine-gun during the last battle at the gates of Moscow.'

The publisher opened his mouth to interrupt and kept it open as the normally mild-mannered monsignor glared and continued.

'He and his companions are harassed by Cossacks, lost in blizzards and saved from partisans by a girl he had saved from the Waffen-SS. This boy,' Emil continued, almost spitting the word, 'loses part of his hand to frostbite and escapes on the last aircraft.'

'Quite a story,' Mario said feebly.

'And not finished just yet,' Emil warned. 'After his recuperation, he is decorated, promoted to captain and appointed to von Kesselring's staff here in Rome. Yes, Mario,' he said in response to the awareness evident in the publisher's eyes, 'in time for the *razzia*. He saves a Jewish family from the Waffen-SS roundup and deserts the army to bring the story of what has happened to the Vatican. And,' he wheezed as Mario raised a hand to halt him, 'he kept a journal.'

'You had already won the race,' Mario said, as the exhausted Emil sank back in the chair, 'the lap of honour was unnecessary.'

'Sorry.'

'He will write this book for me?'

'He will write two books for you.'

'Two?'

'Yes, he will also write a book on the Jews of Rome during the reign of Pope Pius the Twelfth.'

'That's his second book?'

'It's the one you'll publish first – otherwise we go elsewhere.'

'But, Monsignor,' the publisher whispered, 'the pope is still alive.'

'As far as we can determine,' Emil said stonily.

'No publisher would touch such a book.'

Emil leaned forward and waited until the wary publisher was looking directly into his eyes.

'Exactly, Mario,' he said and winked.

'Who is this prodigy?' Mario hedged.

'His name is Karl Hamner.'

'I know that name.'

'Every Jew in Rome knows that name. Every Jew in the world will know it when you publish this book.'

'Where can I find this Karl Hamner?'

'Outside on the pavement.'

'You should have been a Jesuit,' Mario said, offering his hand. 'Tilda,' he bellowed.

THE KREMLIN

Nikita Sergeyevich Khrushchev checked himself in the mirror and grimaced. The Moscow joke was that the members of the politburo checked themselves in the mirror every day to make sure that they were still there. 'I'm still here,' he muttered and tried to smile reassuringly at the man in the mirror. Even in his reflection, the smile wasn't much more than a stretching of the lips; the eyes remained worried.

An officer of the Kremlin Guard had rapped on his door minutes before. 'One hour,' he'd snapped, turned on his highly polished heels and stamped away.

'Bastard,' he told his reflection. 'Jumped up fucking Cossacks think they rule the roost because they protect the cock. One day,' he nodded to himself. Yes, one day, he resolved, there'll be a list of names and I shall draw a line through his. Instinctively, his right hand tightened on a phantom pen. He was good at lists, a splendid organiser. Stalin himself had said so when he'd brought him back from the Ukraine. The Ukraine, he remembered, had been one long list – intellectuals, artists, priests, poets and the thousands of kulaks who thought they owned the land and the thousands of peasants who didn't reach their quota on the farm or in the factories. Stroke! His arm swept before him in a dismissive gesture. Day and night he'd stroked a pen through names, obliterating people – sending them to the slow death of Siberia or the mercy of the firing squad. The end result was the same. 'Purge,' their glorious leader Stalin had commanded the politburo, and purge he had – sometimes two thousand in a day. Molotov, he grudged, had the record, three thousand death sentences signed at a single sitting and then he'd gone to see a film with Stalin. He shook his head in admiration but the eyes in the mirror rebuked him. *What have we become? What will become of us?*

He knew he was trying to evade the 'hour' and the realisation brought him to his desk. The 'hour' was a favourite ploy of the leader. It gave the diligent time to ready an account of their stewardship. The others – the incompetents, intriguers and especially the imaginative – stewed in their juices. Khrushchev was confident he didn't fall into the final category, which was why his star had risen. The grandson of Ukrainian serfs, he had educated himself out of the piss-poor farm in Kalinovka and hitched his career to powerful men within the party. He stood now within grasping distance of the ultimate power. He would not fall.

He was surprised when his secretary interrupted to announce the meeting was just five minutes away. He gathered his notes and crammed them in a filing cabinet. He was on top of his brief – numbers, quotas and statistics at his fingertips. Stalin had an aversion to people who read from 'scraps of paper'. Khrushchev walked towards the leader's office confident that nothing could surprise him at today's meeting.

He was wrong.

Khrushchev was the last to enter Stalin's office and a dark rose of panic bloomed in his chest until he saw the empty chair. There was a long-standing tradition that the man who arrived to find every chair occupied was a dead man. *How Stalin loves his little games*, he thought. The leader stood facing the door through which each man entered. Khrushchev was well aware that Stalin distrusted anyone who didn't look him in the eye and locked his eyes on those beneath the bushy eyebrows as he strode forwards. The hooded, brown eyes regarded him steadily for a moment and then flicked away. He sat.

It was like being in the school he'd gone back to after the

Revolutionary War. He remembered how the teacher called on each individual student to give an account of what they'd studied. The prepared had been ignored and the rest had been degraded. He, Molotov and Beria performed well. Bulganin and Malenkov suffered. Stalin could be charming or coarse, depending on his mood, and his mood could change with lethal speed and consequences. Today, he seemed to be keeping his fires damped, contenting himself with ridicule and sarcasm. 'Know your enemy,' Khrushchev had counselled the defenders of Stalingrad. 'The fascists are armed for full-frontal confrontation. Play by their rules and you die. Hit and run, snipe from cover. Find out where they piss, eat and shit, and kill them there.' It was the knowledge and tactic that brought victory to the poorly equipped, rag-tag defenders and defeat to the most mechanised army in the world. He watched Stalin grow more and more disinterested in the monotonous reports and braced himself for the real agenda.

Like an earthquake, it began with seemingly random rumblings. Stalin growled about factory quotas and growled louder about food production. It was, Khrushchev thought, the preface to *A Tale of Two Russias*. It was also, he considered happily, an indicator of how far he had risen from humble roots that he could recall a book by a foreign author and take liberties with the title. The gap between the living standards of politburo members and the people they served yawned wider every day. The wives of the politburo shopped at the GUM, the huge multilevel store that looked across Red Square at Lenin's tomb. The GUM stocked Beluga caviar and Georgian wines. The shops in Moscow had stringy chickens and industrial-grade vodka – some days. Every day, the GUM extended its range of delicacies for the elite, while the workers queued six-deep for essentials. Typically, the Muscovites grumbled and told bad jokes. 'A worker walks away from his place in a bread queue. "Where are you going?" his neighbour asks. "I'm going to shoot Stalin," the worker replies. "That queue is longer than this queue," his neighbour tells him.' Of course, Khrushchev mused, no worker would ever breathe that name, not when at least one neighbour in every building was reporting to the NKVD. Yet, it was an apt joke, he admitted. Moscow and the entire Soviet Union were crippled with food shortages and simmering with resentment. If that anger ever found a focus—

'Jews,' he heard Stalin say and relaxed. The Jews, he knew, were the usual scapegoats when the pressure needle of economic misery edged into the red. They were also the leader's favoured escape valve for his paranoia. He could rant for an hour against the Jews and then segue seamlessly to armaments or foreign policy or a hymn of praise to the Islamists at Uyghur who were a burr under the arse of Chairman Mao. Not this time though, he sensed.

'Every Jew is a spy,' Stalin said, pacing behind his desk. 'American capitalists have seduced them and they burrow, like weevils, into the heart of the Motherland.'

Molotov may have coughed or not, looked away or not. It didn't matter. Stalin was in search of a target and the stammering Molotov would do. Khrushchev knew there was bad blood between them. He wondered if wounds had been exchanged when they sat together on Lenin's Politburo. They were the only survivors of the Old Bolsheviks, as the young cadres called them. It should have been a glue to bind them together but it wasn't, and hadn't been for a long time. Stalin had misjudged Hitler in 1941 and had blamed Molotov for signing the peace treaty with Ribbentrop, even though it had been his decision. The leader cannot be wrong. Inevitably it was Molotov whom he ordered to broadcast the news of Barbarossa to the nation, ensuring that his name and his voice would ever be associated with disaster in the minds of the people. There was more. Molotov had married Polina and she had befriended Stalin's first wife, a woman who had taken her own life with Polina as a witness.

Khrushchev was turning the pages of the unfolding story, trying frantically to anticipate the conclusion so that he could divert it. Stalin got there first.

'Your precious Pearl,' he snarled at Molotov, making a play on the name Polina, 'is the proof.'

Molotov blanched but remained erect and impassive.

'Whelp of a Jewish tailor – sister to Jews in Israel and America, worming her way to a seat at this table.'

He slammed his palms on the table and every man in the room flinched. Except Molotov, Khrushchev noticed.

'I halted her gallop,' Stalin continued. 'I dug her out of her lair in the committees, held her up to the light of a tribunal, buried her in the Lubyanka for a year, and now she rots in Kazhak. And you,' he spat, pointing a shaking finger at Molotov, 'you didn't have the balls to cut her off. I had to order you to do your duty and divorce her.'

He stopped, his moustache fringed with spittle. It was that moment after a thunderclap when the world seems to hold its breath, when the utter stillness is more terrifying than the clamour that went before. Khrushchev longed to loosen his collar but didn't dare, strained to swallow but couldn't. Stalin stood quite still for a full minute.

'They tried to poison me, those Jewish doctors,' he muttered, as if in disbelief. 'I will scourge them out of Moscow,' he said calmly. 'I will send them all to Kazakh. Then we'll hear what the Americans have to say. I heard them at Yalta, speaking behind their hands, saying they should have finished the job. When we were on our knees they were ready to ride over us. Well, talk is cheap. If they want to talk war, I will give them a real one – if they have the stomach for it. Will Eisenhower go to war for the Jews? Will he mass on our borders for Germans, Romanians and Poles? Is the President of the United States willing to throw the final dice on all or nothing? I think not.' Then he added calmly with dreadful confidence, 'But I am.'

He sat and swivelled his chair away from them. They were dismissed.

ROME; TRASTEVERE

An ache, like the echo of an old wound, brought his palm to massage the back of his neck. *I am being followed.* Karl felt annoyed with himself for having ignored his instincts earlier. Living without war, he'd allowed those survival muscles to become flaccid. Mentally, he retraced his steps. Already, he was on the ornate bridge that would take him via Tiber Island to Trastevere. The parapet was cool to his touch and he looked down into the Tiber, letting the green water sluice away distractions.

After the meeting with Schwartz, the publisher, euphoria had filled his head and dulled his instincts. How many times in Russia had his instinct saved him? How often had he blended with the contours of a frozen tree trunk seconds before he'd heard the heave of Cossack horses in deep snow? Once, his entire patrol had paused on a path and detoured to resume their march at another point, thirty yards ahead. The second patrol group hadn't been so fortunate. Muted by time, he could hear the screaming of the man who'd lost his legs to a Russian landmine. The unwritten rule of the troop had been a simple one; if you sensed danger, you named it, as he had done when a black spot had blossomed over the horizon. His call had tumbled the troop to cover, either side of the road, seconds before the thwarted Russian bomber had growled overhead. His comrades had cheered him, he recalled. Had he been mistaken, they would have teased him and moved on. In Russia, crying wolf was never accounted a fault. The second rule was equally simple. If you were the prey, you led the hunter away from the herd – and he would not inflict this current shadow on his friends. His pace quickened and he wrapped himself in the shadows of high buildings and narrow streets. Instinctively, he used the reflections in shop windows to check behind him and doubled back through arched alleyways to come at his pursuer from behind. In the end, it was his faulty recall of the territory that failed him. Hurrying down yet another alley, he realised that he had broken the first rule of urban warfare, when he found himself in a cul-de-sac. The top of the brick wall that blocked his passage glinted with broken glass. His maimed, left hand tingled in anticipation of the challenge even as he dismissed the option. He turned to retrace his steps.

There were four of them, strung across the mouth of the alley. He had time to measure them as they sauntered forwards. Teenagers, he concluded, from their too-casual gait. Professionals would be more focused but the youngsters, who fanned out as they approached, could prove equally deadly.

'Got yourself lost, *turista*?' the tall one in the centre taunted.

'I have friends in Trastevere,' Karl answered calmly. It would let them know that he knew people who might know them. It was a reasonable ploy, but it was the wrong one. Despite his fluent Italian, the taint of his Austrian accent betrayed him. Instantly, their body-language became more feral.

'Your friends left Trastevere a long time ago, Fritz,' the fat one said. 'Took truckloads of our people with them as souvenirs – people who never came back, Fritz. Maybe you missed a few, last time, Waffen? Coming back now, like a dog to its vomit.'

The tall one came in a rush. Karl stepped inside the wild swing to punch him in the belly. He stepped back as his attacker slumped to the cobble, gasping for breath. It had taken just three seconds to disable that one but three seconds was ample time for the others. From the corner of his eye, he saw someone wield a stick and drifted sideways, turning, so that the stick struck him across the back. Face to face with the startled young man, he butted him on the bridge of the nose and blood jetted over his jacket. The others had pinned his arms and were trying to bend his upper body forward, as a target for the tall one, who was back on his feet.

But they hadn't reckoned on two things. Karl Hamner had survived Operation Barbarossa and the Russian winter. He would not be kicked to death in Trastevere. The second thing was something they didn't know and he wasn't fully aware of himself. Karl had a rancid cistern of anger that he'd kept capped since the war. Deep inside lurked a rage at the death of his father and friends and, deeper still, was his guilt at the loss of Elsa. His daily pilgrimage of expiation to the mine had strengthened his legs and he swept the feet from under the one holding his right arm. He had just enough time to hit the tall one in the chin and he dropped bonelessly. This time, he would stay down. He spun to drag the last one off-balance and grabbed him by the throat. 'Hamner,' the boy wheezed as Karl cocked his fist. For a moment, he was oblivious to everything around him, totally unaware that he was poised to smash this boy's face with his maimed left hand. The boy scrabbled his fingers frantically at the Wehrmacht glove that covered Karl's infirmity.

'Captain Hamner,' he managed, his eyes bulging.

'What?' Karl gasped and the pain in his clenched left fist pried it open.

'Captain Hamner,' the terrified boy repeated.

Karl's vision cleared and he looked closely at the boy. The streets of Trastevere had been terrible that day, with the grinding of Waffen trucks and the screams of their cargo. But every detail of the *razza* and of his flight with the Jewish family had been burned into his memory. He remembered the family huddling outside their restaurant while Waffen thugs battered their father, Enrico. He felt an echo of the shudder in his shoulder when he'd clubbed one of the Waffen unconscious and the scrape of his boots as his comrade dragged him over the cobbles. If he could get them to Tiber Island, he'd thought, they might find sanctuary. Enrico had urged his son to lead the Wehrmacht captain through the dangerous streets.

'Julio,' Karl said faintly.

'*Si*,' the boy nodded.

It was only when Karl offered his hand that he noticed his ravaged knuckles and felt the first needling of the pain that would surely follow. Dumbly, the boy accepted the handshake.

'Glad to meet you again, Julio,' Karl said and smiled.

THE KREMLIN, MOSCOW

Khrushchev kept his composure until he was safely in the haven of his office. He leaned against the desk and allowed his pent-up rage and fear tremble through him. Alexei, his secretary, opened the door to the bathroom and stood aside, his eyes fixed on the floor.

When Khrushchev felt he could walk, unaided, he blundered through and tore his clothes from his body as if they were impregnated with poison. He lowered himself into the cold bath and welcomed the sting. At home, in the village, he'd always been first to the hole in the ice. Always the first to dive without hesitation while his peers high-stepped in the shallows. He grabbed a small towel, soaked it in the bath and draped it over his bald head, as old men did on the Baltic beaches. *We are old men*, he thought grimly, *aged beyond our years by three wars. We are men who have encountered too much, too soon and think that battle is the norm. Why can't Stalin sit in his garden under a tree and marvel at youth at play? Why can't he be charmed by Svetlana, his daughter, and be playfully affectionate with Vassily, his son?* He dragged the towel from his head and soaked it again in the water, pressing it against his eyes. *Why is it that none of us can just stop and retire and become boring old men who talk of the glory days? Old men who've stopped remembering the entrails in the snow, young sightless eyes and the smell of shit and rot and —* He sighed and settled deeper in the water, suddenly resentful that it had lost its invigorating sting. *I could* retire, he thought and laughed a laugh tinged with despair. Nobody had ever retired from the politburo. It was a life sentence for the old men who held the ultimate power. *We are rewarded with dachas in the country and all the trappings of office and the price we pay is self-loathing and fear. Retirement means that one day I will enter the leader's office and there will be one chair absent. Depending on the whim of the leader, I will be demoted and deported, as once I was to the Ukraine. If his mood is vengeful, I will endure a show trial and a bullet in the Lubyanka.*

Alexei stuck his head around the door. 'Visitor,' he announced as he hung fresh clothes on the door and dropped underwear and socks on the laundry basket.

'Tell him to fuck off,' Khrushchev grunted.

'I'd prefer to live,' Alexei said and disappeared.

Khrushchev contemplated emerging naked to greet the visitor. Churchill had done that when Roosevelt had come calling. 'The Prime Minister of Great Britain has nothing to hide from the President of the United States,' he'd said. Khrushchev laughed and a tiny wave lapped at the taps.

The man who waited for him was pear-shaped with a balding head and the smooth face of a successful physician. He affected spectacles without arms that sat on the edge of his nose and made him look like some Tsarist dowager at the Bolshoi. While every man in the politburo had spilled his share of blood for the Motherland, Beria and his NKVD had murdered millions and sent millions more to rot in the gulags he administered. Despite the cold bath, Khrushchev could feel a trickle of sweat begin to run a cold finger down his spine. Beria smiled as Khrushchev entered the room and his smile had all the warmth of the cold room in a morgue. His eyes, an enemy had said, were like two piss-holes in the snow. Khrushchev watched the eyes. Lavrentiy Beria was a serpent. A serpent may dance to a tune but it is always a serpent.

'Lavrentiy,' Khrushchev said warily.

'Nikita Sergeyevich,' Beria replied warmly. 'Your secretary is discreet?' he added.

'Yes,' Khrushchev said, 'and he is mine.'

We are like two dogs marking our territory, he thought. *We will circle and growl until one rolls over in submission*. Beria was a daunting opponent. He had survived the purges and risen to Director of Security of the Soviet Union. He had done this, Khrushchev believed, by becoming a remora that swims in the shark's shadow.

'Sit,' he invited. 'Please, have some coffee.'

Beria filled a cup and sipped at it daintily. 'I take it we will not be overheard.'

'Not unless you've arranged it.'

'I haven't.'

'And you would tell me if you had?'

Stalemate.

Beria took a document from his pocket and placed it on the table between them. Khrushchev read it and handed it back. The document didn't identify the patient and Khrushchev didn't ask. He knew who it was and he hoped Beria didn't notice that his hand had trembled as he'd handed the document back.

'The doctors are concerned,' Beria said.

'If we're talking about the doctors on trial for the attempted poisoning of state officials, then this medical assessment is not to be trusted.'

'Nevertheless,' Beria said smoothly, 'when we are beset by traitors, it is best to prepare for all eventualities. Malenkov agrees.'

Showing his teeth at last, Khrushchev thought. Malenkov and Beria had been appointed deputy premiers by Stalin. They were seen by the citizens as the left and right hand of the leader.

'It is imperative that the state is protected in such treasonous times. I have every confidence in your ability to perform that onerous task.'

'Thank you, Nikita,' Beria smiled. You know Iosif is quite correct as usual. The Americans have no stomach for another war. Roosevelt had to drag them kicking and screaming out of their isolation for the last war. As soon as it was over, they couldn't wait to get back. I met him, you know, Roosevelt.'

It was the sort of self-aggrandising that Beria introduced into conversation, usually at the expense of the listener. It was his I-was-at-Yalta-and-you-weren't jibe. Khrushchev maintained his smile. It wasn't difficult. He was remembering that Stalin had introduced Beria to Roosevelt as 'our Himmler' and Beria had been too star-struck to appreciate the two-edged compliment. If he needed another reason to keep his sunny side in place, he drew it from the knowledge that he was defending Stalingrad when Beria was packing his bags to desert Moscow. He knew it and Beria knew it. He didn't need to say anything, the smile was enough. But he said it anyway.

'Everybody knows that, Lavrentiy.'

Beria's eyes narrowed for a moment and then he relaxed. *Careful, Nikita*, Khrushchev cautioned himself.

'I find the Americans self-absorbed and naïve,' Beria continued easily, 'but not foolish. They like to bark like mastiffs but in reality they're like pampered lapdogs and are much too well cared for to fight over scraps. And then, of course,' he sighed, 'we have our allies.'

He paused and raised his head as if he was looking out over the parapet of the Kremlin at barbarian hordes.

'Allies can be so ungrateful, Nikita. They're like relatives who come to live on your charity and complain about the food.' He barked a short laugh at his own joke. 'We may have spoiled them, given them the expectation that they only had to ask and we'd provide. Malenkov thinks it puts a heavy burden on our own people. It's hard to argue when you think of the sacrifices the Soviet citizen continues to make. Is it unreasonable to raise factory quota in the GDR when our people beggared themselves to buy their freedom? Of course, they are in the front line and vulnerable to Western propaganda.'

He paused as if ticking off items on an agenda.

'I must say, I look forward to the day when those we sent for re-education can be absorbed back into society and make a valuable contribution to productivity. As the West realises the futility of encouraging disaffection, that day will come sooner rather than later.'

He sipped his coffee again and placed the cup and saucer on the table.

'It's always a pleasure to talk with you, Nikita,' he said.

Beria had always been as sincere as a two-rouble whore, Khrushchev reflected.

'I hope we are as one in this, comrade,' Beria continued. 'A bright future is assured for those who are loyal, particularly in these troubled times. I mustn't keep you from your duties.'

He paused with his hand on the doorknob. 'Oh, give my thanks to your Alexei for the wonderful coffee,' he said, and left.

Khrushchev waited until he was certain Beria had left the outer office before he rushed into the toilet and retched in the bowl. As he stood with drool dripping from his chin, he remembered yet another Moscow joke. 'How do you know if a member of the politburo has thrown up in your toilet? There's something in the bowl.' He flushed the bowl and sluiced water in his face at the sink. *Remember, it's a game*, he reminded himself. *That's what you told them in Stalingrad and they survived the fascists. Know your enemy.* Khrushchev had never been known to attend any meeting without preparation or to come back from one without parsing the implications of what had been proposed, discussed and decided. *Think it through*, he commanded himself.

He lowered the lid of the toilet bowl and sat on top. It would sharpen his mind to consider the short distance between success and failure. He felt fear. He felt it was rooted in his bowels and would flourish like ivy to choke him. He'd felt it before every mission against the fascists – he'd learned to face, feel and use its energy to plan how to kill the bastards. There'd been so many times when conflicting reports had come from the commanders in Stalingrad. He'd sat in a basement while other men slept or groaned for a doctor they couldn't have or held their breath at the huff and whine of a mortar. He'd stayed calm. He'd thought through the garbled messages, picked up the pieces of the jigsaw and put them together in a picture he could see and act on. He was never as brilliant as Zhukov or the other generals. Zhukov had been brilliant at Borodino because he'd delayed losing a battle long enough to win a war. *That's why Zhukov had been a general and you'd been a commissar.* But he had been the liaison between the Kremlin and the brilliant generals because he could translate between one and the other and avoid being crushed by the ambitions of either.

He hadn't given in when he'd been banished to the Ukraine after the war. Some men might have sat in the Ukraine and pined for Moscow. He'd gone to a million meetings, slapped backs, drunk vodka and put his people in positions of influence throughout the party. That skill had brought him back to the Kremlin.

So, check the rules of engagement, he told himself. Suddenly he felt it coming and he could have wept in relief. It was the calm that had always come before the deadliest encounters. Fatalism, some called it, but it wasn't that. He'd seen men become fatalistic and it had proved fatal for them because it had neutered their instinct for self-preservation. His task was to distinguish between what Beria had said and what Beria had told him. The former could be replayed a hundred times before a tribunal and be applauded every time for its loyal sentiments. The latter, he suspected, was treason.

He could go to Stalin and denounce Beria. That thought brought cold to his bones faster than a plunge through an ice-hole in the Moscow River. *Evidence? His story against mine. Witnesses? None. Not that the judicial system bothered much with those things.* Also, experience had taught him that the bearer of bad news usually carries his own death warrant. No, the question was what had he been told?

He'd been told that the Americans don't want a war. That was blindingly obvious, but Beria had added that we didn't want one either. The Yalta story had been about meeting Americans, not about meeting Roosevelt. The ungrateful allies were obviously the East Germans, and intelligence reports were agreed that the workers in the GDR were shit-sick of higher production quotas in their factories to stock the shops in Moscow. *There could be a rising there*, he thought, *if the intellectuals ever stopped talking. Did Beria want that? And, if he did, was he covertly encouraging it with repression and aid – the classic stick-and-carrot approach? Or was he willing to trade them their autonomy to ease the pressure on the Soviet economy and have a more stable ally as a buffer against the West?* He ticked the advantages off on his fingers. The Germans get autonomy, the Americans are mollified and we get a better economy. It was a win-win-win situation. He was more certain on the next point. Beria plans to bring prisoners home from the prisons and gulags. It would give a huge boost to public morale and to Beria's public image. And he wanted him, Nikita Sergeyevich Khrushchev, at his side, if he backed the plan. This was the 'if' he'd been avoiding. None of the proposals he'd been considering were possible and all of them were treasonous if the leader remained in power. *They're planning a coup*, he thought and he had to put his head between his knees until the dizziness passed. *It is already midday*, he thought idly. He always took a nap at midday. Stalin often held all-night meetings at the dacha and a man who fell asleep at Stalin's table might wake up somewhere else or not at all.

'Everything all right?' Alexei asked through the door.

'Yes, everything's fine, Alexei. He said to thank you for the wonderful coffee.'

'Good, I picked it up especially at the GUM this morning. Off to lunch now. *Dasvidanya*. Goodbye.'

Khrushchev heard the steps recede from the bathroom door followed, a short time later, by the sound of the outer door closing. 'A policeman is a policeman, even at home, Nikita,' Molotov had told him one time when they'd been discussing the balance between home and work. 'None of us can switch off,' he'd insisted. It was true, Khrushchev acknowledged. Already, he'd been parsing the brief interaction with Alexei through the bathroom door. He thought the door might have played an important part in the conversation. It had blocked eyes, body language and facial expression – only the words had filtered through. He repeated them aloud, 'I picked it up especially at the GUM this morning.' *You were expecting him, Alexei. You are not mine after all.*

'*Dasvidanya*, Alexei,' he muttered.

ENRICO'S RESTAURANT, TRASTEVERE, ROME

Karl felt a disorienting sense of déjà vu as he followed Julio. The boy led him confidently, unravelling the cat's cradle of alleys. Occasionally, Karl looked over his shoulder, and expected to see Sergeant Paulus shambling along behind him with a toddler in his massive arms, remembering a little boy swept from the streets, like jetsam – the boy Enrico had accepted into his family and called Paolo to honour his rescuer.

'How did you recognise me?' he asked Julio.

'Your glove, Captain,' Julio said shyly. 'I remembered.'

'When did you start to follow me?'

'When you entered Trastevere.'

'You didn't see me on the bridge?'

'No.'

It was someone else then, Karl concluded. Someone who had followed him from the publisher's and lost him in Trastevere. He wondered if he should go back and warn Schwartz, but Julio had already raced ahead to open the restaurant door.

Enrico was spreading a chequered tablecloth in the empty restaurant. Karl had time to admire the practised flick of his wrists and the way the cloth billowed like a sail, before it exhaled and lay perfectly aligned with the four corners. Enrico looked up expectantly. Karl saw his expression change from confusion to a mix of joy and pain. *Am I always to be the harbinger of heartbreak?* he thought. The small man stood before him, stroking his face with shaking fingers. 'Oh, my son,' he whispered brokenly, 'you have come back.' Enrico was weeping and laughing, as he rushed to grasp Karl's face, as if to assure himself that Karl wasn't a mirage.

'I am so happy,' he hiccupped. 'Happy to have survived to see this day.'

He was interrupted by a scream from the kitchen. The double doors burst open and Karl was swamped by Julio's mother and sister. They hugged him fiercely, and stroked his beard and hugged him again. Abruptly, Enrico's wife pulled back and looked at him.

'*Caro*,' she demanded, 'what happened to you?'

A sudden hush fell over the group and Julio backed away from his mother. Karl looked down at the blood that dripped from his knuckles. The vision in his right eye was constricted by a lump on his cheekbone and he guessed that his clothes were a mess.

'I got lost,' he said. 'I miscounted some steps and tripped. Julio recognised me.'

Her face hardened, momentarily. 'How very fortunate that my son should find you,' she said evenly, and shrivelled Julio with a look.

'Wine,' shouted Enrico, oblivious to the interlude in the drama of Karl's homecoming. Everything was confusion again. Mama dashed to the kitchen while Enrico and his daughter pulled Karl to a chair. A basin of water, towels and the clucking ministrations of Enrico's daughter repaired the visitor and removed his jacket.

In the middle of the mayhem, Karl saw a young boy pop his head through the kitchen doors. 'Paolo?' he enquired. Immediately, Enrico brought the boy to the table.

'Kiss your brother, *caro*,' he urged gently.

The boy looked confused.

'Perhaps we could just shake hands, until we get to know each other,' Karl suggested.

Paolo shook hands solemnly. 'You're very hairy,' he said in a small voice.

'Paolo is correct,' Karl said to forestall Enrico. 'I have a friend who says I'm like a bear.'

The tiniest smile flickered across the boy's face. '*Scusi*,' he whispered, solemn again, and went back to his sanctuary between the doors.

'He doesn't say much,' Enrico said apologetically. 'We took him to doctors. They say sometimes a child cannot forget and learns to live – inside.'

'His parents?'

Enrico shook his head. 'They were on the train,' he said simply.

'Paolo has been blessed with a new family,' Karl said, 'and a very hairy brother.'

This lifted the sombre mood. There was more happy confusion as plates and serving dishes crowded the tables they'd clustered together. He was touched to see Mama cut his portions to spare his left hand. As they ate, neighbours trickled through the door. Karl thought they were customers until they approached and shook his hand. They were invited to sit and eat and didn't need persuading. The trickle became a torrent as word filtered through Trastevere that the saviour of Enrico's family – the Wehrmacht captain who had offered his mother's wedding ring to help pay the SS ransom – had returned. As the wine flowed, songs erupted from various tables and there were toasts to Captain Hamner. All around him he saw survivors of the *razzia* sing and dance and bounce little ones on their knees. *Survivors*, he thought, *like me*. But they seemed to have discovered a capacity for joy that had eluded him. Something in his face drew Mama to evict the man sitting beside him and take his place. She leaned close so that they would not be overheard.

'Why did you come back?' she asked.

He looked into her calm eyes and rejected the trite answers that were already assembling in his head. 'Because this is the last place I felt alive,' he said.

She nodded and placed a hand on his arm. 'It is difficult to do this,' she said, gesturing at the dancers, 'when we have such sad memories. But it is no honour to the dead if we do not live.'

He was whirled away by a group of young women before he could answer. As he watched their feet to mimic their steps, he glanced at Mama and saw that she was smiling.

The last of the revellers kissed him and departed.

'*In vino veritas*,' Enrico chuckled. 'In wine there is truth. Come,' he said. He took Karl by the elbow and steered him out of the restaurant and into the family sitting room. 'It is quieter here,' he said, 'and if they knew I had this, they would come back.' He laughed as he brought a bottle from a cupboard. 'This is an old cognac,' he said, 'very old.' He splashed the amber liquid into two tumblers and raised his own. '*L'Chayim*,' he toasted. 'To life.' The drink was as smooth as velvet and Karl felt his body surrender to its balm.

'We came back from Isla Tiberna and carried on,' Enrico began as if continuing a conversation interrupted the day before. 'So many didn't come back,' he said, 'so many, and some of those who did were never the same. We opened the restaurant again, and tried to make life normal for the family. Rome is different now. Many Jews work outside Trastevere. My daughter helps in the restaurant and, next year, she will marry.' He accepted Karl's raised glass with a nod. 'Julio wants to go to Israel. He says he wants to be an Israeli. "Israel," I asked him. "Where is that? And who are those Israelis? Israel is younger than Paolo," I said. "We are Romans. We were Romans before Julius Caesar was born." Why do the young always want to be somewhere else?' he asked. Karl sipped his cognac. 'Enough,' Enrico said, exhaling his bad humour, 'tell me about you, Karl.'

Karl wasn't sure if he could, wasn't sure that he could find the words. Even if he did have the words, would saying them somehow reduce those who had died and his sense of loss? Instinctively, he knew that Enrico had no interest in war stories for their own sake. He was a man who had suffered too much to speak easily of it or to demand this of another man. He was tempted to answer as a historian, to take refuge in chronology and facts.

'I loved a girl,' he began, 'her name was Elsa.'

The words came from the deepest part of him. They seemed to fly from his mouth and soar around the room, exulting in their release. He became oblivious to the act of speaking as he bore witness to the girl lost in the mine, a father lost in the snow, the selflessness of Tomas the miner. All the emotion he had held broke through and made the dead alive for the man who listened. Enrico nodded, smiled and wept – a conductor living the symphony he draws from his orchestra. When it was done, they sat in a sacred silence, cherishing and remembering. Enrico said nothing to break the spell. He offered no questions, platitudes or answers, none of the well-meaning words that well-meaning people say to reduce someone's pain to a size they can cope with. Gently, he took Karl by the arm and led him to sit on the couch. He bent and untied Karl's shoelaces before covering him with a blanket. Finally, he stooped and kissed him gently on the head. It was a father's benediction that was so reminiscent of his own father that Karl's throat tightened. When the door closed, Karl began to weep and wept until his eyes stung and his chest ached; then he slept and dreamed.

BERLIN

The identity papers named him as Otto Plummer – *ergo, I am*, Claus thought philosophically. His mother had always stressed the biblical injunction that: 'He must increase and I must decrease.' It had brought him to consider himself insignificant. Perhaps that was why he found it easy to adapt to new names and identities. He wouldn't miss being Claus Fischer for a while longer – he hadn't been Claus Fischer for a very long time. The next page was headed 'Occupation'. A succinct description of an entire country, he surmised. He was described as a 'commercial traveller'. Convenient, he nodded, approvingly. Commercial travellers were ubiquitous and therefore invisible. Ever since mankind had evolved from hunter-gatherers through subsistence farmers to selling their produce to the next village, commercial travellers, like tinsmiths, shoemakers and other wandering craftsmen, had been valuable sources of information. *Spies by any other name*, he reminded himself. Turning to the page, he saw that he would 'purvey leather goods'. *Well*, he reasoned, *one couldn't be too particular in this line of work*. Particularity attracted attention. He'd read the briefing document and knew just enough about curing, lasts, stitching and insoles to pass himself as a bored commercial traveller rather than excite interest as an expert.

He examined the photograph as critically as he knew the Russians would. He looked like he'd been surprised by the experience. *Why are such photographs so universally unflattering?* he wondered. *Is it possible that every subject has been informed of their terminal illness just before the camera clicks?* He had to admit, it was a reasonable likeness, suitably defeated and world-weary. It had been taken in a small storage room behind a grocer's in Linden Strasse. The place had stunk of paraffin and mothballs and he'd helped the photographer shift hessian bags of potatoes so that he could stand before a whitewashed wall. The photographer was a fussy young man with thick-lens spectacles that made his eyes look huge. He acted as if the task was too mundane for his talents. Perhaps his real job was supplying photographs of the great and the good for *Bild* or some society magazine. If his professionalism had been wounded by the job, the solid wad of dollars that changed hands seemed to apply the perfect salve. Claus had thought the amount was overgenerous but it also covered amnesia. The photographer would forget that he had ever taken such a photograph. It was a lucrative sideline for a forgetful man.

So, he was to be Otto Plummer. He checked his watch. The real Otto Plummer was, even now, on his way to enjoying the hospitality of the agency at a remote farmhouse some thirty kilometres west of Berlin. He would be lying across the back seat of a car, covered in a warm rug and doubtless anticipating the fine food at the safe house and the fat stipend he would receive. Claus had to concede that the Americans tended to be overgenerous to their friends in post-war Germany. Berliners agreed that the English sector had the best administration and the French sector had the best cuisine. 'So where do you want the ambulance to take you?' they quipped. 'If the English food doesn't kill you then their doctors can cure you of anything. The French combination of fine food and optional hygiene meant you made a fat corpse. The Americans? Hell, the

Americans just bought you a whole new body.' Or a whole new identity, as his papers proved. Their General George Marshall had injected enough dollars into Germany to cure the whole country. Rather unimaginatively, they'd called it the Marshall Plan and it was working like a charm. They now held half of Germany and generations of Germans would pay, with interest, to redeem their country from hock. Would the new Germany grow from being a grateful vassal to a steadfast ally? 'The poor will never forgive us our charity,' Saint Vincent de Paul had once remarked.

The brand-new Otto Plummer was a man who thought on such things. He thought on them now as he packed his cardboard suitcase with ladies' shoes and handbags. He smiled grimly as he did so. He was remembering a story that had been told to him by a German colleague. During the occupation of Berlin, the colleague said, the Americans ordered a consignment of condoms for their troops. They specified 'large' on the manifest. When the Russians learned of this, they ordered a consignment and specified 'extra large'. 'Like two teenagers playing mine is bigger than yours,' his colleague had laughed. 'Germany gets fucked either way' was the punchline.

The Russian soldiers at the checkpoint would automatically lighten his samples suitcase. It was *droit de seigneur*, a given, that travellers accepted stoically. He'd insisted the shoe sizes of his samples range from thirteen to eighteen and that the handbags be 'small'. '*Nemo me impune lacessit,*' he'd said, when his handler had queried the sizes. When she'd looked unsurprisingly blank, he'd translated, roughly. 'No one fucks with me and gets away with it.'

Formerly of the SD, the intelligence section of the Reich's security arm, Claus had crossed his Rubicon when the Fratres had tried to take him out of the game on the Pont Sant'Angelo in Rome. Why? Because he'd had something they'd wanted buried as deeply in the Pontine Marshes as they planned to bury him. And then, *mirabile dictu*, wonderful to relate, a woman in a fast car had cruised by and made him an offer. It was straight out of *Roman Holiday*. The fact that she had a gun and that a refusal would have dumped him back on the pavement had never ruined the romance of the story.

The CIA had given him sanctuary at the embassy and, after the tanks had rolled in, he'd become an asset. It meant sitting in functional rooms while clean-cut agency operatives interrogated a motley crew winnowed from the chaff of prisoners of war and refugees. They interrogated, in the usual sense of the word, by asking questions. He had seen men and women beaten bloody by truncheons and hung from meat hooks in Gestapo basements. Most of those 'put to the question' by these gentle inquisitors were only too eager to answer and embellish. A few specific questions tended to cool their ardour, but not always. A Prussian major had patronised the young interrogators to distraction until Fischer had walked up from the back of the room and slapped his face. The Prussian was obviously unused to being slapped, judging by the shocked expression on his reddening face. Likely, he had never been slapped by his Vater or Mutter or by his nanny in the baronial schloss. It worked like a bucket of cold water in the face. The major answered the questions.

After that, his American colleagues had given him a wide berth socially, as if they feared some kind of contamination. The agency had responded differently. From that day, he had got to sit in on the high-level interviews. With the slightest inclination of his head, he indicated who should be added to the payroll, who should be returned behind the wire of the POW camps and those who should be repatriated to the Russian zone. The latter were the ones who stalked his nightmares. Ivan had lost six million people in the war and was rabid for revenge.

Claus snapped the suitcase clasps shut with unnecessary force. *I work for the Americans*, he thought, *but the Fratres and Father Max Steiger are my hobby*. Like all Germans, he took his hobbies seriously. It was time to execute the second part of his preparations. He needed transport and the note had been explicit about where he should go.

The foyer of the hotel was where unwanted furniture went to die. He negotiated the maze of over-stuffed armchairs and a moth-eaten chaise longue to lay his key on the desk. He doffed his hat courteously to the woman who sat knitting in a high-winged chair. 'Don't drop a stitch for me, Frau Blum,' he smiled. Like the statue of Justice, she stared sightlessly at him, her wicked needles dragging the wool according to some random pattern.

The Marshall Plan had yet to arrive at the lane that ran parallel with Herbert Strasse. The cobbles sweated beads of dew that gravitated to the turgid trickle that bisected the lane. On either side, dingy buildings with sightless windows teetered over locked garages. *Third on the left*, he reminded himself. He rapped on a yielding plywood door and waited. After a count of ten, he knocked again. Shuffling footsteps grew in volume and a postern gate opened in the door. A figure stood silhouetted in the dim light from within. 'Plummer,' he said and, as the figure receded, he followed. The lock-up smelled of damp and lubricating oil. A single bulb, hanging from a contorted flex, cast a wan light over the den and its denizen – a bald man whose belly strained a grey vest. He had long, powerful arms that ended in delicate hands. His eyes were an innocent blue and they gazed, unblinking, at the visitor.

'Fahrrad,' he said in a surprisingly soft voice. 'Bicycles.'

As his eyes grew accustomed to the gloom, Claus appreciated the understatement. The lock-up was forested with bicycles. They leaned against each other in drunken ranks on the floor and climbed the walls on wooden pegs. The ceiling was haunted with the shadows of bicycles hanging on hooks. He stood in the pool of light and turned a slow three hundred and sixty degree circle, savouring the straight, curved and flared handlebars, angular and oval frames and the overlapping circles of wheels, rippling into the dark.

The man crooked a finger and he followed obediently. Near the rear of the room, the man halted and pointed. Claus looked and tried to swallow his disappointment. This bicycle was the dowdy girl at the Strauss Ball, the chunky country boy among the Olympians. It was the sort of functional, nondescript bicycle a Bavarian spinster would ride over rutted roads bringing eggs to market. 'This one?' he asked.

'*Ja.*'

The man's belly quivered as he heaved the bicycle upright. He leaned it towards Claus, who placed reluctant hands on the handlebars and saddle. The unexpected weight of the monster almost brought him to the floor. The belly quivered again, with what he suspected was laughter.

ENRICO'S RESTAURANT, TRASTEVERE, ROME

'It's arranged,' Enrico said, hanging up the telephone. 'Nice place, nice people. Julio will take you there, can't have you tripping again. Tell your mother Karl is leaving,' he said to Paolo and the boy rushed away to the kitchen. 'Karl,' Enrico said quietly, 'what you said this morning about your book. Are you sure?'

'Yes.'

'You understand that this,' he said, tapping his forefinger on the table, 'is Italy. And that' – he jerked his thumb towards the Tiber – 'is the Vatican State?'

'I understand.'

'Yes, but do you understand that what they say there is still law here?'

'I wouldn't want to get the Jews into any kind of trouble, Enrico.'

Enrico laughed so hard he had to drink a glass of water.

'*Mi dispiace*,' he gasped. 'I'm sorry. You reminded me of something. Sometimes we laugh because the only alternative is to weep, and we have done our share of weeping. A Polish Jew came here sometime after the war. He'd been in Treblinka or Sobibor, I can't remember which. He had so many jokes about the camps, we didn't know whether to laugh or cry. He said that two of his friends had been picked up by the Nazis in Warsaw. In the barracks, they had beaten them with lead pipes. When the beating had stopped, one of the Jews had said, "You Nazis are the scum of the earth", and his friend had said, "Isaac, don't make trouble."' Enrico laughed again and wiped his eyes on his apron. 'We are Italians, *caro*,' he continued, 'and the pope let them put over one thousand of us in the trucks and take us to the camps. Only four returned. Nobody wants to hear that story. They say it could never happen again – but don't talk about that. Nobody talked the last time, Karl. Not the pope, not the Romans. And now you come back to tell our story and you ask if it will cause us trouble. What more trouble can they cause us? The place Julio brings you to, there is a man there called Shimon. Tell him Enrico sent you.'

Karl and Julio turned into a narrow alley and three figures emerged from the shadows. Karl clenched his fists and looked at Julio.

'They wish to apologise, Captain,' Julio said quickly. Karl thought the three looked even more battered than when he'd last seen them. He suspected some of the fresh bruises had been inflicted by the local community. The tall one shuffled forwards.

'Sorry, Captain,' he muttered, 'we didn't know it was you.'

'Why did it have to be anyone?' Karl said. 'I'm an Austrian. Sometimes in the streets of Vienna, people were beaten because they were Jews. It made me ashamed to be Austrian. If you do to others what the Nazis did to you, how are you different?'

'Sorry, Captain,' they chorused.

Karl glared at the three miscreants. 'I'm sorry I knocked you down,' he said to the tall one and held out his hand.

'You have a terrific punch,' the boy said, pumping Karl's hand enthusiastically.

'For a cripple—' the fat one added and froze. 'Sorry, Captain.'

He shook hands with the others and they stood aside to let him pass.

'Why, Julio?' he asked after they'd walked for a while in silence.

'Because I am angry,' Julio said. 'Do you know how that feels?'

'Yes, I do.'

'But do you know what it's like to be afraid, Captain? They beat my father and I was so afraid I couldn't do anything to stop them.'

'You were young, Julio, and you were right to be afraid. My sergeant in Russia warned me about the Waffen-SS. He said they were animals and that some animals should only be seen through bars. Only a fool isn't afraid, Julio. You were afraid the night we brought your family to Tiber Island. Everyone in Trastevere thinks I'm a hero but I couldn't have done anything that day without you.'

Julio was fighting the tears he thought would shame him.

'Come and sit,' Karl said and they hunkered down on a doorstep.

'They come to our restaurant,' Julio said haltingly. 'They even come from across the river and they joke with my father as if … as if nothing had happened. How can people do that, Captain?'

'I don't know, Julio,' Karl said honestly. 'The world seems to be divided between those who don't want to remember and those who can't forget.' He looked at the boy's slumped shoulders. 'Your father tells me you want to go to Israel,' he said.

'Yes,' Julio said fervently. 'The Israelis fought for that country, Captain, and they will never be taken away from it. That's what I want – to live in my own country as a Jew, and not be afraid. I want to be a soldier.'

Karl nodded thoughtfully.

'When the war in Russia was lost,' he began, 'my father, Rudi, and our friend, Tomas the miner, saved me from the snow. Most of me anyway,' he smiled, holding up his gloved left hand. 'There were Cossacks hunting us on horseback. My father took the rifle and hid in a snow-hole to slow them down so that we could escape. He died there. Tomas carried me on his back to an airfield and put me on the last plane. The military police killed him on the runway. A carpenter and a miner saved a boy who wanted to be a historian – someone who would tell their story. An officer wanted to put me off the plane but General von Kluge said that we would need teachers more than generals after the war. I understand that everyone in Israel is expected to be a soldier if the country is attacked?'

'Yes.'

'Then Israel will always have soldiers to defend it, Julio, but it will need historians and teachers and poets and dancers to tell its story. Will you consider going back to school? I could help you, if you like. Will you think about it?'

'Yes, Captain.'

'Call me Karl. My captain days are long gone. Come on,' he added, dragging the boy to his feet, 'let's find this palazzo your father promised me.'

It wasn't a palazzo. The house was three storeys high and seemed to peer across the Tiber over the shoulder of the synagogue. Like an Old Master left out in the sun, sections of paint had flaked from the walls and fluttered in the light breeze from the river. Huge windows, framed between solid wooden shutters, squinted over metal balconies on every floor.

'Signora Visconti.' The woman from the ground-floor apartment introduced herself. 'Clara,' she added, turning to reveal a young girl who clung to her skirts. '*Un momento.*' She began a long rummage in her apron for the key. Signora Visconti eventually produced a huge key that could have opened the door of Saint Peter's. 'Up,' she said triumphantly.

Karl looked down from the second landing and saw Clara

spinning around to follow their progress. He waved and she raised a tentative hand before retreating into the shadows. He was immediately impressed by the height of the spacious room and by the rough wooden beams that furrowed the ceiling. A short set of stairs rose up to an open loft-bedroom. *It will be like sleeping in my attic bedroom in Hallstatt,* he thought. Despairing of the big man's distracted air, Signora Visconti subjected Julio to the tour of the presses and fittings. Karl stood in the centre of the room, turning a slow circle, picturing where he would erect bookcases and where to place the study table to catch the light. The curtain on the window lifted and seemed to wave a welcome. He stepped through to the balcony and let his gaze flow with the river to the tip of Tiber Island. He was unaware of Signora Visconti's presence at his shoulder until she spoke.

'*Bellissimo,*' she said and the beautiful word softened the lines around her eyes.

'*Si, signora,*' he agreed softly. '*Bellissimo, grazie.*'

FRAU BLUM'S HOTEL, WEST BERLIN

The Alsatian tensed when he wheeled the bicycle into the garden behind the hotel. He stood quite still. 'Easy, Goebbels,' he said soothingly. Slowly he moved his hand to the pocket of his overcoat. Goebbels' ears pricked as his ruff flattened. 'Is there a treat for the good dog?' Claus crooned, and was relieved to see the long tongue loll between yellow teeth. 'Yes, I think there is something,' he said, just to see the tail semaphore anticipation. He bent, carefully, and extended his hand, palm upwards. Goebbels lipped the broken biscuit from his hand and turned away to crunch it. The garden shed seemed held together with cobwebs. He brushed at them absently as he leaned the bicycle against a dresser that had been deemed too hideous even for the foyer. 'Carry on, Goebbels,' he said as he pulled the door shut.

'Garden' was a misnomer, he concluded, as he made his way

through a rubble-patch pocked with plants. Onions surrounded a chunk of reinforced concrete in the centre and lettuces flourished within the rectangle of a discarded doorframe. A cluster of cabbages mourned around a fresh hole in the soil and his stomach roiled in anticipation of dinner. There were nettles everywhere. Berliners would never forget the plant that had sustained them in soups and stews while old men and children had resisted the Russians in the final days.

Frau Blum didn't miss a beat with her needles as he presented himself at the desk. Without raising her eyes, she inclined her head to where the keys hung on a rack. Each key was attached to a square of wood that had the room number burned into it, probably with a white-hot poker from the stove, he thought. His key peeked coyly from behind its wooden barricade – he'd placed it the other way around when he'd left. '*Gute nacht*,' he bade her as he moved towards the stairs. He heard her sniff, over the clacking of her needles. Frau Blum had a whole repertoire of sniffs. Did this one betoken disapproval? Was he being paranoid? Of course he was, he decided, it was a necessary part of his armature, like the Luger pistol that bulked in his pocket.

The stairs rose steeply from the foyer to the first landing. Steps three and seven, he knew, were arthritic and groaned when they were stepped on. Framed pictures of Churchill, Eisenhower and de Gaulle bracketed the wall as he climbed. He tilted Churchill with a finger and was unsurprised to find a much-faded patch of wallpaper. '*Sic transit gloria mundi*' – 'Thus passes the glory of the world,' he muttered. He was still mulling over whether Mister Churchill had replaced Rommel or Goering when he arrived at the first landing. The dusty window ledge was speckled with bluebottle corpses. He gave his attention to the top riser. The bluebottle cadaver he'd placed there earlier was squashed into the weave of the stair carpet. He was thinking that the blue, iridescent specks improved the tatty thing as he drew the Luger. At the door, he crouched to look through the keyhole. The tiny ball of paper he'd inserted after locking the door was gone. *Most unlike her*, he thought, as he groped for the light-switch and plunged the landing into darkness.

A slow hand lap commenced from inside. 'You haven't lost your touch,' she called. She was sitting on the foot of the bed and swiped a lighter over the bedspread as he entered. The cigarette tip glowed and she snapped her wrist to click the lighter closed. *The years have not been kind to her*, he thought. She still had the same spare, boyish frame and unsettling eyes, but those eyes had narrowed with time and drawn the smooth skin at her temples into deltas. A tightly bound ponytail added its own pressure so that her cheekbones were more prominent than he'd remembered.

'You're no oil painting yourself,' she said coolly.

He smiled and tried to look abashed. 'You haven't lost your touch either, Medusa,' he said.

She waved the cigarette to deflect the compliment and to signal the end of the small talk.

'You're crossing tomorrow at eight,' she said, as she eased from the bed and went to stand by the window. 'You got everything you need?'

'Yes,' he said.

'The gun doesn't go,' she said and he took the Luger from his pocket and tossed it on the bed. 'You're clear on the objective?'

'Yes,' he said and recited his instructions for her approval. She nodded. 'There is one other thing,' she said slowly. There always was with Medusa. He folded his hands in his lap and sat upright in the chair. 'When was the last time you saw Stradivarius?' she asked.

'About two months ago,' he said, struggling to keep his voice toneless.

'And?'

'And what?' he asked. 'You know what Stradivarius is like.'

'Paranoid.'

It wasn't a question. 'No more paranoid than the rest of us,' he said quietly. He knew that she was staring at him and kept his eyes on his hands. Despite her code name, he didn't believe she could turn a man to stone with a look, but with Medusa it was better not to take chances.

'Word is he's got even flakier,' she said. 'Time he was retired.'

He clasped his hands together to prevent them trembling.

'Is he a friend of yours?'

'We – we don't make friends, in our profession,' he said, and prayed she'd believe him.

KARL'S APARTMENT, TRASTEVERE, ROME

He shifted the table to benefit from the window. He knew that some writers liked to face a blank wall or eliminate all other light except that of the table lamp. He preferred natural light and the lace curtains diluted the sunlight into a soft glow. When he looked up at the window, he saw the faint outline and the muted colours of buildings and trees. Like an altar server preparing the utensils for mass, he arranged the slab of white paper and an array of pencils. The previous evening, he'd taken his old research notes from his rucksack and flicked through them. Unforgiving daylight exposed how paltry they were. Something Enrico had said niggled at his brain – something that had been tossed off, almost as an afterthought. As soon as he began to sketch chapter headings, he remembered.

He knocked once at the door on the top landing and waited.

'Yes?'

'My name is Karl Hamner,' he said, leaning closer to the door so his voice wouldn't echo in the stairwell.

'And?'

'Enrico, the restaurant owner said you would help me.'

'Turn and place both hands on the banister,' the voice instructed.

Sheepishly, Karl retreated to the banister. He heard a bolt slide and a key turn.

'Turn slowly and keep your hands in view.'

A man stood silhouetted in the doorway. 'Where and when did Karl Hamner get his glove?' he asked.

'I … I got the glove in Russia, during the retreat from Moscow. It belonged to my father, Rudi. He gave it to me because I had frostbite.'

'Enter.'

He was blinded by sunlight that streamed from the uncurtained window.

'Sit and place your hands on the table.'

A tall, thin man of indeterminate age looked down at him. The man was completely bald and deep fissures furrowed his forehead and carved a triangle from beneath his nose to the corners of his mouth. He wore rumpled black trousers and a white shirt hung from the bony bar of his shoulders. The Luger pistol appeared enormous in his steady hand.

'Enrico's younger son is named Paolo,' he said. 'Who is he named for?'

'For Sergeant Paulus of the Wehrmacht troop that I led into Trastevere during the *razzia*. Is this necessary?'

The man pocketed the gun and slipped into the chair across the table. 'Have you ever been hunted, Herr Hamner?' he asked softly.

'Yes,' Karl answered, 'by Cossacks and … others.'

'Others?'

'I'd prefer not to say.'

'*Your* preferences are not the issue, Herr Hamner. If others are hunting you, you could have brought them to me.'

After a pause, Karl nodded. 'I was hunted by the Fratres,' he said.

'I was hunted by the Waffen-SS,' the man replied. 'I am still hunted because I chose to become a Nazi-hunter. I apologise for the … precautions but the experience of being hunted marks a man, doesn't it? My name is Shimon.' He extended his hand. 'I should like to call you Karl.'

'Please do.'

'I belong to a network of Jews set up after the war. We are committed to bringing certain people to justice.'

He stood and marched to the far end of the room. The wall seemed to be plastered with photographs of men in uniform.

'I thought that's what happened at Nuremburg.'

Shimon shook his head dismissively. 'Nuremburg was a show trial,' he said. 'The world needed the reassurance of seeing Goering and some of the others hang. Then it could go about the business of forgetting. But there were thousands of others, Karl,' he said, trailing his finger over the faces on the photographs.

'And when will it be enough, Shimon?' Karl asked. 'Will you stop when you get the man who baked the bread for the Belsen garrison or the woman who pretended it wasn't there?'

'Are you sure you're not a rabbi?' Shimon said with the faintest hint of a smile. 'I don't know,' he confessed. 'I don't think I'll have to answer that question in my lifetime. There are enough war criminals out there to keep me busy for a very long time.' He ambled back to his chair. 'I said I belonged to a network. Nets have holes, Karl,' he smiled ruefully. 'Even some of the big fish escaped – Eichmann and Mengele to South America and others scattered across northern Africa. But,' he shrugged, 'we hunt them and they know they're hunted. What can I do for you, Karl?'

Karl told him the title of his book and Shimon nodded. 'I think we can do business,' he said, briskly. 'We can give you access to our archives and maybe to survivors of the *razzia*.'

Karl breathed a sigh of relief.

'And,' Shimon continued, 'you will give us any information you discover concerning the Vatican ratlines. Do we have a deal?'

'Yes.'

'Don't be too eager,' Shimon said, waving a cautionary finger. 'You will place yourself outside the protection of the Vatican and in the gunsights of desperate men.' He walked to the window and waited.

'We have a deal,' Karl said.

CARACALLA, THE ROMAN BATHS

Sergei Radović, the Soviet ambassador to Italy, was in heaven. He was seated at a table near the stage in the ancient amphitheatre of Caracalla and the 'Grand March' from *Aida* was about to begin. Sitting opposite him was Signor Agnelli, the Italian Minister for Foreign Affairs, who raised his glass in a silent toast. The Soviet ambassador acknowledged the toast and reflected on his good fortune. How he loved all things Italian – the wine, the food, the women. He stole a quick glance at his wife Natasha who was sitting beside Signor Agnelli with a dazed smile on her face. *Bloody peasant wouldn't know Verdi from a cow's tit*, he thought sourly, probably using that vodka bottle in her bag to anaesthetise her against culture. His secretary, Yuri, sat on the other side of the minister, tapping the table with a dessert fork, keeping time as the orchestra began to build the musical bridge over which the Grand Procession would pass. There would be elephants, camels, chariots and leashed lions and all the fantastic plumery of an exotic Eastern court – but he was distracted by her fumblings in her bag. Radović had survived the war, thanks largely to his uncle, a general, who had accepted that the best contribution his nephew could make to the war effort was as a junior aide to Molotov – and the old man had taken a shine to him and pushed him up the ladder. After the war, Molotov had shielded him from the purges that had decimated all government departments. The culling of the elite had created a vacuum filled with the faithful and mediocre. Sergei Radović accepted that he was both. Damn, she was at the bag again. He'd wanted to leave her in Moscow with all the other drunken wives, but she wouldn't have it. She'd insisted it was her patriotic duty to accompany her husband. *If she'd been more attentive to her duties*, he thought, *he might not have the expense of keeping a mistress in a fancy apartment on the Esquiline Hill.* Agnelli had been sympathetic. He was a prince among men and understood such things. He wanted to walk over there and kiss him on the lips in the proper Russian fashion, but he was on his third bottle of Chianti and, for pony-piss, it packed a punch. He knew his eyes were glazed and his face was flushed, but he was alive – alive and living in Rome and the orchestra was giving it everything. It reminded him of Tchaikovsky's '1812' and he began to weep. It reminded him of Pushkin, Tolstoy and Dostoevsky and he thought his heart would burst with emotion.

'Ambassador, ambassador.'

Some fucker is whispering, he thought aghast. Whispering as the walls of the ancient baths trembled to the sound of massed voices. He waved his right arm to dispel the intrusive whisper and the brass section responded with a fanfare that turned his bones to water.

'Ambassador.'

There was a face before him. Was it Anatoly? Yevgeni? Fyodor, that was the one. Fyodor the cultural attaché. Fyodor the spy.

'Whatchawant, spy?' he slurred, his left arm bringing in the cymbals. Fyodor leaned closer and mimicked a phone held to his ear. *Go and make your call*, he thought, rising on his toes to nod the entry of the violins. Fyodor leaned even closer and bellowed, 'Beria.'

His timing was immaculate. The single word arrived in the brief pause between 'da da dadadada-dum and da dadadadada'. He saw Agnelli's eyes flicker from merry to wary. Yuri now held the dessert fork frozen upright, like the miniature trident of a hero who has come face to face with Leviathan. Natasha was leering at him, enjoying his terror.

Terror was what he felt. At the name Beria, the blood had rushed to his head and out-pounded the percussion. Then it had drained away to his feet so that he felt a hollow man balanced on elephantine legs. 'Beria,' he mouthed, and an elephant shat on the stage. He wanted to laugh but he was afraid he might become hysterical and shit himself. Fyodor beckoned and walked away. Sergei Radović bowed his apologies to Signor Agnelli, the prince among men, and followed. Outside, the cool air tried to rob him of his senses but he made it to the car, albeit by a circuitous route. Finally, he gained the back seat by sitting ass backwards and rolling in.

'Call back in twenty minutes,' Fyodor said cheerfully from behind the wheel.

A small and hysterical voice was whimpering, 'Beria, Beria, we're all fucked.' He bit on his lower lip when he realised the voice was his.

At the embassy, Fyodor dragged him out of the car and helped him to the secure room in the basement. Adrenalin seemed to pump Chianti through his pores and he tried to stay ahead of his own stink. The phone brooded on a plain, metal table in the unfurnished room. 'Why don't you ring?' he demanded of the black, Bakelite monster. 'Ring, you dumb fucker, and get it over with.'

It rang.

'Sergei Radović,' a voice demanded.

'Good evening, Comrade Beria,' the ambassador replied in a steady voice. Dialogue was not something Beria could be accused of. For the next thirty seconds, Radović felt like a man swatting squadrons of mosquitoes in a swamp.

'Yes, Comrade. I understand. I can meet him— Tomorrow? Yes, Comrade, certainly Comrade. Ostpolitik? Of course I understand. I was just— Yes, Comrade, I am listening. Really! I'm sorry, Comrade, it's just— Yes, I am listening. Could you repeat that, Comrade? It's just the Italian phones— Yes, that's what I thought you said. He's to get— No, you are correct, there is no need to rep— Fyodor? Believe me, Comrade, I am more than capa— Immediately? Yes, Comrade.'

The phone rattled traitorously as he set it on the table and he made shushing gestures at the instrument of his torture. He backed away on tiptoes until his shoulder jarred against the door. 'He wants to speak with you, Fyodor,' he whispered.

The young man walked by him and picked up the phone. 'Fyodor,' he said. Sergei Radović closed the door and leaned his forehead against it. He had been tongue-lashed by the Butcher of the Lubyanka, missed the 'Grand March' from *Aida* and he was stone-cold sober.

He stood in the shower and let the cold water sluice him clean. This was another thing he loved about Rome, taking a cold shower without bits of his body falling off and rolling around the tiles. *How did I ever live in Moscow?* he wondered guiltily, as he pampered his body with soft, fluffy towels. He dressed in an open-neck white shirt and black pants, the formal attire of the Soviet functionary in a capitalist state. At least, he consoled himself, he'd had the pants made by a Roman tailor. Why should the ambassador of the Union of the Soviet Socialist Republics dress like some baggy-arsed *kulak*.

The telephone was picked up on the third ring.

'*Prego.*'

It was probably one of those flunky monsignori who seemed to swarm around churchmen like flies around—

'Tomorrow afternoon, in the usual place,' he repeated. '*Grazie. Ciao*, Monsignor.'

He hung up, vaguely annoyed at the prospect of having to ask Fyodor where 'the usual place' was.

FŐ UTCA PRISON, BUDAPEST

Stefan Nagy knew there was something. The spy-hole cover had scratched against its mounting three times since dawn. The square of sunlight from the high, barred window hadn't yet climbed the table leg and somebody had already checked on him three times. The tiny sound nibbled at what remained of his curiosity. He stood with his back to the wall with the window and examined his cell. The mattress slumbered in the shadows at the base of the wall to his right. A thin blanket made a neat rectangular shape in the middle of the mattress. A pillow, not much thicker, rested on top. The metal table crouched between him and the door. He had learned to place it between him and the door as he had learned to put his back to the window wall so that the table and sunlight could be his allies when they came. There was no stool. In prison, anything that could be picked up constituted a weapon. The slop bucket crouched in the angle of the wall to his left. It didn't have a handle; for the same reason as there wasn't a stool. In the early years, waiting had been their weapon. They would shuffle outside the door or bang on the door with a truncheon and wait. His imagination and the anticipation of a beating would do the rest. It was always a relief when they finally came. That had stopped a long time ago. He wondered if it was because he never resisted. He stood over six feet tall and had worked on the farm before the seminary. Perhaps it was poor entertainment to beat someone as unresponsive as a cow carcass. Or maybe, just maybe, it had been his silence. He'd never made a single sound to satisfy them. Whatever the reason, the beatings had stopped.

Rituals gave him the illusion of living. He followed the seminary practice of rising with the light, folding his bedclothes and washing himself, head to foot, in a basin of cold water. The basin was brought by a guard who stood behind and slapped a truncheon into his palm, measuring out the time it took him to wash. He would then go to the far side of the cell, rest his palms against the wall and splay his feet, while the guard removed the basin. For a long time now, the guard had been an elderly man who puffed under the weight of water and leaned his hip against the table until the prisoner's ablutions were complete. He was the only human being he had seen for— He couldn't remember. No, he hadn't lost his memory. He still had vivid memories of some sequences in his life before prison. Nothing about prison life was worth remembering, except the little lessons on staying alive. Even those memories had faded since the guards had tired of trying to kill him. There was one sequence of memory he played and replayed every day, long after the other memories had circled and slowed like the records on his grandmother's phonograph. He remembered how they'd tire of their endless round and the singing grew strange.

It was 1944. He'd been stacking plates on the sink of the seminary kitchen. Seminarians were required to tidy the refectory after meals. The dean said it would be a good preparation for priestly life. He wondered how that was possible when housekeepers ensured most priests never saw the inside of a kitchen. He liked the kitchen. He liked the homely smells of cooking, the humid atmosphere and the casual conversations of the staff. Most of the lay people there had worked in the seminary for years and treated the seminarians with affection or rough good humour. Their banter was the only access the young men might have to the world beyond the walls.

The talk that day was of the war and rumours flew from mouth to ear. 'The Americans are in the war,' raised a muted cheer. 'The Russians will get here first,' was unwelcome and pots were stirred more vigorously.

He was at the door on his way back to the refectory when someone said, 'They're taking the Jews.' Stefan almost tripped on the hem of his black soutane and only saved himself by leaning against the double doors. Outside, in the small passageway between the kitchen and refectory, he'd gulped cool air, replaying that sentence in his head, oblivious to the students who detoured round him.

'What?' Laszlo asked, puffing by with a soup tureen.

'Later.'

Later, he nudged Laszlo away from the others under the shadow of a linden tree.

'I heard they're taking the Jews,' he blurted.

'I know,' Laszlo said.

He'd been unsurprised. Laszlo's father had some kind of important position in the government. He was a little surprised that Laszlo hadn't told him. Something of that must have shown on his face and Laszlo said hurriedly, 'The bishop knows, Stefan. The authorities informed him.'

'And?'

'Stefan, for God's sake,' Laszlo whispered. 'Stop playing the innocent farmer. You know how things are.' He'd mumbled something about an essay and left.

But Stefan didn't know 'how things are'.

There was a free period after lunch the following day. Despite his misgivings, he strode through the gates. It was important to look like someone on an errand. The man who lived at the gate lodge was known to snitch. Outside the gates, he was beset with second thoughts. *What if I'm caught? What if some priest sees me and reports me to the dean?* It wasn't unheard of for a deacon to be expelled, and being in the penultimate year before full priesthood was no protection. He was already sweating under his soutane when he crossed the Danube into Dohány Street, bound for the synagogue to see for himself. It was the same streak of stubbornness that had caused him to run foul of his tutors. 'Why?' he would ask and they replied, 'Saint Thomas has said it.' Or, more recently, 'Rome says so.' He knew it wasn't an answer, but a barrier against questions.

The synagogue reared up over Dohány Street, as exotic as an orchid among daisies. Already he could see the twin onion domes towering over canted roofs. The Wehrmacht soldiers at the first roadblock after the bridge had been almost deferential. They'd looked at his soutane and called him 'Father'.

'They'd be slow to stop a priest.' The kitchen sages had been unanimous on that point. According to Laszlo, the Church had made an uneasy accommodation with the occupiers. Stefan didn't think a simple soldier would risk a confrontation. He thought they looked uneasy and preoccupied and wondered if the kitchen experts had been right about the Russians. As he drew nearer the synagogue, he noticed something he'd been blind to before. The synagogue was built of coloured bricks and three colours were present throughout the massive building. They reflected the colours of the Hungarian flag. *Why did I never notice that?* he wondered. He'd never really visited the synagogue – it was always just there, in the distance, something constantly at the edge of his vision. *Like the Jews*. He had a vague knowledge of how they'd come to Hungary and risen, from one generation to the next, to becoming part of Budapest life. Even as a boy coming to market with his father, he'd never remarked on the men in black hats and the women with headscarves draped over their wigs who hurried to worship on their Sabbath. To most Hungarians, they had become unremarkable and invisible. *Not to the Nazis*, he thought, grimly, as he approached the final barrier. It was not manned by the Wehrmacht but by the Waffen-SS. He'd heard enough about them to make him cautious.

'Are you lost, Father?'

The soldier who addressed him had silver lightning bolts stitched into his collar.

'I heard the Jews are being taken.'

The soldier had a stubble of blond hair and light-blue eyes. The eyes narrowed at his statement and then relaxed into bemusement.

'Do you see any Jews being taken?' he asked, waving a hand at the empty pavement.

'No.'

'Then I bid you good morning, Father,' he said pleasantly. 'Heil Hitler,' he added and touched his fingertips to his cap.

'I should like to ask more questions.'

He couldn't help himself. He'd always needed to know. His spiritual director had warned him against this stubborn trait. 'It will lead you to the sin of pride, Stefan,' the good man had sighed. Typically, his father had been more direct. 'You'll get your fucking jaw broken.'

The soldier's eyes had narrowed and he'd taken a step closer. 'I'm sure you have many calls on your time, Father,' he'd said tightly, 'why don't you—'

'What is happening to the Jews?' he'd insisted.

The soldier hadn't broken his jaw, he'd done something worse, much worse.

'Very well, Father,' he'd said softly, 'I will tell you. Some of them, the able-bodied, we will transport to Germany. They will serve the Reich in the munitions factories.'

'And the others?'

'The others we will contain in the synagogue.'

'You mean imprison.'

'Precisely.'

'But – they are Hungarians.'

The soldier shook his head slowly. 'No, Father,' he said, 'they are not. They are *Untermenschen*. Do you understand that word?'

Stefan had nodded, ashamed that he did.

'Do you see the Hungarian government standing behind you to protest at this? Do you hear your bishop badgering me with questions? No? Of course not, he has protested through the usual channels. It is what's expected of a bishop – for humanitarian reasons. But we are at war and everyone, government, bishops, even priests, accepts the realities.' He turned to walk away and then spun on his heel. 'I believe Bishop Mindszenty is to celebrate a high mass on Sunday to mark the occasion,' he said. 'I'm sure you wouldn't want to miss that.'

Stefan walked back through the checkpoint and across the Danube in a daze. Laszlo had taken one look at his face and bundled him into a grotto off the cloister.

'Where were you?' he hissed.

'I went to the synagogue.'

'You wha— What is wrong with you? You know—'

'The Nazis say the bishop is to celebrate a high mass in thanksgiving for the deportation and imprisonment of the Jews.'

'Stefan, listen to me. We lost the war.'

Laszlo pronounced every word very slowly and distinctly.

'Yes, but the Church—'

'The Church,' Laszlo interrupted, 'has to – to compromise. The Germans are willing to allow the Church to proceed as before, but there must be an understanding. You can be so naïve, Stefan.'

'What about the Jews, Laszlo?'

'What about them? Do you know any Jews? Have you got friends who are Jews?'

'No – but they are Hungarians.'

'The Jews come and go all over Europe,' Laszlo said testily. 'They stick together. They want to be separate.'

'The Nazis are taking them to work in munitions factories. The rest will be imprisoned in the synagogue.'

'Who told you that?'

'A Waffen-SS soldier.'

'You spoke to a— Stefan, listen carefully.'

Laszlo looked around the little grotto very carefully, so carefully that Stefan almost laughed. Then he remembered the soldier's smile and stopped.

'If word gets back to Bishop Min—'

'Why are we celebrating a high mass, Laszlo?'

Some fierceness must have crept into his voice because Laszlo stepped back.

'Tell me why we are celebrating,' Stefan insisted.

'Because it's not us,' Laszlo said and walked away.

He thought about little else in the days ahead, worrying at it 'like a dog with a bone', as his father had often said. He thought of confiding in Father Bruno, the Dean of the Seminary, but Father Bruno wasn't a friend, like Laszlo – like Laszlo had been.

In the end, it was Father Bruno who'd spoken to him. 'You've been rather distracted, Stefan,' he'd admonished on Friday evening after Compline.

'I'm sorry, Father.'

'Well, these are distracting times,' Father Bruno continued. 'I have some news for you. The seminary has been asked to assist at Sunday's high mass, actually, the deacons will do the scripture readings. You know I never play favourites, so I decided to draw lots. You are to do the second reading.'

'Which scripture passage is it, Father?'

'It's the one that begins "If I have all the eloquence of men or of angels and speak without love, I am simply a gong booming or a cymbal clashing." Do you know it?'

'Yes, Father. I know it.'

'See that you do by Sunday, Stefan. May the Lord be on your heart and lips,' he added piously.

The Roman Catholic Cathedral, Budapest

The three deacons, surrounded by monsignori and other clergy, had vested at the long bench in the cathedral sacristy. Close to the hour, they were bustled away to make room for the bishop. Bishop Mindszenty nodded distantly at the assembled clergy and stood while a flurry of assistants dressed him in golden robes. Mitred, and with the crozier grasped in his right hand, he bowed to the cross and they processed up the centre aisle. The organ cued the choir and the triumphant hymn – 'Ecce Sacerdos Magnus', 'Behold a Great Priest' – filled the cathedral. He'd moved in step with the others.

Laszlo had been chosen to do the first reading. They hadn't spoken in the sacristy. At the conclusion of the first reading, Laszlo stepped back from the lectern and joined Stefan in the centre. They bowed before the altar and Laszlo retired to his seat.

Stefan looked up from the lectern and saw the upturned, expectant faces of the congregation. Raising his eyes, he saw the choir, silhouetted against the great rose window. Taking a deep breath, he anchored his shaking hands on either side of the lectern.

'We are celebrating a high mass because the Nazis are taking the

Jews,' he said. "Who will sing a high mass when they come to take us?'

His face felt like it was melting into sweat and his back made a sucking sound when he pulled away from the wall. He wiped his eyes dry and smiled ruefully. There was a fuss. He was dragged away from the lectern and frog-marched into the sacristy, but Bishop Mindszenty remained stoic and unmoving throughout. There had been informers at the mass, policemen in ill-fitting Sunday suits.

They came for Stefan the following morning. Forewarned, the dean had instructed him to pack a bag because the police would be coming for him. He'd also provided a set of layman's clothes that looked and smelled like they'd been borrowed from the gardener. It might be a source of scandal to the faithful to witness a seminarian being arrested.

Nobody had come since – not his father, his superiors or Laszlo. Not even when the Nazis were defeated and a democratic government installed. The succeeding communist government let him languish. He had committed the cardinal sin – he had spoken out, he might do so again.

BORDER CROSSING, BERLIN

There was a café at the corner of the platz where locals came to watch the checkpoint and place bets on the outcomes. There were only three gambling options – through, back or the hut. The first two were even money. The hut was always long odds. It was common for cheering to erupt when someone was frogmarched to the hut. It reminded Claus of the stories about the ladies who sat knitting around the guillotine during the French Revolution and who dropped a stitch every time a head fell in the basket.

He'd leaned the bicycle against an outside table and sat sipping chicory-flavoured coffee while the queue lengthened. He knew from experience that it didn't do to be up at the front. The Ivans were always eager at the start of their shift, eager to impress the

brass in the hut. Best to wait until the tedium had dulled their edge
a little. Eventually, he drained his cup and wheeled his bicycle to
join the queue behind a woman who was chain-smoking nervously.
As the line inched forward, she lit each new cigarette on the butt
of the last. Dutifully, he trod on the trail of smoking butts. The
Ivans collected them later when the officers had wandered off. It
was, he admitted, a pathetic act of defiance but it made him feel a
little better. It was time to become Otto Plummer. *You are looking
back at fifty*, Claus recited in his head. *The Wehrmacht refused you
because of angina. Your boss isn't happy with your performance –
that's why he sends you across. You wouldn't be a loss if anything
happened and he's got a nephew making a nuisance of himself on the
factory floor. Also, Frau Plummer no longer bothers to mutter when
you hand over your wages. 'At least, if you'd been shot I'd have a
pension.'* The mantra slowed him to a shuffle and caused his face
and body to sag. It drew his attention inside so that his eyes became
glassy and unfocused.

'Papers!'

The soldier was bored. The snap had already leached from his
tone and he looked away from the man dressed even more shabbily
than himself. Don't be too eager, Claus cautioned himself. He
leaned the bicycle against his hip and fumbled in his pockets. At
the precise moment when impatience began to tug the soldier's
head in his direction, he produced the grubby papers. They were
snatched and studied. He knew most of them couldn't read. They'd
been trained to count the pages, recognise the stamps and match
the photograph. The chain-smoker was already becoming shrill as
a second soldier queried her papers and the people at the top of the
queue eddied away from her.

'Bag!'

Awkwardly, he swivelled to support the bicycle on his other
hip and untied the length of rope that bound the samples case.
Rope was better than a belt. It hinted at hardship and wasn't worth
stealing. Impatiently, the soldier tugged it free and dropped it on

the road. Claus turned to face forwards. Courtesy among thieves, he thought, and almost smiled. The soldier walked by him carrying two pairs of shoes and a handbag. He disappeared inside the hut and returned empty-handed.

'I demand to see an officer,' the chain-smoker shouted and he saw his own interrogator pause and look her way, the possibility of entertainment already lightening his face.

'We're all officers in the Soviet army,' someone shouted from the hut and the soldiers culling the queue laughed.

'But my husband is expecting me,' the woman wailed as she was turned back.

'We're doing him a favour,' his soldier shouted and he was already basking in the laughter when he handed over the papers and waved Claus through. Slowly – slowly, he remembered. They watch from the hut for those who drop the mask, like poor actors dropping out of character before they reach the wings. Chain-smoker was a pro, he thought admiringly. She was still berating the Ivans as she reversed to the line. He knew the exact moment she stepped into West Berlin because her language became more salacious and her insults more anatomical. Of course, she was a cut-out, someone planted in the queue to distract from someone else – in this case, him. He hoped she was being well paid. He didn't let anything show on his face and didn't look back.

SAINT PETER'S SQUARE, ROME

Walter Kamf hated Rome, the Vatican and the cassock he was obliged to wear. Seeing the knot of tourists in the square, he added Americans to his hate list. They'd grown fat from the war, he concluded, and paraded around Europe to proclaim their superiority in loud voices. As he passed between the bollards, he watched the thickset American chivvy a woman and girls into a ragged line, with the impatience of an old sheepdog penning a flock.

'Walk slowly,' they'd told him, 'with your eyes fixed on the floor.

That's how real monsignori walk. Remember you're a priest and priests are invisible in Rome – no need to be nervous.' The fact that he was nervous ratcheted up his anger and lengthened his stride until he was kicking the hem of the cassock. The tattoo of black brogues kicking the cassock kept time with his hammering heart. He had been Gehlen's man, for God's sake, the man the intelligence officer relied on for the dirty work. When those being interrogated had ignored all the polite questions, it had been Walter Kamf's boots that had made them sing. Gehlen would turn away as if offended, but he'd been happy enough with the information. With an effort, Walter slowed his breathing and shortened his stride. Gehlen and the others had worn the insignia and taken the plaudits but it was he – he tasted the after-taste of anger on his tongue, bitter as bile – it was he who'd been left behind, surplus to requirements, when Gehlen had read the runes and made a deal with the Americans as they mopped up the last of the Reich. Sure he'd given Walter Kamf a new identity and an introduction to Bishop Hudal and the ratline in Rome. 'Hudal will get you out, Walter,' he'd promised. 'Lots of opportunities in South America for a man of your, er, talents.' The hesitation had said it all. Brawn was all very well for breaking fingers, cracking ribs and lugging metal containers into that fucking mine in Austria. A fresh film of sweat covered his forehead at that last thought. 'You must forget, everything. You don't want the past to follow you into the future,' Gehlen had whispered and, for all his muscle, Walter had felt chilled. Gehlen was a scary bastard. He'd said, yes sir and no sir and thought three bags fucking full, sir – but he'd snapped off a smart Heil Hitler.

Gehlen had smiled that peculiar smile and waved a gloved hand as if dismissing a gnat.

Bishop Hudal had been equally dismissive. He'd given Walter sanctuary in the Anima along with other German fugitives. People turned up at all hours with no names and stayed for a spell and disappeared to Argentina, Brazil, Bolivia and other places – places whose names smelled and tasted of freedom. Walter Kamf had stayed. He'd seen Stangl, the commandant of Treblinka, wined and dined before being smuggled out through Genoa by the Franciscan Draganović. If Hudal had been vague about Walter's passport, the Croatian Franciscan had been acidly direct. 'We export talent, Walter,' he'd sneered. 'They grow their own gorillas in South America.' And when Walter had protested, Hudal and Draganović had played their ace card. 'You don't have to stay here, Walter. You can leave whenever you like.' But he couldn't do that. Eight years after the war, there were people out there with long memories – people in the army, intelligence corps and police dedicated to cracking cold cases. He'd also heard there were hunters, Jews who believed the statute of limitations meant forever. He'd stayed and become an errand boy for Hudal until the stubborn old zealot had published a book and got his ass kicked into retirement at Grottaferatta.

Draganović had survived by becoming a headhunter for the Americans. 'Armament experts, physics professors, mathematicians and chemists,' he'd mocked when Walter had asked again. 'Be a gofor, Walter. You're good at that.'

Walter had promised himself that one day he'd— What? Yes, he knew more than they suspected. Gofors and errand boys hear conversations between powerful people who are blind to their presence. They'd also given him access to documents. What he knew and had collected was his insurance against being kicked out of the sanctuary. That vengeful thought had warmed and reassured him until Steiger usurped Draganović in the San Girolamo.

Walter hated the Franciscan but he feared the Father General of the Fratres. Before Gehlen, Walter had done tours of duty in the camps. He'd seen Mengele and the others close up, and had been frightened. They did terrible things with a dispassion that sickened him. Steiger had that kind of 'absence' about him. For all his bluster, Draganović did as Steiger ordered. And, as the lowest rank in this particular hierarchy, so did Walter. Today, he was Monsignor Albert Schmidt, delivering an envelope to the Director of the Vatican Bank from Father Steiger. At the last minute, as he skirted the tourists, he saw the man ready the camera. Instinctively, Walter Kamf flicked the cape of his cassock over his head.

The road to Genoa

Fyodor loved to drive, particularly in the centre of the road. The ambassador suggested, diplomatically, that he might favour the right lane.

'Bastard Italians drive on the right because they have a Christian Democrat Government,' Fyodor growled around the cigarette he kept clenched in his teeth. 'Next week, they will have a communist government and drive on the left.'

He took his hands from the wheel to make the Italian gesture of exasperation. 'We drive in the middle,' he declared, 'bastards can choose left or right.'

Radović had to admit there was a mad logic to Fyodor's thesis. Even through splayed fingers, he saw oncoming cars make the political decision to veer left or right and their drivers make the universal hand signal of contempt. 'Where did you learn to drive, Fyodor?' he asked, a little breathlessly.

'Tank corps.'

They'd opted for the coastal route, keeping the serenity of the Tyrrhenian Sea to their left and the assurance of Italy's mountainous spine to their right. Radović woke to find a misty Elba sailing past the window. *What would it be like to live on an island?* he wondered. *To be within sight and smell of the sea from dawn to dark?* He imagined himself in a little farmhouse on a hill, looking down on the vine plantations that skirted his land, or writing poetry in the evening by lamplight. Fyodor had followed his gaze in the rear-view mirror.

'Napoleon,' he said, ruining his reverie. 'The first one,' he added helpfully. 'He was – I don't know, king or something, over there.' He jerked his head and half an inch of cigarette ash avalanched towards Elba.

'Are you sure?'

'Yes, very sure.'

So, Napoleon the First lived my dream, Radović thought enviously.

'Stayed almost a year,' Fyodor continued, as he competed with a lorry for the centre of the road. The lorry driver decided to live and surrendered.

There is more to Fyodor than his muscles, Radović thought, not for the first time. It was accepted in the embassy that Fyodor was Beria's eyes and ears in Rome. But why would Beria bother? Italy had escaped communism after the war, persuaded by American money. Few Italians had warm feelings for Stalin. Despite Radović's best efforts, stories of purges, gulags and exterminations had trickled through to the Italian press. The Vatican, under Pius XII, held the Soviet Union as anathema and took every opportunity to denounce 'godless communism' in *Osservatore Romano*. *Pity Pacelli wasn't so vehement against the Nazis*, Radović thought. It was much too nice a day to be—

Damn it to hell, what was going on? 'Ostpolitik,' Beria had said on the phone. Naturally, Radović had made all the right noises, assuring the ogre that he knew what he was talking about. Afterwards, he'd made enquiries, specifically from Piotr, the embassy archivist and resident bore. As he understood it, it meant 'talks with the East'. *That's us*, he concluded. Then there was the enigmatic stuff about news and a gift. His head swam. 'You said it was the next right turn after the church,' he said.

'I know,' Fyodor replied. 'In this country, it's always the next right turn and it's always after a church.'

Fyodor brought politics into everything.

They turned right at Rapallo, after a church, and began to climb. Mount Ebro bulked up on the left and stood sentinel as they negotiated the optional road that hugged the meandering River Trebbia. Just when he was expecting to see grass growing up the centre of the road, they halted.

'Fucking farmers,' Fyodor said and yanked the handbrake savagely. A cart was slewed across the road and a donkey, freed from the shafts, chewed contentedly at the verge. A small man in a large black hat gesticulated operatically to communicate the obvious. The road was blocked.

'He says we'll have to walk from here,' Fyodor reported through the window. 'It's only half a mile up.'

Wearily, Radović got out of the car. He would arrive sweating to the meeting and get dust on his handmade shoes. As they rounded the cart, two men stepped out from hiding, carrying rifles. Fyodor's hand moved to the inside pocket of his jacket and froze. The small man had produced a rifle from the cart and angled the muzzle under Fyodor's chin. With a gesture, he indicated that he should raise his hands. With the ease of long practice, the small man hooked the pistol from its shoulder holster and tucked it inside his waistband.

'Tell me you left the safety off,' Radović whispered in Russian. 'So that this bastard will stumble and blow his ba—'

'*Silenzio.*'

The small man limped back from Fyodor and gestured to the road. One of the men took point, the other two brought up the rear. Radović strained to understand what they were talking about in their rough, local dialect. As far as he could determine, they were discussing the price of cabbages. He peeled off his jacket, draped it over his shoulders and started walking.

SAINT PETER'S SQUARE, ROME

A flicker of crimson tugged at the Swiss Guard's attention. Corporal Dieter Müller had been trained by Captain Markus to notice such things. He'd been the one to ask questions at the end of a training session, a practice that hadn't endeared him to his colleagues. 'There are often thousands in the square, Commander,' he'd said. 'How do we watch so many?'

'Did you fish as a boy, Dieter?'

'Yes, Commander.'

'Good. When you go to fish, you look at the river until you know it, until you have a clear picture of this stretch of water in your mind. Then,' the commander had said, waving his ferrule back and forth like a fly rod, 'you see something that isn't part of that picture. You see a ripple by a rock or a scale flash among the stones on the riverbed.' He'd flexed his wrist and his listeners tracked the flight of an imaginary fly until it landed on Rolf's desk. 'That is where you give your attention. You're looking for the one who is different, the one who goes against the flow of the crowd or who is overdressed on a hot day.' He'd slammed the ferrule on his desk. 'How does an assassin hide?' he'd barked.

'Behind a pillar, sir,' Rolf had suggested and the others laughed.

'Why not?' Markus had challenged. 'Bernini built enough of them.'

'Because we know which pillars afford a line of fire to wherever His Holiness stands, Commander,' Gunther had said.

'Correct. We don't need to watch every place, just the vantage points. The question stands, gentlemen, how does an assassin hide?'

'In plain sight,' Dieter had said.

'*Sehr gut*,' the commander had allowed, 'very good. He is like everyone else. Usually, our barriers and checkpoints keep people at a safe distance. Who could penetrate our defences without raising our suspicions?'

'I don't know, sir,' Dieter had confessed.

Markus had waited as the others shook their heads.

'You and you and you,' he'd said, pointing the ferrule at Dieter, Rolf and Gunther. 'Anyone wearing our uniform could do it. Think,' he'd commanded. 'What other group have the access we have? What other group are such a common sight around the Vatican that we no longer see them?'

'The clergy,' Dieter had said.

'Correct.'

'But there are hundreds of clerics passing in and out of the Vatican every day,' Rolf had protested stubbornly.

'Yes, which is why they must present their papers – no exceptions, gentlemen, from the cardinal to the curate, everyone must produce papers, which is why we memorise the faces of regular visitors. But it is not enough. When is a cleric not a cleric? What signs are there that he is not what he seems? For our next class, you will prepare a list of five signs. Class dismissed.'

Dieter had proudly produced a list of seven and been unsurprised when the commander's list had run to fifteen.

The corporal riffled through his memory as the monsignor crossed the square. His cape has been lifted over his face by the wind, he thought, and then dismissed it. The day was sultry and still.

'How does the subject react to others?' Markus had chalked on the blackboard.

Dieter's eyes strayed to the tableau of tourists the monsignor had passed. He wondered idly if the two young ladies were unhappy or simply tired, and dragged his attention back to the monsignor. Why would the man not wish to be photographed?

'Examine the walk,' had been number eight on the commander's list. 'Clerics wear cassocks from the age of sixteen,' he'd added. 'The cassock dictates a certain kind of walk.'

The man approaching the checkpoint had an erect bearing and favoured long strides. The corporal noticed how he kicked the hem of the cassock as if he found it confining.

'*Buongiorno*, Monsignor,' the corporal said, respectfully. 'May I see your papers?'

The monsignor regarded him with cold eyes for a moment before producing his documents.

'*Un momento, per favore.*'

Dieter retreated to the sentry box. The monsignor hadn't rummaged in his pocket, he'd had the documents ready in his hand.

'People who come prepared,' Markus had written. It was the ninth sign.

The papers were in order and in perfect condition, no creases or bent corners or any other signs of regular use.

'If you have any suspicion, withdraw and observe from afar,' the commander had counselled. 'In your absence, the subject will relax. We learn more from someone who is relaxed than we do from someone who is at attention. This is also true of guards,' he'd added, with a meaningful look at Rolf who was lounging at his desk. 'What do people do while they wait?' Markus had asked. 'They check their watches, shuffle their feet and adjust their clothing. All of that is normal but what is not normal?'

Dieter watched the feet of the monsignor settle into the 'at ease' position. The man's upper body remained rigid and his hands didn't stir from his sides.

'You are German, Monsignor?'

'Yes, is there a problem?'

'Which part of Germany, Monsignor?'

'Bavaria.'

Dieter allowed the pause to lengthen but the monsignor offered no further information. Most people added further information. Dieter had a tin ear and wouldn't recognise a Bavarian accent. Thankfully, Rolf was an irrepressible mimic and was on duty at the next checkpoint. He folded the papers neatly and handed them back. 'Please, proceed, Monsignor,' he said.

Back in the sentry box, he picked up the telephone.

'Rolf! A monsignor approaching your station. Delay him long enough for Hans to get a photograph. And Rolf, see if you can guess where he's from before you check his papers.'

An hour later, Rolf poked his head inside the sentry box.

'Any Russian tanks in the square or snipers on the dome?' he teased.

'No more than usual,' Dieter replied stiffly. He thought Rolf could be alarmingly casual for a Swiss.

'It'll be an inside job,' Rolf continued darkly, 'that's how they do it here. Remember Julius Caesar? Oh lighten up, Dieter, you're getting to be as paranoid as old Markus.'

'Did Hans get the photograph?'

Rolf placed a large brown envelope on the desk. 'Your monsignor,' he smiled.

'Not mine,' Dieter said. He'd noted the sponsor's signature on the papers and details of the office the monsignor was visiting in the Vatican.

'Frankfurt,' Rolf said.

'What?'

'Your monsignor is from Frankfurt. You owe me two beers, Dieter.'

'So he's not from Bavaria?'

'No, definitely Frankfurt.'

'Okay. If you mention this in the barracks, all bets are off and you do double duty for a fortnight, Rolf.'

'You're worse than Markus.'

Commander Markus fished his spectacles from a pocket and held the photograph to the light from the window.

'Bishop Hudal, you say?'

'Yes, Commander, that's what the sponsor's signature said. The monsignor was visiting the Vatican Bank to see a Signor—'

'No,' the commander said quickly, 'I have all the information I need in your report. Thank you, Dieter,' he said warmly. 'Are you on leave this week?'

'Yes, Commander. I've signed up for a course in advanced weapons training.'

'Really? Ah yes, good man.'

Sometimes Markus wished his corporal was a little less – earnest. Still, he reflected, a peacetime army couldn't relax its vigilance. Archduke Ferdinand had been assassinated in peacetime by amateurs and Europe had gone to war. As he dismissed his corporal, he made a mental note to remind the guards of this important fact. He held the photograph in his left hand while he dialed. 'Monsignor Dupont, *per favore*.'

GENOA

The man rose from behind the table in the farmhouse kitchen when Radović and Fyodor were ushered in. He was over six feet tall and solidly built. *As befitted the son of a stevedore*, Radović thought.

Piotr, the archivist, tended to be encyclopaedic. Radović looked closely at the man in front of him. He had a long scholar's face, with a jutting chin that seemed to have been designed for a coarser man. Sharp, brown eyes were magnified behind spectacles. He wore a white, open-neck shirt and black pants – however, Giuseppi Siri could have dressed in sackcloth and still been every inch a cardinal of the Roman Catholic Church.

Radović riffled through the other details of the brief supplied by the archivist. Siri was a doctor of this and a professor of that, he knew he would never understand the various theological disciplines this man was proficient in, and hadn't bothered trying.

Radović's interest had been piqued when Piotr had detailed how, as a young bishop, Siri had been part of the resistance movement against the Nazis. Interest had turned to admiration when he'd learned that Siri had acted as negotiator between the partisans and the Nazi forces surrounding Genoa, a negotiation that had concluded with the Nazis surrendering. And, of course, there was the question of Ostpolitik. According to Beria, this Prince of the Church had rediscovered his negotiation talents and had applied them to Church–Soviet relations.

Radović had met the pope and thought him a candle in a strong wind. He'd met Stalin and thought he'd smelled of blood. Siri had that enviable stillness reserved to a few powerful men. As Siri approached, Radović prepared himself for the formal greeting. He was surprised and a little annoyed to see him greet Fyodor warmly.

'Ambassador Sergei Radović,' Fyodor said, gesturing at his companion.

The handshake was firm and more than perfunctory. 'I'm glad to make your acquaintance, Your Excellency,' Siri said. 'Please, sit with me and have some refreshment.'

The smell of minestrone and freshly baked bread reminded him that he was ravenous and he forgot his wounded pride. He remembered another of Piotr's archival oddities as he spooned soup from a cracked plate. Siri had run soup kitchens during the war and had earned the nickname the 'Minestrone Cardinal'. The wine, poured liberally into clay mugs, was rough but welcome.

'Fyodor and I have been meeting for some time,' the cardinal said apologetically. 'I'm happy that Lavrentiy Beria finds me sufficiently trustworthy to meet his ambassador.'

Radović concluded that Siri had sounded sincere. He'd parsed the cardinal's words for any trace of patronisation or sarcasm, but hadn't detected either. If they had been present, he would certainly have noticed. As a junior ambassador in an ill-starred location, he was expert on both.

'Fyodor and I, with Beria's blessing, have been exploring ways in which the Church and the USSR might progress towards a better relationship,' Siri continued. 'The Church has millions of members within the USSR and is concerned for their pastoral welfare. We, some of us, accept that history cannot be rewritten.'

This is important, Radović thought and refused the wine jug proffered by their limping abductor.

'Détente is not peace,' the cardinal said emphatically. 'Nature and politics both abhor a vacuum. Churchill was correct when he said "better jaw, jaw than war, war". But,' he grinned, 'I forget my manners. I must apologise for the welcome you received.'

Radović waved a hand dismissively, but Siri pressed on. 'Vincente,' he said, nodding at the man who sat behind him, still holding the rifle, 'has been my friend for many years. We were in the resistance together. He and his companions protected me when I went to meet the Nazis. Old habits die hard. There are those, on both sides, who might not favour this meeting.'

Radović nodded and smiled at Vincente, who smiled in return. 'It would seem to me,' Radović began slowly, 'that the main obstacle to better relations might reside in the Vatican.'

'Yes,' Siri granted, 'and it would seem to me that the pope shares that position with the one who resides in the Kremlin.'

'Touché,' Radović allowed. 'Then we have a stalemate, Your Eminence.'

The cardinal poured wine for his guests and refreshed his own mug. 'Within my Church,' he said, 'I am regarded as a conservative, someone who would be rigid in his defence of Church teaching and Church law. I would prefer to describe myself as an independent, a man who walks alone and is not a member of any group. Whether that is bravery or folly I don't know. I do know it's more important to do what is right than to do the right thing.'

'With respects, Eminence,' Radović said, 'what can the Cardinal of Genoa do when the Pope of Rome continues to condemn?'

'With respects, Excellency,' the cardinal replied, 'the Church has a long history of accommodating the real world. The USSR, on the other hand, is a fairly recent political phenomenon. Let me speak plainly. Popes and general secretaries are mortal men – they come and go. The Church and the USSR will both exist for a long time. We must take the long view that the relationship between us can progress through peaceful co-existence to mutual respect and co-operation. And,' he added, 'I have been summoned to serve in the Vatican.'

'Congratulations,' Radović said warmly.

'Some would argue it's a mixed blessing,' Siri said ruefully. 'Vincente doesn't approve.'

This brought smiles from everyone, except Vincente. Radović imagined him toting his rifle into the Sistine Chapel. 'My superiors,' he said, 'are committed to the relationship you speak of. As a token of good faith, they wish to release an ecclesiastic into your care.'

'Mindszenty?' Siri asked hopefully.

'No. I'm sorry,' Radović added when he saw disappointment flood the cardinal's face. 'No,' he repeated, 'the words my superior used were "not yet". We must hasten slowly, Eminence.' He sipped his wine to allow Siri time to absorb what he'd said. 'You have representatives in Finland?' he asked.

'Yes, but—'

'Eminence, please,' Radović interjected, holding up a palm. 'Listen, carefully. Three weeks hence, your representatives should be waiting at the port of Kotka on the Gulf of Finland. That is what I've been instructed to tell you.'

The journey back to the car was a pleasant one. Radović thought it might have been the wine but he was buoyed up by the feeling that momentous events had been set in motion and that he, Sergei Radović, would play a part in them.

FŐ UTCA PRISON, BUDAPEST

A key rattled in the lock and he moved to keep the window at his back. The guard was a man who had survived the changes, a political chameleon who'd adjusted his colours to whatever colours flew from the mast. Today he wore his expressionless face and a clean uniform. He was making an effort to stand straighter. The man who entered behind him stopped inside the door to examine his surroundings. Nothing showed on his face when he removed his hat. He looked like some of the priests who taught at the seminary, kindly and abstracted.

'Two chairs, please,' he said in a hoarse voice, and the guard disappeared.

When he reappeared, he took a noisy moment to discover that he should come in sideways. Carefully, he placed the chairs either side of the metal table. The chair legs rattled on the cement floor as he lowered them and Stefan almost felt sorry for him. With a nod from the visitor, he was dismissed.

'Shall we sit, Stefan?' he asked and sat.

It was the first time since coming to this place that anyone had called him by his baptismal name. He was glad that the man hadn't used his surname. The guards had always called him 'Nagy' in the early days – before they'd grown tired of beating him.

The man took some papers from his pocket and smoothed them on the table. From his inside pocket, he took a pair of wire-rimmed spectacles. There was a vulnerability in the way he wrestled the loops behind his ears and tilted his nose to look through the lens that almost moved Stefan to lower his defences.

'You may call me Gregor,' he said.

He guessed from his breath that the hoarseness came from tobacco. The Hungarian for tobacco is *dohány* – Dohány Street – synagogue. Making connections was how Stefan had exercised his brain in solitude. Consciously, he moved that train of thought into a siding and concentrated on Gregor. He had lived in an unchanging room for so long that his eyes had become superfluous. He could have closed them at dawn and functioned without accident before opening them again when the light died. Something alien and exotic had entered his colourless world and his eyes devoured it.

He started with the hat. Gregor had placed it at the edge of the table. It was a black hat with a broad brim, slightly tilted at one side. Above the brim, a shiny band encircled the hat. It wasn't quite black. Charcoal-grey, some unused part of his brain offered and he accepted. *Charcoal–wood–fire–forge. No! Not now*, he chided himself. Not when there are real things, like the hat. He imagined a little bow tied at the unseen side of the band. The crown was dimpled on either side so that it could be lifted with thumb and middle finger. His fingers twitched in a phantom spasm. There was the usual depression in the top of the crown. *Convex? No, concave*. The coat, which Gregor had opened before sitting, was black. *Wool*. Wool and well-worn, hinted the tiny fuzzy balls that flecked around the cuff. The buttons and buttonholes were stitched tight. Each buttonhole showed a straight mouth. Gregor tied all the buttons, all the time. His collar and the V of the shirt that was visible were spotlessly white. A dark purple necktie bunched under his chin and relaxed on his chest until it disappeared beneath a waistcoat. Stefan sensed that his hands were clammy and rubbed them on his knees under the table. Gregor had a stiff brush of white hair that jutted above his forehead – which was smooth, though thinking, reading or poor spectacles had pinched a pucker between his eyebrows. The whites of his eyes were clear – no hint of yellow, no tiny deltas of red veins. The pupils were as brown as the marsh pools his father had warned him to avoid. 'Fall in there, boy, and you're gone.' Those eyes were looking at him. He dropped his gaze to the table. It was a dull, gunmetal grey, pitted and dented and safe. His eyes relaxed and became unfocused. His awareness moved to his hearing. He had developed the ability to refine door-muffled conversations into clear speech – step inside the tangled threads of tone to identify the dominant one and the emotion it vibrated to. He knew precisely when Gregor was about to speak. The fabric of his sleeve whispered a warning from the surface of the table and there was the slight sibilance of an indrawn breath.

'Nobody came for you, did they, Stefan?'

It was a question that didn't require an answer because it had answered itself. Rhetorical, his teachers had called it.

'Not your father or Father Bruno, your spiritual director, or Laszlo. Not anyone.'

Gregor dropped the page he'd been looking at and tilted his head to look at Stefan. He'd dropped the page as if he had weighed the integrity of those he'd named and found them wanting. *Hand* – manus. *Table* – mensa. *Paper? Not* vellum. *Papyrus?* He couldn't remember. He had translated his entire visible world into Latin but there hadn't been any paper. *Not now,* he cautioned himself. Later, when Gregor is gone and there is time to savour every particle of his newness.

'The Church seems to have forgotten you,' Gregor sighed. 'What did you do that was so terrible? You spoke out against the deportation of the Jews and a high mass held to celebrate it. You managed to offend Church and state in two short sentences. Of course, Mindszenty spoke out against the fascists, but Mindszenty knew how to play the game. He was always the understudy for Pacelli when it came to public pronouncement. Isn't it ironic that Mindszenty ends up in jail for criticising the communist government? Oh, you didn't know? Yes, they accused him of being a collaborator and lots of other things. It was the same game but played by their rules. He confessed everything. The pope says they drugged him, but I think his dignity was so affronted by being hit with rubber truncheons that he begged for the pen. But not you, Stefan.' He was riffling through the pages again. 'Not even after months of beatings, not a single word. It seems,' he smiled, 'you used up all your words at the lectern that Sunday morning.'

He peeled his glasses from behind his ears and kneaded the pucker between his eyes. 'I don't expect you to speak to me, Stefan,' he said quietly. 'You can just nod or shake your head. Do you mind if I smoke?'

The sudden question coming hot on the heels of Gregor's measured talk took Stefan by surprise. He nodded. They hadn't been allowed to smoke in the seminary. On feast days, the dean went to visit his mother, and smoke rose like incense from every window. His father had smoked a pipe and—

Gregor was watching him.

'You were somewhere else, Stefan,' he said. He clicked a lighter alive and drew the flame to the cigarette. He opened his mouth to reveal a ball of smoke, roiling on his tongue. A deep breath and he'd sucked it down, deep. After a moment of suspense, he sighed the smoke through his nose. 'I was saying,' he continued, 'that you were somewhere else. Do you wish you were somewhere else, Stefan?'

It was a direct question. He would have to nod or shake his head. He found he couldn't do either. Immediately after his imprisonment, when the fear and rage had burned off, he'd moved to wishing – wishing for everything he'd lost, wishing so hard it hurt and he had moaned and whimpered. And one day, he'd stopped. Wishing, he'd concluded, was like banging your head on the cell door. It hurt and nothing changed.

'I can get you out of here, Stefan,' Gregor said.

Stefan's ears checked every syllable of that sentence and found nothing false.

'Today,' Gregor said.

'Today' detonated in his brain and he felt a surge of energy through every part of his body. When that first wave of euphoria was spent, he turned unreadable eyes on Gregor.

'Why would I do this for you?'

Rhetorical.

'Because I want you to do something for me.'

Ah!

'Yes,' Gregor said, smiling, 'we understand each other. I don't expect you to agree to do something until you know what that something is. I'll tell you, when I'm ready and when I think you are.'

He was rising to leave, looking for a place to stub his cigarette. He flicked it between thumb and middle finger. It arced to sizzle in the slop bucket. 'You have one hour to consider my offer,' he said, buttoning all the buttons on his coat. 'When I return, I'll ask if you're willing to come with me. If it's no, you can shake your head. But if it's yes, you have to say yes.'

Gregor hammered on the door and, when it opened, he walked away.

'Walked away', the two words pulsed in Stefan's head. Like a dash and dot of Morse code. 'Walked away' – long and short. He looked up and saw the guard staring at him, as if he'd never seen him before.

THE INDUSTRIAL AREA, EAST BERLIN

The workers' paradise could do with a coat of paint, Claus observed, as he pedalled through the dingy streets of the industrial area. Huge chimneys, jutting up from factories, belched clouds of smoke, too soot-laden to soar. The smoke curled down into the streets and teared his eyes. Factory workers, standing on corners in the poisonous fog, bristled as he approached and then dismissed the drab man pedalling an ugly bicycle. Lenin Strasse was a carbon copy of the other grimy streets. Tenement houses lost their top stories in the haze that created a perpetual twilight. The factories, he knew, had their electricity turned off at sunset to cut down on costs. The grimy men who appeared and disappeared on his route, like wraiths, were already working on reduced wages. The GDR was heavily taxed by its Soviet masters. When the reparation tax was added to the bill, it amounted to twenty per cent of the state's income. A double exodus had cut the workforce to the bone. Thousands had already spurned Marx for Marks and moved west. Thousands more had dreamed of something different and woken to the harsh reality of penal colonies. There were no banners here, only the grime of poverty and a smouldering resentment.

He stopped outside number two, ostensibly to check his bicycle chain.

'You have a match, friend?'

The man loomed over him, a brown cigarette dangling from slack lips.

'Does everyone smoke here?' Claus asked.

'Why not?' the man said. 'Everything else does.'

The man led him to the back door of the house. 'Bring it,' he grunted, as Claus went to lean the bicycle against the wall. Inside, a narrow hallway opened out to a large room. He counted ten men. Five were seated at a table and the remainder were ranged behind them, as if they were arranged for a photograph. Some had the smudged look of factory workers, others looked like students. His

interest was piqued by the two clerics who sat companionably, side
by side at the rough table. They all had one thing in common. The
eyes of every man in the room had fixed on his bicycle. One of the
clerics rose from the table and approached. He carried a wicked-
looking knife in his right hand. 'Excuse me,' he said apologetically.
He knelt and began to scrape the blade along the bicycle frame.
Claus palmed sweat from his forehead as the dull, black paint peeled
away, revealing a bright scar. The cleric looked up, his face shining.
'Gold,' he said.

The group boiled from the table to engulf Claus in congratulations.
They continued slapping his back until he felt breathless. Someone
pushed a glass into his hand and it rattled against his teeth as he
drank. An elderly man took him by the arm and steered him to the
sanctuary of the table. 'You didn't know?' he asked quietly.

'No.'

'Sometimes, it's better not to know.'

Their eyes met for a moment and the man smiled.

'We don't use names,' he said, 'for obvious reasons and there are
too many of us for codes.'

'And for secrecy,' Claus added.

'Yes,' his host smiled, 'it's always the first casualty.'

'I thought truth was always the first casualty.'

'Perhaps where you come from,' the man said, and Plummer
dropped his eyes. 'So,' the man continued, 'we have Engineer and
Baker and so on. The factory workers were too many so we named
them for their products – Steel, Bearings, Textiles. Having two
clerics was also a problem. There was a long meeting – yet another
long meeting.' His eyes disappeared for a moment as he smiled.
'One is Gog and the other Magog.'

'Which is which?'

'We've forgotten. We'll have to hold another meeting.'

'And what are you called?'

'Cassandra.'

'So, you are fated not to be believed?'

'Yes.' He turned to face Claus. 'So,' he said, almost sadly, 'it doesn't matter whether you tell me the truth or not. I'm sure that's a weight off your mind.'

Claus sipped his drink and watched the men circle the bicycle like excited children.

'Your bicycle will finance a thousand bicycles for couriers, when the time comes,' Cassandra said. 'You needn't doubt that East Berlin will rise, my friend. It can hardly sink further. I think Ulbricht and his government will reply with promises for a better tomorrow. When this falls on deaf ears, they will remonstrate, like a loving mother surprised and hurt by the behaviour of her unruly children. Finally, Papa will come with the rod – tanks and troops, Herr Plummer, the irrefutable Soviet argument. Berlin will already have sparked other cities across the GDR and there will be a flash-fire of protests. And when it is all over, Ulbricht will blame capitalist saboteurs; over here, it's a knee-jerk reaction if a pigeon shits on a policeman. You will have your revolution – after all, you've paid for it. And we will have more martyrs and meetings, until the next time.'

'What will you tell them?' Plummer asked, nodding at the group.

'It doesn't matter, does it? How can something as abstract as truth compete with solid gold? Anyway, I'm fated not to be believed, remember? Willy will show you out.'

Outside the back door, Willy gestured at a bicycle leaning against the wall. It was identical in every ugly detail to the one he'd delivered.

'You must return as you arrived, Mein Herr,' Willy smiled.

'Yes,' he agreed. Although he doubted he could do that after what he'd just done. And what he was about to do.

FŐ UTCA PRISON, BUDAPEST

Saying yes had been the hardest part. Not because he didn't want to say it, but because the mechanism in his body for making words had rusted through lack of use.

Gregor waited, as solemn and impassive as a bishop waiting for one who wished ordination to the priesthood to pronounce, 'I am willing.'

Stefan parted his lips, pressed his tongue behind his bottom teeth and hissed, 'Ye-es.' The final sibilant sound escaped his lips and most of his breath went with it.

Gergor nodded and went to stand under the high window, looking up so that his white hair dazzled and his segmented shadow stretched behind him. Stefan dressed slowly in the clothes Gregor had placed on the table, savouring the resistance of shirt buttons against his fingertips, the slide, notch and fasten of his trouser belt, the cold firm feel of new shoes. He followed Gregor to the door and paused.

'It's just a single step, Stefan,' Gregor said, 'you can worry about the next step later.'

Stefan raised his foot higher than necessary and leaned forwards, stumbling, until his outstretched hands found Gregor's back. There was a reassurance and strength in that broad back and he relaxed. On the way through the building, he kept his eyes on Gregor's heels, mirroring the lift and set of his feet until his brain recalled the rhythm of walking.

The light blinded him and he faltered.

'I'm taking your arm,' Gregor said, and Stefan felt the sinewy arm thread inside the angle of his elbow. They walked on until shapes hardened and he could see the car. He reversed into the back seat, Gregor's hand pressing gently on his head as he crouched to enter.

As the car peeled away from the pavement, Stefan clutched the seat. He concentrated on the driver. He had black bristling hair and pocked skin on his neck. Encouraged, he surveyed the driver's area. There was an overflowing ashtray and nothing else. Not his car, he concluded. It was a car like the one they'd had at the seminary to bring students to the dentist, doctor or jail. He felt a tremor rise and soothed it by completing the thought sequence. This car is driven by this man but belongs to no one. He risked looking through the window as they sped along, grasping at familiar things like buildings and statues and his stomach floated into his throat as they crossed the Danube.

Everything looked the same and yet strangely different, except the checkpoints and the soldiers. He tensed at the first checkpoint after the bridge, watching the approaching soldier in his peripheral vision – noting the colour of his uniform and the shape of his hat. Gregor lowered his window and held a card for inspection. The soldier stiffened and saluted. He waved them through with exaggerated arm movements. *Was it a sign of self-importance or an acknowledgement of Gregor's?* Stefan wondered.

The railway station was a bedlam of grinding locomotives, steam and hurrying people. Sandwiched between Gregor and the driver, he was propelled into an empty office on the platform. The windows were blinded with dusty curtains.

'Trust me,' Gregor said. 'The driver will bring you to the train. I'll be waiting.'

The driver produced a set of manacles and snapped them on Stefan's wrists. He conjured an outsized fur hat and pulled it over Stefan's head, until it fringed his eyes.

'People never look at a prisoner,' Gregor explained.

The driver reeked of rough tobacco and garlic as he sped him across the platform. Stefan knew precisely where the platform ended and the train began and lifted his foot to quest for the step without being told. When the manacles and hat were removed, he saw Gregor sitting opposite.

'Worked like a charm,' he said. 'Relax, we have the carriage to ourselves.'

Everything was beautiful. He practised the three syllables before giving them breath.

'Yes,' Gregor said, without looking up from his book. 'Beautiful.'

Stefan gazed and dozed and went to the toilet, unaccompanied. The rocking floor skewed his aim and he laughed as he splashed in and around the hole in the floor. It sounded like the noise the gander made on the farm but he'd laughed. The plush seat and the rhythm of the wheels lulled him to sleep. He had always dreamed in pictures. He didn't know it was possible to dream in smells. He smelled borsch – the alkali smell of beet, competing with the ripe scent of meat. Fresh sour cream wove its distinctive odour between both. He woke and it was real. A tray rested on a low, folding table set between the seats. It was crowded with plates, bowls and a silver salver. Gregor had already shifted a stoppered carafe and two crystal glasses to the floor.

'Some of the dishes you'll remember,' he said, snapping out a white napkin, 'like borsch.'

Stefan nodded, his eyes wandering from the soup to the other dishes.

'Pirozhki,' Gregor said, pointing to plump pastries. 'Inside, you'll find potatoes, meat and' – he lifted a pastry and held it under his nose – 'cabbage,' he pronounced. 'Sometimes, they use cheese.'

Stefan saw caviar and dark crusty bread and ….

'Pelmeni,' Gregor supplied, serving the borsch. 'Pelmeni are dumplings with meatballs.' He laughed and when Stefan raised an eyebrow, he said, 'My grandmother always said our eyes were bigger than our bellies. Eat!'

He held each spoonful under his nose until he'd inhaled the flavours. Every mouthful was balanced on his tongue for texture and taste until he felt he couldn't eat another bite.

'Ice-cream doesn't count,' Gregor declared. 'There is always room for ice-cream. This is Morozhenoe with chocolate.'

Firm and yielding, tart and sweet, he felt it melt and slide coolly down his throat. Gregor poured two glasses of clear liquid. 'Vodka,' he said, 'to be sipped, Stefan,' he added, 'we're not in—' He stopped and handed a glass to Stefan. 'Do you know where we're going?' he asked casually.

The farmer's son turned to the window. 'East,' he said.

'Yes,' Gregor acknowledged, 'but we're not in Russia ... yet. Sip!'

Stefan sipped and dabbed his mouth with a napkin. 'Dream,' he slurred.

'The vodka or—?'

'Everything,' Stefan said.

'Go to bed and dream,' Gregor said, 'it will still be real in the morning.'

CARDINAL TISSERANT'S APARTMENTS, THE VATICAN

'And how are the children?'

It was the second time in as many minutes that his old friend had asked the question and Commander Markus struggled to keep anxiety from his voice.

'With their grandmother in Lucerne,' he said, 'polishing their German. Do you know this man?'

Emil tilted the photograph.

'No,' he said, 'despite my reputation for omniscience. Rome is a honeypot for clerics. They come from all over to study or on pilgrimage or to work in Vatican departments. What rings my alarm bells is that this man comes from the Girolamo to visit a Director of the Vatican Bank and Bishop Hudal is named as a sponsor on his papers. You remember how active the good bishop was in spiriting his Croatian friends to South America after the war? I thought the ratlines had run out of rats.'

'No, they've just found a superior strain of rat. Under the new management in the Girolamo, physicists, chemists, arms experts and scientists are the new export, but to North rather than to South America.'

'Is Steiger back?'

'Yes. He's in the Girolamo. If we could find evidence that he's up to his old tricks, His Holiness would be forced to take action.'

Emil didn't share his friend's conviction but remained silent. 'Can I keep this photograph?' he asked.

Stalin's dacha, Moscow

Stalin loved cowboy films. The politburo was arranged before the screen in his office as if posing for a group photograph. Stalin sat in the centre. The film had been stolen in the West. *Stealing from the capitalists absolves us from the sin of enjoying their capitalist products*, Khrushchev thought. There were no subtitles and he filled the time with interpreting the visuals. The 'good guys' rode in from the right; the 'bad guys' from the left. The hero wore a white hat; the villain a black one. Red Indians rode in circles until they were shot and there was no black man. The woman was sometimes killed in the first five minutes and bloodily avenged for an hour and a half. Stalin preferred that scenario. Sometimes he laughed as if he understood the dialogue, or when someone laughed in the film. Whenever Stalin laughed, Beria laughed – always a few seconds later, like a translator.

The drive to the dacha had taken just ten minutes. Someone had joked that the Queen of England thought the whole world smelled of fresh paint. The politburo could have been forgiven for thinking there were no cars in Moscow. From the moment they'd emerged from the Kremlin Gate and crossed an empty, echoing Red Square, NKVD units had clustered on either side of the bridge and at every intersection on the route to Stalin's dacha. The NKVD were the magicians who waved their hands and made the traffic disappear. They were everywhere Khrushchev had looked from the speeding limousine, and they were Beria's. Stalin's paranoia for security was evident in the uniforms around and inside the dacha. Khrushchev suspected there were even more in the woods around the house. The household guards took hats and coats, served drinks and food and then melted into the background. The serious drinking started at one in the morning. Sometimes at these sessions, they discussed affairs of state and drank vodka until dawn. Tonight, there was more of a party atmosphere, the sort of night when old men could put down the burdens of office and pretend to be friends.

While the others milled around the tables, Stalin sat alone by the stove, puffing his pipe. Khrushchev had found a chair by the wall at the far end of the room and contented himself with watching the others. Stalin, he thought, looked his age. There were rumours that he'd had a stroke some time back, but there were no tell-tale signs, no sagging mouth, paralysis or slurred speech. He switched his attention to the others. Sometimes, Khrushchev wished he had Beria's gift for being 'all things to all men' – he could be formal or familiar with Stalin, often in the same sentence. In the Kremlin, he was careful to use proper titles but, tonight, it had been 'Iosif' or 'Koba', the nickname only the chosen few could use. Enviously, he watched Beria listen attentively to Molotov and pour wine for Malenkov. Khrushchev always felt more comfortable holding a wine glass in his fist like a tankard, rather than by the stem or cradled in the fingers. He accepted that, at his core, despite the good suit, shirt, tie and expensive shoes, he was still the farmer's son from Kalinkova. He tended to speak when he was spoken to, and say *da* when he meant yes and *nyet* when he meant no, and he had no talent for small talk. But he was here.

'Nikita Sergeyevich!'

It took him a few seconds to realise he was being summoned. Stalin waved a hand at a chair beside him. 'Sit,' he said.

Khrushchev sat and resumed watching the groups that formed and reformed around the small tables, moving from one conversation to another in the practised choreography of powerful men. Stalin's pipe produced a haze of blue smoke that drifted like a gauze curtain between the politburo and the two men sitting near the stove.

'You don't say much, do you?' Stalin said, never taking his eyes from the others.

'No.'

'Doesn't mean you don't have much to say,' Stalin said, tamping the pipe bowl with a yellowed finger. 'Molotov doesn't say much either,' he continued in a soft voice. 'Some say it's because of his stammer. But he had plenty to say in the old days. Most of it was horse shit, but he said it. Now,' he paused and shook his head, 'I think I preferred the horse shit. Malenkov,' he whispered, leaning conspiratorially towards Khruhschev, 'is trying to look like the Tsar.' He wheezed a laugh that turned into a cough.

'Shall I get you a glass of water?' Khrushchev offered.

'*Nyet*. Water is for pills.' His face darkened and Khrushchev prayed he hadn't started a train of thought that would end in a tirade against doctors. The nine doctors accused of attempted poisoning were still in Lubyanka prison, singing whichever tune they thought the torturers wanted to hear. They were dead men. Everyone knew that. He risked a glance at Stalin and followed the direction of his gaze to Beria.

'Do you have a younger brother?' Stalin asked.

'No.'

'Good,' he grunted. 'My little Georgian brother,' he said thoughtfully, tracking Beria with his hooded brown eyes. 'A younger brother follows you everywhere,' he continued. 'When you laugh, he laughs. He listens when you speak and nods and nods. Every time you look over your shoulder, he's there like your fucking shadow. You kick his ass today, he comes back tomorrow, still smiling. Young brothers grow, Nikita. Then they want to be someone else's big brother. You're better off without brothers, Nikita Sergeyevich.'

He turned and looked Khrushchev in the eyes.

'How many intersections between here and the Kremlin?' he asked.

'Fifteen.'

'Soldiers?'

'NKVD.'

'I like having soldiers around – reminds me of the old days.

Check army deployments around Moscow in the morning. Report to my office at ten.'

'General Zhukov is in—'

'I know where Zhukov is and he stays there. Fucker told me to burn Kiev. Not Zhukov.'

He hadn't raised his voice and no head had turned in their direction yet Khrushchev felt he'd been kicked in the stomach. Stalin slammed a palm on the table and stilled the room.

'I have something to announce,' he said and Khrushchev saw faces struggle to remain impassive. 'Nikita Sergeyevich, our comrade, will dance. Music,' he added and an aide rushed to the record player.

He heard the first strains of the music and knew it had been planned. It was the Pryvit, a Ukrainian welcome dance. The others looked at him uncertainly, and faded back to their chairs. *Why had Stalin done this?* he wondered. Had he said or—? No. If he started on that journey, there'd be a thousand possible destinations and no end. He felt fear. He couldn't remember a time when he hadn't. In time of war, fear for your life is a natural, animal thing. It's the juice that sends you crawling on your belly. He'd seen a different kind of fear in Stalingrad. Some men and women had turned their faces to the wall and waited for death. No amount of shouting or threats or entreaties could bring them back from where they had put themselves. Those who stayed mobile stayed supple inside. They could bend bodies and minds to bear any burden. And there were a few, blessed or damned he didn't know, who were transformed by fear. One minute, a man is wriggling on his belly, staying under the scythe of rapid fire. The next, he's up and running at them. Sometimes, he's laughing or shouting or screaming his mother's name. But in that seven seconds between pushing up from the dirt and smashing into the enemy, he belongs to no army and no country. He belongs to no one but himself. If he survived, the soldiers craved his company and wanted to be in his unit. He'd sat behind barricades with such people. They had a serenity. It was the only word he could think of. They seemed to have been cleansed of fear in the refiner's fire. They had a kind of clarity he'd seen in the faces of some old monks in the gulag. He'd seen the same clarity in the faces of the old women in his village when they danced, and when they danced, he'd seen grown men weep for what they'd lost of themselves.

He was a Ukrainian who was happy to be called a Soviet, always one and part of the other. Stalin was a Georgian who wanted to be a Russian. 'Either or neither,' his grandmother would have said. He looked around at the frightened faces. My grandmother met Vasyl Verkhovynets, he could have told them, as he felt his body ease into the rhythms of the Pryvit. She claimed the dances in his book were the dances she taught him. He could hear her ululating laugh as the tempo began to build – see her toothless grin as he began to spin. He saw their faces blur by as if he were standing still and they were moving, faster and faster. The clapping built like a heartbeat and sweat flew like diamonds from his face when he leapt and reached to finger-touch his toes. The music faded but the clapping continued, faster, faster. He danced the small, almost mincing steps, that tapped the energy from the floor to flow through his body until the floor became a tether, an anchor dragging when the sail is full and he was up, two, three on the table, scattering glasses as he pounded, leapt, whirled and stopped.

He saw as a boy sees who looks through a crystal. There were shapes, shot through with rainbow colours, and fragments of pure white light like silver specks in schist. He heard the sound of pigeon wings, clapping off into the forest, and the surge of his blood like a wind through pines. For a moment, he was afraid that he had gone away, as grandmother claimed her sister had. 'She danced too far to come back,' she'd said. *I am here*, he thought and his vision cleared. He was surrounded by the men he knew, his colleagues on the politburo. They seemed frozen into variations of the same position, as if a spell had fallen on them, mid-dance. Molotov stood erect, his head tilted back, arms extended and eyes wet with loss. Bulganin and Mikoyan held their arms out, caught in mid-whirl. Beria stood on tiptoe, longing to rise free. All of them shone with sweat and excitement and the kind of wordless, breathless joy of boys who have run the race of their lives and won. Molotov started to clap and the others took up the beat, smashing their hands together in appreciation. Behind them, he could see NKVD officers, aides and servants, clapping and turning to smile and nod at each other.

'Enough,' a coarse voice commanded and the spell was broken. The servants were the first to melt away. The NKVD officers stiffened and disappeared behind their policeman faces. Finally, the politburo dissolved into individual men who looked older than they'd been a moment before. They clapped formally now. *I will never be afraid again*, Khrushchev thought, and felt tears prick his eyes. He cleared them on his shirt sleeve and looked up. Beria was clapping with the others but his eyes were alive with questions. Khrushchev swung his arm wide to acknowledge all of them but he bowed to Beria.

STRADIVARIUS APARTMENT, EAST BERLIN

Claus knew where the key was hidden. Stradivarius might be volatile and artistic, but he was also German. Some things never changed, just like the hiding place under the geranium pot on the landing. The apartment smelled of cabbage and rosin, staples in the musician's diet and occupation. He added a shovel of coal to the fire and switched on a standard lamp – Stradivarius didn't like surprises. The light revealed a square of fringed carpet hemmed with a sofa and chaise longue. Two armchairs shouldered each other for space at the fire. Busts of the usual composers gleamed on shelves between rows of heavy books. In the corner near the door, a metal music stand cast a portentous shadow, reaching all the way up to the ceiling and sheet music littered the claw-foot table under the window. The record player looked new. There were no photographs of loved ones. Stradivarius had been spared their fate because Kommandant Stangl had appreciated his genius.

He was fighting sleep when the door burst open and a tall man loomed in the doorway. He had an aged cherub's face, saved from being sybaritic by guileless, blue eyes. He wore a black suit over an open-necked white shirt and held a violin case like a rifle.

'Is that loaded?' Claus asked.

Stradivarius bumped the door closed with his hip without taking his eyes from the visitor.

'The Stasi wouldn't have lit the fire,' he said.

'The Stasi wouldn't bother the leader of the Berlin Radio Symphony Orchestra.'

'That sounds suspiciously like the opening line of a GDR joke,' Stradivarius huffed, placing the violin case flat on the floor. He walked forwards, with arms extended, and they embraced.

'Let us drink to yet another musical triumph,' he proposed and turned to the bookshelves.

'Would that be 'The Tractor Oratorio' or 'The Steelworks Symphony'?'

'You were always a musical philistine,' Stradivarius grumbled good-naturedly as he ran a palm along the book spines. 'No,' he said, pulling a volume and liberating the bottle behind it, 'the programme announced Eisler's *Johannes Faustus.*'

'And you performed?'

'A piece by Meyer, celebrating party politics and more accessible to the masses.'

He magicked two glasses from behind a bust of Beethoven and poured. 'No, friend,' he continued, 'Eisler is persona non grata. No less an authority than the *Neues Deutschland* attacked his *Faustus* – said it was a slap in the face to German national feeling. To German national feeling,' he toasted, 'wherever it might be.'

They touched glasses and he sprawled in the armchair. Claus had been close enough to smell his breath. His friend had played a few bars after the performance, he surmised.

'And how are things in your cultural wilderness?' Stradivarius demanded. 'Lots of decadent oompa oompa, I presume?'

'Lots,' Claus conceded, 'and jazz and cabaret.' He drew out that last word to make Stradivarius wince. 'But,' he added, holding up a hand to forestall the indignant musician, 'we also have wall-to-wall Schoenberg.'

'Schoenberg!' the big man exploded. 'Atonal rubbish – anti-music. Bastard never had any formal training and ends up a professor of composition at a university in California.' He took a long, soothing swig. 'I was hoping you'd come,' he said quietly, 'someone of the old school. I said only you could talk them out of this madness.'

'Which particular madness, Anton?' It was the oldest trick in the book, to encourage revelation by dropping code names and suggesting they had stepped out of the game. He felt ashamed.

'This fucking uprising,' Anton said. 'Christ's sake, Claus, the tail does not wag the dog. Ulbricht is the Ivans' pet puppet, do you think they'll let us cut his strings?'

'No.'

'Good,' Anton sighed. 'I knew you wouldn't swallow that story.'

'Are there other stories, Anton?'

A furtive look weaselled across Anton's face. He shook his head and smiled. 'You're the clever one,' he said, raising his glass. 'You know how it works.'

'I know how it works on our side, Anton, but you're the man on the ground here. You're the one who tours Leipzig, Dresden and Rostok with the orchestra. Nobody on our side has that kind of access.'

'True,' Anton allowed. He leaned forward conspiratorially, although they both knew the apartment was free of listening devices. Locals made fun of the idea that such things could exist in the GDR. They claimed you knew when you were being bugged if you came home and found a six-foot cabinet in your apartment, wired up to a diesel-generator on the street. The GDR could afford to employ an army of informers but it had yet to produce sophisticated surveillance equipment.

'Let's start with the basic score,' the musician suggested. 'The overture is made by our employers. It finds a resonance among the disaffected. Promises and money change hands. Then the *allegro* movement – the feverish planning, contacts and objectives. Up tempo to the *allegro con brio*.' He began waving his arms as if conducting an orchestra. 'Marches, speeches, demands and resistance,' he said feverishly, slapping his palms together like cymbals. He waved his hands to silence the imaginary orchestra. 'A new movement begins to insinuate itself, like the Russian folk music that rises up and begins to overpower the 'Marseillaise' in the *1812*. Remember the guns! The cannons begin to boom after the da-da-das until the world is full of booming and then—'

He dropped his hands and lay back exhausted.

'It will be a massacre,' he whispered bleakly, grinding the heel of his palms into his eye sockets. 'I told them as much in Leipzig, Dresden, Rostok and in Lenin Strasse. Turn the page,' he said, mimicking the movement with a languid hand. 'Story number two is that our masters are singing from a different hymn sheet. I know I'm mixing my metaphors but I'm weary,' he said apologetically. 'The story goes that the agency want what Ivan has always proclaimed – perpetual revolution. Only over here, of course,' he added with a grimace, 'only here and in the other tame Soviet states. Feed their hunger with dollars and let them consume themselves – let them nibble away at different parts of the empire like ants on an elephant, so that it uses more and more resources to keep them at bay. Apart from that, the GDR is rife with rumours that range from the sublime to the ridiculous.'

'Humour me, Anton.'

'Very well. Stalin is to be retired.'

'Oh, for God's sake, Anton, they've been saying that since forty-five.'

'I know, I know,' Anton responded petulantly, 'but this time they're saying the gun will be Russian but the bullet will be ours.'

'You've lost me.'

'Gehlen, my friend. Remember Gehlen?'

'Yes.'

'He was one of yours from the old days. *Abwehr*, intelligence, yes? He read the runes and jumped ship to the Americans, took the brightest and the best with him.'

'Everybody knows that. It's common knowledge that he brought the scientists—'

'And the poisoners and the mind-benders,' Anton interrupted. 'They're the new Praetorian Guard in the agency. You and me? We're just assets. We can be traded or cashed. Remember Kolbe?' Anton demanded as the other man shook his head. 'Kolbe gave the director all that stuff on the rockets. And where is he now? He's a machinist in America. The agency has no loyalty, my friend. You want more rumours? There's a new religious order the agency will finance through the Vatican Bank to buy people in high places. They're called the Fratres. There's even talk of an American pope – a Cardinal Spellman. Do you want some more?'

'No, Anton,' Claus said heavily, 'I've heard enough. Let me get you a drink.' He poured a generous measure and handed it to the sweating Anton.'

'You're not drinking?'

'I'm going back tonight.'

'To you and me,' Anton toasted, 'the fucking expendables.'

'Who did you talk to, Anton?'

The musician opened his mouth and closed it again. He took a quick drink to mask the confusion in his eyes. 'You know,' he said vaguely. 'Sources.'

'Which sources, Anton?'

'Hellman in Rostok, Schweitz in Leipzig – you know those people,' he protested.

'Schweitz was turned, Anton.'

'Wha— Oh Christ,' he whispered. 'I didn't know. I swear to you, on my mother's—'

'It doesn't matter,' Claus said soothingly.

Anton looked at him and Claus saw the realisation widen his

blue eyes. He looked into the fire and, when he turned back, he was relieved to see Anton look so composed.

'I'm glad it's you,' Anton said, resting his head on the back of the armchair. 'I always thought of you as having a soul,' he said drowsily. His eyes brightened suddenly with panic. 'Will it hurt?'

'Do you feel any pain?'

'No. Ah,' he breathed and a sad smile softened his face. 'You were always a true friend,' he said and closed his eyes.

'Is there anything you'd like, Anton?'

'Music.'

Claus rummaged in the rack under the record player. He held the record carefully by the rim and lowered it gently to the turntable. Fouré's 'Requiem' rose like incense in the apartment. He took a rug and draped it over his friend.

'Claus?'

'Yes, Anton.'

'Thank you – thank you for not playing Schoenberg,' he whispered and died.

BASILICA DI SAN CLEMENTE, ROME

San Clemente was a disappointment. Karl thought the bell tower looked like an architectural afterthought, stuck to the side of the church by someone who had more money than taste. Then he stepped into the cobbled courtyard and forgot his reservations. Flowering shrubs edged the area before the church and their scent soothed him as he twisted the circular latch and entered San Clemente. At the top of the main aisle, the enclosure for the choir contained five Dominicans. They were dressed in their traditional garb of cream-coloured, hooded cassocks and black tabards. The plain chant of the Holy Office overflowed the enclosure and echoed around the walls and he waited respectfully until they had finished. As the little group stowed their books, a tall figure detached himself and strode to meet the visitor.

'We're not the Sistine Choir, are we?' he said. He was taller than Karl and the cassock strained to contain his powerful upper body. Karl thought he had the face of Michelangelo's Moses, though without the beard, all high bumps on brows and cheekbones and shadows underneath.

'You Karl Hamner?'

'Yes. Father O'Donnell?'

'Hugh O'Donnell, in the flesh,' he said and crushed Karl's hand in greeting. 'And what do you know of San Clemente, Karl Hamner?' he asked.

'Nothing.'

'Nothing? But Emil said you were—'

'A historian? Yes.'

'And I thought—'

'That a historian knows everything about history.'

'Well, yes, I suppose so.'

'Actually no. We know a lot about a little history, Father – usually what we study for a thesis. What we do know is how to read and research. I plan to start with the books.'

'Good God, man, we have thousands of books. Which one will you start with?'

'The visitor's guidebook.'

Father O'Donnell scratched vigorously at a spot behind his ear.

'D'you drink, Karl Hamner?'

'Yes.'

'Good. It's time for lunch and I could murder a drink.'

He took Karl around the side aisles to admire the paintings and frescos. As they passed the choir enclosure, Father O'Donnell laughed. 'That's been preserved from the sixth century,' he said ruefully, 'you'd think we'd have the chanting right by now. Emil tells me you're writing a book.'

'Yes.'

'And?'

'And?'

Father O'Donnell placed his hand on Karl's shoulder. 'Let me explain something to you, Karl,' he said. 'The Dominicans are the Order of Preachers and the Irish are professional talkers. It's a lethal mix. D'ye follow?'

'Yes.'

'The Irish Dominicans are culturally incapable of monosyllabic or single-sentence answers. If you could see your way to using two sentences in our conversations, I'd be eternally grateful.'

'I'll try, Father. It's difficult for an Austrian,' Karl added.

'Good lad. Now, let's recap. You said you were writing a book.'

'I did.'

'Karl!'

'Sorry. I'm writing a book about the Jews of Rome during the reign of Pius the Twelfth.'

The priest sighed. 'I'll murder Emil Dupont,' he muttered.

'Will that be a problem for you, Father?'

'Karl, lad,' the Dominican confided, 'the Irish Dominicans have been in San Clemente since the sixteenth century. A lot of popes have come and gone in that time. I suspect we'll survive Pacelli. Whether the Church survives him is another matter. Just don't tell the rest of the lads, okay? What they don't know won't trouble them.'

'The lads', Karl discovered, were the four Dominicans already seated at the refectory table. They rose courteously for the guest and their superior made the introductions.

'This is Anselm,' he said, indicating to a frail, elderly priest with a cheerful face. 'He's from County Cavan in Ireland, but no one's perfect. Anselm has been in San Clemente since Adam was a boy. He's encyclopaedic about the place so pick his brains. This young fella is Roberto, hails all the way from Malta. He's really an Irishman with a tan. Roberto is our resident archaeologist, so you two should have plenty to talk about. Canice teaches Canon Law at the Gregorian University, whenever they can roust him from the library.' The owlish, middle-aged priest greeted Karl in fluent German.

'He's also a terrible show-off,' Father O'Donnell sniffed. 'And this is Brother Sylvester.'

Karl sensed a lack of enthusiasm in the superior's voice. It was echoed in the perfunctory greeting he received from the scrawny young man who avoided eye contact.

'Sylvester is our bursar,' Father O'Donnell continued. 'He cooks the books and shakes the tourists down for shekels. Shake his hand but count your fingers.'

The meal resumed and they talked and laughed, except for Father Anselm who was quite deaf and Brother Sylvester who managed to be present and yet apart. One by one, the others drifted from the refectory, leaving the superior to entertain their guest. 'This is all you'll need to get you up and running,' Father O'Donnell said, sliding a thin pamphlet across the table. 'Later on, you can bone up on the second level.'

'Second level?'

'Ah, yes. Father Mulooly, a predecessor of mine in the eighteen hundreds, had a yen for archaeology. Bloody man dug the ground out from under us, you could say. Anyway, he found a fourth-century church and a catacomb under San Clemente.'

'That should be interesting.'

'Did I mention the third level?' Father O'Donnell asked innocently, as he reached for the wine jug.

'It must have slipped your mind.'

'Third floor down, we have an altar to Mithras and a few other bits and bobs. Roberto is burrowing away down there.'

And what is your profession, Father O'Donnell?'

'I'm an archivist at the Vatican Secret Archives,' the priest said with a twinkle. 'Emil didn't mention that, now, did he?'

'No, he didn't.'

'It must have slipped his mind,' Father O'Donnell said and winked.

MOSCOW

A sleek, black car waited for them outside the Moscow train station. It rested low on broad tyres and the door made a solid sound when he pulled it closed. The rear seat was upholstered in velvet. He ran his fingertips over the fabric and they tingled. It smelled of cigars and – perfume! Puzzled, he looked at the driver and saw a bob of blonde hair hanging precisely between a military cap and a slender neck. He turned to Gregor who raised an amused eyebrow. 'A woman, Stefan,' he whispered, 'remember them?' He said something in Russian and the driver laughed and replied. 'I said you find her beautiful,' Gregor translated. 'She said you're no horse's ass yourself. It's a compliment, Stefan,' he added at Stefan's look of confusion.

Stefan felt the colour rise up his neck until his cheeks burned. He glanced in the mirror and, for a second, the driver's eyes locked on his. She nodded and he looked away. Gregor spoke again and she detoured to take them through Red Square. The Kremlin hunkered behind a high wall on their right. Bulbous domes peered above the parapet, like tulips in a private garden. Lenin's tomb crouched under the wall, squat and plain with a ribbon of pilgrims snaking from the entrance. At the mouth of the square, they passed St Basil's and he craned his neck to watch the bubble-domes float past the window. 'Eggs,' he wheezed, 'in a basket.' It was the longest sentence he had said in eight years. He felt exhausted and leaned against the headrest as they crossed the Moscow River, left the city and tunnelled under endless woods.

'Thanks?' he asked Gregor as the driver came around to open his door.

'What? Oh, *spasibo*.'

'*Spasibo*,' he said, keeping his eyes on his feet.

'*Pazhalusta*,' she replied, grabbing him in a bear hug and kissing him warmly on both cheeks.

'She says you're welcome,' Gregor said. 'You are very welcome, Stefan,' he added, 'to the Monastery of Saint Sergius.'

Distance didn't diminish the man who waited for them inside the arch. He was huge, Stefan thought, topping his own six feet by a good two inches. He was enveloped in a Russian Orthodox habit but it stretched at the chest and hung straight at the stomach. A full, grey-flecked beard foamed over the lower part of his face and steady, brown eyes examined the visitors.

'Abbot,' Gregor said after they'd bowed.

'Patriarch,' the abbot rumbled.

Stefan detected a layer of tension in the words and tone and wondered if he really was welcome. That reservation evaporated instantly when the abbot looked directly at him.

'Small little fucker,' he observed pleasantly.

Gregor coughed. 'I should explain,' he said, 'that the abbot learned his Hungarian from Hungarian prisoners of war, during the war against the fascists.'

Stefan nodded dumbly.

'It's peaceful here, Stefan,' Gregor said. 'I'm leaving you with Father Abbot for a while. I'll come to visit and we'll talk.' He embraced the young man and bowed again to the abbot. '*Spasibo*,' he said formally.

'Come,' the abbot said.

Stefan stood rooted to the path.

'What?'

'Sound.'

He had felt it while the two men were saying goodbye. It was a vibration that hummed under his feet and he allowed himself to sink into the sound until he recognised human voices. '*Basso profundo*,' the choirmaster at the seminary had said longingly, when confronted with gangly tenors and baritones. Stefan stepped away to a side path and followed the strengthening sound until he arrived at the closed door of a basilica. He placed his ear against the door and the chanting possessed him. As he listened, the plain chant line fell away to a descant, falling to notes he felt rather than heard. When the full choir joined the leader, the marrow of his bones seemed to resonate. He peeled his ear from the door and placed his fingertips against the wood.

'Enter?' the abbot offered.

He shook his head. He had been there once, he could never go back.

The abbot's quarters resembled an antique shop he remembered in Budapest, a particularly untidy antique shop. The walls were almost invisible behind the glaze of icons. They were mostly Madonnas, only their doleful faces visible through silver visors. Heavy vestments lounged on splay-footed chairs and books. He'd never seen so many books gathered together in the one place, not even in the seminary library.

'Your bunk,' the abbot said, pointing to a door recessed in an icon-crusted wall. 'Food?'

'On the train,' Stefan said.

'What food?'

Stefan searched his memory and the abbot's face. The face had a wistful look and he wondered at the standard of food in the monastery. 'Borsch,' his memory supplied.

'Ah, borsch,' the abbot said disappointed. 'Horse piss.' He motioned Stefan to a chair and sat opposite. 'My Hungarian,' he began slowly, 'not good. Hungarian officer teach me. Fascist bastard, yes. Teach not much,' he added regretfully, 'I shoot him. Tomorrow,

Russian, I teach you. Bunk,' he added.

'Goodnight,' Stefan offered tentatively, and waited in trepidation for the reply.

'Goodnight,' the abbot answered and smiled at the young man's relief.

His bedroom reminded Stefan of the one he'd had in the seminary. He toured the tiny room, touching everything – jug, basin, desk, wardrobe and bed. The mattress was thin but yielding under his fingers. The blankets were woven from coarse wool, but they were thick and the bed linen smelled of flowers. He could have slept on a plough blade. An oil lamp, with a rose-tinted mantle, warmed the whitewashed walls. Thankfully, there was only a single icon. Despite the weight of silver, he could see a young man on a horse plunging a lance into a dragon. Michael the Archangel, he remembered before his eyes closed.

The monastery fare, he discovered, was plain but plentiful. After they'd shared a breakfast of porridge, coarse brown bread, salty butter and stewed coffee, the abbot went off for an hour to deal with community matters. He told Stefan he was free to walk the grounds and explore. There were a number of churches, cluttered with the obligatory icons. He spent most of the hour marvelling at an iconostasis, the decorative metal grille that marked the boundary between the laity and the sanctuary. The monks he encountered were elderly – they bowed when he approached and then went back to their tasks.

Russian language classes took up two hours in the morning and a further two hours after lunch. The abbot proved to be a good teacher, insisting that Stefan watch his mouth as he pronounced the words and reflecting the meaning in his expression, tone and body language. To his surprise, Stefan discovered he had an 'ear' for Russian. He reasoned that it might have been as a result of his enforced abstinence from communication or the hours he'd devoted to listening. Whatever the reason, he was delighted to find that words and phrases began to lodge in his head and trip from his tongue, falteringly at first and then more fluently. When they walked in the grounds together, the abbot made a game of pointing at random objects and asking his pupil to name them. An added bonus, as far as Stefan was concerned, was that the abbot's Hungarian was also improving. At least, Stefan thought gratefully, he was using fewer expletives. The big man seemed genuinely surprised to discover the real meaning of the phrases he'd used so freely. In the evenings, they sat either side of the wood-burning stove in companionable silence or not, as their mood dictated. The abbot smoked a crusty pipe and used it as a conductor's baton whenever he grew animated. As the evenings grew colder, they spent longer periods in the glow of the stove, building word bridges beyond the realm of objects to reminiscence and feelings.

'I was a partisan,' the abbot confided one evening through a haze of pipe smoke.

'How did you become a partisan?' Stefan asked carefully, translating the Hungarian in his head into serviceable Russian. He hadn't yet begun to think in Russian.

'War,' the abbot sighed. It was the word he used most often as if it explained everything. 'I lived in the Ukraine. We were *kulaks.*'

'*Kulaks?*'

'Farmers. The Russians allowed us to own the land and sell what we grew. The Ukraine fed Russia,' he said proudly. 'When the fascists came, they took chickens and bread – it was just food,' he said, waving the pipe dismissively. 'There were others who came later, after the soldiers. Waffen-SS,' he spat and looked at the pipe as if it was responsible. 'They …' He paused and drew his head back into the shadows of the high-winged chair. 'Only Vladimir and I escaped. Vladimir was my brother. We went to the woods, even the Waffen didn't go there – except to bury. And even then, they didn't go to the deep woods. There were men there like us. We took guns from dead soldiers and we fought. What is your father's name?' he asked suddenly.

'Nagy.'

'That is his surname, yes?'

'Yes.'

'Not his patronymic, his—?'

'Baptismal name?' Stefan said it in Hungarian and mimed pouring water over his head.

'*Da, da*, his baptismal name,' the abbot said.

'Michael.'

'Then I call you Stefan Mikailovich. It is the Russian way, *da*?'

'*Da.*'

The abbot settled back into the shadows and resumed his narrative.

'When a man kills another man, he kills part of himself. My brother, Vladimir, liked to kill fascists. The others and myself took them to the Red Army and exchanged them for bullets and food. When the fascists came back from Moscow, they were beaten. They didn't know snow, they'd never seen such snow. Many just lay down. Others came to our camp, to sit at the fire. Vladimir wanted to kill them. He had a wife and daughters before the Waffen came. One day, I see a young fascist soldier in the snow. I am hiding in the woods. There is a girl with me from a place near my village. I take my gun and run from the trees. He is lying, looking up at the sky, so young. I remember – things and I want to kill him, to shoot him in his head. Not like Vladimir. With Vladimir it is always a belly-shot so they die slowly. The girl, she tells me no. I am angry but she looks at me. She says he saves her from the Waffen.' His pained smile gleamed in the shadows. 'She had green eyes. "He save me from the Waffen", she said and she kissed him. I never saw her again. When

I get back to my comrades, Vladimir is excited. "Come," he says, "come." He takes me to the woods. There are fascists hanging – maybe twenty. "Christmas," Vladimir says, "Christmas." After this, I don't talk to Vladimir.' His voice had faded to a whisper and Stefan feared he'd fallen asleep. The story had knotted his stomach but he suspected there was more to come. He thought it might be worse but he needed to know.

When the abbot resumed, his voice was as raw as a fresh wound.

'Vladimir captured a priest. Said he was a fascist. "Vladimir," I said, "he is a priest." "He came with the fucking fascists," Vladimir said. I told him that this man left the fascists to be a priest in a village. It goes on.'

He stopped again and wiped his hands over his face as if to clean a memory.

'I walked away, into the woods. When I came back, they had—' He used a Russian word Stefan didn't know.

'What?'

The abbot held his hands from his body in the shape of the crucified Christ. They suffered together in a long silence.

'Patriarch came the next day with Red Army soldiers,' the abbot resumed. 'Vladimir tells him the story and calls me coward. Patriarch hangs them all. I see Vladimir dancing under a tree. Patriarch says Stalin does not want two armies. I am sent to gulag and then patriarch comes for me and brings me here. This is why I become a priest. You see this cross?' He tipped the crucifix on his chest. 'It was his – the priest's.'

The fire had died and they embraced as they said goodnight.

'Go to bed, Stefan Mikailovich,' the abbot murmured. 'I pray you will not dream.'

FRAU BLUM'S HOTEL, WEST BERLIN

Claus had immersed himself so deeply inside the hapless Otto Plummer that the soldier hardly looked at him when he shuffled through the checkpoint. Hope, he thought, is what makes people stand out from the herd on this side of the wire. He would try to rediscover some, after he'd wheeled his bicycle into the West. He detoured to source a bone for the dog and Goebbels seemed grateful, in a wary way. Nobody gives anything for nothing these days, he thought, when the dog passed on licking the hand he proffered. Feeling rebuffed, he chained the bicycle a bit more tightly than was necessary. The melancholy that had dulled his senses disappeared when he confronted Frau Blum. Not that she said anything. She had pared communication to a limited range of disapproving looks and inclinations of the head. Her attention to her knitting needles was as focused as it had been before he'd crossed over, but the needles seemed to flash a little faster and her high cheekbones bloomed red. A faint tang of cigarette smoke at the foot of the stairs confirmed what he'd suspected and he dispensed with the usual precautions.

Medusa sat on the high-backed chair, just beyond the reach of the streetlight stretching through the window, her cigarette pulsing on and off in the shadows. He dumped the hateful 'samples bag' on the bed and pulled up a stool.

'Sell many shoes?'

'I think boots are the coming thing,' he said, easily. 'Military-style boots are becoming very popular.'

'Our friends?'

'Our separated brethren remain an uncomfortable mix of communism and cupidity,' he said. 'They're delusional,' he continued, 'worshipping an ugly bicycle like the Golden Calf in the desert.' He wasn't sure if she appreciated the biblical allusion – you could never be sure with Medusa. 'They haven't a prayer,' he stated flatly. 'Oh, they have no shortage of excitement and talk – Christ, how they talk – but none of that will matter when the tanks roll in, will it?'

'No,' she agreed.

'Then why—?'

'Oh, Claus,' she said irritably, 'stop playing the fucking White Knight.' The cigarette tip glowed fiercely. 'It's a game,' she exhaled. 'You're the hotshot chess player, so figure it out.' She seemed to relent her outburst and continued in a more I've-told-you-this-a-thousand-times tone. 'Pawns irritate the shit out of the big pieces and get shafted. Think of it as an acceptable level of attrition. Both sides flex their muscles and nobody, of any consequence, gets hurt.'

'It seems a big investment for a small dividend.'

'You've got it assways,' she said tartly. 'The beauty of it is that we get to play with their pawns. We give the foot soldiers the money and turn them loose on their masters. We do it all the time, all across the board – in the DDR, Poland, Hungary, Romania … The other side is so taken up with squashing pawns that they miss the big moves. Get it?'

He nodded to simulate agreement.

'Stradivarius?'

'Like you said – paranoid, all the usual ramblings. Stalin is to be retired etcetera, etcetera. Strad was always a few strings short of a symphony.'

'Was?'

'Was.'

'Good. He play any other tunes on his paranoia?'

'Never stopped,' he grunted. He hoped she'd be satisfied and let the dead rest.

'Like?'

He would need to be careful. He would need to mix just the right amount of world-weariness, incredulity and regret in his answer. She'd expect regret and be suspicious at its absence. Strad had been more than an asset to him, she knew that.

'Like,' he repeated, 'Gehlen and mind control and – oh, yes,' he huffed a brief laugh, 'an American pope and a crusading religious order. Poor Strad, reality was never enough for him.'

The cigarette tip had remained unmoving. Something he'd mentioned had caught her attention.

'Gehlen?'

'Nothing new,' he assured her, 'the usual stuff about their Nazis and our Nazis.'

She'd picked the obvious one to query, the safe option. Where she took it from there would be interesting, he thought.

'You said a crusading religious order?'

'His very words,' he said promptly, 'salted with all the usual tics and mannerisms. He called them … the Fratres, yes, that was it.' The pause would suggest he hadn't given it enough credence to remember the name. Now, it was time to push. 'Know anything about that?'

She stubbed her cigarette and took her time lighting its successor.

'Dime a dozen,' she said, blowing smoke towards the ceiling. 'Nuclear capability, impending apocalypse, religious crusades – you're the scholar, you know how it pans out.'

It sounded rehearsed. They'd both been in Rome when Max Steiger was pushing for power near the end of the war. She'd saved his life from the mad bastards, which is how he'd come to join the agency. And now she was dismissing it all as a kind of millennium fever. 'Who's the American pope supposed to be, anyway?'

'I think he said it was that New York cardinal, Spelling? Spellman, that's the one.'

'Not like you to be so vague, Claus.'

Maybe he'd gilded the lily.

'Strad could be infuriating,' he said, running a hand through his hair. 'You try to argue a point and he's off on another, even more fabulous than the first. That was Strad.'

'What about Stalin?'

'He wouldn't be Strad if he didn't have a variation on the old story. This time, the gun will be Russian but the bullet will be ours. What sort of—? Look, I told him, Stalin is an old man. Why would they go to all that trouble? What would change? Swap Stalin for Beria? *Plus ça change*. They'd never stomach Molotov, not after the Ribbentrop fiasco. Who else is there?'

'They say Khrushchev is playing a good game,' she said.

'No,' he said, flapping his hand in the smoke between them. 'He's Ukrainian. Anyway, he's a party man – good at organising things on the ground. A nuts-and-bolts man, isn't that what Americans say?'

'You may have to go back,' she said, stubbing her cigarette to signal the end of the conversation. 'Get some rest. I'll be in touch.'

And she was gone.

He listened for the creak of the loosened stair riser and relaxed when it obliged. The bed tempted him and he went to sit on the chair she'd vacated. He remembered an old soldier's aphorism and smiled. 'There are brave soldiers and there are old soldiers but there are no brave, old soldiers.' But it wasn't about bravery, it was about brains. He'd been able to think his way into and out of the SD – when the time had been right to hitch his star to a rising man and he'd secured new allies in the Vatican before the inevitable downfall of the Reich. She'd suggested the whole thing was a game of chess and he imagined the board before him, trying to plot the agency's moves. The pawns didn't merit much thought. We finance the uprising to fail. We do the same all across the Eastern Bloc to keep the Soviets busy – too busy with internal bushfires to gear up for expansion. She'd allowed the Gehlen reference to slide by. Why? It was an old story but even an old story might have merited a little exasperation. He'd been an interrogator – still was, when the need arose. The cue not taken, the obvious left unsaid, could be significant. She'd side-stepped the Fratres and the American pope – the former reduced to a symptom of apocalyptic, religious fervour; the latter evaded with an accusation. 'Not like you to be vague, Claus.' Medusa, he knew, was clever, manipulative, lethal and, yes, clinically insane, but sometimes she succumbed to something as ordinary as pride. It was the reflex of the insider to hint at just how inside she was. So, he mused, the big money is on Khrushchev. He filed it away and continued with his reflection. Stradivarius hadn't been retired because he'd talked to the wrong people. He'd been retired because of what he'd heard. He'd only talked about it to – him. He took a few seconds to let that settle in his consciousness. Medusa had effectively put him under house arrest, when she'd suggested he might have to cross over again. *You've been on both sides of the gun, at one time or another,* he reminded himself. *Put yourself in Medusa's chair. How would I go about retiring me?* He could indulge the game for, maybe, ten minutes, he thought – estimating he had an hour before Medusa got things organised and the initiative moved from him to her.

There were so many ways to retire an asset. Putting something in his 'samples bag' next time he crossed and having it discovered by the border guards was as good a way as any – particularly if the guards had been tipped off beforehand. She'd liked the idea of using their pawns to do their dirty work. It was tempting, but he knew she wouldn't choose that option. Claus Fischer knew too much about too many things to ever hand him over to the enemy. It would happen on this side, he was certain of that. He checked his watch again. In about fifteen minutes, she'd get word to the Berlin network that he'd gone rogue. They'd be expected to report any contact or sighting, and they would. It wasn't personal, Stradivarius had understood that. *I'd hit me right here,* he thought. The hotel is a safe house with a guest list of one and Frau Blum could be counted on to see, hear and speak no evil. *Time to go,* he decided. He leaned his back against the door and walked towards the centre of the room until a floorboard protested. Swiss businessman, he thought, as he sorted through the bag of travel papers he'd flushed from the burrow under the floor. The Swiss excited no emotion except envy. The gun might give rise to more passionate emotions but he might need it in the short term.

A small wad of Swiss francs and a larger wad of lira bulked his pockets as he negotiated the stairs. Frau Blum usually went for coffee and apfelstrudel at this time, and he gained the back door without challenge. Goebbels looked up hopefully and he patted him apologetically as he passed. His pursuer wasn't so fortunate – he hadn't paid the toll in titbits and bones and the growling behind him added energy to Claus' flight. He took the time to lock the garden door behind him. It gave him thinking time as the growling escalated to attack. *If there was a backup man, where would he be?* He guessed the backup was the one who'd come around the side of the hotel and met Goebbels. A popping sound and the sudden cessation of barking confirmed his hunch that the assassin in the open would have the silencer.

He started to run, blessing the time he'd spent memorising the maze of alleys behind the hotel. As soon as he hit a busy thoroughfare, he slowed to a walk. A taxi leaned into the kerb and he slid inside one door as a couple exited the other. 'Hauptbahnhof,' he grunted, keeping his chin tucked to his chest so that the brim of his hat shadowed his face. When the taxi joined a queue at a busy intersection, he dumped a pile of bills in the driver's lap and exited the taxi. There was enough money in the pile to keep the driver's head down and he moved purposefully along the pavement to a tram stop. His ticket entitled him to go all the way to the terminus, but he got off two stops short of it and walked along a broad avenue. Large houses stretched either side of the avenue, their top storeys peering suspiciously over high garden walls.

'Frau Geller,' he said, flashing a card at the maid. 'Herr Liszt, come to tune the piano.'

She let him step into the hallway and disappeared. The lady who entered through the double doors of the drawing room had the presence and poise of the true performer. 'Herr Liszt,' she said with a wary smile, 'how prompt you are. Come,' she commanded, 'the piano is in here.'

He followed obediently into the music room and stood, holding his hat in both hands while she raised the lid and began to play. It was 'Tristesse' by Chopin and he found his sense of urgency ebbing away with the rise and fall of the music.

Marta Schiller had been the toast of the GDR concert platforms until he'd offered her a more lucrative tour, west of the wire. In exchange, she'd agreed to become an asset. She might have agreed to become more than that, but he'd nothing more to offer her. After a short time, she'd married Franz Geller, a Gehlen operative currently working as an aide to the West German Chancellor. It had been a marriage of convenience for Marta, a propaganda coup for the government and a rich source of intelligence for Fischer, all rolled into one. It also had the added advantage, as far as Fischer was concerned, of being unknown to the agency. Every handler had agents who were 'off the books'. It was a reality the agency had learned to live with after the war, when the quality of intelligence product was more important than its provenance.

'You play beautifully, Frau Geller,' he said.

'That's what they pay me for,' she said sadly. 'Which piece would you like me to perform, Herr Liszt?'

'"The Ride of the Valkyries",' he said, hoping she remembered the code. Her eyes narrowed but her fingers never faltered on the keys.

'And the venue?'

'I'll tell you on the way,' he said. 'Think of it as a farewell performance, Frau Geller.'

Her fingers fled the piano for sanctuary in her lap.

'The performance fee will be generous,' he continued. 'I've always believed an artist should have independent means and the freedom to choose their own career path.'

He knew she was an intelligent woman and wouldn't need explanations. He also knew that her marriage to Franz Geller was a façade he maintained for political purposes. For the second time in their short relationship, he was offering Marta Schiller her freedom. She closed the piano carefully.

'It has always been such a good companion,' she said huskily, stroking the lid.

'I hope there are – other companions, Marta,' he said.

'Yes,' she said, firming her jaw and looking him in the eye. 'I've wanted to visit for the longest time. There's a cigarette kiosk at the end of the avenue,' she said briskly. 'One hour!'

The car with the diplomatic plates pulled up at the kiosk and he slipped into the back. He lay across the seat and pulled the rug around him.

He slept soundly, confident that the diplomatic plates would shield them from checks and inspections on their way to Switzerland.

When he woke, the mountains crowding the windows signalled that they had crossed the border.

'You can sit up front now,' she said.

'How did you know I was awake?'

'You stopped snoring.'

Berne didn't admire its reflection in a lake, like Lucerne or Geneva. He liked the way the old city sat up proudly in the horseshoe created by the Aare River. They drove by the bank and he directed her to a parking space near the Zytglogge. A hundred yards from the clock tower, they found a coffee shop under the covered mediaeval shopping promenade, where she enjoyed coffee and pastry and he watched passersby from the shadows.

'It's always like this for you, isn't it?' she said, dabbing her lips with a napkin.

'I have a shadow, even at night, Marta,' he said. 'You told me that yourself.'

'Yes,' she accepted.

He wrote a number and code word on a napkin and pushed it across the table. 'You have identification?' he asked and she nodded. 'That's all you'll need at the bank.'

She took it and put it in her purse.

'If they ask, you never saw me,' he said gently.

'I won't be lying,' she said.

The train huffed from the station, as if annoyed that it was departing three minutes after the advertised time. He sat by the window, behind the barrier of a Swiss newspaper, and watched the placenames soften to Como and Milano. Two stops before Rome's Tiburtina Station, he left the train and caught a bus. He planned to contact Monsignor Emil Dupont as soon as he arrived in Rome.

Near the end of the war, he'd made the first contact with the Vatican through a friendly, neutral embassy, offering his services under the code name 'The Good Thief'. It had been his insurance against life after the armistice. The documents he'd passed to the monsignor had slowed the rise of the Fratres, but not stopped them. It was ironic, he thought, as the bus paused at yet another rural village, that Medusa had rescued him from the vengeance of the Fratres. He wondered if even the Vatican could save him from Medusa.

SAINT SERGIUS MONASTERY, STRELNA, NEAR LENINGRAD

Gregor came and the abbot disappeared to allow them privacy. On his first visit, he tried to fill gaps in Stefan's knowledge of the world.

'Your father is dead,' he said. 'I'm sorry. His neighbours told me he searched for you. He went to the seminary and the bishop but they wouldn't talk to him. He wanted to go to the Waffen but his friends stopped him. They said it would make things worse. He died and they buried him on his farm.'

He walked around the room looking at the books until Stefan had composed himself.

'Your friend, Laszlo, is secretary to the new bishop. His father is a minister in the new government. Those who remained faithful to Mindszenty, the government … removed.'

Stefan turned that single word this way and that in his head but didn't ask for an explanation.

'The others, we now call 'Progressive Catholics'. They obey the new Hungarian government, not Rome.'

'Me?'

'They think you're dead.'

'Wha— Why?'

'Because I told them so. It's important they believe that, Stefan. Later, I'll tell you why.'

Gregor drew an atlas from the bookshelf and opened it on the table. Stefan watched, unblinking, as Gregor traced the borders of the new Europe. After an hour, Gregor leaned back and rubbed that familiar spot between his eyebrows.

'It's a lot for you to comprehend.'

'Yes.'

Gregor steepled his fingers under his chin. 'Let's make it simple,' he sighed. 'There is West and East. The West is America and its allies. The East is the Soviet Union and its satellites.'

'Is there … peace?'

Gregor took a long time to answer. 'No,' he said finally. 'There's a different kind of war.'

'I don't understand.'

'Let me explain. It's called the Cold War, the kind of war that is declared but cannot be fought because it would mean the end of everything and everybody. The victor would be waist-deep in the ashes of his own country. There is a bomb,' Gregor continued and the flickering light from the stove danced shadows across his face. 'At the end of the war, the American president, Truman, dropped it on the Japanese — twice. He said it would avoid invading the Japanese mainland and save thousands of American lives. It killed over one hundred and fifty thousand persons in Hiroshima. After the war, the East also developed this bomb. Now, do you understand?'

'Yes.'

'There is hope,' Gregor said softly. 'There are people — many people — in the West who don't want another war. In the East …? — he paused and pursed his lips — 'one in every three of those who died during the war was a Soviet citizen. Our economy wasn't strong before the war, it's a shambles now. Stalin talks of another war. Should he prevail—'

'The Church?' Stefan asked.

'This will be difficult for you to hear,' Gregor said, 'but I must tell you. The Roman Catholic Church is with the Americans. Not all of it,' he qualified, 'and not everyone, but the pope is. He will not make peace with communism. He will not speak to the East and regularly speaks against it. The East cannot return to what it was before the revolution.'

He cupped his hands in the middle of the map.

'There are others,' he said slowly, 'who work for a solution – a third way. East and West, there are people who talk of "peaceful co-existence". In America, it's likely that the new president, Eisenhower, would favour such a solution. He was a general during the war, he can't have any illusions about another one. In the East …' He paused and seemed to wrestle with his thoughts. 'Things could change,' he said eventually. 'If the West sent a signal that co-existence was an option.'

He pushed a forefinger across the map until it rested on Rome.

'Some of us believe that Rome can be the fulcrum, the fixed point upon which the world can turn. If Rome was to soften its stance, the rest of the world – East and West – would listen and might be persuaded. But …'

Again, he let that word dangle and Stefan wondered what other obstruction he would present.

'You are familiar with Church history, Stefan?'

'Yes, a little.'

'Me too,' Gregor said and smiled for the first time. 'I was a Professor of European Languages at Moscow University before the war. When the fascists came, we lost our entire standing army in three weeks. After that, everyone became a soldier – even professors of European languages. I served as an intelligence officer. My father would have found that amusing. But I have always been interested in Church history. That's why the abbot calls me Patriarch. It's a nickname – a nickname that took me to a gulag after the war but it's also the reason I was brought back. I persuaded some people that the Church could have a powerful influence. You remember what happened when a powerful pope became threatened by the rise of Constantinople?'

'Schism,' Stefan whispered.

'Yes. The Christian Church divided down the middle, and it remains divided. If the Roman Church can ... bend, anything is possible – even co-existence, even peace.'

His eyes had grown animated but now they grew more sombre.

'There is a new religious order in the Church called the Fratres,' he continued. 'They are led by a Father Max Steiger and their aim is to create a Europe in the old model where Church and state are two sides of the same power. Steiger ensures they dance to the prevailing papal tune. They speak of a new crusade. Against whom?'

It was his old friend, the rhetorical question, and Stefan nodded.

'They silence those who speak out and they have the ear of the pope. We suspect that if the pope and the Church knew what they do in the Church's name, it would make a difference. But they are secretive.'

'Why are you telling me this, Gregor?'

'Because I think you might be the one to tilt the balance.'

'How?'

'You've more than enough to think on for now,' Gregor said and rose to leave. 'When I come again, I'll answer that question.'

'Did you put that icon in my room, Gregor?'

'I wasn't wrong about you, Stefan,' Gregor said admiringly. 'Yes, I did,' he admitted. 'My grandmother said some people were "old souls". She said they were angels. Perhaps it takes such a one to defeat a dragon.'

BASILICA DI SAN CLEMENTE, ROME

'The church you are standing in stands on the top tier of a three-tier cake.'

The sentence arrested Sarah Walker and she stopped inside the door of the San Clemente. *Novel approach to history*, she thought.

Sarah had 'done' Rome with a group of American ex-pats shortly after her arrival and the guides had ranged from the learned to the ludicrous. She still cringed at the memory of the guy at the Colosseum yelling, 'Can you hear the lions roar?' She'd said 'ciao' to her friends and gone for a gelato.

Her day had started at six with a frugal breakfast followed by a visit to each guest in the Santa Magdalena. At seven thirty, she'd clattered down the stairs to a tiny office and updated their medical files. She'd gone back at eleven for a more informal visit and come down with the girls to the inevitable lunch of soup and bread. 'Go for a walk,' Sister Bartolomeo had ordered. 'Work, work, all the time. Go!'

She'd dawdled in the Campo de' Fiori, savouring the earthy smells from the market stalls. For a few moments, she'd paused under the brooding statue of Giordano Bruno. She'd thought the bustling market had seemed such an odd place to site the statue of a man burned at the stake. 'In the midst of life we are in death.' The phrase had come unbidden to her memory. A sudden chill in the air had sent her walking briskly beside the Tiber, letting the sound and sight of the water wash away thoughts of Bruno's messy martyrdom.

At the Colosseum, she'd joined the queue and deserted it, deciding she didn't want another hour of man's inhumanity to man. Instinctively, her feet began to retrace the route to the Santa Magdalena – *because there isn't anything else in your life*, an inner voice had nagged, *because you were always so focused on being the next Albert Schweitzer that no one could get close. But what guy could compete with Schweitzer? Oh, c'mon*, she'd shot back. *Who are we talking about here? Dicky Pender with his pimples or Seth Fleisch with his infamous halitosis? Gimme a break. It's been a long time since high school*, the voice insisted. *So, med school, huh? The only girl among the hordes of the hormonally challenged. Every time I'd looked at a guy, he'd thought I wanted an anatomy practical. That was a blast.*

She'd shaken her head, looked up and accepted that she was lost. Somewhere after the Colosseum, she'd strayed from the Tiber and taken the way less travelled. Via San Giovanni in Laterano, the street sign said helpfully. Nah, still lost. She saw a café, leaning its canopy over the sidewalk, and sat in its shade. 'Cappuccino, *per favore*,' she'd ordered and when the waiter returned, she'd asked him about the church across the street.

'San Clemente,' he'd said. 'Very historical.'

'Isn't everything,' she'd muttered into her cappuccino.

'Beneath your feet is a fourth-century Christian church,' the voice continued. 'Beneath that is a temple dedicated to the god Mithras, brought home in the second century by Roman soldiers from the wars in the east.'

She could see the tall, bearded figure and his little flock of tourists.

'This whole area has been burned twice,' he said. 'According to legend, Nero fiddled the first time and blamed the Christians, even though a lot of Roman citizens cooked over open fires in high wooden tenements – but why let facts get in the way of a good prejudice? Time passed and a new church was built here only to be burned by the Normans a thousand years later. Did people have short memories then? Just twenty-five years after the Norman fire, a new church was built on this site. You're standing in it.'

A pillar of sunlight leaned at an angle from the high windows to a spot in the centre aisle. Lured by the voice and passion of the speaker, Sarah stepped into that molten space.

'And this,' the young man said, stepping into the Schola Cantorum, 'is a souvenir from the sixth century that the builders decided to incorporate into this building. The clergy have been chanting their prayers from here for over eight hundred years. Come,' he urged and the group filed in to join him.

Karl gave them time to absorb the information. One of the Americans, Mister Wilson, was busy with his camera – again. *Why would someone come to Rome to see it through a lens?* he wondered. Mister Wilson's wife, Myra, seemed weary. He saw her slip, gratefully, into one of the choir stalls while her husband was distracted. Their two teenage daughters seemed marginally less bored than before. He would have been surprised to discover that they considered the young male guide the most interesting thing they'd seen all day. The other two adults in the party, Sam and Mrs Deedes, held hands and seemed genuinely interested in the history of San Clemente.

'Myra,' Mort Wilson barked, and his wife shot to her feet. Karl looked away to spare her embarrassment. Something flickered in the pool of sunlight in the aisle outside the Scola Cantorum and snagged his eye. The young woman who walked towards him was lit from above so that her blonde hair shone like a polished helmet. Her eyebrows, cheekbones, lips and chin were illuminated, the other parts of her face were lost in shadow. His breath hitched and caught in his chest. 'Elsa,' he whispered. As the figure stepped out of the light, it took his eyes a few moments to adjust. The young woman he was staring at had Elsa's strong features and steady eyes – but she was not Elsa.

'So what's the story with the coloured candlestick?' Mort Wilson demanded, pointing at the paschal candle.

Still winded from the experience, Karl answered distantly, 'Mosaic.'

'Seen them in Ravenna,' Mort continued. 'They got mosaics all over the walls up there, never seen it on a candlestick before.'

Karl detected a hint of accusation in his voice.

'You're correct, Mister Wilson,' he assured him. 'The churches in Ravenna were influenced by the east in their design and decoration. By the thirteenth century, a tourist would have stood on mosaic floors and looked up at walls and ceilings covered in mosaic. In the thirteenth century, the artists began to use mosaic on smaller objects. The most famous were the Cosmati family. This candlestick is one of theirs.'

He'd been holding his notes in his right hand and, distracted by the young women who stood at the edge of the group, he took his left hand from his pocket to indicate the paschal candle and its ornate holder.

'Say, isn't that a Nazi glove?'

'Pardon?'

'Your glove, where did you get it?'

'It's a Wehrmacht glove,' he replied calmly. 'I got it from my father.'

'Your daddy was a Nazi?'

'No, Mister Wilson,' Karl said, 'he was an Austrian conscript on the Russian front, as I was.'

'Austrian, German,' Mort persisted, 'same damn difference if you ask—'

'Rein it in, Mort,' Sam Deedes said firmly.

'Dammit to hell, Sam. We didn't come to Rome to be lectured by some—'

'Some kid just doing his job, Mort,' Sam Deedes interrupted. 'Now, let's just settle down here and enjoy the tour.'

'No way,' Mort Wilson huffed. 'We're leaving. Myra! Girls!'

His wife threw Karl an apologetic look before she trailed after her husband. The girls stood their ground for a moment, as if they would defy their father.

'Ellie, Mary,' Karl said, 'I think your mother is tired.'

They hurried from the enclosure, heads down and sandals slapping in protest on the marble aisle. The door slammed behind them.

'Sorry about that, son,' Sam Deedes said. 'Mort tends to get a bee in his bonnet about something and …' – he stepped closer so his wife wouldn't overhear – 'he's also a total prick.' He pressed a folded bill into Karl's hand. 'You do a good job, son,' he said. 'Honey,' he called to his wife, 'let's go catch up with Attila and his happy band.'

Again, the great door opened and closed and Karl stood in the silence.

'Guess that just leaves me.'

He'd completely forgotten about the young woman who wasn't Elsa and felt embarrassed that she'd witnessed the altercation with Mort Wilson.

'We – we were almost finished,' he said, 'except for the mosaics in the apse. Would you like to see them?'

'Wouldn't know my apse from my elbow,' she said cheerfully, steering him towards the door. 'Cut you a deal,' she suggested. 'There's this café right across the street. You pay for the cappuccinos and I promise not to slap you around the head if you mention mosaics. Deal?'

'Deal.'

When the waiter retired to his kitchen, she stretched her hand across the cappuccinos. 'I'm Sarah Walker,' she said, 'I'm an American. Right up to today, that was something I was proud of.'

'I understand the gentleman's reaction,' he said.

'You're using the word "gentleman" a little loosely there, Mister …?'

'Hamner,' he said, taking her hand. 'Karl Hamner.'

She had a firm grip and she looked him in the eye when they shook hands, as Papa had always taught him to.

'They got mosaics all over the walls in Ravenna,' she said.

It was such a perfect imitation of Mort Wilson that he burst out laughing.

'That's better,' she said. 'Drink your cappuccino.'

They sipped their coffee in companionable silence until the waiter began to set the tables for the dinner service.

'I have to get back to the hospital,' she said, turning her wrist to check her watch.

'You're in a hospital? Are you ill?'

'I'm the doctor at the Santa Magdalena.'

'I'll walk you there,' he said and moved around to hold her chair.

She liked the way he did it automatically, without ostentation. Karl Hamner wasn't out to make a big impression, she concluded, he was just a courteous guy.

'Is the Magdalena on your way?'

'No.'

Make that courteous and enigmatic, she thought. As they walked, he pointed out the monuments. She was fascinated by his knowledge of Rome. He could look at a façade and peel it like an onion to reveal the brick behind the marble.

'You're not really a tour guide, are you, Karl?'

'Yes and no.'

'You've been too long with the Irish Dominicans,' she quipped and he smiled. He had a slow smile. It seemed to well up in his eyes and overflow to crinkle his face.

'I'm a historian,' he said. 'Today is my first day working as a tour guide.'

'Coulda fooled me,' she said loyally. She began to notice other things about him, how he always placed himself kerbside of her, as a gentleman should. She remembered that because in high school, Sister Genevieve had said it was the sign of a true gentleman and because Sister Genevieve had an endless list of negative signs. She wondered why he preferred the shadowed side of the street and why he stopped so often to look in shop windows. *Could a historian really be interested in kitchenware?* Karl Hamner was a cultured and courteous man, she didn't doubt that. But his eyes said he'd lived longer than his years. And who the blue blazes was Elsa? She'd heard him whisper the name when she'd walked through the light and she'd seen the light die in his eyes when he'd realised she wasn't Elsa. And why should that matter to her? He was a nice guy but they were 'ships passing in the night' – she was going to Ethiopia.

'Sarah.'

'What?'

'This is the Magdalena.'

MONASTERY OF ST SERGIUS, STRELNA, NEAR LENINGRAD

Gregor came at midnight.

The abbot and Stefan had been talking at the stove, the abbot explaining the absence of young monks.

'Stalin reopened the churches and monasteries during the war,' he'd said. 'It's strange how God becomes popular when the Panzers are shooting up the suburbs of Moscow. We thought it even stranger that the atheist who had been a seminarian would do such a thing.' He'd laughed ruefully. 'He's a wily old wolf,' he'd continued. 'He knew that you can't erase religion by decree. The people played along, of course, as people do. They were communists in broad daylight and Orthodox after dark. He must have known that – Beria has eyes and ears everywhere, even here. So he gambled on that religious feeling. People who believed that God was on their side would fight more fiercely to defend the Motherland. It worked. I saw soldiers stand in the snow while the commissars lectured them on being faithful communists and then kneel in the snow to be blessed with an icon.'

He'd busied himself with his pipe until Stefan prompted him.

'And after the war?'

The abbot had puffed until the bowl of the pipe glowed fiercely, before replying.

'A wolf may suckle a lamb, Stefan Mikailovich, but he is always a wolf.' He'd stared at Stefan until the young man had nodded. 'After the war, it was business as usual. Most of the churches and monasteries were closed again. Did monks object? Yes! They're in the cemetery or in the gulags. The surviving communities were forbidden to take new vocations. God had served the state in its time of need and had become surplus to requirements.'

'Why did Stalin spare Saint Sergius?'

'I don't know,' the abbot had said bluntly. 'Maybe he thought it meant something to the people, like the old icons they keep on the wall of a bedroom. Who knows what Stalin thinks? We were not spared,' he'd stated flatly, 'without young monks, we were condemned to a lingering death.'

'Why did he let you come here as abbot?'

'The monks you see here,' the abbot had replied, waving his pipe stem to indicate the monastery, 'are the ones who said *da* to Stalin and survived, like icons in a museum. I don't judge them. We have all done things to survive. I said *nyet* to Stalin and was brought back from a gulag as their abbot. I am a reminder of the choice they made and they don't love me for it. So we are all together in a different kind of gulag. No one can ever say that Stalin doesn't have a sense of humour,' he concluded sadly.

Stefan had sat silently with the abbot's pain. The knock on the door had come as a relief.

'I thought I heard a wolf,' the abbot said softly, as the door opened and Gregor came in.

Stefan thought Gregor looked haggard. The lines around his eyes had tightened to stretch his skin bloodless over his cheekbones. He dragged his hat off and tossed it on a chair and the gesture, and the way his white hair spiked with friction, signalled tension.

'I will speak with Stefan alone,' he rasped. The abbot took his time knocking the ashes from his pipe into the stove and ambled away without a word. Gregor dropped into the empty chair, hunched forward on his knees and splayed his fingers to the fire. 'Last time,' he said hoarsely, 'I said I'd tell you what's expected of you.'

Stefan nodded and sat straighter in his chair.

'After I've told you,' Gregor continued doggedly, 'ask questions. I may not have answers for all of them. Some, you'll just have to discover for yourself. Understand?'

'Yes.'

Gregor told him the plan in a toneless voice. Stefan suspected that Gregor didn't want to influence his decision one way or the other. Stefan listened carefully, never taking his eyes from the man at the other side of the stove. When Gregor had finished, his shoulders sagged and his head fell forward, like a man who has put down a heavy burden.

Stefan thought it was like hearing his death named and dated by a doctor. He felt a mixture of shock and relief. The enormity of the task stunned him, and yet, hearing it articulated had reduced its potential for dread. Stefan knew from prison that not knowing made him a victim of possibilities. Gregor's toneless incantation had exorcised imagination. The waiting was over. He looked at the man who'd been the bearer of bad tidings. Gregor had brought him back from the dead. But had he done any more than his duty? Yes, he concluded. He'd been long enough in his company to sense his innate decency and long enough in prison to discern and appreciate genuine kindness. When Stefan spoke, his voice was as toneless as Gregor's had been. He resolved to show no sign of the fear that gnawed in his belly. He owed Gregor that kindness.

'Why me?' he asked.

Gregor started as if coming awake. 'Because you have a Church background and the kind of experience they'll believe,' he said. 'Also, you survived prison without dying or going insane. And you have nothing to lose, no one to return to.' He sighed, as if aware of how lacking in feeling he must sound to the young man. 'I'm sorry,' he said softly. 'They ... my superiors use that kind of language all the time. I suppose it shields them from the human implications.'

'Why do you think I'm the one, Gregor?'

There was neither reproof nor sarcasm in his tone and the other man responded immediately.

'Because you care, Stefan. Not about the Church or the Soviet Union or America or any of that, but about the truth – about doing what's right.'

'I think there's something you're not telling me, Gregor.'

Surprised, Gregor looked up then dropped his eyes again. 'Yes,' he said, 'there is. I thought I'd tell you the major part first. When you'd had a chance to think that through, I'd tell you the rest. Sorry, Stefan.'

'No need to be. Tell me the rest, Gregor.'

'If the plan has any chance of succeeding,' Gregor said slowly, 'your story will have to be authentic. Many of the people you meet will be extremely intelligent. Some will be dangerous. If they find a flaw in your story—'

'I understand. What else do your superiors want me to do?'

'To go to prison,' Gregor said. 'They want you to go to the Lubyanka prison in Moscow.' He pushed himself up from the chair. 'I'll be here at dawn for your answer,' he said.

The abbot returned sometime later. 'Do you wish to be alone?' he asked.

'Yes.'

After the abbot had gone to bed, Stefan stacked timber in the stove and sat in its light, staring into the flames. He thought of praying but dismissed the thought. He didn't think he could resume a conversation after an eight-year silence. As he sat, the timber grumbled in the stove, shifting and crackling until it settled in its own soft ash. All around him, saints and angels shared his vigil, awake and watchful in their silver frames.

The abbot returned before dawn and found Stefan sitting in the chair as he'd left him. He was dressed in his travelling clothes and his small bag rested at his feet. They shared a silent breakfast and walked together to the monastery square. It was the time just before dawn when a pearly light limned the buildings and erased all but the brightest stars. He heard the whine of an engine increase in volume and a military truck slewed sideways and blocked the gate. When Gregor walked through the arch, Stefan picked up his bag. 'We will go now,' he said.

'I wish to say goodbye,' the abbot said firmly and Gregor retreated a few steps. Turning to Stefan, the abbot said, 'You must take this.' And he fumbled the cross from around his neck.

'I can't.'

'Take it. You can bring it back when you return.'

'What is your name?' Stefan asked as the abbot leaned in close to loop the chain around his neck.

'I chose Theo. It was his name.'

They kissed on both cheeks.

'*Spasibo*, Theo.'

'*Dasvidanya*, Stefan Mikailovich.'

MOSCOW

The airport smelled of cheap lavatory cleaner and absence. It should have been a vortex, swirling with the flow and counterflow – the coming and going of smiles and farewells. The passengers from Medusa's flight formed a long line that bisected the empty concourse. High ceilings and hard floors hushed conversations. Everywhere she looked, she saw military. 'Moscow is a city occupied by its own army,' someone at the agency had quipped and she'd filed the description under 'hyperbole'. She tried not to stare as she moved to the top of the line. In her wake, she heard the murmurs rise, saw the heads turn in her peripheral vision, felt their hostility like a hot breath on her neck. Just before the murmurs coalesced into complaint, she diverted to the kiosk marked 'Diplomatic Passports'. She felt the tension leak away from the watchers to be replaced with interest. Well, she figured as she laid her passport on the high counter, she was providing a distraction, no one in that line was going anywhere in a hurry.

Neither, it seemed, was she. The uniformed official busied himself with papers, studiously ignoring the passport splayed before him. Languidly, and without raising his eyes, he palmed it from the counter and began riffling the pages. *Checking the stamps of other countries I've visited*, she thought and felt relieved she'd had the guys in documents remove the Israeli stamp. Uncle Joe Stalin had broken off diplomatic relations with Israel and she thought his avatar in the kiosk would savour making things difficult for no other reason than that he could. He began to riffle the pages from the back cover and she settled her feet to wait him out. After a moment, an NKVD officer peeled himself from a pillar to the rear of the kiosk and approached his colleague. 'Problem?' he asked.

'No', the official said, 'everything seems to be in order.'

She heard the mix of disappointment and boredom in his voice and suppressed a smile. *Always a tough duty in the Diplomatic Passports kiosk*, she thought, *no one to harass or send to the back of the line or—*

'Better let the ugly American bitch proceed,' the NKVD officer drawled. The official fought to control his features as he stamped the passport.

'You may proceed,' he said, slapping the passport on the shelf before her. 'Welcome to the USSR,' he added automatically.

'Thank you, comrade,' she said in accentless Russian. 'The ugly American bitch will convey your good wishes and shoulder bar numbers to the US ambassador.'

She allowed herself a brief surge of satisfaction as both men flinched. It was unprofessional to draw attention to herself, she knew, but the bastards were unlikely to report this particular conversation. This was a country were a *mea culpa* could merit a final absolution.

A heavy-set man with more silver than black in his receding hair nodded as she stepped through to the arrivals area. Greg Bates had a mottled, disappointed face and lugubrious brown eyes that missed nothing – drunk or sober. He was the agency man in Moscow, lightly camouflaged by the title cultural attaché. He held the door with old-world courtesy as the driver dumped her bag in the trunk.

'Ours?' she whispered.

'US Marine Corps,' he mouthed and winced as the muscle-bound young man slammed the lid.

'All those pretty uniforms for little old me?' she asked slyly, as they left the airport environs.

'Sorry to rain on your parade,' Greg smiled, 'but it's just part of the everyday paranoia.'

She wondered what it was like to live in a city where every apartment complex housed a resident informer, and segued into considering what it was like for Greg Bates to live in a city where he was shadowed all day, every day. She was too much of a pro to look over her shoulder at the Zil; the Soviet Security car sniffing their exhaust on the way to the embassy. She didn't pursue the subject with her companion. It was 10 a.m. Moscow time and Greg's breath and trembling fingers were all the answer she needed.

'The ambassador won't see you,' he muttered. 'Sorry.'

'I'll do my best to remain unseen,' she smiled, although it rankled that the ambassador, like most of his ilk in the Diplomatic Corps, regarded CIA operatives as something you wiped from the sole of your shoe.

'Asset is in archives,' he said cryptically.

'Best if you ignore me from here on in, Greg,' she said and he nodded with relief. 'You've observed the proprieties by picking me up,' she continued, 'there's no need to put yourself in the firing line. Okay?'

'Okay.' His shoulders slumped and he turned his head to the window.

'Director says the post in Athens is coming vacant in September,' she said. 'Hold that thought, Greg.'

CARDINAL TISSERANT'S APARTMENTS, THE VATICAN

'Please hold for a call, Monsignor Dupont.'

Emil scrabbled among the papers littering the desk until he found a pad. *Pencil*, he remembered. *Why is there never a pencil when—*

'Remember me when you come into your kingdom,' the voice crackled on the phone. It took three rapid heartbeats before Emil recalled the response to the code. 'This day you will be with me in paradise,' he said.

'Have you found an angel for me, Monsignor?'

'Yes. The angel reveals the glories of the San Clemente to those who have eyes to see.'

That elicited a chuckle.

'I think you send me a cherub, Monsignor.'

'Yes, Karl Hamner is an innocent,' Emil said lightly, 'but with the heart and soul of an archangel.'

'*Grazie.*'

The caller hung up and the receiver buzzed in Emil's ear until he quenched it in the cradle. He allowed himself a few moments to recover. His heart rate had increased and his fingers trembled a soft tattoo on the armrest. *I'm too old for this kind of ... farrago,* he thought. *Time was when I would have had the code on the tip of my tongue. Now it takes a few seconds for me to remember that 'angel' is 'messenger' and 'cherub' is the lowest form of angel – 'archangel' was a good recovery,* he consoled himself. *Karl does have all the innocence of a baby angel and the strength of a warrior angel. There's something I must do.* He breathed deeply to quell the frustration until his mind cleared. The photograph slotted neatly inside the large envelope. He scribbled a note to accompany it and printed 'Father Hugh O'Donnell OP, San Clemente' on the envelope. *Now what? Ah, yes, a messenger.*

'Forgetfulness is a cross we must carry,' an old priest had assured him piously, one time. 'I would if I could remember where I put it,' he'd replied. Easy to be whimsical when you're young, he chided himself. Now what? Yes, a messenger.

LUBYANKA PRISON, MOSCOW

The guard who shaved his head moved like a priest. He whipped the lather in a chipped, enamel mug with ritual care and applied it to Stefan's head as if anointing with chrism. Stefan imagined the choir of Saint Sergius chanting an accompaniment to the slow, careful strokes of the razor and smiled. The guard paused, squeezed Stefan's shoulder reassuringly and continued. Finally, he planed his palm across the bare scalp in benediction.

'Your pardon,' the guard said apologetically, 'it is required.'

Swiftly, he notched the top of his left ear and made a small incision at the nape of his neck. Immediately, he pressed damp cloths to the wounds and held them in place until the blood clotted. A different guard led Stefan back to his basement cell.

They came before dawn. The room they took him to was blind and deaf, and the guards who inhabited the space were mute. No window relieved the nicotined walls and the door was thickly padded. The room smelled of urine, sweat and fear. The two guards moved with the ease of old dance partners. One strapped his arms to the chair while the other knelt to secure his feet to the leg bolt in the floor. The larger man stepped aside and assumed the 'at ease' position. His partner began to bind his right hand in Hessian strips. As the man with the bound right fist stood before him, Stefan watched his shoulders.

'Don't watch the hand,' his father had advised, 'watch the shoulders. A man's shoulder will move before his fist does. If you can't parry a punch, roll with it.'

This lesson had been delivered behind the farmhouse on that bare patch that passed for a garden. It had been prompted by a growth spurt that had attracted the attention of older boys eager to prove themselves.

'Feet apart for balance,' his father had grunted. 'Left foot forward and left hand cocked at your cheekbone for the block. Keep your right hand lower for the counter-punch. Remember, most fights are fast. They last maybe two or three blows.'

He'd illustrated this with light, lightning cuffs to Stefan's ears before grappling him close; his bristly jaw sanding against Stefan's cheek. 'When you're this close, bring up your knee,' he counselled. 'You're a good lad, Stefan,' he'd whispered, without breaking the clinch, 'a bit on the soft side, like your mother. If they come at you, put them down, Stefan. Otherwise the bastards will never stop coming. You hear me?'

'Yes, Papa.'

His father had squeezed him tightly and walked away to the barn.

The right shoulder twitched and Stefan twisted his face to the right. It was a glancing blow but it rattled his teeth. He managed to ride a flurry of blows until he hurt too much to concentrate and let them land until he stopped feeling.

A bucket of water brought him back. His face felt like a mask that hung before him. He knew if he could touch it with his fingertips, it would feel like rubber. Through the slit of his right eye, Stefan saw the puncher strip the Hessian from his fingers and flex his fist. He nodded to his companion. They reversed their dance routine to free him from the floor bolt and the chair. With surprising ease, the smaller man hugged Stefan around the chest as he sagged and hauled him upright. He felt the burn on his heels as he was dragged across the stone floor. Puncher held him steady as the other raised his arms and locked his wrists in the manacles dangling from the ceiling. He heard a mechanical clicking and was tugged upward until his toes twitched just above the floor. The big man beat his body with a rubber truncheon. He shifted his feet as he worked, shuffling around the hanging body, until every inch of Stefan's skin seemed to burn and he ground his teeth on the scream that filled his mouth.

He was aware of errant stalks of straw poking him from the pallet. In the hayloft, he would have circled, like a dog, to smooth the space for sleep. Moving was not an option. He'd tried and lost consciousness. The rasp of the spy-hole cover brought him back and he sensed an observer. *Déjà vu*, he thought and let the darkness take him.

Gregor pressed his face to the door for a full minute. He stepped back and nodded to the guard to close the spy-hole. 'Smoke?' the guard asked, shaking a brown cigarette from a pack. He bent to inhale the flame until the cigarette tip glowed white. They smoked in silence.

'Did he say anything?'

'No, Colonel, not a word.'

'Did he—'

'No. No screams – nothing. I'd say it's not his first time,' the guard added, studying the tip of his cigarette. It was a question, Gregor knew, and he let it pass. The guard was the one who'd shaved Stefan as he'd watched through the spy-hole. He'd felt grateful for the small kindnesses and sickened at the thought of what was to follow.

'It's necessary,' the guard said, as if reading his thoughts. 'Where he's going an unmarked man is a dead man. The *zeks* would take him for an informer – you know that, Colonel.'

That knowledge didn't salve his soul.

'When?'

'Tonight. He's a tough lad.' The guard stubbed the butt beneath his heel and dropped it in his pocket. 'Think he'll last, Colonel?'

'He must.'

'What about the cross?'

'It goes with him.'

The guard's normally placid face creased into disapproval. 'It's trouble, Colonel,' he said flatly. 'I heard of a *zek* nailed to a wall because he wore one. Maybe—'

'It stays.'

US EMBASSY, MOSCOW

Vernon Andrews, according to her brief, was a life-long scholar. He had already accumulated a string of degrees from prestigious universities and was hell-bent on accruing more. 'A textbook asset,' the director had said with a wry smile. The only child of deceased parents, his inheritance allowed him to wander the world of academia without financial worry. An agent in Oxford had seen his potential and nudged him towards 'Agrarian Reform in the USSR' and bumbling, alcoholic Greg had been the perfect mentor – always listening attentively as the lonely scholar passed on his observations. Vernon – not 'Vern' as he was quick to point out – had the stereotypical domed forehead, thick spectacles and rounded shoulders of a student. He also had the kind of innocent owlishness that invited confidences. Everyone, from disaffected managers of collective farms to displaced kulaks and lesser officials, shared information with Doctor Andrews that could have earned them a berth in a gulag. When she entered the archives, he was standing on a spindly, antique chair reading the spines of dusty volumes.

'Doctor Andrews,' she said respectfully, 'I hope I'm not disturbing you?'

'What? Oh no, not at all, young lady,' he said, gazing at her approvingly through thick lenses. 'Not disturbing,' he said, stepping down and extending his hand. 'But definitely distracting,' he added, as he prolonged the handshake. The briefing notes hadn't been coy about the good doctor's libido.

'I've brought the books you requested from the States,' she said sweetly.

'You are an angel of deliverance,' he said happily. 'This' – he waved a dismissive hand at the shelves – 'is an academic wasteland. I'm sorry. Do I know you?'

'I haven't had the pleasure, Doctor.'

'We'll have to rectify that as soon as possible, won't we?' he twinkled.

'Business before pleasure, Doctor,' she said, lifting her book bag and placing it on a reading table. 'There is an additional volume,' she said as he reached eagerly for the bag. 'When you go for lunch tomorrow, to your usual bench in Gorky Park, leave the bag on the seat beside you. Our friend will pick it up.'

'The bag?'

'The book, Doctor Andrews.'

'Just teasing,' he smiled. 'And can we celebrate the hugger mugger with coffee afterwards?'

'I was counting on it.'

THE VATICAN SWITCHBOARD

Brother Cletus plucked the earphones and let them dangle around his neck. He breathed carefully on his spectacles and polished them with a white handkerchief which he refolded and placed in his cassock pocket. Only then did he read the transcript of the call. Brother Cletus was well aware of his intellectual shortcomings, they had been enumerated and emphasised by various superiors since he had entered religious life. Only the Father General of the Fratres had seen his true potential. 'You are meticulous in everything you do, Cletus,' he'd said in that wonderful voice. 'Humility will be your shield in the service of the Church.' Father General had arranged to have him employed in the Vatican Telephone Exchange. 'You will be in the frontline of our intelligence service, Cletus,' he'd said. No one had ever used 'Cletus' and 'intelligence' in the same sentence, and he glowed at the memory.

He pleaded a headache and the supervisor excused him for the rest of the day. It was not the truth, he admitted, as he squeezed himself into the public telephone box on the Via della Conciliazione, but he would confess it later. When the connection was made, he began to read from the page he held in his left hand.

'Remember me when you come into your kingdom,' he began in a slow, clear voice.

PRISON TRAIN, MOSCOW

The guard came before dawn and dressed him with rough efficiency. It was how he remembered his father doing it when he was a small boy. He allowed his arms and legs to be threaded into long underwear, trousers, two shirts, a roll-neck pullover and a greatcoat. The socks were rolled up over each foot and he felt the crackle of paper when the guard tied his shoes tightly. There were scratchy woollen gloves and a fur hat with ear flaps that tied under his chin. He needed a push to mount the truck.

The twelve prisoners were rousted from the truck at the railway station and rifle-butted into a ragged line. The NKVD officer looked and sounded like he'd been punished with this particular duty and snapped through the formalities. Stefan ignored the bureaucratic stuff until he began to list the names and crimes. Stefan Nagy was listed as a petty thief. *Farm boy, seminarian, prisoner and petty thief, how low the mighty have fallen*, he mused. He must have smiled because the officer paused in his recitation to glare at him. *You know the game*, he chided himself and assumed a vacant expression. The officer continued. The group comprised eleven criminals, including petty thieves, a burglar, a fence, a forger and a political who held himself slightly apart from the others and had the kind of scared look that invited trouble. 'Yanov,' the officer named him. 'Dereliction of duty.'

The officer was on the point of leaving when he turned to the forger. 'Back again, Yuri,' he sneered and the guards laughed. Some instinct prompted Stefan to shadow the forger as they boarded the cattle wagon. The little man waddled to the engine end of the carriage and commanded a corner. Stefan promptly squatted beside him.

'Snore?' the man asked and Stefan stared at him. His lips hadn't moved.

'No,' he replied, pushing his tongue against a spot above his top teeth and snorting the sound so that his mouth hung open and unmoving. The little man nodded approvingly. They exchanged names and the lesson began. For a man who never moved his lips, Yuri was amazingly talkative and informative. 'Always back to the engine,' he instructed, as the train began to grunt and gather speed. 'Wind comes through the door at the other end. Corner is best – supports the back and you see what's coming. The 'political', Yanov, he gets stove duty – permanently.' He tapped Stefan's fur hat. 'Hat for pillow or plate. Coat for blanket. You have newspapers?'

'Why would I—'

'Heat,' Yuri grunted. He untied one button of his greatcoat to show a padding of newspaper. 'Also trade,' he added. 'Even old news is news in the gulag.'

'This isn't your first time.'

'No. I'm not a very good forger.'

The greatcoat shook and Stefan realised that Yuri was laughing.

The 'political' had some difficulty with his status as 'stoker' until a kicking from the fence and one of the smugglers persuaded him otherwise.

'He won't last,' Yuri muttered. 'Politicals are the lowest form of life in the gulag.'

On the second day, Stefan helped the "political" with the stove.

'That's his fucking job,' the fence snarled and subsided when Stefan hefted a cord of wood and stared him down.

'You can't care,' Yuri advised. 'If you care, you die.'

'We all die sometime, Yuri.'

'Yes, but that only happens once. There are other ways of dying.'

'Where are we going?'

'I'll know tomorrow.'

On the third day, the train stopped.

'Are we there?'

'No, just changing to a spur line. Fuck. We're going west.'

'Is that bad?'

'The worst. We're going to Camp 213 in Karelia. It's just a

spit from the Finnish border. Every day, you wake to the smell of freedom.'

The gravelled road gave out at the forest and they walked a rough path hemmed with trees for another two hours. The trees were losing their shape in the twilight when Stefan smelled the camp. At first, it was a faint whiff of decay that lurked under the resinous smell of the forest. As the trees thinned and the outline of the camp grew sharper, the smell gained strength, like the gases that belch from a bog. He expected the sentry boxes, raised on stilts at each corner and the barbed wire that looped between them. The seemingly random scattering of the huts surprised him until he realised the area had been cleared from the forest and the huts were sited between amputated tree stumps. The absence of order and the shabby appearance of the guards led him to conclude that this was a place where Moscow's writ didn't run. They slumped in a ragged line before the only building that looked reasonably maintained and waited in a torment of flies.

'Camp commander in his cups,' Yuri whispered. 'The *zeks* have a still in the forest and he's their best customer.'

The door of the hut slammed open and a scarecrow swung out on crutches.

'Fucking Adolf,' Yuri sighed, 'hoped he was dead.'

'Adolf?'

'Commander's pet Nazi,' Yuri muttered, 'souvenir of Barbarossa. Left his legs and his wits behind him. Sees, hears and speaks all evil. Fucking spy.'

Adolf swung to attention before the guard and snapped off a salute that the guard didn't acknowledge. He produced a document and passed it over before spinning to face the prisoners. The guard shouted names and hut numbers and they dispersed to their billets.

Stefan, Yuri, the fence and the political had been rostered together and pushed into their appointed hut. They were confronted by implacable faces and a sudden, unnerving silence. Bunks bracketed the walls and a stove shimmered in the centre of the floor. Yuri strode confidently to the bunks in the left-hand corner and stared at the occupants. Standing behind his shoulder, Stefan saw the man in the lower bunk return Yuri's stare and lean sideways to look at someone behind them. His eyes hardened and he began to gather his possessions. Yuri raised his eyes to the man in the top bunk who swung his legs to the floor and followed his companion.

'It seems our rooms are ready,' Yuri chuckled and patted the lower bunk for Stefan to sit beside him. 'Unpack and listen,' Yuri whispered. 'The one eye in the bunk nearest the stove is Pavel. He's the alpha-wolf. When he barks, the pack follows. Pavel and I have an understanding. I alter the orders and Pavel skips work-detail. Don't cross him unless you're ready to kill him.' He inclined his head to the others. 'Top bunks are for top men after Pavel. Bottom bunks are for the tolerated and the floor is for politicals and goners.

'Goners?'

Yuri inclined his head and Stefan shook out his coat to cover a glance. A skeletal man with a slack mouth and faraway eyes was slumped in the no-man's-land between the stove and the bunks.

'Food equals work,' Yuri said. 'Don't reach your quota, you get less. A kind of prolonged execution – too weak to work, too hungry to live. Wash yourself.'

'What?'

'Strip, wash, do it.'

Conscious of his nakedness, Stefan hunched over the bucket and palmed cold water under his armpits. The talk faltered and then resumed among the bunks. He thought he felt Pavel's one-eyed stare linger between his shoulders. He was tucking his shirt in when Yuri spoke again. 'He saw your bruises. You're in.' Yuri rolled into his bunk, fully clothed. 'Nights getting colder,' he muttered.

'Where do we … defecate?' Stefan asked.

'De-fe-cate,' Yuri mimicked, savouring each syllable. 'In here, we use a bucket at the back of the stove. Out there, anywhere from here to Moscow. Pleasant dreams, Stefan.'

He seemed to sleep immediately. In the top bunk, Stefan lay awake, listening to the snores and the grumbling stove and the restless movement of the men on the floor.

GORKY PARK, MOSCOW

The craft was in becoming someone else. It was a cliché, worn smooth with overuse by agency instructors and regarded by neophyte agents as a dressing-up game for adults. To her, it was instinctive, something she'd employed as a survival technique for as long as she could remember. Leaving the embassy, she was Professor Elaine Brown of the Iconography Department at the Smithsonian, a middle-aged academic who dressed soberly without thought for style or colour and consulted a street map through thick-rimmed spectacles. The 'tail' had shadowed her from the embassy, staying the regulation distance behind. Old Russia hands joked that every foreigner in Moscow had a shadow, even at night. She determined there was only one after a series of seemingly random detours. She was a low-risk, high-boredom assignment for the tail. He would expect to trail the dowdy American academic around the usual galleries and museums.

At the public toilets on Godunov Street, she placed a coin on a battered table and accepted a sliver of soap and four carefully counted sheets of toilet paper from the old lady attendant. The babushka didn't establish eye contact or offer a greeting. There was nothing about the woman on the other side of the table to excite interest or invite conversation. In the stall, Professor Brown became Ekaterina Kazakov, changing with the ease of long practice into a plain knee-length skirt, white shirt and home-knit, navy cardigan. Her scholar's bag, turned inside out, sported an embroidered flower and consumed the clothes she'd been wearing. The removal of four hairpins loosed the severe bun at the nape of her neck and she recaptured it with a ribbon into a careless ponytail. As she washed her hands, the mottled mirror reflected her new identity. She was a young woman from Vereya, a town close enough to Moscow to explain her presence and far enough into the 'sticks' to be ignored as a 'hick' by the natives. When she emerged, she walked with the loose-limbed stride of someone unused to the rhythms of city life. At the flower market, in the shadow of the Brandenburg-style arch, near the Gorky Park Metro, she chose a babushka. The grandmotherly babushki were ubiquitous in Moscow, an informal militia of elderly ladies who swept streets, sold at market and watched everything and everybody.

'Mother,' she said respectfully to the grey-haired woman, shapeless in shawls, 'a man is following. On the Metro, he tried to—. When I wouldn't, he followed.'

The babushka's weathered face went prune-like with annoyance.

'What does he look like, daughter?'

She entered the oasis of Gorky Park safe in the knowledge that if the 'tail' made it as far as the flower sellers, he'd wish he hadn't.

The path paralleled the Moscow River. At this time of day, it was busy with men and women using their lunch hours to savour the open air and each other. A lime tree provided the perfect cover for observing Vernon Andrews. He sat, hunched over a book, on a park bench, his bookbag lying open beside him. He seemed oblivious to the procession of young women who strolled by, arm in arm in the pale sunlight. She was thinking it must be an engrossing book when she saw the contact. No NKVD agent would wear a heavy overcoat and wide-brimmed hat on such a mild day, she concluded, and stopped checking the people behind and in front of him on the path. 'Amateur,' she sniffed as he minced back and forth before the bench before sitting stiffly beside the bag. She was relieved when he stayed a few minutes after lifting the book before easing back into the flow of walkers. Vernon Andrews seemed unaware of the little drama playing itself out on the bench beside him. There was no ostentatious looking the other way or sudden-discovery-of-the-missing-book moment, like some old ham in a silent movie. She nodded in grudging admiration and left him to his reading.

She caught up with the contact as he crossed one of the ornamental bridges, touching his elbow and asking for a light. While he rummaged with his right hand for matches, she leant closer and spoke around the cigarette in her mouth.

'I have news of Natasha, Alexei. Light my cigarette,' she insisted quietly as he froze. He broke the first match. The second flared and she put her hands around his as he cupped the flame. 'At the coffee kiosk in the children's area,' she added. 'Six minutes.'

'The six-minute window' the instructors had called it. It was the critical period during which a contact might decide he was a patriot after all and blow your cover. After six minutes, he would have to explain why he hadn't acted immediately. Her instinct assured her that Alexei wouldn't go to any of the uniforms in the park. But, then again, there had been that woman in Kiev. Mistress to a powerful party official and wife of a famous general, she'd listened to the offer, excused herself and blown her brains all over the wall in the ladies' room. There had been an inquiry – a roomful of starched shirts from Ops and Psych, chaired by the director. She remembered the relentless questioning and how the individual interrogators had clicked and pocketed their pens and asked to be excused until only the director remained.

'They don't get it,' she'd muttered fiercely. 'They look at me like I'm some kind of fr—'

'Medusa,' the director had interrupted, 'stay focused. They're desk jockeys. Most of them have never gone over or made a play. What they think of you or me or the agency isn't worth a bucket of spit.'

It was so unlike the patrician director to use that kind of language.

'The pointy-headed guy said I was acting in a moral vacuum,' she'd persisted. 'What the fuck is that supposed to mean?'

'It means he'll probably write a paper on it to be read by other pointy-headed academics,' he'd said. 'It's what they do. We' – and the inclusive word had mollified her – 'do what needs doing in a war. Our gallant allies flattened Dresden and our president gave an executive order to erase Hiroshima and Nagasaki. Needs must, Medusa.'

Something the Psych guy said still scraped a fingernail along her brain.

'There are always consequences, lady.'

'Are you threatening me?' she'd asked, just for the buzz of seeing him pale.

'You miss the point,' he'd said. 'I meant there are personal consequences resulting from our actions. If they're not dealt with, they accumulate until—'

'Thank you for your contribution, Doctor Edwards,' the director had interrupted and the guy had shuffled his papers and left the room. She hadn't asked the director to explain. Sure, there were times when she had flashbacks, faces at the moment of death and blood. There was always blood.

'Fuck!' She checked her watch. Twelve minutes – too long.

He was there, pacing like a caged animal in his long coat and stupid hat. She could see some of the mothers in the playground looking at him. It would only be a matter of minutes before they started looking for a uniform.

'Alexei,' she called breathlessly and, when he spun in her direction, she put her arms around him. 'Hug me,' she whispered. 'You thought I wasn't coming and you're relieved. Do it.' After a brief hesitation, his arms tightened around her. She sensed the wave of relief that rippled through the watchers. *Everybody loves a love story*, she thought. 'Come,' she said, linking his arm and leading him off among the trees. When they were on a quieter path, he tried to free his arm from hers. 'No,' she said. 'Sharp actions attract sharp eyes – everything slow and easy.'

'Natasha?' he whispered.

He had the facial features of a fallen cherub, a round, boyish face tightened with worry lines at the eyes and mouth. She steered him off the path to admire a ragged stand of sunflowers.

'Alive,' she said.

'Who are—'

'No,' she said, tightening her arm on his. 'You must remain calm and listen. Your boss plays an unsubtle game, Alexei – your *real* boss,' she added. He gave a long, shuddering sigh and she eased the pressure on his arm. 'Look at the flowers, Alexei,' she said soothingly. 'Your boss says do this thing for me, and Natasha will return from the gulag. Correct?'

He nodded.

'It costs him nothing to release Natasha,' she continued. 'He can't afford to leave you alive, not after you deliver.'

She turned to look at him and saw the eyes of a dead man.

'Unless,' she offered.

'Unless?'

'Unless you confess your sin,' she said and pressed her case before confusion replaced hope on his face. 'Two huge rocks are rolling from opposite directions. You don't want to be in the middle when they collide.'

'What can I—'

'Listen. Listen, carefully. You have choices. You can play out the game according to the rules and you'll disappear from the board. Or you can go back to the other side of the board and be protected.'

'He'll never take me back,' he said woodenly.

'Not as you were,' she countered. 'Not as a trusted aide and confidant, that's true. But he will take you back as a weapon, because of what you know.'

'For how long?'

'For as long as you're useful,' she said bluntly. 'You won't be going back to him empty-handed. We can feed you copies of all the communications that have changed hands up to today. Think of what that's worth in the right hands. And you know the hands I mean, don't you, Alexei?'

'Yes.'

'I'm going to take a hairbrush from my bag,' she said, 'and you will hold my bag like a proper gentleman while I brush my hair. The papers you need are inside. Time to choose.'

She thrust the bag against his chest. He grasped it with both hands, like a drowning man.

BASILICA DI SAN CLEMENTE, ROME

'I couldn't better that myself,' Father O'Donnell said admiringly, as the tourists trooped out the door.

'I'm sure you could,' Karl demurred.

'I damn well couldn't, boy,' the Dominican insisted. 'In fact, I think I'd benefit from your tour myself. Come inside for a coffee.'

The elderly Father Anselm sat alone at the refectory table.

'Ha,' Father O'Donnell said, 'there's Anselm skiving off as usual. They say a drop of that man's sweat could shift any sickness.'

'They say he's deaf too,' Anselm riposted as he rose from the chair. 'Would you give an old man your arm, Karl?' he asked. 'Just as far as the door.'

'You can run but you can't hide, Anselm,' his superior roared.

'I wish I'd joined the Jesuits,' Anselm confided to Karl with a smile. 'The Dominicans take any old ruffian.'

It had taken Karl some time to understand that insults were a form of affection among the Irish.

'Messenger from Emil brought this,' O'Donnell said to Karl when he returned, slapping an envelope on the table. 'Have a look while I get some stuff.'

The photograph was a mystery and the enclosed note as enigmatic as only Emil could write.

'A shadow awaits in Trastevere,' he read. 'Hear his tale and show him the photograph.'

'I couldn't make head or tail of it either,' Hugh admitted, as he returned with a sheaf of papers. '"Paul IV on the Jews of Rome",' he said. 'Read it with a good bottle of wine. It'll take the bad taste out of your mouth. Have it back tomorrow so as I can smuggle it back into the archives.'

Karl thanked him and put the documents with Emil's envelope in his rucksack.

'You had a visitor yesterday.'

'A visitor?'

The priest had a talent for taking him off-guard.

'Ah, a lovely girl. Seemed disappointed to miss you. For the life of me, I can't see—'

'Father!'

'Doctor, she said she was. Now, what was her name at all?'

Karl glared at him.

'Walker, that was it. Sarah Walker. If I was only thirty years younger—'

'She wouldn't have been born, Father.'

'Now, that was cruel, Karl – cruel and uncalled for. She said she's at the Magdalena. You could do worse than drop in there on your way home.'

'Perhaps tomorrow,' Karl said, lifting his rucksack from the table.

'You're too bloody Austrian for your own good, Karl,' the priest protested.

'But I *am* Austrian.'

'That's exactly what I mean. That's a really lovely girl we're talking about here. A fella should take her out for a coffee or to a restaurant and tell her she's beautiful and—'

'And you know this how?'

'I wasn't born a bloody Dominican.'

Father O'Donnell was still talking as Karl left. 'A grand girl like that doesn't come around twice in a man's lifetime,' was the last sentence Karl heard through the closed door. Father O'Donnell was right, he admitted. 'A grand girl like that' had come into his life only once before – but he wasn't sure he could risk that kind of loss again.

WORK-DETAIL, GULAG 213

'Gulag 213 was a camp designed by Hieronymus Bosch.'

'Who?'

'Bosch! You know? Dutch, one of those bloody lowlanders who can't go up in a hayloft without getting a nosebleed. Saw his woodcuts when I was at university. 213 was mud and mayhem. Water?'

Yuri was on water detail for the forestry gang. Yuri was always on water detail. Stefan swung the axe and splinters flew.

'Go slowly,' Yuri grumbled. 'We have no shortage of trees.'

Stefan armed sweat from his eyes and accepted the mug of water. 'Smell of snow, Yuri,' he said.

'Snow, this early?'

'We're farther north, it comes earlier. Don't you smell it?'

'Nah, never could, Moscow born and bred. Give me pen and paper and I could forge you some. You want snow, real snow, you need to go to 258 or 340, up near Murmansk or Perm. Have to shit over a fire in winter. Go outside for a piss, come back wearing a three-foot icicle on your—'

'Which way is Finland, Yuri?'

'Will you stop asking me about Finland? Drives me crazy.' He huffed and his breath plumed before his face. 'From where I'm standing, it's about thirty kilometres west. From where you're standing, it might as well be on the moon.'

'Are there villages that way?'

'Stefan, listen to me. Do your time. Do whatever it takes to survive but don't dream.'

'Do the uniforms run patrols that way?'

'Are you deaf as well as stupid? Yes, there are villages that way and they are full of bounty-hunters. They pick you up, they bring you back dead or alive, same bounty. Are there patrols? No.'

'No?'

'No. N and O, Stefan. Patrols yes, pursuit no. Hunting dogs. Once they're loosed they can't be called off.'

'Suppose someone was to go the other way, to the Gulf of Finland.'

Yuri threw his arms up in disgust.

'C'mon, Yuri, humour me.'

'Fine,' Yuri nodded. 'You're a believer. At least you have that cross swinging around your neck. So, this is what you do. You get to the coast and walk right out into the Gulf of Finland until some fucking reindeer-lover picks you up.' He walked away a few paces and walked back. 'How can an atheist ask God for patience?' he grumbled. 'Can you sail a boat, Stefan?'

'No.'

'I rest my case.'

'Maybe someone else can.'

'Start chopping, there's a uniform coming.'

In the evenings, they were allowed to congregate at open fires dotted around the compound. Stefan noticed that a caste system applied there too, and sat behind his mentor. 'Take the tour,' Yuri advised. 'You might find a sailor.'

Stefan wandered from one group to another listening to their stories. The conversations centred on their experience of other camps. No one spoke of home or family. At Pavel's fire, a bottle circled the front row and then spiralled back to those behind. The liquor smelled of turpentine and the aftertaste smouldered on his tongue. When it came again, he passed. By the fourth night, he hadn't found a sailor. On the tenth night, he found a priest.

It was the smallest fire, tucked almost up against the wire. He might have missed it but for the fact that the wind changed and a flicker between two huts caught his attention. He paused on the path and recognised the rhythmic cadences of prayer. There were three figures at the fire – the priest, the political and the goner. The priest dressed like any other *zek*. He wore a hat with ear flaps and a shapeless greatcoat but he turned to look as Stefan approached and his eyes marked him off from other men. Somehow, he had managed to salvage a measure of hope. It glowed in his eyes and suffused and softened his face. The political wept quietly and the goner simply sat as the priest recited the sonorous phrases.

'Out of the depths I cry unto thee, O Lord,' he intoned.

'Let thine ears be attentive to the sound of my pleading,' Stefan answered automatically.

The political flinched at the sound of Stefan's voice and then relaxed when he recognised his champion on the train.

'Be welcome,' the priest invited and Stefan sat cross-legged at the fire. The prayer concluded with a blessing and the others wandered off. The priest leaned to place another branch on the flames and something flickered at his chest when the pine needles flared.

'That cross,' Stefan said. 'Where did you get it?'

The man measured him with his eyes before answering. 'I am a German priest,' he said, softly. 'I tagged onto Barbarossa and jumped ship at a village near Bryansk. My mission was to save their souls,' he said wryly. 'I like to think I saved their lives when they handed me over to the Cossacks. The cross was a gift from Cardinal Tisserant. We were each presented with one before we left on our mission.'

Stefan saw something move in the shadows beyond the firelight.

'It's just Adolf,' the priest reassured him.

'Isn't he a spy?'

'Yes. But like most of us, he's more than he seems. You can come now, Corporal Steiger,' he called in German. Warily, the small man swung in from the shadows. He hung on his crutches and stared intently at Stefan.

'Karl?' he said suddenly. 'Is that you, boy?'

'No, Herr Steiger,' Stefan replied. 'My name is Stefan – Stefan Nagy.'

The crippled man sagged on his crutches.

'You remind me of Karl,' he whispered. 'Karl was a good Christian and a real son.'

'Herr Steiger?' Stefan asked. 'Did you have a son, Max?'

Steiger flinched back and crabbed away a few yards on his crutches.

'You know my son?'

'No, mein Herr, not personally. I've heard of him. I heard he is a priest.'

Steiger stared at him. 'A priest?' he said and shook his head savagely. 'No,' he growled, still shaking his head like a man attempting to shake loose a painful memory. 'Max is a … killer,' he said and his eyes clenched closed on the word.

He rocked back and forth before speaking again.

'I told Karl,' he said defensively, 'and the miner, Tomas. Told them it was Max who killed …' – he had difficulty making himself to repeat the word – '… Elsa,' he said in a strangled voice. 'Elsa … in the mine.' He turned his back to the men at the fire. 'I was the policeman,' he continued. 'I had my duty. But … I loved him.'

He became agitated again and the priest interrupted. 'Will we pray for him, Herr Steiger? Will we pray for your son?' Steiger stumped reluctantly to the fire. 'Yes,' he said in a small voice. 'Say the prayers for the dead.'

'When did he die?' the priest asked.

'Long ago,' Steiger whispered in a singsong, storytelling voice, 'when he was just a boy.'

'*Ego sum,*' the priest sang softly, '*resurrectio et vita*' – 'I am the resurrection and the life.'

Stefan left the fire with the final phrase echoing in his ears.

'And whosoever believes in me shall never die.'

GORKY PARK

'You mentioned coffee.'

'What?' Vernon closed the book and rose slowly to his feet. 'Look at you,' he said, admiringly. 'Just this morning, I was distracted by a beautiful American lady and now I find myself disturbed by a fresh-faced Russian peasant girl. Even Tolstoy didn't have that kind of luck.'

She sat beside him on the bench.

'So,' he whispered, 'who are you now, if I may ask?'

'It doesn't matter. I'll be someone else later.'

'Extraordinary,' he breathed. 'You know the American Indians believed in shape-shifters? Yep, it seems some of them could change into a wolf or a coyote or pretty much any animal that took their fancy. Most ancient cultures have some version of that story but they all have one thing in common. If the shape-shifter stayed too long in any particular form, it stuck.'

'What are you getting at, Doctor Andrews?'

'Actually, I'm just getting on, dear,' he sighed. 'The older I get, the greater a bore I become. Shall we walk?'

She was the one who had shape-shifted, she thought, yet he was the one who had changed. He seemed less abstract and more focused. He wasn't any less talkative. Vernon kept up a seamless commentary as they walked the path beside the river. Country niece spends a day with city uncle, she decided and began to enjoy the role. She knew from the file about his expertise in agrarian reform but she was surprised at how well-versed he was in the history of Moscow.

'Italian masons built that,' he said, nodding at the wall across the river.

'The Kremlin!'

'No, just the walls. And then the Poles came every couple of hundred years or so and tried to knock them down – never managed it.'

They crossed a bridge and circled around to enter Red Square.

'The word "red" has nothing to do with the colour and it isn't a proper square,' Vernon confided. They stopped to watch a wedding party go by. 'She'll place her bouquet at the tomb of the unknown soldier,' he said quietly. 'No other people can mix romance and tragedy like the Russians.'

'You promised me coffee,' she reminded him as they left the rowdy wedding party and the oddly named square.

'And I have promises to keep,' he quoted, turning her into the doors of the GUM. The odour of freshly ground coffee lured them to a café tucked into a corner on the second level of the gigantic shopping arcade. It was mid-afternoon and there were a few customers sprinkled around the tables. A cadaverous young man scribbled furiously in a small notebook. Poet, she concluded, and swung her gaze to the middle-aged couple in expensive leather jackets. They were sipping their coffee in silence. Married! Near the door, an older man with round, wire-rimmed spectacles read *Pravda* with a faintly amused expression.

'This place is really nice,' she said. 'Look, they've got real sugar cubes.' She plucked four cubes from the bowl and began to amuse herself by building a tower. 'Pisa,' she laughed as her sugar-tower tilted and fell.

'Or Babel,' he smiled. 'Pisa was built on sand and Babel was buttressed by hubris.'

He tipped the waiter and held the cup under his nose to savour the fragrance. 'This is the only place in Moscow where you can get really good coffee,' he said with satisfaction.

'Two lumps?' she asked.

'Beautiful and omniscient,' he smiled.

'Aren't you going to drink your coffee, Vernon?'

'No, Ekaterina, I think not.'

She lowered her cup and looked at him stonily.

'With Alexei you were Ekaterina Kazakov from Vereya,' he said tonelessly. 'When you left the embassy this morning, you were Professor Elaine Brown of the Smithsonian. Before that, you were Medusa. Do you wish me to continue?'

'No.'

'Very well. Revelation should be mutual, don't you think? This morning, you met Doctor Vernon Andrews.'

'Who are you now?'

'It doesn't matter,' he said, 'I'll be someone else later.'

She leaned back and dabbed at her mouth with the napkin.

'Very good,' he murmured appreciatively. 'Now that you've checked the other patrons, perhaps you'd favour me with your impressions.'

'The poet and the married couple are good,' she said, 'although the GUM is a little out of his league.'

'Excellent,' he said. 'Proceed.'

'The guy by the door is reading yesterday's *Pravda*. He looks over his spectacles when he reads.'

'He's near retirement,' Vernon sighed. 'You know how it is – the young try too hard and the veterans get careless. Relax, enjoy your coffee,' he said. 'This is not your day to die. Not this day,' he added. 'Don't come back. Some of my colleagues are from Kiev. They have long memories.'

KARL'S APARTMENT, TRASTEVERE, ROME

His guardian angel was waiting in the hallway as always.

'*Buongiorno*, Signorina Clara.'

'*Buongiorno*, Signor Karl.'

Now that the daily ritual was concluded, Karl could proceed. His foot was on the first step of the stairs when she touched him shyly on the elbow.

'*Che cosa, cara*?'

She gazed at him solemnly before pointing up the stairwell, like a guiding angel in some mediaeval tapestry.

'*Grazie*,' he murmured and she moved back to watch him ascend.

A broad-shouldered man in a rumpled suit sat behind the table in his apartment.

'You're very hairy for an angel.'

'You're very substantial for a shadow.'

The man eased himself upright and extended his hand. 'My name is Claus Fischer,' he said. 'Monsignor Emil knows me as "The Good Thief".'

Karl shook his hand warily. 'Karl Hamner,' he said. 'You must be a good thief, Herr Fischer, my door was still locked when I returned.'

'I'm a better shadow,' Fischer said. 'Better than the one shadowing you.'

Instinctively, Karl moved to the window.

'No,' Fischer said sharply. 'Don't alert him. He isn't very good and they might replace him. Shall we to business, Herr Hamner?'

'Karl.'

'Claus,' Fischer nodded. 'You are a historian, Karl.'

'How—'

'Your books betrayed you. Also, I read your edition of von Kluge's war papers.'

'I was just a collaborator.'

'It was a very readable collaboration.' Claus sighed and rubbed his eyes. 'You'll understand if I don't tell you about myself,' he said quietly. 'What you don't know you can't be forced to tell. Also, no one must know of our … collaboration.'

Karl nodded.

'Firstly, they are things Emil needs to know.'

Karl reached for the rucksack.

'No! No notes, Karl. We'll have to trust in your historian's memory.'

He sat back to gather his thoughts.

'Stalin is to be removed,' he said.

'But – but there's nothing in the newspapers.'

'Yes. Let us say I know people who know such things,' Claus said. 'They also say he will be poisoned, most likely warfarin. Another source told me the poison will originate in America.'

'Rumour or fact?'

Claus nodded approvingly. 'I can see why you are a good historian. Let us say just hearing that story killed the man who told me.'

He seemed to lapse into reverie.

'Can I get you something?'

'What? No … No, thank you. Where was I? Ah, yes. Khrushchev is the one expected to fill the vacancy.'

'Khrushchev? Is he a senior member of the politburo?'

'No, but the people I spoke to play a patient game. There will be a popular revolt of the workers in the DDR. The CIA are funding it and they've warned the Soviets to expect it.'

Karl thought his brain was swelling.

'Why don't the Soviets take steps to prevent it?'

'Because the eventual suppression will serve as a salutary lesson to all the other Soviet satellite states. It is also rumoured that Father Max Steiger is being funded by the CIA.'

Karl stared at him.

'You know this Max Steiger?'

'I knew a boy by that name,' he said woodenly. 'He … He was a friend. I don't know the man.'

Claus raised his eyebrows and pressed on. 'The money he is receiving is most likely being channelled through the Vatican Bank – Steiger has gone that route before. If it's true, the CIA will use the Fratres to influence European politicians. The Fratres will also become information-gatherers for the CIA. Tell Emil that Gehlen might hold the key to the structures already in place. There is also talk in the East that the American Cardinal Spellman is being promoted as a successor to Pacelli. I think that's everything.' He leaned back in his chair.

'Why are you telling Emil this?' Karl asked.

'Because I'm blown, Karl,' Claus replied tiredly. 'I'm ready to accept the sanctuary Emil offered me in the Vatican but I'm not sure I can make it there alive.'

'You could stay here,' Karl said impulsively.

'Emil was right about you,' Claus smiled. 'Thank you, but no. The people who want to eliminate me wouldn't hesitate to kill anyone who stood in their way.' He shrugged his shoulders and sat forward again. 'Do you have something from Emil?'

Karl eased the envelope from the rucksack and passed it over the table.

'Do you know this man?' he asked.

Claus adjusted his spectacles and held the photograph in the light from the window. 'No,' he said finally. 'I'm sorry.'

He handed it back and Karl studied it, tapping his finger on the face in the photograph.

'Do you know him?' Claus asked.

'No, but I know someone who might.'

'Best if you keep your back turned and your hands on the banister,' Karl whispered when they reached the landing. Claus looked bemused but didn't argue.

'Shimon, it's me, Karl Hamner.'

'And the other one?'

'A friend of Emil.'

'Karl, you come inside when I open the door. The friend comes in when I say.'

Karl expected the gun but it still bothered him. Shimon waved him into the room before turning to the door. 'Turn and walk slowly,' he said. 'Keep your arms away from your sides.'

As soon as Claus was inside, Shimon slammed the door and spun to press the muzzle behind Claus' ear.

'Shimon,' Karl said hurriedly, 'this is—'

'I don't care *who* he is,' Shimon grated. 'I know *what* he is.'

'Please, Shimon,' Karl said, struggling to remain calm. 'Emil sent him. He knows the code.'

It took a long time for the madness to drain from Shimon's eyes. 'You,' he said to Claus, 'you get up and sit here.' He hooked a chair from the table with his foot and kicked it into the centre of the floor. 'Keep your hands palms up on your knees. Do it!'

He edged to the other side of the table and gestured to Karl to sit beside him.

'What do you want, boy?' he said, without taking his eyes from Claus.

'Do you know this man?' Karl asked, placing the photograph before him. Shimon shifted his gaze to the photograph. 'Need to check my files,' he muttered. There was an awkward moment while he seemed uncertain how to access his files while keeping Claus covered.

'Why don't you check on me first?' Claus suggested helpfully. 'My name is Claus Fischer, formerly of the SD.'

Shimon hesitated and then snatched the telephone. He dialled and waited. '*Shalom aleichem*,' he said. 'Claus Fischer. SD.' Karl saw his eyes tighten and held his breath. '*Toda*,' Shimon muttered and hung up. He tucked the gun in his waistband and walked to the filing cabinets that shouldered up against the wall near the window.

'Shadow outside,' Claus called. 'Don't cross the window.'

'Yours?' Shimon asked.

'His,' Claus replied, nodding at Karl.

Shimon removed a file and spread photographs and documents on the table.

'That's him,' Karl said, stabbing his finger at a uniformed figure in the second row of a group photograph. Shimon twisted the photograph for a better look. He checked the writing on the back. 'Walter Kamf,' he read. 'Mean anything to either of you?'

'Name doesn't mean anything, but I'd like a look.'

'Know him?' Shimon demanded impatiently.

'No, not him,' Claus said. 'But I think I know some of the others.'

'Who are they?' Karl asked.

'The Gehlen Group,' Claus answered. 'Can you run a trace on Walter Kamf?' he asked Shimon. 'Ask them—'

Shimon cut him off with a raised hand. Silently he padded to the

door and listened. 'Someone on your landing, Karl,' he whispered.
'I'll cover you from up here. If it's someone you know – whistle!'

'Julio, what are you doing here?'

The boy jumped and then smiled. 'My father sent me with documents,' he said. 'He got them from the rabbi.' Inside the apartment, Karl locked them in a drawer.

'Can I get you something to drink, Julio?' he asked.

'No, Karl, my friends are waiting.'

Karl gave him a questioning look.

'I don't see them often,' Julio said defensively, 'not since school started.'

'That's good news, Julio,' Karl smiled, following him to the landing. 'Will you excuse me for a moment?' he asked before leaning over the banister to whistle. 'A friend upstairs,' he said to the puzzled boy.

'Oh, Karl, my father says there will be a party in our restaurant for your book tomorrow night. You can come?'

'Yes … yes, I think so. My book, you said?'

'Yes. To celebrate.'

'But it's not finished, Julio.'

'He says we'll have another party then.'

Karl threw his hands up in surrender.

'Also, my father says you must bring something to make Mama happy.'

'What?'

'A lady.' Julio winked and leaned over the banister to whistle. 'Perhaps your friend upstairs,' he said, before skipping down the stairs.

Shimon closed the door when he heard Karl's whistle. 'I must apologise,' he said stiffly. 'I didn't know who you are.'

'Who I was.'

'Yes, I understand you helped Jews, when you could. They … they said Doctor Baruch of Vienna owes you his life.'

'It's all in the past now. Well, for me, perhaps.'

'Why did you do it? What you did for the Jews, I mean?'

'It was all a long time ago, Shimon. It doesn't matter—'

'Please, Herr Fischer. In my … line of work, I hear only evil. It coarsens a man.'

Claus leaned back and stretched his arms over his head.

'Anything to drink?' he enquired.

When they'd both tasted their tumblers, Claus studied the surface of his drink. 'It was such an honour being selected for the SD,' he said softly. 'I remember I walked all the way across Hamburg to tell a friend. We went to a restaurant to celebrate. That was before … before things changed. I did well in basic training. Anyone with half a brain would have. There was one particular test they set us at the end of our basic training.' He turned his glass a few times and began to rub his forefinger on the rim until the glass hummed. 'We were to investigate the family tree of someone we knew without them becoming aware we were doing it. I was so enthusiastic then.' He laughed humourlessly.

'You chose the friend who lived across Hamburg.'

Claus nodded.

'And a parent or grandparent was a Jew?'

'Grandparent. It was enough. I received a commendation.'

'And your friend?'

Claus Fischer's face was bleak. He drained his glass and set it on the table. 'What do you suggest we do about Walter Kamf?' he asked.

'We?'

'Yes, we. You want information for your purposes and I for mine. Can you have him lifted?'

'That can be arranged,' Shimon said as he refilled their glasses.

Karl arrived in time to see them raise a toast.

WORK-DETAIL, CAMP 213, KARELIA

The snow decided him. The first flakes filtered through the trees and freckled his shoulders as he swung the axe. It was a light dusting, but he saw it as a portent of what would come. Quietly, he shaved leg-length sections from a fallen tree and bundled them with the other offcuts, set aside for the stove. Later, he bartered his second shirt for a knife. It was no more than a spoon handle, stone-honed into a shiv, but the fence struck a hard bargain. While the others slept, he salvaged the pieces while tending the stove and worked on them under the blanket. Before dawn, he slid them under the mattress.

'When?' Yuri whispered.

'Soon. I need a map.'

Two days later, he persuaded Yuri to take the other end of the bowsaw. The screeching blade masked their conversation.

'I have the details,' Yuri wheezed. 'I can sketch them for you. Can we stop this fucking sawing?'

'Not yet. Do you want to come?'

'No. It's twenty years too late. I'll see you at prayers tonight.'

The priest prayed a little louder than usual while Yuri and Stefan conversed. The spectre of Steiger lurking in the shadows had persuaded the political to opt for an early night. The goner was present but somewhere else.

'We are here,' Yuri said, using a pencil stub to scratch a map on the margin of one of his precious newspaper pages. Stefan measured the distance from the pencilled X to the broken line of the Finnish border.

'It's so close,' he breathed.

'Use your brain, boy,' Yuri snapped. 'You think the uniforms and the border patrols don't know that? You must go south, along the corridor between the frontier and Lake Ladoga. Your best hope is to catch a train. The line skirts the lake and runs all the way to Vyborg.'

'Tell me about Vyborg.'

'Handed over by the Finns after the war, along with half of the Karelia, for a few shitty islands in the gulf.'

'Where did the Finns go?'

'Home. Thousands of them evacuated across the new border. Not all of them. Some of the old fishing families still operate out of Vyborg, near the Old Fort.'

'What about the dogs, Yuri? How can you arrange for the dogs to go west?'

'You ask too many questions.'

'I have other questions, Yuri,' Stefan whispered and let the silence lengthen.

'Someone else is going west.'

'Who?'

'The political.'

'Why—'

'That's three questions, Stefan, let it go.'

'He won't make it.'

'He has to go. He's a dead man if he stays.'

THE KREMLIN. KHRUSHCHEV'S OFFICE

'I knew,' Khrushchev said to his secretary. 'I've known since Beria's visit. It wasn't difficult to find the reason. She's up near Murmansk, isn't she?'

His secretary nodded.

'You're a dead man either way,' Khrushchev said bluntly. 'Beria can't let you live and I have no reason to keep you alive.'

'Is it true,' Alexei began slowly, 'in the Ukraine people make offerings to the dead?'

Surprised, Khrushchev narrowed his eyes and nodded.

'Suppose the dead could make an offering to the living.'

'For what purpose?'

'For a time in purgatory before resurrection.'

'What the fuck are you—'

'Nikita,' Alexei interrupted, 'I have a document. I bring it to you as an offering. It's not sufficient to clear my debt, I know that. But there will be more.'

He pushed the papers across the desk and drew his hands back to his lap. Khrushchev made no effort to take them.

'Why should I trust that this isn't disinformation?'

'You shouldn't,' Alexei said simply. 'I ask you to consider the circumstances of my ... betrayal and the nature of the material I'm putting before you. You were the target, I was the weapon. Under any other circumstances, I would have warned you and trusted in your protection. You were not in a position to offer that protection – not then.'

Khrushchev looked at the younger man for a full minute before he picked up the papers. He read them through and then started at the beginning again.

'I need to think about this,' he muttered.

'Shall I draw you a bath?'

'Yes, I think I can trust you to do that.'

THE SAN GIROLAMO, ROME

'"Yes, Karl Hamner is an innocent but with the heart and soul of a seraphim."' The secretary placed the message slip on the desk. 'That is all, Father General,' he said and waited.

Max Steiger sat as if carved in stone, the vivid twin welts marring his marble cheek from eye to mouth. Silence sifted down like dust to deaden the room. It was the kind of silence the secretary had grown accustomed to, and yet it had an underlying hum of tension that made him uncomfortable. He missed the quiet of his Benedictine monastery. Near the end of the war, it had been host to refugees from Austria and the constant hubbub had driven him to stay with his bees from dawn to dusk. When the time came for them to go home, the refugees had made a great effort to restore the monastery to what it had been before their arrival. It had taken the monastic community a full month to regain their precious silence. More and more often, he found himself yearning for that silence, for the quiet companionship of community and the security of regular hours and duties. Some monks came to the life attracted by the possibility of mysticism and some for the opportunity to devote themselves to study. Others confessed that they'd come to escape some painful reality. Brother Cyprian had come because he was a loner.

The abbot had been unperturbed. 'Think of us as a hive,' he'd said. 'We work, each according to his ability, for the benefit of all, but we retain our individuality.'

When he'd first heard Max Steiger preach about the adventure of a new crusade, his brothers had seemed compliant and docile by comparison and the monastic lifestyle unchallenging. He'd felt guilty asking permission for a leave of absence to spend time with the Fratres. 'Why not?' the abbot had responded. 'Francis of Assisi went on a crusade when he was forty years old and he had ambitions to convert the Saracen Sultan. If it's self-mortification and rigour you're after, our own Benedict lived the ascetic life of a hermit before he founded our order. Go, with a good heart and my blessing, Cyprian. If you find fulfilment with the Fratres, why would your brothers do other than rejoice? If you do not, consider it a discovery rather than a failure and come back to us. Idealism is a wonderful thing, Cyprian, but remember when Francis reached Damietta, he found that not all the Saracens were devils and not all the Christians were angels.'

Were the Fratres all that Max Steiger had promised? he mused. *Was the new crusade everything Max Steiger had preached?* In the quiet of his heart, he had to admit a growing disillusionment. Religious life in the Schloss had seemed to revolve around extreme personal mortification and blind obedience to Father General. If anything, his experience of religious life in the San Girolamo was even more dismaying. The Fratres students seemed almost fanatical in their devotion to the Father General and to the new cause. He suspected that some of the older residents wore religious habits for reasons other than strictly religious ones. And what of Max Steiger, the man? As his secretary, Cyprian had had the chance to observe him closely and had become increasingly disenchanted. Stripped of the glamour of his charismatic public persona, Max Steiger could be cruel and manipulative. 'Judge not lest you be judged,' the scriptures cautioned and yet the same scriptures also declared, 'By their fruits shall you know them.' The image of a young sister sitting on a hard bench outside Max Steiger's door flashed into his mind and his soul shrivelled with shame. He'd known what was happening. She hadn't been the first novice he'd seen elated at Steiger's summons and left isolated and confused, waiting on his whim. He'd known and done nothing. Rather than facing the facts and the challenge posed by them to him as a religious, he'd twisted his own sense of betrayal into a contempt for the betrayed.

'*Mea culpa, mea culpa, mea maxima culpa*,' he prayed. 'Through my fault, through my fault, through my most grievous fault.'

Max Steiger's absence in America had given him an opportunity to reflect. He'd managed to find quiet in his forays to the church of San Luigi dei Francesi in the Piazza Navona and in the public gardens that rewarded those who scaled the Spanish Steps. The trees had leached some of the ache from his soul and the flowerbeds had given him the benediction of bees. How he missed the bees. In retrospect, Steiger's absence had been a reprieve rather than a pardon and his return had plunged Brother Cyprian into a frenzy of activity. Journalists from *Der Spiegel* and other prestigious European newspapers had besieged the San Girolamo for an interview with the Father General. He'd been present for most of the interview, ready to fetch coffee for the visitors, ubiquitous and invisible.

He'd listened to Steiger's impassioned exposition of the Fratres' ideals, painfully aware of the reality behind the rhetoric. Max Steiger seemed to have become infatuated with America and enthused at length about American leadership of the free world. He'd also taken every opportunity to laud the vision and zeal of Joseph Spellman, an American cardinal of whom Brother Cyprian had never heard before the invitation had come for Steiger to visit New York.

And there was the money – amounts he could hardly comprehend, millions of dollars that passed through his hands to those of the German monsignor and into the vaults of the Vatican Bank. He'd typed letters to powerful political people, exhorting them, in Father General's name, to favour the political rise of one candidate and stymie that of another until no amount of washing at the end of a day could help him feel clean. He wondered if—

'Read it again.'

Brother Cyprian picked the message slip from the desk and read it again.

Max Steiger lunged from the chair and snatched it from his hand. He leaned forward until his face was mere inches from that of his secretary. It was the face of a wild animal and Cyprian steeled himself. He'd experienced Steiger's fugues before. The priest would rage at his reflection in the window or at some random object in the room or at him. He knew, at an intellectual level, that he was the butt and not the source of that ravening anger, but he felt afraid. He did what he always did when he felt fear, he reached inside himself to take the hand of the four-year-old boy whose mother was dying upstairs. Together, they walked out of the farmhouse kitchen to the orchard and the bees. Surrounded by bulbous hives, he wrapped the boy in his arms and listened to the bees.

'"The innocence of a cherub,"' Steiger sneered. 'Your innocence was ignorance, Karl. You were so protected by Rudi and Mama and that El— El—' He seemed to choke on the name and ground out 'girl'. 'You never smelled the sewer that was Hallstatt, did you, Karl? Never had to sit deaf, dumb and blind to the policeman and his poisonous wife?' He spread his hands beseechingly. 'I offered you … everything,' he wailed, like some evangelical preacher. 'I took you to the top of the mountain and showed you the kingdoms of the world ... begged you to take my hand and leap from the pinnacle of the temple and you turned away from the vision.' A look of utter incomprehension filled his eyes with confusion. 'For Hallstatt, Karl?' he whispered. 'For Tauber, the Jew teacher's life. Oh, yes,' he nodded slyly, 'I know. I see you ... see you all the time. My ravens watch and whisper from the trees and eaves. They see you, Karl, wandering like some penitent pilgrim from school to grave to mine. Let the dead bury their dead,' he urged. 'I did.' His voice dwindled to a whine. 'Why couldn't you have stayed away, Karl? Why couldn't you have stayed in Hallstatt where I could see you and not have to see the accusation in your eyes? What will I do with you? You are my *nemesis*. Remember that, Karl? You are my black beast, and you nose and sniff and snuffle at my heels and I have no rest.' His eyes brimmed and tears flooded his scars. 'We were friends, Karl. Remember?' he pleaded. 'Always you and me, and me and you. Remember?'

He shuffled away like an old man and slumped in his chair, his eyes glazed and unseeing.

'Father General,' Brother Cyprian ventured.

Max Steiger started at his voice. Slowly, his eyes frosted and his face smoothed into a white mask.

'Maintain the surveillance on Karl Hamner,' he said.

'Sister Pilar is waiting—'

'Sister Pilar is to return to her post and remain there until she is summoned. Send for Barth.'

A short time later, Cyprian showed Barth into the room and withdrew gratefully.

Cyprian feared Steiger and yet he could find a place to hide inside himself when Steiger raged. Barth terrified him. The monks chanted the same cautionary verse every evening.

'*Fratres, sobrii estote et vigilate* ...' – 'Brothers, be sober and watchful. For your adversary, the devil, goes about seeking whom he may devour. Resist him, steadfast in the faith.'

It was a verse Cyprian knew by rote and chanted without thinking. Far from the sanctuary of his monastery, he knew with chilling certainty that there was no resisting Barth. Even among the hard-eyed men lodged in the Girolamo at Steiger's pleasure, Barth was a byword for cruelty. The self-effacing monk overheard their whispers whenever Barth passed. 'Burned them in the church ... buried him alive ... girls to the forest, never came back.'

Cyprian was painfully aware of his compliance in the past and resolved not to sin by omission again. Steiger liked to keep a window open at all times. Standing near his own window, Cyprian sometimes heard snatches of conversation from Father General's quarters. 'Jew,' he heard and leaned closer to the window. 'Writing a book' had no meaning for him and he elided it from his memory. 'Fire.' He pricked his ears in time to catch a whole sentence. 'Everything burns, Barth, everything burns,' Steiger said and Barth laughed that terrible laugh. Cyprian hurried to his desk.

Barth passed him without a glance. Cyprian thought he smelled the way a stove smells when the fire has been banked too high.

Barth had just disappeared from view when the telephone shrilled and Brother Cyprian grasped it gratefully. '*Prego?*'

He clamped the receiver to his ear for a few moments and replaced it.

'Well?'

'Father Leiber, the pope's secretary, says you are to cancel all appointments for the next two weeks. You will be summoned to a papal audience.'

Steiger appeared stunned – anxiety and elation warring across his disfigured face.

BISHOP SHEEN'S TELEVISION BROADCAST, NEW YORK

'Full house, Bishop,' the producer said, straddling a chair in the green room. Fulton Sheen met his eyes in the make-up mirror.

'We've had full houses from the start of the series, Tom,' he said easily. 'What's on your mind?'

The producer blew out his cheeks.

'The script is a little …'

'Different?'

'Yeah.'

'That bother you?'

'You can carry it.'

'Thanks, Tom. I think I can. It's not my usual … schtick,' he admitted, 'but we don't want to fall into "same old, same old", do we?'

'No. Still, you know what they say. If it ain't broke—'

'They say a lot of things, Tom, and when all is said and done—'

'I know. There's a lot more said than done. I'll send Suze to fetch you backstage at the five-minute mark. Knock 'em dead, Bishop.'

The guy from Imperial Soap, the company sponsoring the programme, had a reserved seat in the auditorium but opted to sit at the back of the mixing booth. 'Like to be at the centre of the action,' he said – every time.

'Don't buck the sponsor,' the producer cautioned his crew. 'If he wants to stand on the stage and hold the bishop's hand, that's A-Okay.'

That led to a little eye-rolling. The mixing team worked as a tight unit and didn't appreciate 'the money' looking over their shoulders.

'Coming up to five minutes, Suze,' the producer murmured into the microphone, 'time to fetch the talent. Hold the wideshot, Harry.

Tim, just a tad closer. Perfect. We'll be going to you for close-ups of audience reaction, Leroy. Three minutes, folks, to opening caption after the Imperial commercial.'

He could feel the tension rising among the people who flanked him at the desk.

'Nice and easy, everyone,' he said lightly. 'Remember, we got God on our side.'

They were still chuckling when the floor manager counted down to a single finger before the camera and the on-air light blushed red.

'What the hell is this?'

The sponsor's rep was standing at the producer's shoulder.

'Close-up on lady sitting third in the row and hold. And go.'

Satisfied she was on screen, he leaned back a little, without taking his eyes from the monitors.

'Shakespeare,' he said shortly. 'Coming back to the wideshot … now. Ready to go to close-up.'

'We didn't pay for Olivier,' the man behind him grumbled.

'Close-up … now.'

'Who cleared this?'

'Let's talk about it later, okay? Stay with the close-up.'

The producer had his own misgivings about the script but he didn't intend sharing them with the sponsor's rep. Adapting the burial scene from Shakespeare's *Julius Caesar* and changing the names of the protagonists to Stalin, Beria, Malenkov and Vyshinsky was novel, but it risked losing a large slice of the viewers. If anyone could pull it off, Sheen could, he'd persuaded himself. The bishop had the looks, the presence and the *chutzpah* to carry the lines. 'Final kicker-line coming up. Steady on the close-up and … go.'

The producer looked up at the central monitor as Bishop Sheen intoned the final line. 'Stalin must one day meet his judgement.'

'Cue applause and fade to final credits,' he murmured.

SOVIET EMBASSY, WASHINGTON DC

The Soviet ambassador to the US nodded and his aide hurried to switch off the television set. The young man had only a rudimentary grasp of the English language and absolutely no idea about who Shakespeare was and the broadcast had largely passed over his head. He had recognised the names Beria, Malenkov, Vyshinsky and Stalin and wondered if the priest was making fun of the leadership. American television shows sometimes spoke disrespectfully of the Soviet Union, and he hoped the ambassador would lodge a formal complaint with the State Department.

'I need to use the telephone,' the ambassador said huskily, mopping his face with a large white handkerchief. Eagerly, the aide went to the coffee table and lifted the handset but the ambassador was already heaving his bulk from the chair. '*Nyet*,' he snapped irritably, 'the telephone in the basement.'

The ambassador closed the door in his face and he paced outside the basement door. Easing the ambassador's life was part of his function as an aide. Observing and reporting on the ambassador was part of his function as an NKVD officer. Lavrentiy Beria would not be pleased, he thought, and that thought chilled him.

Inside the stuffy basement, the ambassador pressed the receiver to his ear. When the connection was made, he read a Shakespearean quotation from the slip of paper that wavered in his fingers.

'"If it were done when 'tis done then t'were well it were done quickly,"' he recited. The line went dead and he replaced the receiver carefully. Unlike his aide, the ambassador was a highly educated and cultured man. He had been a Shakespeare reader for years and seen most of the plays performed on the Washington stage – except *Macbeth*. He wondered why Beria had chosen a quotation from that unlucky play. As a young man, he had tried to read *Macbeth* and got no further than the murder of King Duncan. Even now, the thought of assassinating a head of state made him nauseous.

THE MAGDALENA CONVENT, ROME

Sarah Walker shifted the stethoscope a centimetre and listened. She slid it back to the original spot on Laura's abdomen and listened again. Finally, she lifted it away and absentmindedly squeezed Laura's hand.

'Is the baby okay?' Laura asked.

Sarah started, as if her mind had been called back from somewhere else. She took Laura's hand in a firm grip and laid the palm of her other hand against the girl's cheek.

'They're fine,' she whispered.

'Did you just say … they?'

'Yes, they, you're going to have twins, Laura.'

'Are you—'

'Yes, I'm certain. Here, blow your nose.'

Laura blew her nose and blotted her eyes with Sarah's handkerchief.

'What …? How will I …?'

'No problem,' Sarah assured her. 'Same deal as having one baby – only twice, if you get my drift.'

Laura nodded uncertainly.

'How did you feel about your baby when I examined you this morning, Laura?'

'Feel? I guess I loved him … her.' Her eyes began to brim again.

'Think there's enough of that love for a brother or sister?' Sarah asked gently.

The young woman drew in a deep breath. 'Guess so,' she said.

'Good! It's a shock, huh? Believe me, honey, everything's okay. Those babies have won the lottery. They've got the most wonderful Mama in the world and their mama's got this most amazing doctor. We're in the third and final round,' she said in a commentator's nasal voice, 'boxing like crazy and way ahead on points.'

Laura's laugh encompassed wonder and tears.

'Give me my handkerchief,' Sarah said. 'I think I got something in my eye.'

A sharp knock sent her flying to the door. Sister Dorothea was red-faced and breathless from the stairs.

'Oh, Dottore,' she gasped.

'Is it—'

'No, Dottore,' the little sister quavered. 'It is a man.'

'A man? What man?'

Sister Dorothea looked at a loss for a moment, and then her face creased into a foolish smile. 'Barbarossa,' she said and her face became even redder.

Karl heard the mad tattoo of footsteps on the stairs slow to a measured pace on the landing. Sarah Walker glided sedately down the final flight and held her hand out. He shook it formally.

'Good morning, Sarah,' he said and bobbed his head.

Was that a bow? Her left hand made a treacherous attempt to touch his cheek and she rerouted it to the stethoscope around her neck. 'Good morning, Karl,' she said.

'I would like to ask you something,' he said.

'So, ask,' she prompted when the pause seemed to sag.

'I would like to ask you if you would accompany me to a party.'

She opened her mouth and closed it again. 'When?' she managed.

'Tonight. I could call for you at seven.'

Not 'around seven' or 'sevenish', she thought. *God, he is so Austrian*. 'I … I don't know if I can. The guests might—'

'Certainly,' a voice said and they jumped. Sister Dorothea huffed into view. It was obvious to Sarah that she'd overheard their entire conversation and she felt a blush creep up her neck. 'Sister Dorothea will care for guests,' Dorothea declared. 'Dottore will leave telephone number. If there is problem, I call you.'

'Thank you, Sister,' Karl said, but the happy Dorothea was already bustling up the stairs.

'Seven is fine, Karl,' Sarah said.

'At seven then.'

'Yes,' Sarah said. 'And Karl.'

'Yes, Sarah?'

'Could I have my hand back, please?'
'Sorry.'

THE KREMLIN, MOSCOW

Khrushchev struggled to stay awake during the cowboy film. Stalin sometimes quizzed the audience after the credits had rolled to a standstill. As the lights came up, he remembered the main actor had been a decorated tank commander during the war, a small man who now fought outlaws and Indians for Hollywood. He couldn't remember his name. No matter, if Stalin asked he'd say, 'He was better in tanks.' Furtively, he stole a glance at his companions. Beria had the glazed look of someone who'd been tossing vodka. Before the film, he'd been restless and talkative. Khrushchev had seen the quelling look Malenkov had directed at Beria and felt a worm of anxiety coil in his belly. The documents he'd received from Alexei wouldn't hang Beria – yet. *What the fuck was going on here?* he worried. Instinctively, he looked at Bulganin and was reassured by his bland expression. Nikolai Bulganin was not a man he'd get drunk with but he admired the bastard's ability to survive despite his wealthy parents and private education. He was at ease in social situations and a smart dresser but all of that could be forgiven because he was a survivor. *Like me*, Khrushchev thought. He wondered if he and Bulganin could—

'You've read the report on the Jew doctors?' Stalin asked and they nodded. Khrushchev had read and re-read it in the bath until he felt more chilled than the cooling water warranted. It was classic Beria, he'd thought, admiringly. A female doctor files a complaint against a number of Moscow's most eminent medical men. The fact that they are Jews adds powder to the pan. The fact that they are accused of plotting to poison the leadership is more than enough to fire Stalin's paranoia. He'd read the instructions Stalin had scribbled in the margins for the interrogators. 'Beat, beat, beat again.' It was a foolproof method of obtaining confessions, he'd thought cynically.

Khrushchev braced himself for one of Stalin's outbursts and was unnerved by the leader's measured tones. Stalin's rages could be terrifying but even the worst storms blow over at some point. A calm Stalin was a truly dangerous animal and he set his face in stone.

'A Zionist-CIA plot,' Stalin intoned. 'They dare not meet me face to face and so they plant saboteurs to attack us from within.' He looked with contempt at the silent group. 'Are you men or kittens?' he asked. 'How will you recognise the enemy after I'm gone?'

Was it possible that the Man of Steel even considered the possibility of dying? Khrushchev wondered. If so, he was the only person in the entire Soviet Union who dared even think such a thing.

Pyotyr Lozgavech stood beside the door in the at-ease position. If Stalin wanted him he would know where to find him but as long as duty required him to remain in the room, he would do nothing to attract that attention. *Best to be prudent*, he reminded himself.

'Prudent'. His wife had let the word curdle on her tongue before she'd spat it out. He'd understood her frustration. Prudence demanded that he never spoke of his work in the dacha. To her, it meant her husband appeared for two weeks after a two-month absence and behaved as if he'd ceased to exist in the interim.

'You don't trust me,' she'd accused.

'I trust you, Anna,' he'd assured her, 'but who do you trust? And who do they trust? A secret is something known to one person, Anna.'

'You think I'd tell others what you do?'

'No, you'd tell them I did something different and you were never a good liar.'

'It's no secret, Pyotyr,' she'd said tiredly. 'You are a guard and we are the prisoners.'

Pyotyr knew every man in the room. He'd taken their coats when they'd arrived, offered them food and poured them drinks, as he'd done many times before. He doubted that any of them knew his name. He preferred it that way, a guard shouldn't become familiar with people he might be required to arrest. At some point in the evening, the brown eyes would find him and he would fade from the room to the guard room. There, he'd go through his ritual of hanging his uniform jacket while trying to divest himself of everything he'd seen, heard and sensed in the room. It wasn't easy to erase the evidence of his senses, but it was prudent. His reverie was interrupted by the touch of the brown eyes. Pyotyr Lozgavech straightened to attention before slipping away soundlessly.

CAMP 213, KARELIA

The snow fell vertically, piling up on the firs until a branch twitched like a sleeping dog and dropped a silent avalanche. He watched the branch rise again in anticipation of a fresh load. Towards the end of their shift, Pavel started bawling out the guard and Stefan drifted into the trees.

'The trees are freezing,' Pavel shouted. 'The axe head kicks back and takes your fucking eye out.' It was the wrong argument and the guard was unmoved. 'Better switch to water detail,' the guard grumbled, 'while you still have one eye.'

Pavel stuck his one good eye in the guard's face. 'The bowsaw jams in the cut; snaps the blade. We don't want pieces of blade lying around. Do we, comrade?'

Reluctantly, the guard gave the order to return to camp and the work-detail whooped, like children released early from school. A running snow-fight lasted all the way to the camp gate and when the guard tried to stand them up for roll call – they rolled him in a drift.

'What's the problem?' Pavel demanded, as he pulled the man upright and dusted snow from his uniform. 'They're running *into* the fucking camp.'

When the sun dipped and shattered in the treeline, Stefan

started walking. 'Walk,' Yuri had counselled. 'Stay under the trees as much as possible – less snow, easier walking. Remember, ice is your friend. Cut across ponds and small lakes. The ice kills your scent and delays the dogs. In the open ground, use your skis. The snow will cover your tracks. Remember the train, Stefan. It's one hundred and fifty kilometres to Vyborg. The uniforms will telegraph ahead so drop off before the station. Okay, tell me the meeting point.'

'The Vyborg Fort on the waterfront. I'm to ask for Ante Hakkonen.'

'Who are you?'

'I'm Mika, his cousin's youngest. I want to work on the boat.'

Two hours into the trek, the trees thinned and he pulled the home-made skis from his back. His spare pair of socks had bought him a lump of lard from the kitchen and he smoothed it along the undersides of the skis. Two whittled branches served as makeshift ski poles and he pushed himself into motion. At the first small lake, he kept the skis on to distribute his weight on the ice and crabbed across to the next landfall. He forced himself to rest and drink water before pressing on. The pre-dawn light outlined a long, low rise to his right that was too regular to be natural. At the foot of the slope, he buried his skis and poles in the snow and bellied to the top of the embankment. The tracks wound below him before climbing a steep gradient, through a stand of trees. It seemed to take forever to crab-crawl below the top of the rise to the trees. The grunts of an oncoming train breathed urgently in his ears as he floundered into the cover at the foot of the gradient. He counted eight freight cars, mounded with grain, and picked the second last, weaving in to catch the rear of the wagon. Feverishly, he hauled himself up and toppled over the rim before a bridge knifed overhead. When he'd regained his breath, he made a hollow in the grain and covered himself to his chin.

The sun was higher when he woke and he was relieved to see farmland interspersed with woods and lakes. He felt exposed by the bright light and feared an idle eye snagging on something in the grain-car until the sun dimmed and snow sifted in from the west. Blowing in from Finland, he thought and let it land and melt on his upturned face. A blast from the engine alerted him that there were more houses springing up in his eyeline. Rolling to his side, he scanned the line ahead. As the engine twisted right and lost sight of the rear wagons, he lowered himself to the track, trotting to maintain his balance before veering off into a stand of rushes. The roadway beside the railway line showed an unbroken skin of snow. Dogs barked and a curtain twitched as he passed houses close to the road, but the falling snow and his shuffling gait seemed to render him unworthy of interest or effort.

His nose led him to the sea front. It was no challenge to find the Vyborg Fort, a squat, rounded tower under a cone-shaped roof. An old man, darning a net in the lee of a wall, angled his head to a slipway when he asked for Ante Hakkonen. A younger man, packing fish in ice, directed him to a warehouse favoured by resting gulls. He felt the man's eyes boring into his back as he pulled the doors open. While his eyes were adjusting to the dim interior, something cold and sharp pricked under his chin.

'What do you want with Hakkonen?'

'A berth on his boat. I'm Mika, his cousin's youngest boy.'

He was pushed into a small office, strewn with charts and blue with pipe-smoke. A thickset man with a wind-tautened face straightened from a chart table.

'How is my cousin, Bert?' he asked around a pipe-stem. 'Still married to that beauty from Helsinki?'

'Never met him,' Stefan answered. The man behind him stepped closer but was stilled by a shake of the head from Hakkonen.

'Who sent you?'

'Yuri.'

'Ah, Yuri,' the man smiled, 'is he still a bloody smuggler?'

'More like a bad forger,' Stefan said.

The blue eyes bored into his for a long moment.

'We go tonight,' he said, turning to the chart table. 'Joel, put him somewhere safe and get him weather gear.'

Joel seemed reluctant to dispense with the knife. 'Are you worth it, *zek*?' he said, as Stefan pulled on the waterproof leggings and jacket.

'Worth what?'

'Worth another man's life.'

'What?'

'Dogs got a *zek* a kilometre from the western border. Uniforms called off their patrols as soon as word came through.'

He locked the door of the gear store as he left.

A small window set high in the wall dimmed as the day faded. When the sky had blackened, the lock turned. Strong arms guided him over the gunwale of the boat nuzzling the dock. 'Ante's in the cabin,' Joel whispered.

'Coffee in the pot,' the skipper said and flattened a chart on the table. 'We go here,' he said, tracing a route from Vyborg into the Gulf of Finland with his pipe-stem. 'The border runs here,' he added, tapping an imaginary line across the gulf. 'Sometimes the patrols are busy, sometimes not. If we're boarded, we put you in the freezer. If they stay too long, you die.'

'Why do you do this?'

'Put you in the freezer?'

'No.'

'Ah, because one hand washes the other, boy. Vyborg is where we've always lived, for generations before the evacuation. Some of us chose to stay. Let's just say we're paying rent for that privilege.'

The snow thickened as they left the harbour and swung right to hug the coast. It seemed to tamp the surface of the sea so that the boat shouldered steadily through calm and unresisting water. Once, they heard the throb of engines swelling in the dark and he was on the threshold of the freezer before the sound ebbed again.

Later, the two men spilled the net aft and motored in a lazy circle. When Stefan looked askance, Hakkonen smiled. 'Fishermen fish,' he grunted. 'That's what we're expected to do. No sudden dashes for freedom. We fish here until my brother finds us.'

'Will he find us in this weather?'

'No,' the skipper chuckled. 'Varno couldn't find his arse with a lantern in broad daylight. But Pennti will.'

THE PUBLISHER'S OFFICE, ROME

Tilda saw herself as the castellan of the House of Schwartz. At the appointed hour every evening, she walked the house from top to bottom, righting whatever careless havoc Schwartz had wrought during the day. She stooped, with difficulty, on the top landing and shuffled scattered papers into a pile. *That bloody man is deciduous where papers are concerned,* she fretted, *shedding sheaves wherever he walks and shouting blue bloody murder when they go astray. Perhaps it was time to employ some 'young thing' who would trail the ogre and stack the shelves and do the hundred and one things I do to save him from being trapped, pressed and petrified in paper.* Schwartz was still 'at his last', of course, probably vivisecting some hopeful manuscript. She listened to his happy grunting through the office door and smiled contentedly. *Say what you like about Schwartz,* she admitted – and then balanced that admission with the unkind thought that saying what you liked about Schwartz would take all of ten seconds – *but he was the Paganini of the red editing pencil.*

Safely ensconced again in Alexandria, she paced her ritual round of the bookshelves. Some older folk she knew reminisced through the medium of photograph albums. She preferred to trail her fingers along the spines of her books and let the titles prompt her memories. She paused and made a little extra space to allow a thin volume to squeeze between two presumptuous neighbours. Foxe's *Book of Martyrs* always reminded her of her father's library.

The descendant of staunch Catholic recusants, he'd granted tenancy on his bookshelves to Foxe and other Anglican writers. She recalled a Catholic neighbour's protest and her father's response. 'My dear Giles,' he'd said, 'Anglicans burned just as brightly under Mary as Catholics did under Elizabeth.' Mother abhorred books, 'dust-gatherers' she called them. 'You'll ruin your eyes, Mathilda. The other girls are—'

Father had been Catholic with a small *c* and catholic in the very best definition of that word. 'In Shakespeare's time,' he liked to say, 'it was the feigned blindness of Anglican neighbours to our absence on Sunday that saved us from the gallows. We reciprocated by burying our dead at home, in the family vaults, thus saving them the embarrassment of barring us from the cemetery. Accommodation, Tilda,' he'd say. 'It's a little less than love and a little more than hate but, in the long run, it keeps us all alive.'

Her fingers strayed over the books and stopped. *The Crucible*, by Arthur Miller was a play that had given her nightmares. Even the bright lights of Rome hadn't shielded her against the bleak fundamentalism that erupted into hysteria and death between the covers. Perhaps it was precisely because she had read it in Rome, she reflected, where the ghost of Torquemada still found substance in a repressive and dogmatic Church. *Cold men*, she shivered, *recreating God in their own image and likeness*.

The very next book exorcised those demons and warmed her. Ian Fleming reminded her of Emil. Her little monsignor revelled in Vatican intrigue. He was a Gallic Pimpernel, puncturing the pompous with his wicked wit and sharp tongue. He was also her oldest and dearest friend. *They might have— No*, she chided herself. Emil was a rare edition, a combination of intellectual passion and childlike innocence. Emil was to be cherished. Near the end of the shelves, she spied another old friend. *Ah, there you are, Oscar, darling*, overshadowing a neighbour again, leaning a louche half inch outside the other volumes, eager for attention. She adjusted her spectacles to identify the volume lurking in Wilde's shadow.

It was Bradbury's *Fahrenheit 451*, a book that had attracted and repelled her in equal measure. It was a book about burning books. The very idea filled her with—

It was the faintest scent. It touched her nose and, almost before she was aware of it, faded. She stepped back from the shelves and raised her head. The mildewy incense of books lay heavy on the room. There it was again – a short, sharp tang that could only be ... *Schwartz! He wouldn't dare. Not after the last time.* She'd threatened to make him eat that vile cigar and he'd promised by all he held—. *That's it*, she resolved as the odour grew too distinct to be denied. She cut a swathe through stacked books and strewn papers to pause at the door. She felt certain she'd extinguished the light in the hallway. Schwartz said it attracted authors. And yet, a light shimmered along the crack below the door. *Intruders? What would it profit a man to burgle a publisher?* she thought whimsically. *What were words worth?* It was such a dreadful pun that she really must remember to inflict it on Emil. She wanted to laugh but her throat had tightened. *Oh, for heaven's sake, Tilda*, she thought, *open the damn door.*

She dragged the door open and screamed.

STALIN'S DACHA, MOSCOW

Krustalev, the chief guard, was the only one not in his bunk. Dimitri and Vladimir would be rousted when the guests were leaving to take up positions around the dacha. Stalin was like a child that way, Pyotyr thought. He liked to know others were awake and watchful while he slept. And, like a mischievous child, he delighted in catching the watchers napping. He could appear at any hour and stare directly into your eyes. 'You'd like to sleep, Pyotyr,' he'd whisper. People claimed he could tell if you were lying by looking in your eyes. Pyotyr had been saying 'No, comrade Stalin' for years, in response to that question. He never considered it a lie because it was a game Stalin played and they both knew the rules.

'Everything okay?' Krustalev drawled without raising his head from a newspaper.

'Yes.'

Pyotyr drew tea from the samovar and sat near the stove. Dacha-duty was largely watching and waiting. He knew some might consider it a privileged position and envy him. As he sipped his tea, he remembered a neighbour had asked his father, 'What is your idea of heaven?' The old peasant had answered immediately. 'A job indoors, where the stove is always stacked and the samovar is never empty.' He felt he should be grateful that he'd achieved his father's heaven without dying, but this heaven wasn't guaranteed for eternity. This paradise was a minefield of pitfalls. A guard could be cast out for waking Stalin before Stalin was ready to wake. A guard might enter Stalin's quarters without being summoned or fail to look him in the eye or speak without permission. There were many 'sins' that could lead to the fall from grace that was 'redeployment'. But the greatest sin was to appear interested in what was said and done inside the dacha when 'the others' were gathered. That sin would be branded 'treason' and the penance for treason was death. 'One cannot bid the eye but see,' his grandmother had liked to say and, despite his studied blankness, Pyotyr Logzachev saw, heard and sensed. Tonight he'd sensed that Stalin seemed more tired and irritable than usual. He'd gone to the bathroom three times and returned looking even more disgruntled. 'The others' had appeared subdued and yet the room had thrummed with tension. During Stalin's third trip to the bathroom, they'd discussed 'The Doctors' Plot' and Bulganin had said, 'If I have a heart attack, please take me to the Lubyanka.' His companions had pretended not to hear him and Bulganin appeared abashed.

He started awake in the chair when the bell rang in the guard room. He struggled into his jacket to attend the departing guests.

'I'll do it,' Krustalev said and left. Pyotyr returned to his place at the stove and listened to the sounds of departure. Car doors slammed, engines revved, gears engaged and the headlights interrogated the guard-room window as the motorcade swept down the drive.

'Comrade Stalin said we should go to bed,' Krustalev said from the door. 'I told Dimitri and Vladimir earlier.'

'But—'

'But what, Pyotyr? D'you want to argue with the boss or go to bed?'

He went to bed but sleep was slow to come. This had never happened before. Who would stand in the anteroom and keep watch while Stalin slept? If he wanted his pills or vodka during the night, who would—

He woke at six and padded immediately to the guard-room window. Stalin's window showed no light and he busied himself with dressing and breakfast. At ten, the window showed nothing but the reflection of weak daylight from an overcast sky. By now, the other guards had risen and were lounging around the guard room. Pyotyr checked his watch at three in the afternoon and approached Krustalev.

'Don't you think we should—'

'No, I don't,' Krustalev said. The chief guard seemed unperturbed and Pyotyr returned to his vigil by the window.

As the afternoon edged into evening, Pyotyr began to pace from the window to the stove and back again.

'Have your supper,' Krustalev growled.

The food was tasteless. He forced himself to chew and swallow. After he'd washed the dishes, he sidled back to the window.

Six thirty, his watch accused him. Six thirty and nothing happening. No one had seen Stalin since four the previous morning. What—

The light came on. He blinked. One moment, there had been nothing but the dark smudge of the window and now a glow filtered through the curtains.

'Comrade Krustalev.'

Krustalev looked annoyed until something in Pyotyr's tone drew him across the room. Pyotyr stood aside to let him look. He was perfectly positioned to see the look of anxiety that aged his superior's face.

'Should we—'

'No! We haven't been summoned. The bell hasn't rung.'

Waiting was torture. He'd known that exquisite pain during the siege of Moscow. When the foxhole was dug and the camouflage net hung in place, he'd climbed into the earth, pulled the netting over the mouth of his burrow and waited. It was always a relief when the flare went up and the madness began. He looked at Dimitri, who widened his eyes in a gesture of helplessness. Vladimir sat at the table, his forehead resting on his folded arms. 'If you close your eyes, the terror isn't there,' Pyotyr had assured himself in the foxhole. But it was there and it was waiting.

At ten twenty-five, Pyotyr stood abruptly and tugged at his rumpled jacket.

'Where do you think you're going?' Krustalev asked.

'To do my duty.'

'On your own head then,' Krustalev muttered and turned to the stove.

His courage almost failed him at the door to Stalin's quarters. He pressed his ear to the door and heard the rapid beat of his own heart. Awkwardly, he put his nose to the keyhole, scenting for pipe-smoke. *What would I do if Stalin opened the door now?* he wondered and choked the urge to laugh.

'Comrade Stalin,' he called, and the quaver in his voice frightened him further. The door opened so smoothly under his hand that he stumbled two paces inside before regaining his balance. Nothing seemed amiss in the familiar room, but the smell brought his hand up over his nose and mouth. Stalin lay curled on the floor, like a child surprised by sleep. 'Comrade Stalin,' he whispered. The rheumy eyes were narrowed to slits in a yellow face. Pyotyr thought he was dead and was retreating when a thin sound escaped from the pallid lips.

'Dz— Dz—'

It sounded like he had a fly trapped in his mouth. Pyotyr saw that his trousers were stained and he was lying in a pool of urine. His first impulse was to run from the foetid room and keep running, but then the soldier in him took charge. He noticed two items either side of the prone body – a copy of *Pravda* and a pocket watch. A crack marred the face of the watch and the hands stood locked at six thirty. Breathe, his brain commanded, and a huge gulp filled his chest. Carefully, he backed to the door.

Dimitri took an involuntary step back when he saw Pyotyr's face. Vladimir raised his head from his arms and placed his palms over his ears. Krustalev stood motionless and expressionless.

'Come,' Pyotyr said hoarsely.

Krustalev risked a look inside the room and ran for the telephone in the guard house.

'Help me,' Pyotyr whispered to Dimitri. The big man's face was the colour of piss and his eyes looked wild.

'Help me,' he repeated. 'Lift.'

He slid his arms under the body and waited until Dimitri's icy fingers clutched his. 'Now,' he said, and they carried Stalin to the sofa.

'What are you doing?' Krustalev asked from the door.

'It isn't right,' Pyotyr said. 'Not on the floor. Dimitri, fetch a blanket from the bedroom.' When he returned, Dimitri draped the blanket over the figure on the sofa. He looked expectantly at Pyotyr.

'That's good, Dimitri,' he said and the words flushed a little colour into the man's cheeks. 'Did you call them?' he asked Krustalev.

'Beria is coming.'

Dimitri looked jaundiced again.

Pyotyr wrung the cloth and smoothed it on Stalin's forehead. The yellow eyelids flickered and Pyotyr held his breath until the face relaxed.

'Is he dead?'Dimitri whispered.

'No!' He spoke more forcibly than he'd intended. 'Why don't you take a break, Dimitri?' he said more gently. 'I'll be here with him.'

Dimitri didn't argue and Pyotyr felt relief when the door closed behind him. He believed the dying sometimes hear the voices of the living. He'd learned that in the war when a boy beside him had cried out and crumpled. He'd held the boy upright in the shelter of a burned-out tank, whispering encouragement – willing him to live. The wound in the boy's thigh had seemed innocent. He'd wrapped it tightly with a belt and loosened it regularly to thwart the rot, all the time whispering in his ear and waiting for the medics to arrive. It was a commissar who'd come. 'He's dead,' he'd said. 'No, I'm not dead,' the boy had whispered, and died. Just two words, Pyotyr remembered – two words spoken in the hearing of a dying boy had loosed his grip on life. He checked his watch. *It is seven in the morning*.

The guard-room door stood ajar and he straight-armed it fully open.

'Go and sit with him, Dimitri,' he said. 'Change the compress every few minutes. If he vomits, turn him on his side.'

'But Pyotyr, what if—'

'Do it.'

Dimitri left and Pyotyr closed the door.

'Where is Comrade Beria?'

'Don't take that tone with—'

'Where the fuck is he?' Pyotyr demanded, closing the gap between them.

'He's com—'

'Not fast enough. Stalin needs a doctor.'

'Beria will—'

'Beria's not here.' He brought his voice under control before continuing. 'You are the superior officer,' he said slowly. 'If *he* dies – it will be on your watch and there will be questions.'

Krustalev's cheek twitched.

'Telephone the doctor.'

'I'm not authorised.'

'Fuck you,' Pyotyr said and picked up the telephone.

'Put it down,' Krustalev said. The pistol was wavering in his hand when the headlights speared the window.

KOTKA, FINLAND

Varno Hakkonen's boat had left the Finnish port of Kotka two hours earlier. A clear night had become snowblind until Pennti dimmed the cabin lamps to cut the glare from the glass.

'Russian snow,' Varno grumbled. 'I hate it.'

'Russian snow or Finnish snow,' Pennti sighed. 'What's the difference?'

He'd been crewing with Varno for twenty years and the script never changed.

'There is a difference,' Varno insisted. 'Why don't you go out to the bow and make yourself useful?'

It was well known in the Kotka fleet that Varno was too short-sighted to recognise his wife. Pennti went to the bow. The old bastard wasn't short of courage, he grudged, as he peered into the dark. Not many skippers would run so close to the border. Bad visibility wasn't an excuse that washed with the patrols. As if on cue, an engine throbbed in the dark.

He ran back to the wheelhouse and waved his arms before the glass. Miraculously, Varno seemed to see the signal because he throttled back and eased her to the left. The engine sound began to die away again and Pennti filtered its fading sound, straining his ears for something else. He hung in the bow, like a cormorant sensing the water. Suddenly, he raced the deck and slammed his hand against the wheelhouse. Varno cut the engine and they wallowed – waiting.

Santa Magdalena Convent, Rome

He stood in the hallway at seven. Sarah didn't appear until ten past, although she'd been ready an hour before. Laura and the other girls had bombarded her with conflicting fashion advice and Dorothea had brushed her hair until static crackled and her scalp tingled. She settled for a simple blue dress she'd brought from America and forgotten to unpack. Dorothea ran to the laundry room to press it and then ran back again to check Sarah's shoes. 'Dorothea,' she'd said finally, 'sit down. You'll give yourself a heart attack and ruin the evening. Okay, now let's run a check. I gave you the phone number?'

'*Si.*'

'You know you're to call me if any of the guests are feeling unwell?'

'*Si.*'

'It's ten after seven and I'm pushing my luck. Karl's a really nice guy but he's very—'

'Austrian,' they'd chorused.

His turn-ups were a little shy of his shoes and he'd have to unbutton the jacket or asphyxiate, she thought, but his eyes were smiling.

'You look very nice, Sarah,' he said.

She thought 'very nice' was probably an extravagant compliment from an Austrian and took his arm. The cab dropped them at a restaurant that seemed to be doing a roaring trade. 'Some party,' she said as they stepped to the pavement. 'Who's it for?'

'Me,' he said.

Italians sure hug a lot, she thought. Some of the signorinas are coming for second helpings. 'Popular guy,' she said, taking him into custody and punching his arm gently. They sat between Enrico and his wife and she concentrated on getting the family names down pat. Julio was the young guy who kept whistling and giggling every time he caught Karl's eye. Elena, the daughter, was engaged to be married to a young rabbi and the little kid who seemed grafted to Karl's elbow was Paolo. *Kid doesn't like me a lot*, she concluded. Mama directed servers, greeted guests and showered Sarah with extravagant compliments, without missing a beat.

'How do you know Karl?' Sarah managed to ask during a lull between courses.

'He is our son,' the matronly lady replied, and turned away to greet some latecomers.

It was some time later before she had Mama to herself. Karl was trailing Enrico round the tables exchanging handshakes and even more kisses.

'What did you mean when you said that Karl was your son, Signora?' she asked.

'He hasn't told you?'

'No, the first and only conversation we've had was about frescoes,' Sarah said, smiling.

The older woman laughed and took her hand. 'Come, help me in the kitchen,' she said loudly. In a small, private parlour, Mama eased her feet from her shoes and sighed with pleasure. 'The kitchen will survive without Mama,' she said. 'Sit! What do you know of Karl, Sarah?'

'He's Austrian,' Sarah began. 'Very,' she added. 'He was

conscripted with his father to fight on the Russian front. Karl didn't tell me that, I overheard a conversation. Apart from that, I know he works as a tour guide in the San Clemente and he needs a shave.'

After they'd stopped laughing, Mama leaned back in her armchair and began to talk.

When she finished, Sarah sat silent for a long time. 'He never mentioned any of that,' she said softly.

'He will, if you give him time,' Mama said confidently. 'Karl has known many losses, Sarah. A man like that grows cautious ... about love. But you see him with my family, especially the way he is with Paolo. He has so much love in him. Karl risked everything for us, Sarah, and suffered for it. We admire Captain Hamner for what he did, but we love Karl for who he is.'

'And Elsa?'

'It is for Karl to tell you that story, *cara*. Tell me what you like about him.'

'Well, he's kind, courteous, patient – sometimes maddeningly so. He's reserved. I thought that was him being Austrian but when he laughs—'

'You like him?'

'Yeah, I like him.'

'Like is good,' Mama nodded. 'I liked Enrico for a long time before I loved him.'

'Isn't it a little soon to talk of love?'

'Perhaps you're right,' Mama sighed. 'It was different for my generation. In wartime, everyone had to learn to live today. Tomorrow wasn't a time we could be sure of.'

'I had planned to work in Ethiopia.'

'It is good to have plans, Sarah. Come, or he will be dancing with someone else.'

He was dancing with someone else. Paolo stood on Karl's shoes, basking in the smiles of other dancers as Karl shuffled around the floor. It reminded her of standing on her Mama's shoes while they danced in the apartment, and she smiled. 'Left hand here, right hand here,' Mama had instructed. 'Let's boogy, honey.'

Karl was holding the little hands as tenderly as Mama had held hers. She felt a lump rise in her throat. As he disentangled himself from Paolo, she reached out to take his hand.

A thunder of applause swept them to the dance floor.

'I'm not a very good dancer, Sarah,' he whispered.

'I'll stand on your shoes if you like,' she offered, and he smiled. 'Why don't you just hang on and let me do the driving?'

He did. His hands felt warm and the warmth spread through her as they circled slowly. At first, she looked over his shoulder, steering him away from potential collisions. Gradually, her eyes found his and she became oblivious to the music and the other couples and the fact that they had yielded the floor to the young couple who danced so well together.

'Papa!' Julio's voice pierced the moment. 'Papa, Karl, come.'

She trailed them outside and saw a red glow in the sky across the city. Julio led them to the Tiber and Karl draped his jacket across her shoulders against the chill. They stood on the high embankment as a crowd gathered. 'Schwartz!' a late arrival announced. 'A carabiniere said it was Schwartz.'

'What is it, Karl?' she asked.

'Schwartz is my publisher,' he said.

'We'll hail a cab.'

STALIN'S DACHA, MOSCOW

Pyotyr had met a wolf once. He'd been fourteen years old and taking huge strides to stay in his father's footprints. His father had stopped suddenly and Pyotyr had crashed into his back. 'Come up beside me,' his father had whispered, easing the axe from his shoulder. The wolf was crouched in the snow between them and the trees. Pyotyr had sensed the open space stretching back behind them to the farmhouse and he fought to control his bladder. 'Be brave,' his father had whispered. 'He'll smell your fear so you must stand tall, boy, and face him down.' He'd stared into the yellow eyes for what seemed like an eternity. Those eyes seemed to say, 'you are nothing to me but meat'. He'd watched the wolf weigh his hunger against the chance of injury until it had flicked around and vanished in the trees.

'Who is this?' Beria asked.

The eyes are the same, Pyotyr thought.

'Comrade Stalin needs a doctor,' he said before Krustalev could reply.

Beria's eyes hardened, held and flicked away to Krustalev's empty holster before he stalked outside. Krustalev jerked after him, as if on a leash. Pyotyr followed.

'Who found him?'

'I did.'

'Like this?'

'No, comrade. He was on the floor. We moved him to the sofa and covered him. He needs—'

'Thank you, comrade.' Beria circled the sofa warily. 'Comrade Stalin is asleep,' he pronounced. 'He is not to be disturbed. Return to the guard room.'

Automatically, the others turned to the door.

'You also,' Beria said.

'I would like to sit with comrade Stalin until the doctor comes,' Pyotyr said.

Beria moved towards him until he was uncomfortably close. Pyotyr stared into the wolf's eyes, willing himself not to show fear.

'Your dedication and concern does you credit, comrade,' Beria said smoothly. 'You have done your duty and may step down. It's out of your hands now.'

HAKKONEN'S BOAT, GULF OF FINLAND

'Can you swim?'

'Yes.'

'Better get out of that gear or it will drown you.'

They eased him into the icy water.

'Keep swimming until Pennti finds you or until you reach Finland.'

CARDINAL TISSERANT'S APARTMENTS, THE VATICAN

'I'm coming, I'm coming,' Emil grumbled, wrestling with his dressing gown.

'*Pronto!*'

'Yes, Monsignor Cosmas. What can I do for you?' He rolled his eyes in exasperation. Cosmas was the master of the non-sequitur, a man who launched into sentences only to abandon them at the earliest opportunity.

'It's only that I thought ... well, I mean, everyone knows ... not that it's anyone's business but your own ... the Jews are our brothers in faith ... people are much too quick to—'

'Cosmas.'

'Yes, Monsignor Emil.'

'I am an old man, Cosmas. I may not live to hear the entirety of this message.'

'I beg your pardon, Monsignor Emil ... it's just that Damian, from Archives, was passing ... always first with the news, Damian ... and I—'

'Cosmas. Before the last trumpet sounds, I beg you – say it!'

'Schwartz is burning.'

Emil pressed his hand to his chest at the spot where his heart was hammering to get out. 'Tilda,' he whispered.

STALIN'S DACHA, MOSCOW

Dimitri had spent the intervening hours looking from Pyotyr to Krustalev and back again. Vladimir had buried his head in the sanctuary of his arms on the table.

'If you don't call the Kremlin,' Pyotyr said, 'I'll walk to the checkpoint and tell the Spetsnaz Commander we have a Code Red.'

He waited for a slow count of ten and stood.

'I'll shoot you,' Krustalev said.

'You were a commissar during the war, Victor Andreyevich,' Pyotyr said, buttoning his jacket. 'You have experience of shooting soldiers in the back.'

Dimitri towered over Krustalev.

'There will be no shooting,' he said fiercely. 'Make the call.'

The Zils roared into the compound and disgorged their passengers. Beria raced directly to Stalin's quarters with Malenkov at his heels and Krustalev at his. Pyotyr was leaving the guard room when Khrushchev approached. Pyotyr thought the party boss looked awkward in the suit and half-strangled by his necktie. Bulganin had drifted away to look at something among the trees.

'Name,' Khrushchev demanded.

'Pyotyr Lozgavech, comrade Khrushchev.'

'What happened here?'

'Comrade Krustalev is the senior—'

'I know who he is. I saw him yapping after his master. Krustalev will raise his leg and piss on the rest of you. Tell me what happened.'

Pyotyr told him in the inflectionless voice he reserved for verbal reports. He told him everything.

'Have you told this to Beria?'

'No.'

'Why did you tell me?'

'I saw you dance.'

'Wha— Oh, that. Stalin ordered me to dance.'

'Yes, I remember. But you didn't dance for him. You danced for yourself and for us. It was … it was the first time since coming here that I forgot to be afraid.'

'Are you married?'

'Yes.'

'Children?'

'No.'

'Good. You'll be redeployed, you know that?'

'Redeployed', Pyotyr knew, was a fancy word for a transfer to somewhere far from Moscow. He nodded.

'I'll do all I can to make sure your wife goes with you,' Khrushchev said. 'When this is over, if you're still alive, I'll bring you back.'

THE PUBLISHER'S OFFICE, ROME

They stepped from the cab and into a scene from Dante. Bombardiers wrestled with snaking hoses on a wet street that flamed with the reflection of the fire that was eating the publisher's building. Carabiniere locked arms at the edge of the pavement, swaying against the press of a crowd drawn to the spectacle. The heat rolled in billows from the building and Sarah covered her head with Karl's coat.

'Karl! Karl!'

Emil was trapped in an eddy of spectators at the mouth of the street, struggling to keep his feet against the press of bodies. Karl lifted him over the carabiniere line to the sanctuary of the pavement. A scream dragged their eyes to a window on the second floor. A woman stood there, her face pressed against the glass. Her fingers scrabbled frantically at the window as flames limned her body.

'Tilda,' Emil moaned. 'My poor Tilda.'

He went to break through the cordon but Karl held him tightly.

'No, Emil,' he shouted over the roaring. 'Stay with Sarah.'

Before she could react, Karl peeled his coat from her shoulders and bulled through the crowd. A carabiniere moved to intercept him and was shoved reeling into a colleague. She saw him trail his coat in a puddle as he ran and whip it around his head and shoulders, before disappearing inside the building.

'Karl!' she shouted. 'Karl!'

He found the hallway miraculously free of fire. The draught from the open door, funnelling up the stairs, fed the flames on the second floor. Karl crouched and ran through dense smoke until his shoulder banged painfully against a banister. He clutched it and began to climb. Blistering varnish stung through the glove on his left hand as he used the banister to guide him higher. Burning scraps of paper sifted down the stairwell in a deadly snowfall that settled on his arms and hands and stung. He was still climbing when his foot found space and he sprawled headlong on the landing. Somewhere to his left, someone screamed. The sound brought him scrabbling on all fours through dense smoke, dipping his head near the floor to suck a breath under the choking mantle. Blindly, his outstretched hands quested before him until his right hand touched and grasped an arm.

Sarah held tightly to Emil as her eyes watered from staring at the open door. Tendrils of flame had started to lick from beneath the lintel. She felt a shudder run through her feet as the fire inside found a fresh cache of tinder and roared. A shadow shifted in the wall of flame that reared behind the doorway.

'Karl?' she whispered as the shadow solidified.

Karl burst from the building and fell into the embrace of two bombardiers. One flapped at his smoking clothing while the other peeled Tilda's body from his shoulder. 'Dottore,' Sarah shouted and the magic word cleaved a path through the crowd.

She crouched over Karl, her eyes and fingers frisking him for signs of injury. He coughed, spat and coughed again. 'Sarah,' he gasped.

'Here,' she said, pressing her cheek to his. 'I'm here.' He smelled of destruction but she inhaled the foetid odour happily. He was alive.

They draped a blanket on the pavement of a side street for Tilda. Someone attempted to place a blanket over her but Sarah waved him away. 'Not yet,' she said as she bent to examine her. Tilda's clothes had been charred and welded to her body. Her hair and eyebrows had disappeared and the left side of her face looked like melted wax. She turned stricken eyes to Emil and shook her head. 'Morphine,' she said and a bombardier dug a syringe from his bag and prepared to fill it.

'I'll do it,' Sarah said. It took her a long time to find an unscorched patch of skin. Tilda whimpered as the needle sought a vein and then relaxed.

Emil sank to his knees beside her. 'Tilda,' he said, 'it is Emil. I am here, *cher amie*, to take care of you.'

Her left eye trembled and opened a crack. 'Emil,' she said hoarsely, 'I can't see you. I was in … Alexandria.' Her mouth mangled the word and Emil bent his head lower. 'Emil … pray,' she whispered.

'The Lord is my shepherd,' he began in English, 'there is nothing I shall want.'

Tilda's mouth twisted into the semblance of a smile as he spoke the words of her favourite psalm. 'Fresh and green are the pastures where he gives me repose.' His voice cracked and Emil began to sob like a child. Karl put his arm around the old man and held him as the bombardier covered Tilda's body. He held out his other arm and Sarah leaned into his embrace.

'If you ever do anything like that again,' she whispered, 'I'll kill you.'

On the way back to Santa Magdalena in the cab, Sarah did running repairs on Karl with a first aid kit charmed from the bombardier. Apart from cuts, scrapes, bruises and burns, he was miraculously intact.

'Sorry, Karl,' she said, as she smeared salve where his left eyebrow had been, 'the beard's kaput.' She shook pills into his palm and closed his fingers over them. 'When you wake, tomorrow, you'll wish you hadn't. Take these with lots of water and go back to bed. I'll call the San Clemente.' She leaned up and kissed him.

He told her he'd bring Emil to the Vatican and hand him over to Commander Markus of the Swiss Guards.

'You know him?' she enquired.

'Yes. He took me into custody one time.'

'Guy sure gets around,' she mumbled as she fumbled with the key to the Magdalena. Inside, she kicked off her ruined shoes and was tiptoeing down the hallway when the light snapped on. *Lord*, she thought, when her eyes had adjusted, *Dorothea wears a tent to bed*.

'Dottore?'

Dorothea was swathed head to toe in a voluminous dressing gown. Her eyes blinked and focused. '*Cara*,' she gasped. 'What happens?'

'Well,' Sarah muttered, as she was steered to a chair in the refectory, 'we had at least four dinners and we danced and then there was a fire and Karl saved a lady, but she died and I kissed him and …' Her face crumpled and she began to cry.

'Is terrible,' Dorothea said, patting her on the head.

'It's worse,' Sarah wept. 'I think it's love.'

VARNO HAKKONEN'S BOAT, GULF OF FINLAND

Pennti hung precariously over the bow, a long gaff hook poised in his right hand. He closed his eyes and angled his head, letting his ears grow accustomed to the rhythm of the water – waiting for the sound that didn't belong. He opened his eyes and kept them open until a blob, bigger than the snowflakes, blurred and resolved into a white face. Expertly, he manoeuvred the swimmer midship and landed him over the rail. Stefan felt the deck move under his feet as Varno engaged the engine and spun the wheel for home.

KOTKA, FINLAND

Arvid Morne returned to the harbourmaster's window. Visibility had reduced to two feet beyond the glass where the snow fell as mute and unruffled as his mother's lace curtains. The call had come before his alarm clock and he'd stumbled downstairs to grab the receiver, hushing his voice. 'Who? Spell it please. Yes, monsignori are minor Roman Catholic prelates.' It was the sort of thing he'd know and someone in Helsinki headquarters knew that. As he replaced the receiver, he imagined the conversation in police headquarters. 'Give it to Morne the Encyclopaedic. Anyway, his mother's Catholic. Really? Morne has a mother?' They were correct, of course. He had a mother and she was a Roman Catholic and he had sensed her standing on the stairs.

'Trouble?' she'd asked.

'Something's come up,' he'd said. 'I'm going to the harbour.'

'A body?' she'd persisted.

'I'll call you later,' he'd said and had begun to climb the stairs. 'Why don't you go back to bed, Mother?'

'Why? I'm awake now. Wear a warm coat,' she'd said, as he stood aside to let her pass. 'And a tie, a policeman won't get promotion without a tie.'

It was one of her aphorisms, he thought as he dressed, one of many. He wondered if his father had joined the Finnish army to fight the Russians or to escape his mother's aphorisms. The Russians had rolled the Finns back to the negotiating table and swapped a few frozen islands in the gulf for half of Karelia. They had also taken Eino Morne. 'Missing in action' meant 'dead' to Arvid. To his mother, it meant vigils, rosaries and masses for Eino's release. 'He will come back,' his mother had assured him since 1941. 'God is good and, anyway, why would the Russians keep Eino Morne?'

He'd knotted a tie. It wasn't one she favoured and he'd felt annoyed at his pettiness.

'Take your coat off when you're inside and hang it up,' she'd said before sprinkling him with holy water at the door.

He checked the reflection in the window and saw his coat hanging dutifully on the back of the harbourmaster's door. The two monsignori opted to retain theirs and sat like oversized penguins on the parlour chairs the harbourmaster had fetched from his living quarters. This was after he'd roused his daughter, Edith, to see to the guests and before he'd taken refuge behind the closed door of his office. The door opened and he saw Edith enter sideways with a tray. He counted three cups and turned from the window.

'Thank you, Edith,' he said in Suomi and she smiled.

The older monsignor was Italian, corpulent and talkative. The other was harder to pin down. He could have passed for Scandinavian, but Arvid wasn't convinced there were enough Roman Catholics in Scandinavia to produce a monsignor. He spoke perfect, accentless Suomi and condensed the Italian's flow into the bare essentials. Arvid knew this because he spoke Italian. It was one of the six languages he spoke fluently – something which had earned him the 'encyclopaedic' tag in headquarters. It was also something he didn't share with the monsignori.

'Two sugars, Arvid,' Edith said, stirring his cup before handing it to him. Edith Canth knew more about the gulf and its busy shipping traffic than her father. It was her voice that crackled on the wheelhouse radios, warning of ice or fog and keeping the Kotka fishing fleet wide of the merchant vessels that ploughed from Vyborg, Leningrad and Tallinn. And it was Edith who kept the belligerent or foolhardy skippers on the Finnish side of the invisible border that stretched across the water. Rumour had it that she also knew the frequencies of the patrol boats that policed the border on the Russian side.

'Is he the best Helsinki can offer?' the fat monsignor complained in Italian.

'Have you been long in the police force?' his companion translated.

'Long enough for what?' Arvid asked innocently.

'He's evasive,' the man with the high cheekbones and arctic eyes translated.

'Aren't they all,' his companion sighed. 'It must be the weather here.'

Arvid had gleaned a certain amount of information from their casual and, as they thought, confidential conversation. They belonged to the Diplomatic Corps in the Vatican. A Cardinal Siri had instructed them to be in Kotka on this particular day to receive someone who would come by sea. Helsinki, he knew, had tried to elicit more information without success. Someone in the government had contacted headquarters and instructed them to ask no further questions and provide every assistance. Helsinki had delegated the matter to Arvid's boss, who had dumped it on him. *So far, so typical*, he thought.

'Edith, a moment please,' he said and touched her elbow to ease her to the other end of the room where a chart of the gulf hung framed beside the window. The glass reflected her shoulder-length, blonde hair and strong-boned face. It didn't do justice to her eyes, he thought. The police inspector and the harbourmaster's daughter had been thrown together by duty. He had been delegated responsibility for the harbour by his boss and she had been told to 'keep that fucking nuisance out of my office' by the harbourmaster. She had quoted her father verbatim to Arvid at their first official meeting. There had been an amused glint in her eye that had taken the sting from the quotation. Their friendship had developed from sailors' brawls through fishing disputes to bloated bodies coming ashore from the Baltic. *It is not the stuff romances are made of*, he thought. And, of course, there was her father and his mother – the irresistible force and the immovable object. And yet—

'Arvid?'

'What?'

'You wanted to ask me something?'

'Yes.' He wanted to ask her to go for coffee with him sometime. He wanted to talk to her about all the normal things normal people talked about. He wanted—

'Arvid?'

'Sorry. Any shipping expected in port tonight?'

'No, except for Arne Hakkonen's fishing boat. I talked to his partner, Pennti, before they left. I told him quite clearly that there would be snow, poor visibility and the possibility of ice. It was like talking to my father.' She leaned closer and inclined her head towards the visitors. 'Who or what are they waiting for, Arvid?' she whispered.

'I don't know,' he confessed. 'They haven't said.'

'Have you asked them?'

Edith had the uncanny knack of asking the obvious and awkward question.

'It seems it's *sub secreto*,' he whispered, 'a secret.'

'I know what *sub secreto* means, Arvid.'

'Sorry.'

A dimple puckered her cheek and he felt absolved.

'Let's hypothesise,' she said, turning to the chart. 'Let's say it's a "who". Coming from where?'

It was a rhetorical question. They both knew where people wanted to come from.

'Not Leningrad,' he ventured, and felt absurdly pleased when she nodded.

'And not Tallinn,' she said, 'their fishing fleet hugs the coast. It must be Vyborg.'

'Logic or female intuition?' he asked.

'Local knowledge,' she said. 'Arne Hakkonen has a brother in Vyborg, also a skipper. They're … close. I'll listen in and let you know when they're coming in.'

'It might be best not to get the visitors' hopes up,' he suggested. 'I could meet them at the berth and check it out.'

'Of course.'

KARL'S APARTMENT, TRASTEVERE, ROME

Karl was contemplating the perils of climbing the stairs to bed when his foot found the note.

Shimon opened the door just as he was about to knock. Shimon looked at the reddened patches on his beardless face and risked a tiny smile. 'Sharpen the razor,' he said. He held a cautionary finger to his lips and closed the door behind him. 'Walter Kamf, just arrived,' he whispered.

A blindfolded man sat shackled to a chair in the centre of the floor. Claus Fischer favoured the shadows in the corner but it was the muscular men in identical white shirts and black trousers who caught and held Karl's attention.

'Uri and Lev. Friends,' Shimon whispered and pushed him into a chair.

'We know who you are,' Shimon said, standing before the prisoner.

'I am Monsignor—'

'You were Walter Kamf, a gofor with the Gehlen Group,' Shimon snapped and whipped the blindfold from his eyes. 'Observe, Walter,' he continued, holding up a photograph before the man. 'In the second row, the story of your life,' he sneered and tossed the photograph aside. 'We have bigger fish to fry, Walter,' Shimon said tiredly. 'Why would we concern ourselves with you? Gehlen used you and left you. Of course, he did give you a forwarding address, like you were some unwelcome parcel. First you go to Hudal at the Anima, then to Draganović in the Girolamo and then to Steiger as his runner boy. "When do I get to sunnier climes?" Walter asks. "When do I get a new name and travel documents from the Red Cross and follow Eichmann and Barbie and Gehlen and all the others?" "Maybe tomorrow," Hudal says. "Maybe next year,"

Draganović says. "Maybe never," Steiger says. "If you don't like it here, you can always go back to—" Where, Walter? To Germany? Which Germany? In West Germany you are something they want to forget. In the East, they have long memories. Russia?' he said in a loud voice and Walter flinched. 'I didn't think so,' Shimon said and began to circle the chair. 'What's that you say? America? Walter, Walter. Are you a scientist, chemist, psychologist or doctor? No? Do you have knowledge of mind-altering drugs or advanced interrogation techniques? Big boots are not what they advertise for, Walter. And so, Walter stays and runs his errands in a black skirt until someone spies Walter and brings him for a little ride and ties him to a chair and that someone is Shimon the Nazi hunter.' Shimon was standing directly before the prisoner, staring into his eyes. 'You know me, don't you, Walter? Before your superiors took the boat, they whispered of Shimon the Jew. The second-class Nazis hiding behind Steiger's skirts in the Girolamo know of Shimon. He's a hunter, they say, and when he finds us—' He stepped back and Uri and Lev raised the chair and placed the prisoner before the array of photographs. They untied his right hand and stepped away.

'A little game, Walter,' Shimon proposed. 'You pick a face. Yes, just point at any face and I'll tell you what we did with him.'

Walter pointed to someone and Shimon leaned close to the photograph.

'Brandt?' he said. 'We hanged him in Israel, Walter.'

The pointing finger moved to the faces in the photographs and Shimon recited their epitaphs. 'Schroeder was strangled in Bolivia. Schmidt is in the foundations of a new building in Bavaria. Heine is down a well.'

The finger trembled uncontrollably. Suddenly, it stopped shaking and stabbed at a face.

'Ah, now you're cheating, Walter,' Shimon chided. 'You know very well where Eichmann is. And so do we. And one day … You did well in that game. Now we play a new game. I ask you a single question. If you get the answer right, my friends dust you off and take you back to the Girolamo. Why? Because you're already serving a prison sentence, Walter. Why would we punish you further? But Walter might run to his superiors and tell them a tale of Shimon the Jew. No, I don't think so. What would Steiger do if he discovered that Walter talked to Shimon?'

Karl saw that the sweat stains that had arced from Walter's armpits had spread to join at his spine.

'Listen carefully, Walter,' Shimon said. 'This is your question. Before he surrendered to the Americans, where did Gehlen dump his files?'

Shimon allowed the silence to stretch for a full minute.

'Lev,' he snapped. The big man walked forwards and grasped the small finger on Walter's left hand.

'Austria,' Walter gasped, and Lev paused.

'Good,' Shimon nodded, 'but Austria is a big place. Try again.'

'It was in Austria,' Walter protested, 'that's all I remember. The army was in retreat and—'

'Lev!'

'No,' Walter gabbled. 'There was a lake and the troops wanted to dump everything in the lake. Gehlen said no. He said the fishermen would bring it up in the nets.' His voice rose to a whine. 'There was a mine in the mountain above the village.'

Karl stood and surprised Lev into immobility. Shimon raised an eyebrow as Karl moved to stand behind Walter.

'It was a salt mine,' Karl said.

'*Ja*,' Walter said quickly, 'it was a salt mine; the walls were shining.'

'Paper and pencil, please,' Karl said. When Shimon fetched them he drew a sketch of the mine entrance and the large chamber. Carefully, he detailed the tunnels leading from the chamber deeper into the mountain. 'You entered here,' he said, tracing a line from the entrance to the main chamber. 'Do you remember this place?'

'Yes.'

'Do you remember anything unusual about it?'

For a moment, Walter looked blank, then he nodded. 'There was a – fossil, in the floor of this place.'

'The four shafts lead away from the chamber,' Karl said. 'Which one did you enter?'

Again, Walter paused. 'Perhaps the first on the left,' he said tentatively.

'No, Herr Kamf,' Karl said. 'I know that shaft.'

'Think carefully, Walter,' Shimon muttered. 'If you send us the wrong way, we know where to find you.' Sweat beaded on Walter's forehead. 'The second from the right,' he said.

'Sure?'

'Yes, sure.'

'How far inside the shaft did you dump the material?'

'Perhaps thirty … forty metres. There was a deep hole.'

After Uri and Lev left with Walter, Shimon and Claus studied the sketch.

'Is he lying?' Shimon asked.

'I don't know,' Karl shrugged.

'How did you know it was Hallstatt?' Claus asked. 'There are hundreds of lakes and mountains in Austria.'

'Yes,' Karl acknowledged, 'but not lakes, mountains and a salt mine. Also, I remember a friend in Hallstatt who hid in the mines at the end of the war. She said troops threw all they didn't want to carry in the lake. One of the other women heard voices in the mine and a rumbling sound.'

'Is it enough to go on?' Claus asked.

'Yes,' Shimon said slowly, 'I think we should go first thing in the morning. Our friend Walter may try to barter this information for a visa.'

STALIN'S DACHA, MOSCOW

Finally, the doctors came. Pyotor led them to Stalin's bedroom and read their faces as they hovered over the patient. He thought they looked like men who had heard a knock on the door at four in the morning.

'Examine him,' Beria hissed.

'May we strip him?' one of the doctors asked nervously.

Beria waved a dismissive hand. While they were prodding the left side of his body, Stalin vomited blood.

'We must consult with our senior colleagues,' the nervous spokesman said to Beria.

'Call them on the telephone,' he said, indicating to the telephone in the room.

The doctor hesitated before leaning forward and whispering in Beria's ear. Beria laughed. 'Yes,' he said, 'there are telephones in the Lubyanka.'

Pyotyr saw Khrushchev lurking in the anteroom. He hadn't entered the sick room since arriving.

Beria was still chuckling when Dimitri eased inside to whisper in Pyotyr's ear. 'Two arrivals.'

A young man with a mottled face staggered past them in the anteroom. Pyotyr smelled alcohol as he brushed by. 'Vasili, the son,' Dimitri confided and followed Pyotyr outside.

The driver of the second car hurried to open the rear door and a young woman stepped out. Pyotyr didn't need Dimitri to identify Svetlana Alliluyeva, Stalin's only daughter. She's not pretty, he thought, but she has a fearless face. Her mother, Stalin's second wife, had taken her own life when the girl was six years old. She hesitated beside the car and he stepped forwards. 'My name is Pyotyr Lozgavech,' he said. 'May I escort you inside?'

She looked him squarely in the face for a moment and nodded. Khrushchev dropped his eyes as they passed. Bulganin half-rose from a chair and nodded. Beria was still chuckling when they stepped inside the room.

'Ah, Svetlana,' he said, twisting his face into a grimace of sympathy, 'the doctors are doing everything they can.'

The doctors were preparing to attach leeches behind Stalin's ears and Pyotyr moved to obstruct her view and guide her to a chair.

Vasili had already been rerouted to another room and he could hear him shout that they were killing his father. As the hours ground by, Stalin seemed to deteriorate and the doctors became more frantic. They applied compresses and administered injections, all the time asking permission from Beria for every procedure. Stalin seemed to be paralysed on one side. His breathing became more laboured and erratic and he was still vomiting blood. Pyotyr detected a change in the rhythm of his breathing and tensed. Instinctively, he placed his hand on Svetlana's shoulder. The doctors retreated and the room stilled. Stalin fought for every breath, the interval between one breath and the next lengthening until Pyotyr felt a painful constriction in his own chest. Svetlana had begun to weep when Stalin opened his eyes and raised his hand as if calling down a curse. Then Iosif Vissarionovich Stalin took one last furious look at the world and died.

Tentatively, the senior doctor approached the body and placed two trembling fingers at the neck. He held them there for a few breathless seconds before he turned to Beria and nodded. For a moment, Beria seemed as stunned as the others. Slowly, his expression changed to one of triumph. He hurried from the room shouting for his driver. Malenkov immediately jerked upright from his chair and followed. The doctors converged on the body.

'Come,' Pyotyr said.

She clung to his arm as they walked to the guard room. Dimitri gaped and then hurried to fetch a chair. Pyotyr filled a clean mug at the samovar and placed it in her hands, cupping her hands in his until she raised it to her lips. She took a long, shuddering sip and closed her eyes.

'He called me his "little sparrow",' she said in a small, breathy voice. 'He said … he said I looked like his mother.' Her face contorted. 'Beria was laughing,' she said.

'Hush,' Pyotyr whispered. 'Don't speak. Not now, not here. You understand?'

Her face relaxed into an expressionless mask. When she looked at him, he saw the glint of steel in her brown eyes. 'Thank you, Pyotyr Lozgavech,' she said firmly. 'I think I'll leave now.'

He watched the car until the trees hid it from view. Tightly wrapped buds stippled the branches. *It's spring*, he thought.

'Krustalev has gone with Beria,' Dimitri whispered.

When will we stop whispering? Pyotyr wondered. Anna claimed she couldn't hear his voice for the first few days of any furlough.

'What should we do, Pyotyr?' Dimitri asked.

'Pack,' Pyotyr said and embraced the big man.

KOTKA, FINLAND

He spent an hour pretending not to eavesdrop on 'the visitors'. In that time, he learned that clergy like to pass the time talking about other clergy. Cardinal Siri was going to Rome. He was regarded as 'papable'. Arvid made a mental note to check that word with his mother. The pope was ailing and if all Finns were like the police inspector, it shouldn't come as a surprise that they danced to the Russian's tune. His ears were flaming red when Edith put her head inside the door.

'The typewriter is jammed again, Arvid,' she said. 'Can you help, please?'

She closed the door firmly behind him. 'Hakkonen has rounded the breakwater,' she said. 'Come!'

He didn't protest as she shrugged into her heavy coat and pulled a woollen cap over her hair. 'Don't go back inside,' she said. 'Take my father's coat and we'll go out the back way.'

'Your father is bigger than me, Edith,' he said as she held the coat for him.

'Maybe taller, Arvid,' she said and turned up his collar.

Arvid placed himself on the windward side of Edith as the fishing boat materialised out of the snow. Pennti jumped from the rail and looped the hawser around a bollard. Hakkonen feathered the engine until his craft nestled snugly against the harbour wall.

'Edith, Arvid,' Pennti nodded. 'He's in the wheelhouse.' Hakkonen was holding a mug of broth to the young man's lips when Arvid and Edith arrived. 'I think he's thawing,' he said without looking around. 'Easy, boy,' he said gruffly in Russian, 'there's plenty more where that came from.'

'Where did you find him?' Arvid asked in Suomi.

'Swimming across the border.'

'You were fishing there?'

'No, I was baring my bum at Leningrad.'

'Another of the joys of living in Leningrad,' Edith said dryly.

'I think that will be all for now, Captain Hakkonen,' Arvid said evenly. He opened the wheelhouse door and stood aside to let him pass. Impulsively, the fisherman hugged the young man. The blanket slipped from around his torso and Hakkonen wrapped it around him again. 'Welcome,' he said. Then he turned to Edith. 'You want to talk to me?' he asked truculently.

'You went fishing and you returned safely,' she said. 'That's what goes in my log.'

After Hakkonen had grumbled his way up the gang plank, Arvid fetched two stools and they sat.

'I am Police Inspector Arvid Morne,' he said in Russian, 'and this is Acting Harbourmaster Edith Canthe. May I ask your name?'

'Stefan Nagy.' His blue lips blurred the words.

'You are not Russian?'

'No, I am Hungarian.'

'Where have you come from?' Arvid asked in Magyar.

The young man's eyes widened momentarily. 'From a gulag in Karelia.'

Arvid searched the map table until he found the one he sought.

'Where is the gulag?' he asked, holding the splayed map before him.

'There.' Stefan Nagy put his finger on a spot north of Lake Ladoga and pressed it to the map to still its trembling.

'I assume you left from Vyborg?' Arvid said, running his finger south from the gulag to the port. 'That's a long way.'

'I hid on a train and then walked.'

'And at Vyborg?'

'I stowed away on a fishing vessel.'

Arvid nodded and rolled up the map.

'How many fishing vessels are registered in Vyborg?' he asked Edith in Suomi.

'Thirty.'

'The lady says there are thirty fishing vessels registered in Vyborg,' he said, reverting to Magyar. 'You were very fortunate to stow away on one that fished so close to our border. And at the border, what did you do?'

'I swam, until Captain Hakkonen's boat rescued me from the sea.'

'Do you wish to claim political asylum in Finland, Mister Nagy?'

'No.'

Arvid was still processing that answer when the wheelhouse door slammed open. The harbourmaster glowered in the doorway, shadowed by two irate monsignori.

'They want him, Arvid,' he said.

'I haven't quite fin—'

'We have authorisation from Helsinki,' the younger prelate snapped, brushing the harbourmaster aside and thrusting a document into Arvid's hands. He read it slowly before handing it back.

'May I ask—'

'No, you may not. It was discourteous of you not to inform us of his arrival and—'

'I'm obliged by Finnish law to interview persons coming to Kotka from another jurisdiction,' Arvid replied evenly. 'As to courtesy,' he added in Italian, 'I gather it is not a prerequisite for a curial appointment.'

The younger prelate had the grace to blush. 'Come,' he said, and Stefan Nagy followed him from the wheelhouse.

'Would either of you like to tell me what the hell is going on?' the harbourmaster demanded.

'Not right now, Papa,' Edith said, linking her arm through Arvid's. 'Arvid and I are just going for a walk.' She steered the bemused policeman to the door.

'A walk,' the harbourmaster spluttered. 'It's after midnight and it's snowing.' He was speaking to a closed door. 'And that's my bloody coat he's wearing,' he shouted.

The snow had eased and the moon was struggling to assert herself.

'What are you thinking, Edith?'

'I'm thinking that freedom is such a … a fragile thing.'

He heard tears in her voice and tightened his grip on her arm.

'What are you thinking, Arvid?'

'I'm thinking I'll go to Helsinki at the weekend to make my report and they'll file it under "Forget". And—'

'And?'

'And I'm also thinking that the Helsinki University Choir perform Sibelius' 'Origin of Fire' on Sunday night. I have a colleague who can get me tickets.'

'Plural?'

'Two to be exact. Do you think the Gulf of Finland could manage without you for a weekend?'

'Possibly,' Edith Canthe said, and smiled.

Cardinal Tisserant's apartments, the Vatican

Emil sat in a chair, a suitcase on the floor beside him. He wore his cassock under a long black travelling coat.

'Where are you going, Emil? Tisserant sighed.

'Into retirement,' the little monsignor replied.

Tisserant's initial shock gave way to annoyance.

'Do I have any say in this?' he growled.

'I am your secretary, Eminence,' Emil snapped, 'not your chattel.'

The cardinal took a deep breath and released it slowly.

'Where will you go?' he asked.

Emil looked nonplussed for a moment. 'Away,' he said firmly.

'And may I ask why?'

'Because I failed you and Karl and … and Tilda,' he said in a rush. His voice broke and tears rolled down his cheeks.

Tisserant sank to his knees before him and took his hands. 'Tell me,' he said and listened until Emil had no more to say. 'But it's not your fault,' he said gently.

'Eugène, please. I should have anticipated what happened. Ti— Tilda practically spelled it out for me. A book is to be published written by Karl Hamner. It will, most likely, be critical of the pope but that wouldn't bother Steiger unduly. It wouldn't matter to him if Karl was writing a book on … fungi. But it is an opportunity for him to hurt Karl and enjoy his own Night of the Burning Books. The – the Führer of the Fratres burns the books and the Zionist Schwartz … and poor Tilda. I should have seen it and taken precautions but—' He looked up with such a depth of anguish in his eyes that Tisserant's heart quailed. 'I have grown vague, Eugène,' he said.

'No!'

'Yes, Eugène. Sometimes I can't remember who you are. Put me aside, Eugène,' he begged. 'Please.'

'And what would I do?' Tisserant said huskily. 'You are my father, Emil. What sort of son would put aside his father?'

'But others will notice and—'

'Others!' Tisserant shouted and reared to his feet. 'Who are those others and when did we set our course by them? Show me these others – let me hear the faintest whisper from them and I will … I will—'

'You will burst a blood vessel, Eugène,' Emil sniffed and dabbed at his cheeks. 'You were always too tetchy.'

'Tetchy!'

'Well, perhaps tetchy is the wrong word – a tad too close to petulance.'

'Petulance!'

'No? I have it – irascible. Now that's a whipcrack word.'

'Irascible?' Tisserant savoured the word and nodded. 'Irascible it is, then. I'll have no more talk of retirement, mind.'

'No, Eugène.'

'Like a brandy?'

'Perhaps a *soupçon*.'

'Not like you to be so … vague, Emil. Do you really think a book on fungi would sell?'

'Yes,' Emil said sweetly, 'as a primer for poisoners.'

The Magdalena Convent, Rome

'No, Dottore, no message,' Sister Dorothea told her for the third time in an hour. 'No telephone,' she added quickly before Sarah could ask her, again. 'Soup?' Sister asked hopefully.

Okay, Sarah told herself, *take a deep breath and let it out. Good! Say, "thank you, Sister", and walk away with dignity. Remember, you're not some love-struck sophomore. You are Doctor Sarah Walker MD, so be a good little doctor – go and cure someone.* 'Thank you, Sister,' she said so sweetly that Dorothea looked uneasy. Her dignified withdrawal held until the first landing. Dorothea heard the angry slap of sandals on marble and took refuge in the kitchen.

'*Amore*,' she sighed.

'Sarah?'

'Huh?'

'Is everything okay? You've been taking my pulse for ages.'

'With you and the babies, yes. With me – so-so.'

'I'm sure he's got a good reason for not—'

'Sure he's got a good reason,' she growled. 'He's probably busy talking about mosaics or busy writing his damn book or—'

'Or maybe he just forgot?'

'Forgot! He's a historian, Laura, for crying out loud. Karl can remember stuff God has forgotten. Sorry.'

'It's okay. You really like him, don't you?'

'I'll kill him.'

'Like him that much, huh?'

'Laura, believe me, if he came crawling—'

'Dottore!'

She was halfway down the stairs before her dignity kicked in.

Julio stood in the hallway, a silly grin halving his face. 'Sarah,' he said uneasily as she paced towards him, 'a message.' He held the note before him like a shield. 'For you, Signorina,' he added in a small voice.

She snatched the note from his hand.

Sarah. Sorry. Had to go away for a few days. I hope you are well.
Karl.

'When you see him, Julio, I want you to tell him something for me.'

'Yes, Dottore.'

'Tell him I'm going to take a claw hammer to his precious San Clemente. After that, I'll work my way through Bernini and—'

Julio had fled.

'Sorry,' she muttered. 'Everyone's so damn sorry.'

THE VATICAN. CARDINAL TISSERANT'S APARTMENTS

'When do we go to Cahors, Papa?'

Tisserant laid his pen aside and rubbed his eyes wearily. Emil's periods of lucidity had become shorter and less frequent. He'd brought a professor friend from the university medical faculty to observe him, under the pretext of a casual visit, and had made an excuse to leave them alone together. On his return, the professor had looked at him with profound regret. 'Irreversible and progressive,' he'd sighed, as the cardinal saw him to the door. 'He's not in pain, Eugène,' he'd assured, 'he's just … going somewhere else. I'm so very sorry.'

'We'll go to Cahors, tomorrow,' he said.

'I'd like to see the Pont Valentre,' Emil said wistfully.

'Doesn't the Camino de Santiago pass through Cahors?' Tisserant asked hopefully.

'You know very well it does,' Emil snapped. He sighed. 'Really, Eugène,' he said, 'Cahors has been on the camino route since before John the Twenty-Second.'

Tisserant let his shoulders sag with relief. Emil had returned – but for how long? And what if— The knock on the door startled him. 'I'll get it,' he said.

'I must apologise for coming without an appointment, Eminence,' Cardinal Siri said, 'but I would appreciate your counsel.'

'Do you know Monsignor Emil Dupont, my secretary?' Tisserrant enquired as he arranged a chair for the guest.

'Only by reputation,' Siri smiled, taking Emil's hand.

Emil looked at him keenly for a moment, before returning the smile. 'Minestrone,' he said.

'I see that the monsignor's reputation is merited,' Siri said ruefully, and sat. 'I am called Giuseppe by my friends,' he said.

'Eugène,' Tisserant said. 'We are brother cardinals, I hope we may be friends.'

'Let me be direct,' Siri began. 'It is rumoured that His Holiness is considering appointing me as mentor to the Fratres in Maglione's place. I understand you have not been favourably disposed to the Fratres.'

'Yes. I advised against a formal recognition and cited canon law to support my proposal that there be a period of trial.'

'That period seems to have become … extended,' Siri sighed. 'Why has it taken the pope so long to appoint a successor?'

'When did you last see His Holiness, Giuseppe?'

'I had an audience with him a month ago, when I arrived from Genoa. His Holiness asked me to be available to Tardini and Montini, who share the Secretary of State position.'

'Have they availed of your counsel?'

'No.'

'I see. Let me also be direct. Montini and Tardini are monsignori. With respects, dear friend,' he continued, patting Emil's hand, 'the appointment of monsignori to share such a prestigious post does not endear them to some of our brother cardinals. A number of, shall we say, the disaffected have attempted to bend the monsignori to their will. Others have made themselves available. Montini and Tardini walk a diplomatic tightrope between both factions. They are good men, Giuseppe, trying to do an impossible job with few resources.'

'And they see me as yet another prelate foisted on them?'

'Yes.'

'Thank you for your candour.'

'He's renowned for it,' Emil said dryly, and Siri smiled. 'How would you recommend I proceed in this matter, Eugène?'

'Concentrate on Montini,' Tisserant replied immediately. 'There are matters he's investigating – troubling matters that may involve Father Max Steiger and the Fratres. In your capacity as mentor to the Fratres, Montini will not deny you access to all the relevant documentation. If you want a more complete dossier, give him a letter, under your seal, empowering him to demand what he needs from each department.'

'Negotiating with the Nazis was probably a good apprenticeship for dealing with Vatican politics,' Siri said with a grimace. 'There is one other matter, Eugène. A Hungarian seminarian has escaped from a gulag in Karelia. I will present him to His Holiness at an audience at noon. I would be most grateful if you would attend and interpret. His Russian and German are quite good but Magyar is beyond me.'

'I am persona non—'

'Also,' Siri persisted, 'it is only proper that the cardinal with responsibility for relations with the Eastern Churches be present.'

'Are you flattering me, Giuseppe?' Tisserant asked.

'Just a little,' Siri admitted. 'Will you come?'

'Speak, O wise one,' Tisserant said, when the door had closed behind the cardinal.

'He has a reputation for pragmatism and candour,' Emil said thoughtfully. 'Not as caustically candid as some I could mention, of course. The letter for Montini was a clever move, Eugène. It will open doors and files to him. What do you make of the fact that he hasn't seen the pope for a month? It suggests that the circle around Pacelli is becoming more exclusive and that's not good for the Church or the pope. You'll have to do something, Eugène.'

'Me! They won't let me—'

'He goes for a walk in the garden every day, Eugène. Alone!'

'Oh.'

'Oh, indeed,' Emil nodded. 'This matter of the escapee intrigues me. What is a Hungarian seminarian doing in a Russian gulag? How does he manage to escape and come to be in Rome under Cardinal Siri's wing?'

Emil spent some time mulling over his own questions before he leaned forward and spoke softly. 'You know there were rumours some time ago that Siri was soft on communism?'

'Witch-hunting,' Tisserant said dismissively. 'That's just the sort of thing Pizzardo would "let slip" to bolster his conservative credentials and damage those of a rival. Come, Emil, you know how it works.'

'I do,' Emil said pensively, 'but we both know that Pacelli's total rejection of any rapport with the East is not to the benefit of the Church, over there or here. If we know it, why wouldn't Siri? And if Siri in Genoa has more freedom to do something about it than we do in Rome—'

'You could be right.'

'I often am,' Emil said smugly.

'He said he doesn't speak Magyar.'

'Yes, he did,' Emil agreed, 'but he also inferred that he spoke German and Russian. German would have been convenient in his dealings with the Nazis. Perhaps he also negotiates with someone in Russian?'

'Pacelli would never allow—'

'If Pacelli knew,' Emil said and rose from the chair. 'I think I'll take a nap now,' he said. 'Being so brilliant can be quite exhausting.'

PAPAL AUDIENCE CHAMBER, THE VATICAN

The drawbridge seems to have been lowered for the occasion, Tisserant thought cynically, as he mingled in the crowded anteroom to the papal apartments. He saw Pizzardo's red face looming in a corner – 'like a full moon in a fog', as Emil liked to say. Tardini was being solicitous with Leiber while Montini stood alone. Tisserant made his way to the monsignor's side, aware of Pizzardo's cold stare on the back of his neck. *The inquisition is always with us*, he thought.

'It seems we're destined to be dance partners, Monsignor,' he said and Montini jumped.

'Do you know what's happening, Eminence?' he asked anxiously but before Tisserant could answer, Siri entered with a young man and everyone turned to stare.

A little robust for a zek, Tisserant thought, observing the well-built young man critically. The beard was interestingly Orthodox but it was his eyes that caught and held Tisserant's attention. *The eyes of an old soul*, he thought sadly, and felt moved to approach the young man as Siri abandoned him and circulated.

'Eugène Tisserant,' he said.

'Stefan Nagy,' the young man answered and attempted to kiss the cardinal's ring. Tisserant held him upright. 'I don't think you've had much practice at that,' he said in Magyar.

Stefan's face relaxed into a slow smile of relief.

'I would appreciate the opportunity to speak to you sometime, Eminence,' he said. 'Cardinal Siri said I may.'

At that moment, the pope's secretary clapped his hands like an imperious dance master and they shuffled into pairs to process inside.

Pius XII sat in an elaborately gilded chair. Less elaborate chairs formed a semi-circle on the floor before the dais and the guests bowed before the pontiff and sat. Tisserant glimpsed an empty chair on the periphery of the row, sat and then turned his attention to the pope. *He's perched rather than sitting on that ugly chair*, he thought. *He's too damned fragile to dent the cushions*. The skin on his face seemed to be stretched so tightly over his cheekbones that they glowed like ivory, and sepia-coloured deltas fanned under his eyes. Even as they waited for the assembly to be seated, he saw the pope place the flat of one palm beneath the pectoral cross he wore and contort his mouth. Tisserant thought the pope looked like a man whose insides were sucking the substance from his frame. *They're killing him*, he fumed. Those quacks and sycophants are sucking like leeches on his life while we stand idly by. His rage kindled and suffused his face. Suddenly, he felt a cool hand on his own.

'Are you well, Eminence?' Montini enquired.

'Yes,' he grunted and took a deep breath. 'Yes, thank you, Giovanni,' he said more calmly. Leiber fluttered to the pope's side and knelt to whisper. The pope stiffened and clasped his hands so tightly that his knuckles bleached bloodless.

'Dearly beloved brothers,' he said in a small, breathy voice and the room stilled. 'We have been informed that Josef Stalin is dead.'

'*Deo gratias*, thanks be to God,' Pizzardo said in the profound silence that followed the announcement.

'We do not rejoice in the death of any man,' the pope said sharply. 'In particular, we do not rejoice in the death of one who turned his back on God. It behoves us to commend his soul to our Saviour's mercy. *Requiem aeternam dona eis, Domine, et lux perpetua luceat eis. Requiescat in pace.* Eternal rest grant unto him, O Lord, and may perpetual light shine upon him. May he rest in peace.'

'Amen,' they chorused.

Pius nodded and Leiber scuttled to open the door. Father Max Steiger entered the audience chamber and knelt before the pope.

'It is our desire,' Pius said, 'that the order known as the Fratres be placed in the care of a mentor, a position vacated on the death of our dear brother, Cardinal Maglione.'

'I thank Your Holiness,' Max Steiger answered. 'It is our desire that Francis Cardinal Spellman be appointed over us.'

There was an audible gasp from the assembly. It was customary for a pontiff to appoint a prelate to such a position without consulting the order in question. It was unheard of for an order to nominate their mentor. *God forgive me*, Tisserant thought, *I'm going to take pleasure in this.*

Pius straightened in the chair and fixed his skull-cap with trembling fingers.

'It is our wish,' the pope continued frostily, 'that our beloved brother, Cardinal Siri, assume this responsibility.' He inclined his head to Siri. 'Are you willing?' he asked.

'*Volo.* I am willing,' Siri replied in a strong voice.

Leiber tapped Max Steiger twice on the shoulder before the priest stumbled to his feet and seated himself on the empty chair. Pius deflated again.

'Holy Father,' Siri said gently, 'we have cause for great joy.'

The pope roused and looked expectantly at the cardinal.

'Holiness,' Siri continued, 'I wish to present Stefan Nagy of Budapest, a seminarian who was imprisoned for eight years by the Soviets and who has recently escaped from a punishment camp in the Karelia region.'

Stefan rose and stepped forward to kneel at the pope's feet. Tisserant saw Pius transformed before his eyes. A childlike expression of pure delight suffused the drawn face and sparkled in his eyes. He held out his hands and grasped those of the young man.

'God has gifted us today, my son,' he said fervently.

'Holiness,' Siri interjected, 'Stefan speaks Magyar, his native language. I have petitioned our brother Cardinal Tisserant to interpret for us.'

Pius turned to where Tisserant now stood and the cardinal felt shamed by the gratitude in the pope's face. 'Please, Eugène,' Pius whispered and repeated what he'd said to Stefan.

Tisserant translated the short conversation between the pope and the seminarian.

'How may we serve you?' the pope asked, and Tisserant's heart constricted in his chest. He struggled to keep his voice from breaking as he translated.

'I have been granted freedom and sanctuary,' Stefan replied. 'If it be Your Holiness' will, I ask to spend time in a religious house where I may experience again the life of a community and be of some small service.'

'You have only to name it, my son,' Pius answered. 'Any of our communities would be honoured by your presence.'

'His Eminence Cardinal Siri welcomed me to Rome,' Stefan said. 'I would be honoured to spend time with the order he has been chosen to mentor.'

During the spontaneous applause, Tisserant stole a look at Steiger. Max Steiger wore the look of a man reprieved at the foot of the guillotine.

CIA OFFICE, NEW YORK

Cy fussed with the projector until the image sharpened into focus. He sat to the side as the newsreel played, his scribbling on a clipboard the only soundtrack to the silent footage. The director watched impassively, until the screen blanched and Cy switched the projector off.

'Better than we'd hoped for,' the director muttered.

'Pardon, sir?'

'Tied up seventeen divisions,' the director said, as if he hadn't heard.

'That's twenty thousand Soviet soldiers, sir,' Cy said promptly.

'Factor in the DDR police and—'

'Eighty thousand *Polizei*,' Cy supplied.

'Thanks, Cy. And it ripples out from East Berlin to more than four hundred other centres in the DDR. Hungary and Czechoslovakia get antsy and Ulbricht gets hauled to Moscow to have his ass kicked by Molotov. Yep, definitely better than we'd hoped for.'

'The, eh, joint chiefs aren't too happy, sir,' Cy offered tentatively. 'Word from the Pentagon is that they'd have pushed for military intervention if they'd had more notice.'

Cy, the director thought, had a knack of finding every cloud in a silver lining. 'Well, they would say that, wouldn't they?' he said, returning to his desk. 'When the only tool you've got is a hammer, everything presents as a nail.'

'Sir?'

'A peacetime general is an oxymoron, Cy,' he explained. 'No general ever wants a war to end. Well, not when he's on the winning side. Ike did the right thing by going into politics. He lets Dick Nixon sweat the local politics while he keeps an eye on the generals and his finger on the button.' He sighed and stretched his legs. 'What's the latest on our friends in East Berlin?'

'Picked up in the first wave of arrests, sir.'

'All of them?'

'All of them, present whereabouts unknown.'

Probably scattered around the gulags if they're alive, the director thought, but didn't say. Cy was a genius with statistics but he could be a little ambivalent when it came to casualties.

'When is the meeting with the president and the joint chiefs of staff?'

'The White House says they'll let us know. Secretary says it's a bi— it's a nightmare arranging a time when they can all get there.'

'Raptors don't flock, Cy,' the director said cryptically

'I, eh, believe vultures do, sir. Flock, I mean.'

'Only to feed, Cy.' He thought it seemed as good a time as any to see Medusa. 'Ask Medusa to come by in about five minutes, Cy.'

He stood at the window, looking out over the New York skyline. The view had ceased to amaze him, but whenever he had a meeting scheduled with the powerful, he liked to stand here to marshal his thoughts. The view reminded him of how quickly the awesome becomes ordinary.

The meeting with the joint chiefs would likely develop into a brawl. Ike was committed to the covert war that had segued seamlessly from the end of the last one. Sure, 'the boys' had come home and, eight years down the line, the birth rate and economy was booming. America Militant had been transformed into America Triumphant. Not all 'the boys' had come home, of course. Some were still looking over the line in Berlin while others watched the North Koreans watching them across the DMZ. The Harvard hotshots in state talked about *détente. Fancy French word for a ceasefire*, he thought. Now that both sides had the bomb – or 'The Bomb' as Cy would say – he knew a foreign policy based on 'I won't if you won't' wouldn't work in the long term. *Maybe*, he thought cynically, if the jingo meisters had come up with a slogan like 'If you do, I sure won't be able to', it might puncture the national complacency. And then there were the generals. Eisenhower had been politician enough to go with the good-time flow while keeping a wary eye ahead for rapids. Some of the others were hungry for action –

'We should have gone all the way in 1945'; 'We could launch first and get that Red monkey off our backs for good and all' – these were the familiar refrains that were sung in the war room. 'Hawks,' Eisenhower called them. 'And what do you suggest I do to keep those damn hawks in check, Mister Director?' he'd asked. 'If you want to have hawks sit quiet on your wrist, Mister President,' he'd answered, 'you have to keep them hooded.'

The president could live with that – he was four-square behind the agency and its director. He had introduced one caveat. 'You know the old gag, Mister Director?' he'd said. 'When in Rome, do as the Romans do, only don't get caught.' Well, the Reds were still 'doing', over there and over here. Stalin's death had given rise to mixed feelings. Some of the joint chiefs had acclaimed it as the end of a belligerent era. Wiser heads had worried about 'the Devil you know'. *Well*, he thought, as he returned to sit behind the desk, *that was in hand, as Cy would say*.

Medusa opened the door. Knocking or waiting to be called was not in her modus operandi. She sat and lit a cigarette. He'd watched her closely from the moment she'd opened the door. *Vulnerable*, he concluded. That was a word he never thought he'd tag to Medusa.

'To lose one asset, Medusa, might be considered unfortunate. To lose both—'

'I can finish the quotation,' she snapped.

'Start with your own guy,' he suggested.

She didn't fudge, fade or dump the blame. He gave her credit for that.

'Fischer blindsided me,' she admitted.

'He must be very good.'

'Best I ever had. Slipped Berlin and disappeared. We trawled both sides of the line. Zilch.'

Terser and terser, he thought. 'He's in Rome,' he said, and rage sucked her eyes to slits. *Blindsided twice*, he noted. *She lost the asset and someone else found him. Two strikes.*

'I'll terminate him myself,' she said and dragged at her cigarette until the tip glowed white-hot.

'Okay,' he conceded after a pause, 'I'll tell Rome to give you—'

'I don't need anything from Rome,' she said through a cloud of smoke.

He waited for the cloud to rise. 'I'll tell Rome you have the tiller,' he said. 'Assistance to be given if requested.'

She nodded. She was still in the game.

'And Moscow?' he asked, angling his chair so's she'd see him side on and lose his eyes.

'He was never ours,' she said, grinding the cigarette in the ashtray and lighting another. *A tad more tightly wound than usual*, he observed. Fischer had done his job across the line and hadn't gone back to undo it. That boded well for the long-term success of the operation. *Let's see how she handles the Moscow affair.*

'I figure he was Beria's asset,' she continued. 'No one else has the muscle or the resources to run that kind of operation. Let's work back from that premise. Beria gets the stuff and Alexei passes it on. We achieve our primary and secondary objectives. Case closed.'

'Not quite,' he murmured and let her stew before continuing. 'Father Steiger has been paying his dues.'

'He delivered Spellman for the Fratres?'

'No, he cocked that up in spectacular fashion. I guess he was anxious to make up for lost ground.' He left that sting in her ego until it delivered its full load of venom. 'Steiger says Fischer, and accomplices, is after something Gehlen left behind. I guess you could call it insurance he took out in case the deal with us turned sour.'

She coughed on the cigarette. 'Gehlen,' she gasped.

Blindsided again, Medusa, he thought. 'If they find it before you find them—'

He didn't have to spell it out. Medusa was enough in the loop to understand the implications. There would be lists and charts, he knew. Christ, the Germans were so obsessed with lists. He'd read them in Nuremberg where the lists had hanged their authors. Gehlen's lists would include names of people who'd been willing to switch their allegiance from Hitler to Uncle Sam. They were employed in every department of the US defence forces. Also, they would identify assets whose wartime actions had been 'sanitised' by the CIA to dupe Truman into granting visas. If Gehlen's insurance policy ever saw the light of day, the fallout around the world would be nuclear and the Geiger counter would tick all the way back to the agency.

'Scorched earth, Medusa,' he instructed. 'Second chances are no longer a luxury we can afford.'

THE SAN GIROLAMO, ROME

'Come,' Barth said, and he followed. Following was what he'd been good at. That's why he'd been in the second row of the photograph.

'Come on, Walter,' Gehlen had invited, 'join us.' Gehlen was like that, always an officer who'd share success with the lesser ranks, always eager to include – except when he'd disappeared with the others and left a note with directions to Hudal's door.

Barth forced the lock of the basement door and the dark yawned at their feet.

'Wait,' Barth said and bent to light the lantern, 'wouldn't want you to have an accident.'

The basement smelled of decay and discarded things. He thought he detected the sour smell of sewerage and remembered someone had said there was a tunnel under the basement that led to the Cloaca, the ancient Roman sewer. He'd said that after the talk of Bolivia and Argentina had stopped and they'd started talking about escape, a few had taken their chances under the basement but had never come back. He wondered if they were lying in the sun in La Paz or Buenos Aires, or just lying under the floor. Barth placed the lantern on a table in the centre of the room. The surface of the table was scarred and some of the welts in the wood appeared to be fresh.

The light from the lantern exposed a processional banner leaning
against a cobwebbed wall.

'Sit,' Barth said, and he sat on a tea chest beside the table. Barth
sat opposite, his impassive face animated by the flickering flame
between them. 'Walter,' he sighed, 'a little bird says you've been
singing. Will you sing for me, Walter?'

He looked into the pale, empty eyes and saw his death. In a flat,
monotonous voice, he told him everything.

'Make a map,' Barth said, pushing pencil and paper across the
table.

Walter's hand betrayed him. It was shaking so badly that the
pencil skittered on the first stroke and gouged the paper. Barth
replaced the page and nodded.

'Four shafts,' Barth said when Walter had finished. 'Which one?'

Walter felt drained. The accumulated fear of capture, Hudal,
Draganović and Steiger had leached from him with every step on
the basement stairs. He leaned forward and marked an X on the
map. Barth folded the page and put it in his pocket.

'It's time,' he said.

HALLSTATT

The sun had yet to climb the Dachstein peaks and the valley savoured
the last, sleepy hours under a mist blanket. Claus and Shimon paced
the small pier, trying to kick start their circulation after the train
journey. Karl sat at the end of the pier, his feet dangling just above
the water. He felt the train had added bruises to his bruises and
the burned places stung. Again and again he'd run the reel of the
day before in his head. It had all begun so well. Sarah had looked
beautiful on the Magdalena stairs. 'Beautiful' was the word he
should have used – 'very nice' was inadequate and withholding.
He'd dreaded the idea of dancing. It hadn't been a feature of his life
in Hallstatt. At first, his feet felt like they belonged to someone else
and then … And then, Sarah had taken charge and he'd forgotten

his feet and the others and the— The fire bloomed in his memory. He closed his eyes against the memory of Tilda lying burned on the pavement while Emil looked so lost. He'd seen men die in Russia, seen the terrible things war could do to a human body but there had been no time to absorb the experience and no one to give comfort. The tip of his nose tingled and he put his fingers to it as if he could hold the sensation. Rome, as he'd said to Enrico, was where he'd last felt alive, but it was Sarah Walker who'd moved him from alive to living. 'And losing?' he asked himself. He raised his head to look in the general direction of the mine. *She's a lovely person, Elsa*, he thought. *I wish you could have*— The creak of oarlocks and purling water brought him back to the present.

'Suits you,' Johann said, peering at Karl's chin, 'never trusted men with beards. Always thought the bastards were hiding something. The other two with you?'

'Sit down, Johann,' he said. Awkwardly, the one-armed man lowered himself to sit on the pier. Karl told him as much as he could. 'There are people who don't want us to find the container,' he murmured. 'I don't want to put you and Erich in their way.'

Johann nodded thoughtfully. 'Does this involve that bastard Steiger?'

'I don't know,' Karl admitted

'Okay, this is how it goes,' Johann said. 'Erich will take us across and you'll come to my house. I have ropes and lanterns in the basement. Your father asked me to store them when we stopped looking for ...'

'It's okay, Johann,' Karl said. 'I like hearing Elsa's name, it means she hasn't been forgotten.'

Johann's wife had marked their progress across the water from her kitchen window and the smell of breakfast welcomed them into her home. After they'd eaten, Johann led them to the cellar. Coils of rope looped from nails hammered into the support beams and lanterns stood sentry along the walls but it was what was stacked on shelves and racked on wooden pallets that drew Karl's eye. 'Where do you keep the tank, Johann?' he whispered and Johann laughed.

'Bastard Germans dumped everything they didn't want to carry in the lake,' he said, shaking his head. 'We kept snagging the net on the stuff. Had to haul it out so as we could fish, of course.'

'Of course,' Karl agreed dryly.

'Any strangers come around recently?' Claus asked.

'No one stranger than you,' Johann grunted.

'Best to take precautions,' Shimon said.

'Which precaution would you prefer?' Johann smiled, hefting a rifle from the rack.

'Guns and me don't mix,' Shimon said quickly.

'I'll take the rifle,' Claus said.

'Which leaves pistols for me and Captain Karl Hamner, the hero of Moscow,' Johann smiled.

Before the sun had burned the mist from the valley, they climbed to the tree line. The rapid pace and steep gradient was already telling on Shimon. 'Seems you and mountains don't mix either,' Johann said cheerfully. 'We'll have to take it more slowly when we get among the trees.'

Karl was unhappy with the pistol. The Luger seemed to be in perfect working order but it weighed more than it should have. The gun he'd carried in Russia had welded itself to his hand at thirty degrees below freezing, and when he'd stumbled and dropped it, it had taken most of his left palm with it. His palm twitched at the memory. The first time he'd killed a man, Sergeant Josef had slapped him hard on the back. 'Aim, breathe and squeeze, boy,' he'd said. That mantra had shaken him from the shock of the crumpled figure in the snow, as the sergeant had intended, but the killing had never become routine. He knew that whatever blood he'd spilled had pooled in his heart and anything he'd tried to do for the Jews of Rome, and the daily pilgrimage to the mine in Hallstatt, was an attempt at expiation. He was hoping this day would not add to that reservoir of pain when the trees thinned and the bare mountain loomed up before them. Shimon slumped gratefully against a tree. A bullet sang through the space he'd occupied and gouged a splinter from the bark. Before the splinter had stopped spinning, they were prone and crawling for cover.

'Where?' Claus called from behind a boulder.

In answer, a second shot sprayed him with stone chips.

'Near the mouth of the mine,' Johann yelled from between the trees. Karl risked a look from where he lay among the roots of a tree that had lost its grip on the thin soil. A bullet tugged at his sleeve and shredded a sapling behind him.

'He's covering the scree,' he shouted. 'Can't go up. I'll work back – find another way. Keep him distracted.'

'Bastard doesn't seem distracted to me,' Johann growled.

Karl wormed back from his position until there was enough cover to crouch and run. He ran diagonally in short bursts, waiting for when it was safe. He clung to the bole of the tree until his breathing eased and began to run again. He knew the sniper had the advantage of elevation and a clear field of fire. The scree was a perfect killing ground, treacherous underfoot and almost totally bare of cover. He also knew the mountains. This had been his playground as a child and his pilgrim route since coming back from the war. His feet retained their memory of the terrain and he made good time to the logging path. Memories dogged him every step of the way, and he struggled to keep his focus. 'Stop gawking, boy,' Sergeant Josef had shouted as they skirted a forest that was mantled in snow. 'The fucking scenery can kill you, idiot.' He'd got another thump on the back for that. But he'd learned, learned to blend with the background, use the cover of mounds and hollows, even the meagre cover available on the steppe. Stay alive, had been the basic skill, followed closely by hunting and killing. He was hunting now, angling across the mountain, using its curve to shield him, staying shy of the skyline where he'd present a perfect target. Some part of his mind admitted that he was immersing himself in the role of hunter to avoid contemplating the next step. Killing was something he'd never sought to do, but he had done it before and would do it again to stay alive. 'Sarah,' he whispered, 'Sarah, Sarah' – a mantra that forced his leg muscles to keep their rhythm and carry him above the mouth of the mine.

'Never run down a slope,' they'd been cautioned in childhood, and that memory braked his impulse to hurry. His path to this point had been punctuated with shots, and the vulnerability of his companions pleaded for speed. 'Measure twice, cut once,' his carpenter father had advised. He sat on the slope and waited – waited until his breathing steadied and the pounding in his chest muted. Cautiously, he rose to a crouch, the Luger in his right hand, and started to descend, using the edge of his leading foot as a brake. A shot boomed from beneath and his foot jerked, sending a small avalanche of pebbles skittering a few feet before they stopped. Motionless, he listened – hoping the sniper might be deafened temporarily by the sound of the gun or distracted by the echoes ricocheting among the peaks. A few yards short of the lintel, he lay flat and inched to the overhang.

The sniper had always been the bogey-man to the troops on the Russian front. They'd feared him even more than attacking tanks and troops – at least they could be seen and engaged or evaded. The sniper was insubstantial and haunted the shadows. Any tree, mound or declivity could harbour one. Even the featureless snow could hide a sniper in winter-white camouflage, and so the troops walked wary and watchful, as if traversing an endless minefield. Constant vigilance wore them down until fatigue set in and someone forgot and – crack! In barracks or under canvas, the stories multiplied and the sniper's prowess grew more mythic in the telling. 'They could wait for days in a tree, unmoving. They could bury themselves in snow and let a patrol walk by before taking them from behind.'

The sniper sprawled before the mine was a man. He wore a black knitted hat and camouflaged fatigues tucked into studded boots. As Karl watched, the man took his finger from the trigger to scratch behind his ear. Every sniper, he knew, chose a firing position that could be vacated when superior numbers made it untenable. Very rarely did a sniper undertake a suicide mission, holding a position until he was outflanked or overrun. This man, he concluded, was a delaying tactic, holding them at bay until someone else arrived. Infinitely slowly, Karl extended the Luger in his right hand and sighted down the barrel. 'Stop,' he barked. The man's head jerked up from his weapon. 'Push the rifle down the slope,' Karl said in an even voice.

The man shrugged, eased to his knees and then, in one fluid movement, swivelled and fired. The round spanged the stone lintel of the mine entrance and shards scythed over Karl's head. He squeezed the trigger.

'You okay?' Johann enquired. Karl nodded. 'It was a clean kill,' Johann muttered gruffly before going to join the others.

'Asshole,' Medusa muttered to herself as she looked at the man spreadeagled before the mine. She'd been doing that a lot lately – talking to herself – and it bothered her. She'd always talked aloud when alone but she'd seen her partner pretending not to notice her mutterings as they'd climbed. They'd come from a different valley and approached the mine from the opposite side to the four climbers from Hallstatt. She'd watched through binoculars from a stand of trees while the asshole let himself be outflanked by a 'civilian'. 'Asshole,' she said again and kicked him in the thigh. 'If the kid hadn't shot you—' Still, the kid was something,' she grudged. 'Savvy and guts are a rare combination in a man. Add a cool eye under fire and the one-shot-wonder might even grow up to be an asset. Too bad,' she sighed, as she entered the mine. 'And Claus,' she said, as the walls twinkled in the lantern light, 'boy, I enjoyed watching you haul your sorry ass up the mountain. Then you go and disappear inside the mine. Tut and tut again, Claus. An asset never goes in without another way out. Strike one, Claus.'

'Stop.'

The sinkhole was a black eye in the shaft floor.

'We can cross on that side,' Karl said, raising the lantern to reveal a ledge that skirted the hole. 'I'll go first.' He tied the rope around his waist while Shimon and Claus took up the slack. The urge to flatten himself against the wall of the shaft was almost irresistible. 'Stay upright and face the wall,' Tomas, the miner, had advised the men who searched for Elsa. 'If you cling too tightly with your hands you'll forget your feet.' Balanced on the balls of his feet, and trying to ignore the drop behind him, he sighed with relief when his left foot found purchase on the other side. Johann came next, surprisingly light on his feet, barely touching the wall with the tips of the fingers of his remaining hand. Claus followed, carefully, and took up a position on the rope behind Karl as Shimon began to edge across.

'Look at the wall, Shimon,' Karl instructed, 'and keep moving left until I tell you to stop.'

Shimon began to shake and within a few feet of safety made a lunge for firm ground. 'No, Shimon,' Karl called and threw himself back on the rope as Shimon fell. He thrashed like a fish at the end of a line until Karl shouted at him to be still. Johann hovered at the edge of the hole as they eased back on the rope. 'Your hand,' he said and lifted Shimon to safety.

'Sorry,' Shimon gasped.

'You'll do better on the way back,' Johann assured him and Shimon looked as if he might be sick.

Karl checked the map. 'Next one,' he said and walked ahead with the lantern. He tightened the knots at his waist and took the spare lantern in his right hand. 'Claus and Shimon on the rope,' he said. 'Johann, you hold the lantern over the edge when I go down.' He sat on the edge of the hole and eased himself into the earth.

The walls were polished smooth with the passage of time and water. The lantern sparked reflections from below, tiny glowing lights flaring in the salt crystals. After a long, vertical descent, the tunnel gradually sloped to the side and he was able to slide a stone chute into a small cavern. He heard the sound of rushing water from somewhere just beyond the light of the lantern and stalactites bristled from the roof. As he quested over the debris-strewn floor, his leading foot found something solid and he scrabbled to free a metal case. It was about the size of an ammunition box, he judged as he unlooped the rope from his waist and tied it through the box handle. 'Slow and steady,' he called up the chute, hoping the sound would travel to the surface. He tugged the rope and it tautened. Slowly, the box began to disappear from view, sliding along the smooth chute until it reached the vertical shaft.

After a few moments, he followed the light of the lantern towards the sound of running water. The narrow river rushed through an opening in the wall of the cavern to his left and was sucked into the mountain by another to his right. Directly across from where he crouched, he could see debris piled against the wall. Timber spars latticed the wall with shadows as the lantern found them and they sparkled with a frost of salt. He wondered which part of the mine they'd come from and how long they'd— 'The rope,' he whispered. The rope wouldn't travel around the bend in the sink-hole. Carefully, he eased his body into the chute and began to climb. It was like climbing a slide in a children's playground, he thought, until the gradient became steeper and he used knees and elbows to find purchase against the walls and crab along. He'd abandoned the lantern at the lip of the chute. He needed both hands to climb, and carrying it in his mouth by the handle or hanging it from his waistband were not options that appealed to him. His joints were grinding painfully when the vertical shaft appeared above his head like the moon emerging from an eclipse. The rope swung in the dim light. 'Brace,' he shouted. After a slow count of five, he shot his arms away from the walls and grabbed the rope. It burned through his fingers until he held hard and braked his fall. 'Pull,' he shouted and the long ascent into the light began.

Salt gleamed like sparks in the wash of her lantern. The director had been so damn ... superior. She'd clocked the 'five minutes' and the oh-so-careful questions and the swivel of the fucking chair. She was Medusa, nobody tried that kind of shit with her. '"Second chances are no longer a luxury we can afford." What was that – a threat? Back-up in Rome?' she laughed. 'What an oxymoron. This guy was the best Rome could offer and gets himself offed by a rookie?'

'Blindsided by Claus?' a voice in her head questioned.

'He knew the rules,' she whispered fiercely, 'know more than you need to and you're dead.'

'You know too much, Medusa,' the voice insisted.

She shook her head violently. 'No, that's not how it works. I'm in the loop – hear me. The director talks to me – everything – the DDR, Stalin, Khrushchev, the Shah. I know—' She froze and the lantern swung, distorting her face. She lurched forward and fell, screaming, into the dark.

She dreamed she was flying down a starry tunnel. Suddenly, the floor sloped and she was sliding on her back. 'Look at me, Momma,' she shouted at the woman with the burned face. 'Lookame.'

Her eyes snapped open. She saw lights wavering across the ceiling and breathed a sigh of relief, the lantern had survived the fall. 'S'good,' she slurred, 'don't want to be in the dark with no burned lady.' Carefully, she flexed her limbs and bit down on a scream. She raised her head and saw her left foot angled the wrong way. 'No major problem here,' she said, fighting the nausea that threatened at the back of her throat. The gun lay beside her and she picked it up. 'Feeling better already,' she said. Stretching, she lifted the lantern and began to inch along, holding her left leg high from debris on the floor. 'Thunder?' she wondered, confused by the constant rumbling sound that battered the walls of the cavern. 'Water. Three weeks without food and three days without water, that's what the survival manual says. Good odds.'

The river poured out of a hole in the rock and ran twenty yards before disappearing into another hole. She ducked her head and came up gasping. 'That's good,' she said and scooped a palmful to her mouth. 'Salt,' she spat, 'should have remembered, the whole fucking mountain is made of salt. File that problem with the busted ankle and check the perimeter.'

A jumble of boulders formed a small cairn near the river's exit point. That's where she found the girl. She lay on her back in a depression, encased in a solid pool of salt. She seemed to float, like a body under river ice.

'Well, look at you, honey,' she crooned. 'You come shooting down that tunnel and wander over here to rest and then the lantern dies and the salt drips, drips from the roof until—' Nearby, she found what looked like a drawing pad, salt-encrusted and solid as a brick. She held it to the light but couldn't decipher the pencil marks. 'Guess you were following a map too, honey,' she whispered. 'Map' brought Walter Kamf to mind. 'When I get out of here …' but the echoes mocked that threat into silence. The lantern dimmed, flickered and burned steady again. 'I could yell up the shaft,' she said. 'Claus might hear me and drop a rope? Yeah, and pigs might fly.' The gun felt heavy in her hand. '*You* are plan Z,' she told it and tucked it in her pocket. She watched the rushing water until the lantern dimmed and died. Medusa took a deep breath and rolled into the river. *Here's to nothing,* she thought as the mountain swallowed her.

The Kremlin. Khrushchev's office

Alexei looked like a shadow wearing a suit. Khrushchev thought there was room in there for at least one other person. 'Sit,' he commanded. The chair cushion appeared undented by Alexei's weight. 'How are you, Alexei?'

'Fine.'

'Fine? I was in Leningrad during the siege, Alexei. When people looked as fine as you, we stacked them up as sandbags. In the parts of the city where they'd run out of rats, you'd have been on the menu.'

'I have the papers,' Alexei whispered. With infinite slowness, he dipped in the inside pocket of his overcoat and withdrew a sheaf of documents. The front of the coat seemed to deflate a full inch before it reached the resistance of his ribcage.

'Shall I fill your bath?' he wheezed.

'No. I need a hot bath and you'd drown in the steam.' Khrushchev paced around the desk and plucked the papers from his fingers.

'I forgot to congratulate you on your new position,' Alexei said.

'There were ten positions available,' Khruhschev grinned. 'I came in at number ten. Hardly a ringing endorsement, wouldn't you say? Well, it beats the hell out of the alternative. Coffee?'

'I seem to have lost my taste for coffee,' Alexei said ruefully.

'See if you can crawl as far as the samovar,' Khrushchev said and started reading. He read the first page quickly, and then read it again, running his finger down the page, a throwback to inadequate and intermittent schooling. He felt a swelling sensation in his chest and rose abruptly to walk to the window. 'Bastard,' he muttered, before returning to his seat and his reading. 'This all of it, Alexei?'

'Yes, I must replace it by lunch. Beria is distracted by many things just now, but—'

'I understand. It's best to be cautious,' Khrushchev agreed. He sat back in his chair and tapped his foot rhythmically against the desk. 'I wonder where the hero of Borodino is these days?' he mused.

It took Alexei a few moments to align his brain with the shift in their conversation.

'Not very far away, I imagine,' he said softly.

Khrushchev picked up a page and held it at arm's length before letting it seesaw to the desktop.

'There's a vacant office at the end of the corridor,' he said. 'Comrade Beria sometimes uses the telephone there to make … special appointments.'

It was an open secret in the Kremlin that Lavrentiy Beria had a harem of mistresses in Moscow. Most of the women were the wives of men who owed their position or even their existence to Beria.

'That telephone is not connected to the Kremlin exchange,' he added and smiled. He savoured the thought that Beria might finally be fucked because of that particular telephone. Hastily, he scribbled a name and message on a slip of paper and tossed it on the desk for Alexei to read. When Alexei left, he drew tea from the samovar and popped the scrap of paper in his mouth. Someone observing Nikolai Khrushchev at that moment would have been struck by how savagely he chewed. Returning to the desk, he lifted the telephone.

'Molotov,' he said.

TRAIN TO ROME

'Trastevere is compromised,' Claus assured them. 'Karl had a tail when we first met and they were already hunting for me.'

'Most of my boltholes are in or near Trastevere,' Shimon added. 'We need a secure place where we can get the material photographed. Any suggestions, Karl?'

He had been withdrawn since Hallstatt, and his companions had given him space.

'I know a place,' Karl said quietly and went back to looking out of the carriage window.

Shimon raised his eyebrows at Claus, who made a 'let it pass' gesture. Shimon grew more restless as the train rattled closer to

Rome and began to pace the small compartment. He reached up regularly to touch the metal case on the rack, until a look from Claus pushed him to leave and pace the corridor.

When they arrived in Rome, he was relieved to see Uri and Lev shadow them as they moved through the crowded station.

'I must make a call,' Karl said and disappeared inside a telephone booth. Shimon seethed as they waited. 'Come,' Karl said and led them to the pavement outside.

'We're very exposed here, Karl,' Shimon grumbled.

'Soon,' Karl replied.

Shimon's nerves had gone rogue by the time a black limousine nosed out of the traffic. They bundled hurriedly into the plush interior and the driver wove seamlessly back into the ribbon of cars. Uri sat beside the driver, his eyes sweeping the pavement for signs of undue interest.

'Where are we going, Karl?' Shimon asked.

'To safety,' Karl replied, as if surprised at the question.

Shimon became increasingly nervous as the limousine sped up the Via della Conciliazione and Saint Peter's Square began to fill the windscreen. They veered right at the edge of the square and then sharp left. He gulped when the Swiss Guards raised their halberds and they raced inside the Vatican.

Commander Markus spirited the group to Tisserant's apartments using stairs and corridors swept free of human traffic. Once his charges were safely inside, he stood guard outside the door. Tisserant embraced Karl and shook hands with the others. 'I'll leave you to your business,' he said briskly. 'If you need anything, ask Emil or Commander Markus.'

Uri and Lev commandeered a table and began to photograph the documents Shimon and Claus relayed from the metal case. 'Two copies of everything,' Shimon reminded the photographers.

'Two?' Claus queried.

'Yes, two. One for the Israeli embassy and one for the cardinal. Where's Karl?'

'He said he had something to do.'

They left Uri and Lev to their work and went to sit with Emil at the window. 'The Good Thief returns,' Emil said, smiling broadly and clasping Claus' hands. 'And the Nazi hunter,' he added, looking keenly at Shimon. 'Plenty of quarry for you in that lot, I'll wager.'

'Enough for two lifetimes,' Shimon smiled.

'The brandy is in the cabinet by the door,' Emil said. 'Eugène keeps the best bottle hidden behind the cheap champagne.'

Claus related the story to Emil as they sipped their drinks.

'Poor Karl,' the monsignor said sadly, 'he'll find it hard to bear the hurt of taking a man's life.'

'That's why he is the man he is,' Claus said softly, and the others nodded.

'Where do you go from here, Shimon?' Emil asked to break the sombre mood.

'To Israel, I think. I need Israeli Intelligence to help me sort the material.'

Emil turned to Fischer. 'And you, Claus? You know you can stay here for as long as you wish. We can find asylum for you somewhere … in time.'

'I appreciate your offer, old friend,' Claus said. 'I probably should stay until the furore dies down. The long term is more problematic. The agency neither forgives nor forgets and it has a long reach. There are very few governments who would resist pressure from the United States.'

'There is one state that might resist a demand for your extradition,' Emil said slowly, 'particularly if you offered your expertise to their intelligence service.' He turned to Shimon. 'Would you agree that the Israeli Intelligence Service would benefit from the knowledge of Herr Fischer?' he enquired.

'Why – yes,' Shimon stammered. 'Would you, Claus?'

Claus Fischer studied his empty glass for a long time before replying. 'Yes,' he said finally. 'I … I have things to atone for.'

Molotov's dacha, Moscow

'Polina?' he enquired when they were ensconced in the living room. Khrushchev had passed on the offer of vodka to prolong the taste of paper in his mouth.

'I went to Lavrentiy this morning,' Molotov said, 'and demanded her release.'

There was no denying Molotov's love for his wife, Khrushchev thought, *but it was early days yet for demands. Still*, he grudged, *the old bastard has balls – even if he did hand them on a platter to Ribbentrop*. He withdrew a folder of documents from his valise and offered it to Molotov. 'I'm as happy about Polina as you are, comrade,' he said, 'but Lavrentiy plans to release thousands.'

'What?'

Molotov read the pages feverishly, and sat back with a glazed look in his eyes. 'Why is he doing this?' he breathed.

'Because he can,' Khrushchev said mildly, 'and because it will sweeten his image, at home and abroad.'

'What are *zeks* to the West, Nikolai?'

'You're right, of course,' Khrushchev agreed, 'but a new deal on the DDR might impress them.'

'What?'

Khrushchev flourished a batch of fresh papers. 'Page twenty-seven,' he said helpfully.

'Madness,' Molotov hissed, as he read. 'The party would never agree to this. It's – It's a blueprint for—'

'The end of the union,' Khrushchev supplied. 'There is one final document, comrade,' he said slowly. 'It came from the same source as the others. If you read it and believe it – there is no going back.'

Molotov stared at him. The clock ticked loudly in the silence until he stretched to take it. *Molotov always looked anaemic*, Khrushchev thought, watching him closely. *Now he looks like a week-old corpse.*

'Murder,' Molotov gasped.

'Treason,' Khrushchev added and waited.

Molotov and Stalin had been the only survivors of the Lenin era and Stalin had hung his Minister for Foreign Affairs out to dry when the fascists crossed the border in 1941. Khrushchev remembered the night Stalin had humiliated Molotov before his peers; baiting him about his wife's Jewish connections. He hoped Molotov had not forgotten but he knew the old man was faithful to the party and loyal to the leadership. 'He controls the NKVD,' Molotov said cautiously, and Khrushchev felt relief course through his body.

'Josef Stalin was aware of that, comrade,' he said. 'Only recently, he asked me to find out how many military units were stationed in the greater Moscow area. I suggested contacting a particular general but our leader vetoed him.'

'The man who refused to retake Kiev from the fascists and was demoted for it,' Molotov mused and Khrushchev nodded. 'But, would Zhukov—'

Khrushchev held up a hand to forestall the question. 'I think I heard his car pull up outside,' he said.

THE MAGDALENA, ROME

Sarah Walker opened her door and froze. Sister Pilar stood outside Laura's door, her upper body bobbing forwards and backwards, and gibberish streaming from her mouth. Sarah listened intently. When she heard the word '*puta*', she placed herself between the deranged woman and the door. 'Can I help you, Sister?' she asked.

Sister Pilar's glazed eyes focused and narrowed. She opened her mouth to reply and then snapped it shut so violently that Sarah heard her teeth click. Her face spasmed from anguish to anger and she hurried to her room and slammed the door. Sarah heard the muttering start up again, like an angry wasp in a window. She waited until the stream of sound segued into slapping sounds.

Sister Pilar was strange to begin with, she thought, *and had become stranger*. In the beginning, she'd sat apart from the others in the refectory, methodically tearing a bread roll into tiny pieces and sipping a glass of water. Lately, she'd just sat, mostly mute, but liable to start muttering. It bothered the guests and Sarah had mentioned it to Dorothea, but the little nun had thrown her hands in the air. 'Fratres,' she'd whispered as if that single word explained everything. Sarah had become accustomed to the chanting and slapping sounds from Pilar's room but seeing her at Laura's door tuned her anxiety to a higher pitch. *I'm an obstetrician*, she reminded herself, *not a psychiatrist*. But the thought of another human being suffering like that appalled her. She tried to push what she'd seen and heard to the back of her mind as she pushed at Laura's door.

'Aloha, Laura,' she said with forced levity. Everything was well with mother and child – children, she corrected herself, as she finished the examination.

'Not too long now, honey,' she pronounced, 'time we had our birthday talk.' She explained, in simple terms, how the babies would be delivered and Laura seemed to relax.

'Sarah,' she asked, 'could something go wrong?'

Sarah Walker's old mentor had always advised against certainty. 'Someone who say's "no problem" sometimes doesn't see the darn problem. Yes,' she said easily, 'there's always that possibility. If it happens, we ditch plan A. Babies haven't read the script, Laura,' she smiled, when the girl's eyes clouded. 'Most of my training was focused on what to do when the unusual happens. Obstetricians are a bit like airline pilots. Usually, the pilot lifts it up and puts it down, no sweat. Occasionally, stuff happens. That's what the pilot gets trained and paid for.' She sat on the edge of the bed and took Laura's hand. 'If something happens,' she assured her, 'I'll be right on it.'

'If – if something does happen,' Laura said, 'will you do something for me?'

'Apart from delivering two healthy babies, sure. Shoot!'

'I – I have a journal,' Laura whispered, as if afraid of being overheard.

Sarah leaned closer and lowered her voice. 'And?' she prompted.

'It's in my wardrobe,' Laura confided. 'Wrapped in a bathrobe. I didn't want anyone to find it.'

By 'anyone', she means Pilar, Sarah thought.

'I never,' Laura began and then hesitated and broke eye contact. 'You know how girls like to share secrets and stuff,' she continued. 'I never had … someone, you know?'

'Sure,' Sarah said, 'I know.'

'I'd like you to have my journal,' Laura blurted.

'I'd be honoured to have something so special,' Sarah said and then grinned and tilted the girl's chin. 'But it ain't gonna happen, honey, because I'm the hottest-shot dottore in the universe and nothing bad happens on my watch.'

'Dottore!'

Sister Dorothea's yell startled them.

'This time, Julio eats the message,' Sarah fumed.

It wasn't Julio. Karl stood in the centre of the atrium while Dorothea jigged around him like a happy puppy.

'You shaved,' she said. 'It suits you. Makes you look … less like a bear.'

He smiled and Sarah almost forgot she intended to kill him. 'Sorry,' he said.

Sarah stepped up close and looked him in the eye. 'You know, Karl,' she said softly, 'sorry is wearing a little thin.'

His mouth opened but she placed a warning finger to his lips. 'I know it's a reflex,' she muttered, 'but if you say sorry again I'll—'

He put his arms around her.

'*Scusi*,' Dorothea squeaked and raced into the refectory.

'Can we walk?' he whispered and his breath tickled her ear.

'Walk and talk, *hombre*,' she said, easing out of his arms. 'Is there a telephone number I can give Dorothea?'

'Yes,' he said and recited it slowly as she scribbled.

'Is that the restaurant number?' she asked as he helped her into her coat.

'My apartment,' he said.

They were midway across the Ponte Sant'Angelo when he broke the silence. 'There was a girl in Hallstatt and I loved her.'

She felt her heart trip and took a steadying breath.

'Elsa?'

'Yes, Elsa. We were very young.'

'You're never too young to love, Karl.'

'She was killed,' he said, and she tightened her grip on his arm. 'She was killed by my friend, Max Steiger. I – I don't think he meant to kill her, but he was jealous and …' His voice trailed away.

The little girl exchanged formal greetings with Karl without taking her eyes from Sarah. That stare itched at her spine all the way up to the apartment. *What is it with this guy?* she wondered. He's got Paolo in the restaurant and this little signorina in his apartment building, both watching his back like sawn-off bodyguards. She forgot her misgivings when she entered the apartment. *Spare but not Spartan*, she thought, as she looked around the room. It was functional rather than fancy – a writer's room, she concluded, as neat as only Karl could make it. Two armchairs faced a high window that filtered shadow-patterns through lace curtains. A faded rug nestled like a cat on a chair and she knew he'd brought it from his home in Hallstatt. A small kitchen peeped through beaded curtains and wooden stairs climbed to a half-loft. *That's where he sleeps*.

'Coffee?' he called from the kitchen and she was glad of the distraction.

They sat in the armchairs by the window, watching the curtains bell in the breeze to reveal facades, balconies, the dome of the synagogue and a green glimpse of the Tiber. Karl began to talk. As the story progressed, she closed her eyes, trying to see him so young in Hallstatt and Russia. He recounted his war experiences and, though it was a tale told by a historian, the telling wasn't dispassionate. At some stages, his voice grew husky. Sometimes, it failed him completely and he seemed to wrestle with his emotions, waiting for them to submit to the narrative. The sun was tinting the rooftops when he told her why he'd come back to Rome and how he'd killed a man in Hallstatt since their last meeting. He told that part with no attempt at self-justification but with palpable regret. When he finished, she gathered the coffee mugs and rinsed them in the kitchen. Sarah, the domestic goddess, she imagined her mother saying and smiled. When she returned she stood behind him and leaned forward to hold him, resting her chin on his head. He lifted his hands to cover hers.

'And what's the next chapter in this story, Karl?' she asked softly.

'It's whatever we agree to write,' he said.

'You know I planned to go to Ethiopia?'

'I love you, Sarah,' he said.

Dammit, she thought, *didn't he just tell me of all the madness in his life and didn't I tell him about Ethiopia? How the hell can he just –*

'Say it again,' she said.

'I love you, Sarah,' he repeated.

His eyes never left hers – not when they climbed the stairs to the loft or when they explored each other's bodies with trembling fingers or when they kissed and she welcomed him inside her. She drifted into sleep, safe in the knowledge that Karl watched over her in the dark.

MOSCOW

On the return journey to the Kremlin, Khrushchev played and replayed the scene. Again, he saw Molotov's face going from white to grey as he read the documents and the way he polished his spectacles so furiously as if they'd been soiled by what he'd read.

Zhukov was made of sterner stuff. When the Defender of Moscow had read the papers through and then aligned the pages neatly before closing the folder, he'd stood to attention in Molotov's cosy living room and uttered one word. 'When?'

Alexei sported sweat in his eyebrows when Khrushchev returned. It was an hour before noon and he was fretting about returning the documents. He jumped to his feet when Khrushchev entered the office, his eyes riveted on the party boss.

'Return the documents and come back,' Khrushchev said brusquely. 'You are finished in Moscow.'

Alexei swayed on his feet and Khrushchev helped him sit.

'I am sending you to the Ukraine,' Khrushchev said, 'for health reasons. Your papers will state that you are investigating private enterprise activity among the kulaks. Unfortunately, your duties will require you to travel into the interior.' Khrushchev smiled. 'Even a resourceful man like you could get lost – and stay lost until I need to find him.'

Alexei stared at him with uncomprehending eyes until his brain decoded what Khrushchev had said. A single tear eased from the corner of his eye and hung on his cheekbone. 'Nikita,' he said throatily, 'I would like—'

'Vodka,' Khrushchev supplied with a gruff laugh. 'I'll join you,' he added. 'I've had a taste of paper in my mouth all morning.'

THE SAN GIROLAMO, ROME

Brother Cyprian found a vacant table in the corner and sat with his back to the refectory. Coming early to breakfast meant that he could enjoy some quiet time and avoid listening to the growling talk of the others. The kitchen staff didn't object – Father General's secretary could have his meals sent up on a tray if he wished. He didn't want that. As difficult as it was to endure the refectory, he would rather starve than eat in the toxic atmosphere that infected Max Steiger's apartments. However, he felt guilty for accepting preferential treatment and for his lack of charity towards the others and welcomed the intrusion as an act of penance.

'May I sit here?'

He was tall with sallow skin and dark hair. *Hasn't done much work outdoors*, Cyprian thought and felt guilty again.

'Of course,' he said. 'My name is Brother Cyprian.'

'Stefan Nagy.' He gave a brief bow and began to cut the loaf.

So, this is Stefan Nagy, Cyprian mused. He'd read the terse document from Cardinal Siri and overheard the expanded story in the refectory. '*Zek*,' they'd called him. Brother Cyprian gathered he'd been monosyllabic with the others and they'd tired of him. *Good*, he thought approvingly. He also noticed that Stefan Nagy had cut two slices from the loaf and taken just one, as a good monk should.

'May I ask you something, Brother Cyprian?'

Cyprian's spirits fell. *Here it comes*, he thought. Father General's secretary will now be asked to use his influence. Resignedly, he nodded.

'Thank you. I find I'm welcome and comfortable, but not useful,' Stefan Nagy said. 'You seem to be very busy, Brother. May I be of assistance?'

Stefan Nagy had spoken simply and to the point, Cyprian admitted, and the good Lord knew, he was weighed down with paperwork. And … and there was a stillness about the young man that soothed a part of his spirit rubbed raw in Max Steiger's service.

'If you could come at ten, Brother, it's quieter then.'

Cyprian realised he'd automatically used the monastic title, but didn't correct himself. Stefan Nagy ate slowly and frugally. After a short time, he excused himself, and took his dishes to the kitchen.

'A fellow brother,' Cyprian marvelled. '*Deo gratias*. Thanks be to God.'

THE MAGDALENA, ROME

So, this is purgatory, Sister Pilar thought.

When the demons began to trouble her waking hours, she'd increased the number of strokes with the 'discipline' but to no avail, even when the blood ran from her back and buttocks. The lascivious whisperings and leering faces tormented her, appearing and disappearing until only one face remained – his. Prayers for deliverance brought no respite nor had the pages she'd torn from the *Dark Night of the Soul* and pinned to the walls like a talisman. The wounded pages fluttered ineffectually on their pins like the butterflies she'd mounted as a child – silly, frivolous creatures who wasted their short lives preening gaudy wings. The sound of Sister Dorothea's voice echoing in the stairwell made her wince. 'Dottore – Dottore.' It was followed by the sound of footsteps descending. She cracked her door open and listened. *So*, she thought, *the lover has returned and taken the witch away*. 'The coven has been deserted by its dam,' she whispered.

When she roused again, the dark had come to claim her. She felt no fear. 'I gave myself to the dark,' she whispered, 'it has come to claim its own.' She stood painfully and began to dress, welcoming the sting of coarse cloth as it abraded her wounds. *There must be a purgation*, she thought, and that thought flashed like fire in the darkness. He had cast her into this desert to try her soul. She had endured the torments of looks and whispers and the lash of the dottore's tongue. Blood, the voices demanded, we can be saved only through the expiation of blood. You shall not suffer a witch to live, the voices urged. 'He will embrace me when I am cleansed,' she whispered, exultation rising and spreading through her body. 'If it be thy holy will,' she prayed and opened the door.

Laura cringed in her sleep.

'You are not bright, Laura,' her father said. 'I never had any real hope that you might be. However, I did expect you to grow into a proper person – a lady. It seems even that was too much to expect.'

She had always kept her eyes fixed on the floor when Papa said hurtful things. That was okay for a child, she reasoned. Children find a place to hide from cruel things, but she was a woman now and she was going to be a mother and no one would ever hurt her babies the way he— She opened her eyes and blinked at the figure beside her bed. 'Sarah?'

'The dottore has sacrificed her duty to indulge her lust,' Sister Pilar whispered.

Laura opened her mouth to yell for Dorothea but the attack began. A fist smacked her in the side of the head and rocked her in the bed. *Mustn't fall*, she thought automatically, as she tasted copper in her mouth. Pilar's attack was a flurry of blows and Laura covered her abdomen with her arms, stoically enduring the savage beating until a surge of outrage swept through her. She'd been timid before her father's verbal abuse and had abased herself before the power of Max Steiger. *Well, fuck that*, she thought fiercely. Sister Pilar seemed momentarily paralysed by the roundhouse punch. She screamed and attacked with renewed ferocity. Laura tried to fend her off with her arms but the walls were beginning to pulse and fireworks bloomed in her vision. She thought she glimpsed Dorothea charge through the door, like a tiny vengeful angel and then—

KARL'S APARTMENT, ROME

A phone rang somewhere deep in the house, and she tightened her arms around him. The phone insisted until someone picked it up and she listened with a sense of resignation to the footsteps pattering round and round until the soft knock sounded on the door. Karl pulled on trousers and shirt and cracked the door open. A small voice spoke and he disappeared. She was already dressed when he returned, alerted by the urgency of his steps on the stairs. 'The Magdalena,' he said breathlessly.

So much blood was her first, panicked thought. She ground her teeth until they ached and then tapped into a pool of calm at her core. 'Dorothea, the bag from my room,' she said and the nun vanished. 'You two,' she said, turning to the ashen girls cowering outside the door, 'go back to bed. I'll call by later when I've fixed Laura. Go now.' She took Karl's arm to steady her. 'Her waters have broken,' she said with forced calm. 'I need you to talk her back, Karl. Bring her back so she can push.'

He went to Laura as Dorothea returned with the medical bag. Dorothea wrung a cloth under the tap and took up a position opposite Karl at Laura's head. 'She bathes, you talk,' Sarah grunted as she spilled instruments from the bag. 'Her name is Laura Morton,' she added, 'and she … she comes from Chicago.' Her voice broke and she struggled to recover her calm. Dorothea washed blood from the girl's face with infinite tenderness. Every swipe of the cloth revealed terrible damage. Laura's face was swollen grotesquely and her nose appeared to be broken. Her eyes were closed and short, panicked breaths puffed from her open mouth. Dorothea hooked a finger inside Laura's mouth and fished out the broken stub of a tooth.

Karl found Laura's hand and held it in both of his. 'Laura,' he said in a clear voice, 'it's Karl Hamner, remember? The man who ran from the train.' Laura's eyelids twitched. He read it as a hopeful sign and squeezed her hand. 'You do remember,' he said. 'I lifted your bag down from the rack and you told me who you were. You said, "I am—"'

Laura opened her eyes. 'I am Laura Morton,' she slurred through swelling lips, 'from Chicago.'

'Push, Laura,' Sarah commanded. 'Karl, brace her,' she added, and Karl eased the panting girl into a sitting position. He sat behind her and locked his hands on her shoulders. Sarah felt panic rising inside her. There was so much blood and Laura lapsed in and out of consciousness. She considered the array of instruments strewn on the bed and—

'Trust your hands, Sarah Walker.'

Her head snapped up as if her old mentor had spoken right beside her. 'Instruments are just extensions of the hands, Sarah,' Professor Green had said. 'Sometimes you gotta bring a baby into the world with just hands and heart.'

She could hear Karl whisper in Laura's ear and drew comfort from the warmth in his voice. Laura arched her body and groaned and a tiny scalp appeared. 'That's it, honey,' Sarah called, 'keep pushing, sweetheart.' Nothing in her life ever matched the thrill she felt when a new baby eased into the world. She checked his airways, tied off and cut the cord with the efficiency of long practice. 'Dorothea, down here,' she breathed and passed the baby into the sister's care. 'He's perfect, Laura,' she said encouragingly, as a thin cry came from the bundle in Dorothea's arms. Laura strained and Sarah delivered the second male infant while Dorothea cleaned up the first baby. Sarah deliverd the afterbirth and joined Karl at Laura's side. It was the first chance she'd had to examine Laura close up. 'Karl,' she gasped and his steady eyes held hers.

'Sarah is here, Laura,' Karl said.

'Sarah,' Laura whispered. 'Babies?'

Dorothea passed the babies to Sarah and she held them up close to Laura's face.

'See, honey,' she whispered, 'your boys.'

'Are ... are?'

'Perfect,' Sarah assured her.

'Beautiful.' The effort it cost Laura to say that word and the wonder in her voice broke Sarah's heart.

'Your beautiful boys,' she said brokenly. 'You're their momma, Laura Morton from Chicago.'

Laura's eyes glazed and refocused with anxiety. 'He ... take them.'

'No way,' Sarah said. 'They have a momma now and—'

Laura's eyes widened and waited for her friend's eyes to meet them. Sarah Walker recognised what some doctors saw just once in a lifetime's medical practice, the accepting and grateful look of a patient who senses death's arrival. 'No way,' she repeated fiercely.

'Promise?'

'I ... we promise,' Sarah said, and Karl shifted beside her so that Laura could see them together. Laura Morton's ruined face relaxed and she sighed.

Sarah felt hands either side of her face and blinked Dorothea into focus.

'Sarah,' the nun said, 'Laura is gone.' Sarah tried to twist her head away but Dorothea held her firmly. 'No one could have saved her, not even you, *cara*,' Dorothea said gently. 'And you are a true dottore.' She leaned up and kissed Sarah on the forehead. 'Now,' she added, 'you must say goodbye to Laura and go.'

'Go?'

'They will come for her sons,' Dorothea said firmly. 'The Fratres.'

Karl held Sarah as she looked at her friend's face. 'Come,' he said. Dorothea fussed with the babies and finally they were ready.

'Wait.' Sarah rushed to the wardrobe and fumbled through Laura's meagre stock of clothing. 'I'm ready,' she said and took one of the infants from Dorothea. Karl had the other cradled in his right arm.

'Where are we going?' she asked but a look from Karl silenced her.

'San Clemente,' he told the driver when they reached the car.

'Karl, won't he tell?'

'Perhaps,' he whispered as they sped away from the Magdalena. 'It doesn't matter. They'll find us, sooner or later.'

SAN CLEMENTE, ROME

'I always said you were a dark horse, Karl Hamner,' Father O'Donnell said when he saw the baby in Karl's arms. His eyes widened when Sarah emerged from behind Karl. 'Two babies, by God,' he breathed.

'We don't have time, Father,' Karl said and shouldered by him. 'The Fratres will be coming soon,' he added when they had reached the refectory. 'We need to find a sanctuary for the babies.'

'And who, exactly, are the little lads?' the Dominican enquired. His eyebrows climbed into his hair as the story unfolded. 'Settle down,' he said. 'I need to send for Canice and I need to make a telephone call. Within minutes, he was back with Father Canice, the canon lawyer. 'Repeat your story, Karl,' he said, taking the baby from Karl and retreating to sit beside Sarah at the far end of the table.

'We can't go on meeting like this, Doctor Walker,' he whispered and she tried to smile. 'Listen up now, girl,' he said, suddenly serious. 'We can delay the Fratres but I don't think we can stop them. I've made a call. There's a Sister Catherine in the Irish College just up the road a ways. She ... she arranges adoptions,' he said and saw Sarah's face fall. 'You and Karl are marked,' he said gently. 'Steiger will hound you at every turn. If ... if the little lads are ever to have any kind of normal life, it'll have to be well away from Rome. I'm sorry, girl,' he sighed, 'but that's the truth of it.'

'But ... but Karl—'

'I know,' he nodded, 'he's Austrian and stubborn as they come. He'll listen to you, Sarah.'

A buxom, pleasant-faced nun arrived soon after and took charge of the twins while Sarah huddled with Karl out of earshot of the others.

'No,' Karl protested, 'we can—'

'Karl,' she interrupted, holding his face in her hands. 'The priest is right. You know what Steiger is capable of.' She spoke for a long time before he nodded. 'Can we hold them?' she asked Father O'Donnell. They held the babies in their embrace until the Dominican said, 'It's time.'

They sat in silence at the refectory table until the Dominican returned with the Maltese Brother. 'Quickly now,' he said. 'Roberto will guide you out. It's best we don't know where you're going.' Impulsively, he hugged the young couple. 'Remember what I told you, Karl,' he said, gruffly. 'A great girl like that ...'

The pounding on the San Clemente door drowned his voice and spurred them to follow Brother Roberto. The passageway sloped under the church and they hurried to stay in the glow of Roberto's lantern. 'Down here,' he whispered and disappeared through an opening in the floor. *Fourth-century Christian church*, Karl registered as they skirted crumbling walls and descended even lower. *Mithras*, he thought as the lantern light washed over an inscribed altar, *favourite God of the Roman legions who'd brought*

the cult from the east. He knew he was keeping the pain at bay.
There would be time to deal with that later, he assured himself. The
lantern wove this way and that through catacombs serrated with
niche tombs. Bones encrusted the slits in the walls and occasionally
the light swept across a skull, spilling shadow from the eye sockets
as if the dead marked their passage. At last, Roberto stood before a
massive door. 'Outside is an alley that leads to the Via Labicana,' he
whispered. He turned the key and edged the door open. 'Go with
God,' he said, and they stepped into the night.

The Dominican took a long measuring look at the two men at
the other side of the refectory table. Father Leo looked like an
administrator or a scholar of one of the dustier areas of theology.
Probably a half-arsed canon lawyer, he mused and shifted a guilty
glance at Father Canice who sat beside him. *Canice is a canon
lawyer, but not a half-arsed one*, he thought grimly. The other
cleric was squat and swarthy and smelled of violence. He'd been
introduced as Barth – no prefix of 'Father' or 'Brother'. *Brute, more
like*, O'Donnell thought and begged God's forgiveness for his lack
of charity. No child of God should be dubbed a brute but he was
willing to make an exception in Barth's case.

'We have reason to believe that you gave sanctuary—'

'Believe,' Canice interrupted the Fratres priest. 'Come, Father
Leo, the word of another is deemed hearsay. Hearsay is hardly a
sufficient basis for belief.'

The tall priest glowered and cleared his throat. 'It is only logical
to assume they came here,' he insisted. 'Father Superior,' he appealed
to O'Donnell, 'surely you understand that the illegitimate child of a
Fratres Novice should, under the circumstances, be restored to the
care of that order?'

'I'm no canon lawyer,' O'Donnell said gruffly, 'but I have a few
things to say about that. The first is that there are no illegitimate

children, Father, only illegitimate parents. The second is that given that this girl was impregnated while a Fratres Novice, wouldn't it be reasonable to assume that she was abused by someone within the Fratres? If,' he said, raising a hand to forestall an interruption, 'if we can assume that, then surely we must assume that a Fratres house is no fit place for a novice.'

'We will appeal to the Vatican,' Leo said ominously. 'We are not without influence.'

'That is your right, Father Leo,' Canice said equably. 'However, I doubt very much if the Vatican would wish to become involved. Think of it, Father, a canonical tribunal of investigation into the circumstances of the girl's pregnancy and her eventual death at the hands of a Fratres Sister is hardly something Father Steiger would desire. And, of course, there is the Italian police to consider.'

'The police?' Leo faltered.

'Of course, Father. Ever since the Concordat with Mussolini, all crimes committed outside the Vatican walls must be investigated by the Italian police. I imagine the police have already been summoned to the Magdalena. The matter gets really complicated when you factor in the Americans. Laura Morton was an American citizen.'

'But she left America to join the Fratres.'

'One certainly renounces the world to enter religious life,' Canice said smoothly, 'but I have yet to meet a religious who also renounced their citizenship. It's not required, Father Leo. The American embassy will show a keen interest in this matter, I assure you.'

'So, you refuse to assist us in determining the whereabouts of the child and of this Doctor Walker?'

'Who mentioned a child?' O'Donnell snapped. 'This is another assumption, Father Leo. As to the whereabouts of Doctor Walker, why don't you enquire at the American embassy?'

The tall priest stood up from the table. 'So be it,' he said. 'If you will not assist us then the consequences—'

'Are you threatening me?'

'No, Father Superior. The Fratres do not threaten – we act and you will rue that fact.'

'I'm trembling already.'

'Our message for Doctor Walker is a simple one. Stay not too long in Rome.'

'What was all that about?' O'Donnell asked when the door slammed behind the emissaries.

'Oh, canon law is quite clear when—'

'No, Canice, not that stuff. The last thing he said puzzles me.'

'Actually, I think it refers to a conversation Octavius had with a senator who thought he was being too ambitious and said, "Stay not too long in Egypt, Antony." Supposedly, Octavius replied, "Stay not too long in Rome."' Canice rubbed a spot between his eyebrows before continuing. 'Octavius was ambitious, Hugh. He wanted the empire and nothing was going to stand in his way. I think Doctor Walker has been threatened by Max Steiger and we would be very foolish to take that lightly.'

THE SAN GIROLAMO, ROME

Brother Cyprian tapped on the door and waited.

'Come.'

Steiger was preparing for yet another press interview and didn't look up from the desk.

'Stefan Nagy has offered to assist me, Father General,' Cyprian said. 'I asked him to come at ten.'

Steiger fixed him with a flat stare. 'It is customary to ask permission before rather than after, Brother,' he said caustically. His head dipped to the papers again. 'I suppose we can find some use for Siri's *zek*,' he grudged, stuffing papers in a briefcase. 'I'll be at the Vatican Bank until mid-afternoon.' He waved his hand dismissively.

Brother Stefan, as Cyprian automatically thought of him, was industrious and efficient. He seemed to have an intuitive grasp of what was needed and anticipated without being presumptious. Most importantly, from Cyprian's point of view, he was blessedly quiet. In the absence of Father General, Cyprian took him on a quick tour of Steiger's office and was impressed by his attention. At noon, he ordered lunch from the kitchen and they shared it in companionable silence. For once, it was Cyprian who spoke first.

'What exactly is a *zek*, Brother?' he enquired.

Stefan answered simply and concisely and continued chewing in that slow, methodical manner. Cyprian's brain reeled at what he'd heard.

'What happened in the event of an escape?' he asked when he could muster enough breath.

'A lucky *zek* would be found by villagers and returned for a bounty,' Stefan answered.' An unlucky one would be run down by the dogs.'

Cyprian realised his mouth was hanging open and he dabbed it quickly with his napkin.

'But, you ...?' he began and was unsure how to complete the question.

'I was very lucky, Brother,' Stefan said with a small smile. 'I swam to Finland. Some more water?'

After lunch, Cyprian asked him to file some papers while he tidied Steiger's office. The mayhem in the office appalled him and Steiger's absence was an opportunity to put it right. After mid-afternoon coffee, he declared a break. 'I like to visit one of the churches in the city,' he told Stefan. 'You may accompany me if you wish.'

Cyprian found the company of Brother Stefan made Rome seem less aggressive. Mostly, they walked in silence. Sometimes, Cyprian ventured a snippet of information about a monument or an observation about the city and its people. He confessed to being oppressed by the bustle and noise of city life. They rested on a bench in the Piazza Navona. Pigeons strutted around their feet, like self-important monsignori, Cyrprian thought uncharitably. Hawkers shouted their wares from ramshackle stalls that filled the open spaces between the fountains.

'I remember when I was taken from the prison,' Stefan said. 'I was overcome by the verve of everything.' He took a crust of bread from his pocket and crumbled it for the pigeons. 'I wanted my cell and the silence and the security of knowing that tomorrow would be exactly like today.'

'Do you miss it?'

'The silence, yes,' Stefan answered, shooing an ambitious pigeon from his arm. 'The cell – no.'

'I usually visit the San Luigi dei Francesi when I come to the Navona,' Cyprian said, as they strolled from Bernini's Quattro Fiume past the obelisk in the centre of the piazza. 'There are Caravaggios in the Francesi,' he added. 'Would you like to see them?'

The Calling of Saint Matthew hung in a side chapel. Where the Christ appeared in the painting was almost stark in its simplicity. The other half seemed crowded with people, Matthew among them.

'How difficult it must be to step away from riches,' Cyprian murmured.

'Even a *zek* can be rich,' Stefan said quietly. 'A *zek* can barter socks for a shiv or a spare vest for a lump of lard. A *zek* can own things, even other *zeks*. Anyone can make a gulag within the gulag.' He shook his head as if he'd surfaced from a pool. 'I'll leave you to your prayers, Brother,' he said. 'You'll find me with the dolphins.' He bobbed his customary bow and faded into the shadows. Cyprian stared at the Caravaggio. 'Have I exchanged my cell for a gulag?' he pondered and tried to pray.

As Stefan approached the fruit stall before the Sant'Agnese Church, he slipped a folder from the deep pocket of his cassock. A man turned from the stall and bumped the Brother. '*Mi dispiace*,' he apologised. 'I'm sorry.'

They both bent to retrieve the items they'd dropped in the collision. 'A *zek* should look where he's going,' Fyodor whispered in Russian.

'A *zek* should go where he's looking,' Stefan replied.

'*Mi dispiace*,' Fyodor repeated loudly and hurried away.

Cyprian watched the young man sitting near the fountain. Stefan seemed oblivious to the shouts of the stallholders or the screams of children who rushed to touch the lip of the fountain and retreat before the wind shifted the spray and soaked them. *He looks like a Bernini afterthought*, he mused, *like one of the bees he carved into the Fontana delle Api for the Barberini pope.*

'You bought fruit,' Cyprian said.

'A *zek* barters, Brother,' Stefan said.

ENRICO'S RESTAURANT, TRASTEVERE, ROME

When Karl came back from the telephone, Enrico listened to the story. Sarah had been spirited away by the women and the two men sat in the small parlour.

'I'm sorry, Enrico,' he concluded. 'I knew they'd follow but I didn't know—'

'No,' Enrico interrupted 'no apologies, please. You came to us in our trouble.'

'But—'

'And where else would a son in trouble go but to his parents. Let them follow, Karl,' he said, 'we will never hide in the cellars again.'

When Sarah returned, her bloodstained clothes had been replaced with a simple blue dress supplied by Mama.

'You sure know how to show a girl a good time,' she said when they were alone, but he didn't smile.

'I called Father O'Donnell,' he said and reached for her hand.

'That bad, huh?' she said in a small voice, and he nodded.

'The Fratres want your silence,' he said bluntly. 'They want you to leave Rome and go to Ethiopia.'

'And what do we want, Karl?'

'It's not what we want, Sarah. It's what the Fratres are willing to give.'

'And what's that?'

'Your life, Sarah,' he said and his eyes were haunted.

'I could go to the US embassy,' she said. 'We could—'

'No, Sarah,' he said. 'They will know. You'd have to stay there or go to America. Max Steiger has powerful friends in America – friends who don't want him exposed.'

'This is America we're talking about, Karl, you know? The land of the free and the home—'

'Sarah.' He waited until her eyes met his. 'It would be an accident – not tomorrow or the day after but some day. You would walk out of a restaurant or be driving to the hospital and … I know them, Sarah.'

'But Ethiopia means I'm not here, with you.'

'Ethiopia means you're alive, Sarah. While you live, there's still hope for us.'

A tap on the door disturbed the silence that had settled on them. Mama entered with a tray and stood over them until they had eaten something. Karl excused himself and went to use the phone. When he returned, Sarah was alone.

'I've spoken to Cardinal Tisserant,' he said and she nodded. It was much later when the telephone rang again. She looked at his face when he returned from the hallway.

'When?' she asked.

'Tomorrow.'

SAN GIROLAMO, ROME

'Setting up your own Subiaco, Brother Cyprian?'

Cyprian understood Steiger's taunting allusion to the early Benedictine monastery and his growing friendship with Stefan. He chose to ignore it.

'Our dear Monsignor Kamf decided to leave us,' Steiger said

lightly, 'through the sewers. Appropriate, wouldn't you agree, Brother?'

Steiger's tone sawed at Cyprian's nerves. He breathed deeply and tried to think of bees. 'Be you hot or cold,' Steiger continued, mangling the scripture text, 'but if you are insipid, I will vomit you out of my mouth. Insipid and blank, Cyprian – you and that mute *zek*. Take a leaf from the book of Brother Barth, Cyprian,' he whispered, raising a cautionary finger before the monk's face. 'Brother Barth is an avenging angel,' he continued, wagging his finger from side to side. 'He is the Hound of Heaven who sniffs out the insipid and the vacillating and – strikes.' Steiger stabbed his finger painfully into Cyprian's chest and the monk jumped. 'Clean up those files,' he said and left.

'Are you upset, Brother?'

'No … yes.'

'Why don't you sit by the window?'

'I can't. He wants his files tidied and—'

'Leave that to me, Brother.'

When Stefan emerged from the office, he joined Cyprian at the window.

'What do bees do when they're threatened?' he asked.

'Bees? They, eh, defend the hive.'

'And if they can't do that?'

'They swarm to some other place until it's safe to return – or they find a new place to settle.'

'Would you like to swarm, Brother Cyprian?'

'Oh, God.' Cyprian put his face in his hands and kneaded his cheeks. 'This is such an angry place.'

Stefan tapped him lightly on the shoulder. 'Come.'

The taxi grunted up the Janiculum Hill and stopped at the Garibaldi monument. Cyprian stood in the sunshine and took the deepest breath he'd taken since coming to Rome. It tasted and smelled of pine needles. Looking down on the city, he understood why men who sought God favoured high places. The inscription on the monument snagged his attention as they walked by. '*Roma o Morte,*' it read. 'Rome or Death.' He wondered if the Latin *o* should be replaced with *et* so that it would read 'Rome and Death'. The chill of that thought left his bones when they entered the Corsini Gardens. He strolled in a daze along paths bordered by flowers and shaded by trees. He stopped suddenly and looked up in amazement. 'Is that—'

'A sequoia,' Stefan confirmed.

An hour passed. For Cyprian, it was a period of peace that refreshed his soul. The old guilt threatened to distract him with thoughts of all he had to do and all he'd left undone in the San Girolamo, until he remembered the abbott's counsel. 'A monk too busy to take time for beauty starves his soul.'

Stefan finally steered him to the tiered fountains and insisted he rest. 'I'll go and keep an eye on Rome,' he said and disappeared along the path.

Fyodor stepped from behind a palm. 'They say the *zeks* are coming home,' he said with a grin.

'Where is home for a *zek*?' Stefan answered. It wasn't the agreed response but Fyodor didn't react.

'The ambassador is very pleased,' he said as he slipped the folder inside his coat.

'That should please him even more,' Stefan said. 'It's the last of it,' he added. 'Steiger is mad, not foolish.'

'Plenty of room in the embassy,' Fyodor said.

'No,' Stefan said. 'This time, I'll choose my own gulag.'

TRASTEVERE, ROME

Barth was hunting.

It had been so long since he'd hunted that his body tingled with anticipation. He remembered the excitement of the old days with the pack – the thrill of picking up the scent or spoor of Jews in Russia, as the pack coursed in the wake of the Wehrmacht. How the regular soldiers had despised them. Waffen, they spat but never too loudly and never too close. *Well, a stupid man will kick his dog*, he mused as the bridge over the Tiber hunched in the dark. *He'll chain the dog to a post outside and sleep safely in his bed only because the dog will be awake and watchful.*

His Waffen pack had ignored the looks and words. They'd endured the place outside the camp. Endured? No, they'd savoured the distance from the domesticated dogs who barked and begged at some officer's command. *We were wolves*, he thought as the river rushed beneath his feet, *Waffen. We hunted Jews from the shtetls to the steppe to the forest and when we brought them down, we strung them up.* 'The Beast', the pack had called him – 'Barth the Beast'. He could scent a Jew from a day-old track and sniff to where he'd gone to ground. 'Come out, come out, little Jew,' he whispered as he crossed the bridge and padded through the shadows of Trastevere.

There were four of them. They ranged before an archway, blocking his path. *Cubs*, he thought and smiled. 'Back to your burrows, Juden,' he called mockingly, 'Barth the Beast has returned to the ghetto but not for cubs like you.' He felt elated when they turned tail and disappeared. He knew the burrow that hid Karl Hamner. Max Steiger had slipped his leash and set him on Hamner's trail. 'Don't kill Hamner,' he'd ordered. 'Follow, watch and report.' He was Waffen. There is no 'no' for Waffen. No one tells the hunter how to hunt. But this was Steiger – Steiger who had found him in the camp, Steiger who had saved him from the rope and brought him leashed to Rome. He could not disobey Steiger. If he disobeyed Steiger, he would be driven out, hunted down and hanged. Could he kill Steiger? No. Steiger had no scent, as if he was already dead. That thought chilled him back to the present. He couldn't kill Hamner but Hamner had a bitch. He stopped to sniff the air and savour that thought of killing.

The whistling started.

It seemed to come from his left, but when he cocked his ear that way, it echoed from the right.

'Juden,' he whispered, 'calling like frightened birds roosting in the dark when the wolf—'

The whistling came from the right and then the left and then it was all around him as he circled.

'I am Barth the Beast,' he roared. 'I have returned to the Jew burrow to smell out your sisters and devour them.'

He laughed manically, and the whistling stopped. Slowly, figures emerged from the dark, figures who multiplied until he stood in a ring of silent men.

'Waffen,' he barked and the circle rippled back a pace. 'Waffen,' he roared again and they surged forwards. They dragged him squirming into a pool of light spilled from a streetlamp and someone tugged his hair, twisting his head so that the light shone full on his face. A man's face came close and he growled.

'He is Barth,' the man said. 'I remember.'

They dragged him writhing to the bridge. 'I am Barth,' he shouted as they lifted him high and cracked his back upon the balustrade. When they toppled him over, he opened his mouth to howl but the water rose and took him by the throat.

San Girolamo, Rome

Time to swarm, Stefan thought. The screaming had gone on for some time and showed no signs of stopping any time soon. Max Steiger had stormed into the office and launched into a tirade. From what Stefan could glean through the door and open window, something had gone seriously awry with Steiger's plans.

A Sister Pilar had arrived in a dishevelled state, and had been shown in by Cyprian. As soon as the door closed behind her, the shouting had begun. It had escalated to screaming, Steiger and Pilar out-swearing each other and poor Cyprian caught in the storm. The door flew open and Steiger dragged Pilar from his office. Cyprian laid a restraining hand on Steiger's shoulder. Enraged, Steiger shook it off and turned on the monk.

'Enough,' Stefan said.

Steiger looked in amazement at the hand that gripped his wrist. 'Let me go,' he growled.

Stefan tightened his grip until Steiger's scars turned white against his livid face. He pushed Steiger back and placed himself between the enraged priest and Cyprian, who looked deathly.

'You,' Steiger snarled at Pilar, 'you are cast out.'

'*Puta*,' she spat and ran.

'You,' Steiger spun to confront Cyprian, and Stefan raised a cautionary hand.

'*Zeks* fight to the death, Father Steiger,' he said evenly. 'A leader who loses is hunted down. The pack is howling, Father Steiger. Can you hear them?'

Angry shouts reached up from below. Steiger rushed into his office and slammed the door. Stefan put a comforting arm around Cyprian's shoulders.

'Time to swarm, Brother,' he said.

The frantic state of Sister Pilar had not gone unnoticed. The men cooped below sensed a crisis that threatened to overturn the stone of the San Girolamo and expose what hid beneath. That, along with the screaming from Father General's office, was enough to ignite them to violence. Cyprian held grimly to the back of Stefan's cassock as he butted a path through the brawling men. A man in a torn cassock swung a blow that Stefan countered on his forearm before delivering a solid punch that sent his assailant to the floor.

THE VATICAN

'Tisserant,' Stefan said to the Swiss Guard. 'Stefan Nagy and Brother Cyprian.'

While the guard telephoned from the guard house, Stefan

nudged Cyprian and pointed at the crest above the great door of the basilica.

'It's the Barberini crest,' he said. 'Bees.'

'You asked to see me.'

'May we speak in German, Eminence? Brother Cyprian is Swiss.'

Tisserant nodded and gestured at the elderly man bundled in rugs by the window.

'My secretary, Monsignor Emil Dupont.'

'I think you should read this.' Stefan said and offered the folder to the cardinal.

'Why should I?'

'It's material from Max Steiger's files.'

The cardinal's hand moved forward and then withdrew.

'Why would you offer me stolen goods?'

'Because you sent brave priests to Russia as part of Operation Barbarossa. One was my friend in the gulag. Another was crucified. They trusted you.'

Tisserant paled. 'How do I know this is the truth?'

'A man who saw him crucified said his name was Theo, that same man took his cross and gave it to me.'

Stefan reached inside the neck of his cassock and lifted the gold cross from its hiding place. Tissserant's face seemed to age before his eyes.

'Look at the back, Eugène,' a thin voice quavered from the elderly monsignor. 'We had them numbered, remember? The list is in the red envelope, bottom drawer of your desk.'

The cardinal turned the cross over as he went to his desk.

'Theo Brandt,' he read, 'Archdiocese of Cologne. Requiescat in pace,' he murmured. 'May he rest in peace. Why are you doing this, Stefan Nagy?' he asked. 'What is Max Steiger to you?'

'It's not who he is but what he represents, Eminence,' Stefan said. 'You know I was a seminarian in Budapest. You must wonder how I got from there to a gulag, eight years later.'

'The thought did cross my mind,' Tisserant said dryly.

'Your mind?' Emil said, and laughed. 'Go on, boy,' Emil insisted. 'Tisserant is actually listening.'

'Mindszenty gave a high mass after the Jews of Budapest were deported,' Stefan said. 'I was asked to read one of the scripture readings. Instead, I asked the congregation why we were celebrating and if we didn't speak up for the Jews who would speak when the Nazis came for us? I was in solitary confinement for eight years.'

There was a collective gasp from the other men in the room.

'I was very young, Eminence,' Stefan continued. 'I spoke out against an injustice and the Church was politically embarrassed. After I was put in prison, I think the Church forgot me. Someone has to speak out against Max Steiger.'

He offered the folder to the cardinal for the second time, and Eugène Tisserant took it.

'Sit with Emil,' he instructed as he moved to his desk.

'This is Brother Cyprian,' Stefan said to the monsignor.

'Steiger's secretary,' Emil said, and smiled at their reaction. 'There are no real secrets in Rome,' he smiled. 'Except yours, Stefan Nagy.'

Stefan looked into the pale, intelligent eyes and smiled.

'What do you wish to know, Monsignor?' he asked.

'Who did you send copies to?' Emil asked promptly, and Cyprian gasped. Tisserant joined them before Stefan could reply.

'Is it sufficient?' Emil asked.

'Yes,' Tisserant said slowly. 'I think so.'

'Send for Siri and Montini,' Emil instructed. 'And send for our archangel,' he added.

While Tisserant spoke on the telephone, Emil turned to Brother Cyprian. 'Where does the Benedictine wish to go?' he asked.

'Back to my bees,' Cyprian said without hesitation.

Siri closed the file and placed it on the floor beside his chair as if he didn't want to handle it any longer than was necessary.

'Together with the material collected by Monsignor Montini,' he said, 'I think it should be enough to persuade His Holiness.'

Tisserant thought his brother cardinal sounded less than convinced.

'Do you agree, Giovanni?' Tissertant asked Montini.

The balding, young monsignor twisted his hands in his lap.

'The documents are sufficient cause for an inquiry,' he said cautiously, and Tisserant snorted. 'But,' Montini continued, 'an inquiry could go on for a very long time. His Holiness is unwell. He may not wish to embark upon such a lengthy and upsetting process.'

'Their eminences and I would like to confer privately for a few minutes,' Emil interjected smoothly. 'Would you gentlemen like to take refreshment in the anteroom?'

Stefan, Cyprian and a clearly miffed Montini bowed and departed.

'Emil,' Tisserant hissed, 'this is no time for—'

'*Ecoutez*,' Emil said with steel in his voice. 'You too,' he said to Siri and the snap in his voice straightened the cardinal's spine. 'There are copies in other hands,' Emil stated when he was sure of their full attention.

'How do you know that?' Tisserant demanded. 'Did Stefan admit to it?'

'No. But he didn't deny it. Eugène, listen to me,' he went on urgently. 'How does a seminarian find himself in a gulag? We questioned that from the start. How does he escape Karelia, cross the Gulf of Finland and find his way to Rome? Now, let us look at a parallel scenario. While Stefan serves his time in Fő Utca Prison, Stalin grows older and more belligerent. Waiting in his shadow are Beria, Malenkov and maybe Khrushchev, who plan a future without him. What do we know for certain?' He lifted a finger. 'We know that the USSR is a broken economy. Two' – a second finger joined the first – 'we know that Stalin wants another war and his top officials know it would annihilate the Soviet Union.

These are intelligent men. They know that Stalin can't last and they want a détente with the West because aid will follow. But there is something and someone standing in the way of that détente – the same something and someone who didn't stand in Hitler's way.'

'Pacelli,' Tisserant breathed.

'Pacelli and the Church,' Emil corrected. 'Standing against any rapport with the Communist East. The Soviets need a vulnerable spot in that obstructive logjam and a lever to shift it.'

'Steiger and the Fratres,' Tisserant said, 'are the vulnerable spot and Stefan Nagy is the lever.'

'About time,' Emil said in exasperation. 'They know about the Croatian money Steiger lodged in the Vatican Bank, but they can't prove it. They know that Steiger has friends in Washington as reactionary as himself. If the Russians had evidence of Steiger's malfeasance and could reveal it to the world, what then?'

'The scandal would rock the Church to its foundations,' Tisserant said.

'That scandal would split the rock, Eugène,' Emil insisted, 'and put the Church under a cloud of distrust for generations.' He turned his fierce gaze on Cardinal Siri. 'The maxim of the law is that silence gives consent, Eminence,' he said bluntly. 'I conclude your silence betokens you know about this. No,' he said sharply when Siri attempted to reply. 'I take it that you had good reasons and acted in good faith. But consider the implications. If the Church does not move to discipline Steiger before the Russians reveal the documents—'

'What do you suggest we do, Monsignor?'

It was the first time Siri had spoken.

'There are two things that must be done and one thing that should be done,' Emil said briskly. 'Your Eminences and Montini must present the evidence to the pope and press him for immediate action. In that way, we clean our own Augean Stables and steal the Soviets' thunder. Agreed?'

They nodded.

'And the second thing, Emil?' Tisserant enquired.

'We need to listen to the voice of someone who has suffered at the hands of Steiger.'

'Would this person give testimony before the pope?' Siri asked.

'She is dead, Eminence,' Emil said sadly, 'but her testimony survives her. You will have to decide if the pope needs to hear it.'

'Shouldn't we hear it first?' Siri asked.

'Yes,' Emil said. 'Will you call the others, Eugène? And fetch the visitor from outside.'

His Eminence Eugène, Cardinal Tisserant hurried to obey his secretary.

'"My name is Laura Morton,"' Karl read. '"I'm from Chicago."' His voice roughened on that line and he cleared his throat. '"I wanted to give my life to something good when my parents were killed in an automobile accident, so I gave my life to the Fratres."' As he continued, the innocent, trusting testimony of Laura Morton captured the attention of every man in the room. The details of the money she had signed over to the Fratres in Zurich brought frowns to many faces. As the tragic tale of her rape, pregnancy and expulsion from the order unfolded, some grimaced and others wept unashamedly. Sarah Walker's name, and Laura's affection for her, occurred and reoccurred in the final pages and Karl laboured to finish.

A profound stillness settled on the gathering. Montini broke the silence, speaking in an uncharacteristically firm voice.

'We will go to the pope,' he said.

CIA OFFICE, NEW YORK

'Still no word from Medusa, sir, should I organise a, er, search or something?'

'No,' the director said. 'If Medusa wants to be found, she'll be in touch. You know, Cy, with Medusa awol, I'd like you to handle her network.'

The young man did a good imitation of a small rabbit staring into the headlamps of a very large truck. 'Not the field stuff, of course,' the director added, and Cy rediscovered his ability to breathe.

'Er, yes, sir, if you really think—'

'I do, Cy. A helluva lot of work, though. Think you can handle that?'

'Certainly, sir.'

'Good. Still, work-life balance is important, Cy, keeps a man stable. Kinda hard to keep things on the level if there's no one to go home to. Know what I mean?'

Cy blushed and held the clipboard to his chest, like a shield. 'Well, er, sir, there's this girl I met and, er—'

'That's great, Cy. She an agency employee?'

'No, sir, absolutely not. It doesn't really work if the, er, person is in the agency, sir. Boundary issues and, er, she's from out of town; local rep with a clothing company – travels all over. Moved into my apartment building a few weeks ago – well, thirteen days ago to be exact. Kinda fortuitous, sir.'

'You could call it that.' The director nodded and walked to the locked filing cabinet. *Fortuitous we do well*, he thought, as he retrieved the code book. Elizabeth Swan was one of the brighter agents from the Cleveland office. Her report on Cy had been comprehensive and he'd skimmed over Cy's hobbies – 'biographies of powerful men'. Sexual orientation – 'heterosexual but inhibited' and all the other titbits that made up Cy. Occupation, he was pleased to see, was listed as 'researcher at the state department'. The temptation to impress the opposite sex with the agency connection was irresistible to some. It sometimes segued into pillow talk and that path led to Leavenworth Maximum Security Facility for a very long period of reflection. 'I'm going to encode a message, Cy,' he said, sitting at his desk, 'and I want it delivered to our man at State.'

'Yes, sir.'

'He'll reroute it to the embassy in Moscow and they'll see that it gets to Nikita Khrushchev.'

Cy was having respiratory problems again. In this 'need to know' world, he didn't need to know this level of detail unless … unless? *She's not coming back*, he thought and almost swayed with relief. *She's not coming back.*

'I think that should cover it,' the director said and pushed a slip of paper across the desk. Cy took the unprecedented step of putting his clipboard down before he picked up the message.

'I'll get on it right away, sir. You can count on me, Mister Director, sir.'

'I think I can, Cy,' the director responded.

He pushed some papers around until the door closed, then he laced his fingers behind his head and swung the chair to face the window. He'd keep the surveillance in place for another month, he decided. Sometime during that period, Agent Elizabeth Swan would terminate her relationship with Cy, citing his secretiveness and its inhibiting affect on his sexual performance. That barb could sting a guy like Cy into saying more than he should. In which case—

He stood up from his desk and went to the washroom. 'Cy is a good guy,' he assured his reflection as he shaved. 'He's got a bright future ahead of him at the agency – if he passed this test.' If he did, maybe some girl would come along who'd give him a home and kids and be content to believe that her husband 'worked for the government', and that he really was the man he said he was. Someday, maybe, he might be in a position to trust her with the truth. It had worked for him and Mary. She'd listened until he'd trailed away to silence. 'Okay,' she'd said, 'this is where we renew our marriage vows. You vow never to talk about what it is you do and I'll vow never to ask you. Agreed?'

They'd stuck to their vows, even when their boy had been posted to active duty in Korea and he could have pulled strings for a home assignment. And when he came back the way he was, there had never been any hint of recrimination. *One in a million*, he thought as he sluiced the basin clean. 'Long odds, Cy,' he admitted as he pulled the stopper.

TRASTEVERE, ROME

The black saloon car flying the papal flags drew stares as it negotiated the winding streets of Trastevere. Tisserant had delayed the delegation long enough to make the arrangements. Sarah sat at a table in the restaurant, surrounded by Enrico's family.

'It's time,' Karl said and they kissed and hugged her in turn. Mama and Elena clung to her until Enrico took her gently by the hand and placed her hand in Karl's. Paolo watched from his usual spot by the swing doors to the kitchen, his anxious eyes following Karl all the way to the door.

He held her hand in his as they journeyed out of Rome to the port of Ostia. She broke the silence just once.

'Did you read it, Karl?'

'Yes, I read it.'

'That must have been hard,' she sighed and squeezed his hand. 'Will they—'

'Yes.'

'My arms ache for her babies,' she said, and he folded her against him.

'What will become of them, Karl?' she asked, but he couldn't answer.

'And us?' she whispered. 'What will become of us?'

He stood on the dock while others waved and wept. He could see her standing at the handrail, fading sunlight glinting in her hair. The ship dwindled and the dock emptied and still he stood, unmoving.

When the ship veered to clear the lighthouse and disappeared, he raised his maimed hand and cried, 'Sarah.'

The gulls took up his cry and reclaimed the empty dock.

THE PAPAL APARTMENTS, THE VATICAN

It was Leiber who opened the door. On any other day, Tisserant would have been amused. Confronted with such an array of senior clerics, the poor man blanched.

'We will see His Holiness,' Siri stated and stepped forwards. Leiber retreated, flapping his hands frantically before him until his back struck the door of the pope's office. He scrabbled for the handle and slipped inside, attempting to close the door behind him. Siri blocked the door with his foot and the delegation followed the secretary inside.

'Holiness,' Leiber gasped, 'I couldn't … forgive me …'

'You may return to your desk,' Pacelli said softly. Leiber was already wheezing asthmatically before he reached the door and pulled it closed.

The pope had been signing documents. He blotted the document before him and cleaned the nib of his pen before replacing it in its box. Only then did he turn steely eyes on the intruders.

'Holiness,' Siri began, 'we apologise for this intrusion. The matter we've come about was too urgent to allow for protocol.'

The pope nodded almost imperceptibly.

'I have here a collection of documents sourced by the Secretary of State from various Vatican departments. They relate to financial transactions undertaken by Father Max Steiger. Also, I have documents from Father Steiger's personal files which—'

Pacelli silenced him with a raised hand. 'We do not read stolen documents,' he said frostily.

Siri returned his stare. 'Copies of these documents are being read in the Soviet embassy at this very moment,' he said.

The pope's eyes widened and he nodded.

'The documents from Father Steiger's files detail his dealings with the Central Intelligence Agency of the United States,' Siri continued. 'They also outline his actions on behalf of that agency throughout Europe. It is imperative that the Church act on this matter immediately.'

Tisserant wished that Siri had adopted a more conciliatory tone. Pacelli considered himself the avatar of Jesus Christ and didn't take kindly to counsel or opinion from his clergy. After a long, tense pause, the pope extended his hand and took the folders.

'You may sit,' he murmured and they retired to chairs on either side of the door.

Tisserant's eyes quested around the room for distraction. Pacelli's office was as Spartan and cold as a hospital waiting room. Everything was so neat and spare and functional that the cardinal began to feel big and angular and completely out of place. Montini suffered in silence beside him. He wondered how the gentle monsignor was coping and when their eyes met briefly, he was heartened by the determination he saw there. Siri sat upright and stoic to his other side. Finally Pacelli closed the folder and rested his forearms on the desk.

'We could initiate an inquiry,' he said uncertainly.

'Details would leak to the press, Holiness,' Siri said. 'Even if the inquiry was held *in camera*, this story would have scandalised the world before the ink had time to dry on recommendations from an inquiry.'

The pope seemed to hear just one word in that sentence.

'Scandal is something we must avoid,' he said firmly. 'We must not provide our enemies with ammunition.'

'But, Holiness,' Siri insisted, 'these are grave matters and—'

'If I may,' Tisserant interrupted. 'These documents deal with financial and political matters. We may lose sight of the fact that there are also people involved – many people who have suffered grievously. Your Holiness,' he continued, holding the pope's eye, 'some time ago, a young American lady pledged her life and fortune to the Fratres. She went to their headquarters in Switzerland to live the life of a novice.' He took the journal from his pocket and rested it gently on his lap. 'According to her journal,' he continued, 'she was raped and impregnated by Father Steiger.'

Pacelli's face tightened and he sat upright in his chair.

'When her condition was discovered,' Tisserant resumed, 'she was expelled from the novitiate and brought to the Magdalena in Rome.'

He paused as the pope leaned forwards.

'This could be discounted as some form of female fantasy or as a result of a mental derangement,' the pope said.

'There are witnesses to her condition and sanity, Holiness,' Tisserant countered. 'A Sister Dorothea has records of her admission to the Magdalena, naming her sponsor as the Fratres. She was attended by a Doctor Sarah Walker, an American obstetrician, who confirmed her pregnancy. She arrived in the company of a Fratres Sister, a Sister Pilar, who stayed in the Magdalena during her confinement and whose assault on her led to the novice's death. Sister Pilar's whereabouts are unknown but her detention should not prove too difficult. This would inevitably lead to a trial. I have depositions from the American doctor and Sister Dorothea if you wish to read them.'

The pope had grown more and more horrified as Tisserant had recounted the story. He waved his hand weakly. 'If this is true,' he said, 'it is a great sin. That a priest would—' Words failed him and he dropped his head in his hands. When he raised his head again, he had recovered his composure.

'We recommend our brother, Cardinal Siri, take whatever action he deems appropriate in this matter,' he said tonelessly. 'As mentor of the Fratres, His Eminence is ideally placed to evaluate the culpability of those involved and the nature of the consequences that may arise from their actions. His Eminence will also take into account the potential for scandal among the faithful and the damage that may be inflicted on the Church's good standing, throughout the world. We have every confidence in His Eminence and wish him God's blessing. Go in peace.'

CARDINAL TISSERANT'S APARTMENTS, THE VATICAN

'Vintage Pacelli,' Emil crowed.

Tisserant and Siri sipped their cognac in silence.

'You Three Magi arrive unannounced and determined,' Emil continued. 'What is the pope to do? Should he summon the Swiss Guards? Prepare to be defenestrated? There are precedents,' he insisted when Tisserant snorted. 'Pacelli was nursed by his predecessor. He was weaned in the Vatican. And so he listens carefully to the cardinal's presentation. He expresses appropriate outrage at the wrongdoing. No,' he said as Tisserant opened his mouth to protest, 'I'm not being cynical. I don't doubt that Pacelli was genuinely moved by that poor girl's story and horrified by the treatment she suffered at Steiger's hands. But ... what to do? Action must be taken immediately to forestall the Soviets. You made that very clear,' he said, nodding approvingly at Siri. 'But what sort of action and by whom? The "whom" is you,' he told Siri. 'It's your football, as the Americans say, you run with it. That passes for delegation in Pacelli's mind. And then the caveats. If I can reduce all the folderol to simple language, it goes like this: he expects you to protect the Church – that's the bottom line. Stalin did it with Molotov after Operation Barbarossa, putting him before the microphone to be the bearer of bad news. So Molotov becomes synonymous with the catastrophe and Stalin carries on with the war.'

'That's very heartening to hear, Monsignor,' Siri said dryly.

'I wasn't finished,' Emil said tartly. 'You must do this without anyone finding out.'

'What do you suggest I do?' Siri asked.

'What have you done already?'

'We've made contact with Laura Morton's parish priest, a Father Reilly. He's flying in tomorrow to take her home.'

'And the *polizia*?'

'I've told them this is a crime committed on Italian soil. The Vatican will guarantee full co-operation with the investigation. Also,

I've spoken to the US ambassador. He's satisfied with our statement to the *polizia*. Now, Emil, what do I do about Steiger?'

'No one can answer that question,' Emil said. 'But from what you've told me, I think Pacelli made a mistake. Cardinal Siri of Genoa is no Molotov.'

THE ROOM OF THE SEGNATURA, THE BELVEDERE PALACE, ROME

For the first time in his life, Tisserant was early. *Siri has done well*, he thought as he paced the empty room. The Room of the Segnatura was where a special council met in days gone by to sign documents. Not exactly awe-inspiring in itself, but the room was more than a bureaucrat's back parlour. Pope Julius II, the Warrior Pope, had raised his visor long enough to commission a young man to paint it – and not just any young man. Raphael had worked his magic on the frescoes in this room, even putting the faces of da Vinci, Bramante and Michelangelo in the frame. *Clever*, Tisserant thought, *soften the sting for those who didn't get the contract. I'm distracting myself*, he confessed. *I'm worried about Emil and when I see Steiger I know I'll get angry. Emil says I shout when I'm angry. I will not shout. I may raise my voice a little—* Montini and Siri entered and the trio took their places behind the polished table.

Max Steiger entered the Segnatura as the great bells of the basilica heralded the hour. *Like the leader of some imagined host*, Tisserant thought, *wearing his livid scars like a badge of honour*. There was no chair for Max Steiger.

'Father Steiger,' Siri began in a dry, emotionless voice, 'you are charged with accepting monies from the intelligence agency of a foreign state and of using the personnel and resources of the Fratres to work on their behalf. How do you plead?'

'I do not plead,' Steiger answered scornfully. 'Neither do I admit or confess. To do so would be to admit to a crime. By my actions,

I allied the Church with the pre-eminent temporal power on earth. It was the alliance with the Emperor Constantine that won the Roman world for the Church at the Edict of Thessalonika. As to the second charge, did the Church not use that alliance to place Christians in positions of power throughout the empire?'

'Until, of course, the empire fell and the Church found refuge in Constantinople,' Tisserant said dryly.

Steiger reacted to the barb with a contemptuous silence. *Maybe Emil is right,* Tisserant thought. *Steiger thrives on confrontation. Anger is the fuel he feeds on and if that supply is cut—*

'You are also charged with the rape of a young novice in the care of your order,' Siri continued.

'A female fantasy,' Steiger said dismissively.

'Her pregnancy was no fantasy, Father,' Tisserant said mildly.

'She could have been impregnated by any one of a hundred men,' Steiger continued.

'Really?' Tisserant said in feigned amazement. 'It is your considered opinion, Father, that there are a hundred potential rapists in the Fratres?'

'I did not say that,' Steiger snapped. I … suggested that an immature girl, prone to fantasies, might seduce—'

'Except that her journal states very clearly that she was taken, against her will, and by you, Father Steiger.'

'Fantasy! Do you think I'd lower myself to have sex with a novice?'

'Are we to understand then that you would consider having sex with a sister in solemn vows? A sister more advanced in religious life?'

'You're putting words in my—'

'A sister such as Sister Pilar, perhaps?'

'Sister Pilar is clearly insane.'

'If you are so clear on that fact, Father, why did you appoint her as a companion to a pregnant novice during her confinement – an appointment that resulted in a murderous attack?'

'Sister Pilar would never testify against me.'

'The "clearly insane" would not be required to testify, Father Steiger, you must know that. What you don't know is that a number of other novices have declared, under oath, that you—'

'Lies,' Steiger said savagely, stung by Tisserant's relentless pursuit. 'Lies from the mouths of hysterical women. Are we re-enacting the Salem witch trials here, Eminence?'

'Yes,' Tisserant said, to Steiger's surprise. 'Yes,' he repeated. 'We would be re-enacting that infamous trial if the young women in question are also confessing to sexual encounters with warlocks and devils. But they are not, Father Steiger. They claim, under oath, to have had them with you. *You*, Father General,' Tisserant goaded, 'the charismatic leader of the Fratres and bannerman for the New Crusade.'

'And what of you?' Steiger shouted. Tisserant felt Siri tense and laid a restraining hand on his arm. 'You and you and you,' Steiger ranted, using his pointed finger to strafe the tribunal. 'You,' he said, reverting to Tisserant, 'you have frittered your life away, tilting at Pacelli's court and for what? To become Tisserant the Untouchable. Tisserant the bannerman for intellectuals and liberals, conspiring with your pet monsignor to keep those heretics from the flames. And you,' he roared, spearing Montini with his finger. 'A monsignor who is half a man and half a Secretary of State, a buzzing, bureaucratic fly. The world comes to cataclysm while you dither, my timid Monsignor. But come the day of my destiny you'll buzz too close and—'

Clap! The smack of Steiger's palms striking echoed in the room.

'Let us not forget our ... mentor,' Steiger said, savouring the word. 'Siri the Genovese, Saviour of the City. Siri the red cardinal, the Trojan Horse who'd bring the East inside our walls. I know you. I know you all as blind moles who burrow beneath our foundations.

When my day dawns, I'll see you paper-men burn to ashes on the bonfire.'

Siri waited for the echoes to die.

'By the authority invested in me,' he said, 'I revoke the status granted by His Holiness Pius the Twelfth to the Fratres.'

Steiger staggered as if he'd been dealt a physical blow. 'The pope will not sanction—'

'I am the pope here,' Siri thundered. 'There will be a root-and-branch examination of the Fratres carried out by officials from my department,' he continued. 'My department will co-operate fully with the Italian police in the investigation of these and other matters and have already provided them with copies of all documents in our possession.'

Steiger shrugged and turned to leave.

'I am not finished,' Siri said icily.

Tisserant noticed the two monsignori who had entered the back of the room. 'I remove you, Father Steiger, from your position as Father General of the Fratres. You will not return to the San Girolamo or take up residence in any religious community of Fratres. My associates,' he said, and Steiger turned his head at the approach of the monsignori, 'will escort you to the Carthusian Monastery at L'Aquila, where you will remain under strict supervision and available to the *polizia* at all times. This matter is ended,' Siri declared and closed the folder.

'How did Steiger become such a ... monster, Eminence?' Montini asked when Siri departed and they were alone in the Segnatura.

'He's not a monster, Giovanni,' Tisserant said tiredly, 'he's a man who did monstrous things. As priests, we must be clear about the distinction.'

'But he said—'

'Whenever I listen to Steiger, I hear a frightened boy. I think of him as a boy who was betrayed – betrayed by those who should have loved him.'

'I must go, Eminence,' Montini whispered.

'Then go in peace, Giovanni,' Tisserant said. *I should have kept some of that peace for myself*, he thought ruefully as he paced the empty room. He felt restless, as if something had been left undone – like a shutter left unlatched, that would bang throughout the night and spoil his sleep. He stopped before a portrait of Julius II, the bearded, warrior pope. 'This matter is ended,' Siri had declared. But was it? Had he witnessed the exorcism of Max Steiger? He looked at the bearded pope as if he might answer that question. Julius had vowed not to shave until Italy was rid of its last usurper. *He has a very long beard*, Tisserant thought.

Sheremetyevo airport, Moscow

'You are even more handsome than I remember,' the driver said and kissed him noisily.

'She said you—' Gregor began.

'I know what she said.' Stefan hadn't meant to snap. Saying goodbye to Cyprian had been difficult and Tisserant had been stubborn.

'You can go back to Hungary.'

'No, Eminence. I did not leave Hungary, Hungary left me.'

'At least let us accompany you to the airport.'

'Eminence, how would that look? The prodigal arrives in a Vatican limousine with a cardinal for an escort.' And just when he'd steeled himself to walk away from these good people, Tisserant had insisted he keep Theo's cross and had hugged him.

'We don't want to lose you, Brother,' he'd said huskily and kissed him Russian-style.

Gregor had been waiting in Sheremetyevo. Their greeting had been perfunctory. Fyodor had impressed on him the need to be low-key. 'You gave with one hand and took with the other, *zek*,' he'd said, smiling that indestructible smile. 'Everything worked out okay but things are tense at home.'

Things were tense between Stefan and Gregor. He wasn't happy with that but—

'Where do you want to go?' Gregor asked and Stefan told him.

'Are you sure?'

'I'm sure, Gregor.'

Gregor issued instructions to the driver and she rolled her eyes. 'Such a waste,' she grunted and slammed the car into gear.

Father Abbot stood framed in the archway, the shoulder of his habit already mantled with snow. When they embraced, he said, 'Fuck me' and began to cry. 'I thought I'd never see you again, you little bastard.' Gregor stood in the background, near the car.

'Do you want to say goodbye to Gregor?' the abbot asked.

He crunched through the snow as Gregor eyed him warily.

'Do you like Italian wine?' he asked.

'Yes … yes,' Gregor stammered.

'Send the car away and come inside. I have six bottles in my bag. Do you object to drinking wine from the Vatican cellars?'

'Maybe this one time, I'll make an exception,' Gregor said with a slow smile. 'Just to prove that it's inferior to Georgian wine.'

The abbot woke him before dawn. 'Come,' he said.

An honour guard of monks, chanting softly, led him to the church. As they neared, a swell of voices reached through the open door to claim him. Stefan was home.

ENRICO'S RESTAURANT, TRASTEVERE, ROME

Paolo sat in Karl's lap. He'd climbed up as soon as Karl returned from Ostia and refused to budge. While Karl and Enrico talked, Paolo picked thoughtfully at the shreds of the Wehrmacht glove.

'Does he still want to go?'

'Yes, Enrico sighed, 'it's all he talks about, Israel, Israel. What should I do, Karl?'

'I have no sons, Enrico.'

'What would your father have done?'

'My grandfather was a miner, my father a carpenter and I'm a historian. Does that answer your question?'

'Yes, I think it does. Sooner rather than later, I think. He's getting restless.'

'Shimon might be able to help,' Karl suggested. He lifted Paolo from his lap and set him on his feet. 'Would you like to go for a walk?' he asked. The boy looked doubtfully at the door.

'Outside?'

'Yes.'

'Will you hold my hand?'

'Yes.'

'All the time?'

'All the time.'

They stopped at the Tiber and Karl told him the story of the Isola and pointed to where the ancient Romans had built a stone prow to make the island look like a boat. They strolled home under the washing lines of Trastevere.

'Papa said you brought us to the island when I was little.'

'Yes, I did.'

'Will you tell me that story – sometime?'

'Whenever you wish.'

Julio's going away party threatened to become a two-day event. When the last of the guests had dragged themselves home, the family set everything to rights and sat together, over the wine that had survived.

'Tomorrow we sleep,' Enrico said.

'Tomorrow we go on a trip,' Karl said.

'To Ethiopia?' Paolo asked and the family glared at him.

'No,' Karl said and lifted him to his shoulders. 'Tomorrow we'll go on a long journey. It will take over a thousand years. Tonight, you are going to bed.'

THE KREMLIN, MOSCOW

Khrushchev wished he could have told Alexei what the message contained. They'd been at the railway station and Alexei had passed him the message through the carriage window, almost as an afterthought. 'The drunk from the American embassy,' he'd said, 'maybe he wants to defect.'

'We have a full quota of drunks at the moment,' he'd remarked dryly and Alexei was still smiling at the window when the train left the platform.

He'd read the message in the car and wished the American drunk had delivered it personally. They could have got falling-down drunk together and he might have been able to forget the contents of the message he'd tucked in his jacket pocket. He'd expected it, or something like it, but the slip of paper between his fingers stippled his arm with goosebumps. 'Two bears won't live in one lair,' his grandmother had liked to say. She had a Russian proverb to cover every eventuality. *It was apt*, he thought. *They'd divided the world and would survive so long as they stayed divided*. Stalin's war had been averted because they'd made an accommodation. *I wonder what proverb Grandmother would dredge up to cover the message in my pocket*, he wondered. *It would surely read something like 'one hand washes the other' or that other one about mutual back-scratching*. He didn't need the old babushka to remind him that gifts are exchanged between people and the powers that rule them. He fingered the paper slip one last time as the others filed into the room.

It's now or never, Khrushchev thought. *If it's never, I won't live to regret it.* He studied the faces of the men at the table, especially Molotov and Malenkov. Molotov looked even more sombre than usual. *He's wearing his hangman's face*, Khrushchev thought and suppressed a smile. Malenkov, he worried, was a different matter. Everybody knew whose dog he was. But would the dog bite the hand that fed it?

Pounding footsteps in the corridor outside intruded on his thoughts. The door crashed open and Beria bustled in, a fat briefcase clutched to his chest. Something in the faces around the table caused him to pause inside the door. A shadow of anxiety flickered over his face before his normal imperious expression returned. *What has he to fear?* Khruhschev mused. He and Malenkov had carved up Stalin's legacy before the body was cold. The puppet had inherited an empty title while the master had awarded himself the combined ministries of State Security and Internal Affairs – effectively placing him at the head of the Secret and State Police. He knew Beria controlled every guard in the Kremlin. It is we who have reason to fear. He held his breath as Beria's expression slid back to irritation and then to fear. *Took the bastard long enough to notice*, he thought. There was no vacant chair at the table. He saw Beria wrestle with that fact and with the implications.

'Wha … what—' he stammered and, before he could frame the question, Khrushchev was on his feet.

'There is only one item on the agenda,' he said. 'I propose that the cynical careerist and imperialist spy Lavrentiy Beria be dismissed from this council and expelled from the party immediately.'

Beria wheezed as if he'd taken a punch to the gut.

'What's going on, Nikita?' he gasped. He turned his dazed,

beseeching eyes to Malenkov, his mouth moving soundlessly. Malenkov dropped his eyes to the table.

'I vote in favour of the proposal,' Khrushchev said and raised his hand.

He experienced a heart-stopping moment until Molotov's hand rose and then the others. Panicked, Malenkov's hand flitted up before crashing down to press a button on the table. The doors burst open and General Zhukov, flanked by armed military officers, stormed into the room.

'Gag and hide him until nightfall,' Khrushchev directed. 'The Kremlin is infested with his collaborators.'

Once Beria was secured in a military compound, Khrushchev knew General Zhukov would cull those who had been closest to him. Beria, he vowed, would be the last to die. *Let him live with the certainty of it*, he resolved. He sat and scanned the faces of his ashen companions. 'Any other business, comrades?' he enquired. 'No? Then I'd like to discuss something not on the agenda.' He waited to see if they'd quibble about protocol, but the scene they'd witnessed seemed to have left them drained. 'The traitor Beria mishandled the DDR crisis,' he said bluntly. 'That debacle raised the confidence of our enemies and damaged that of our allies.'

'The DDR business was just a local bushfire, comrade,' Malenkov said dismissively.

'Sparks travel from the smallest fire, comrade,' Khrushchev said evenly. 'They find dry tinder and new fires catch and blaze until we fight fires on every front. No. We need a show of strength the likes of which has never been seen before, so that no one – ally or enemy – will ever dare question our commitment to the ideals and unity of the USSR.'

He paused to read their reactions. Molotov sat as impassive as ever, satisfied that he had saved Polina and revenged himself on Beria. Down the road, Molotov might flex his political muscle but he was yesterday's man, the dupe of the fascist Ribbentrop. No, Molotov is forever tethered to his past and Malenkov cowed by Beria's fate. It was he, Nikita Khrushchev, the party man and youngest man at the table, who had been David to Beria's Goliath. He felt the others look at him with a mixture of wary respect and fear. It was a good feeling.

THE ARCH OF TITUS, THE FORUM, ROME

The limousine sped out of Trastevere.

'Where are we going, Karl? Mama asked, reduced to whispering by the plush interior.

'A thousand years away,' Paolo answered solemnly.

'I have never been to the Forum,' Enrico confessed as they trooped through the entrance by the Regia to walk the Via Sacra. As they skirted the Temple of Vesta, Karl kept them distracted with historical titbits until they arrived at the Arch of Titus and pooled in the shadow of the massive arch spanning the flagstoned roadway.

'A thousand years ago,' he told them, 'your ancestors were led through this arch as slaves. They vowed never to walk under it again until they could return to their own country.' He took Julio by the arm and walked him to the mouth of the arch. 'You have a long journey before you to Israel, Julio,' he said, 'take your first steps here, as a free man returning to a free country. This is my gift to you.'

Julio looked at his father and Enrico nodded. To tears and applause, he marched proudly through the Arch of Titus.

They were resting on the steps of the Basilica Julia when Karl excused himself and walked away under the trees. He stood in the shelter of the canopy, watching the sunlight dapple patterns on the earth underfoot. '*Guten abend*, Herr Fischer,' he said softly and Claus Fischer materialised at his side. They stood together, watching Paolo scamper up and down the ancient stones.

'I'm sorry, Karl,' Claus said quietly.

'Thank you, Claus.'

'The boy goes to Israel,' Claus said after a pause.

'Yes, he wants to be a teacher,' Karl said.

'I'll keep an eye on him,' Claus murmured.

'I hoped you would.' Karl was distracted when Paolo jumped from a big stone and barrelled towards him. He fielded the boy and swung him up in his arms.

'Who were you talking to, Karl?' Paolo asked.

'A friend.'

'He's disappeared,' Paolo whispered.

'He's very good at that,' Karl said, and they walked back to join the others.

THE WHITE HOUSE, WASHINGTON

He read the coded message carefully, and read it again. His hands trembled as he folded it and placed it in the inside pocket of his jacket.

'Everything okay, sir?' Cy enquired anxiously.

'Yes and no,' he murmured.

'Meeting of the joint chiefs in thirty minutes, sir.'

His driver had him at the White House in five.

He waited on a chair by the door while President Eisenhower signed documents at his desk.

'That it, Henry?' the president asked.

'That's it, Mister President,' the aide replied, shuffling pages into a pile.

'Better run them by Nixon before they go,' Eisenhower said.

Good play, the director observed. Keeping a vice-president sweet wasn't easy. Most of the ones he'd known had either grumbled about being out of the loop or prayed fervently for the demise of the incumbent. Eisenhower had given Nixon responsibility for local politics and the shifty-eyed guy had taken to it with gusto. 'I like Ike', he remembered had been a popular slogan during the presidential election, simple and effective. *Just like the man*. Ike brought a pragmatism and energy to the White

House that Roosevelt had in his first term and Truman not at all. He and the president were not friends and never would be. The President of the USA and the Director of the CIA operated in two different worlds. *Like the different worlds we've come from*, he mused. He had been born into wealth and all the opportunities money afforded. Dwight Eisenhower had worked a dead-end job for two years to put his brother through college before taking his turn as a student.

'Mister Director,' the president said, offering his hand.

'Mister President,' the director replied and shook it.

'You ready to face the firing squad?' the president asked, with a hint of a smile.

'Some of the joint chiefs haven't fired a shot in anger for a very long time, Mister President,' the director replied. 'I'll take my chances.'

There were the usual 'housekeeping' items that fill up the first few minutes of any meeting and the director used the time to reconnoitre the brass in the room. General Omar Bradley sat at the president's right hand, in recognition of his unique five-star status. The British field marshal Montgomery had described him as dull, conscientious, dependable and loyal. *Faint praise indeed*, the director thought. He might have added polite and courteous. Bradley had been unique among the wartime generals in that he'd never given a command without adding the word 'please'. That might have marked him as weak for some, except that he'd fired a whole slew of under-performing officers as against General Patton's one. Bradley, he knew, was army to the marrow of his bones and not shy about criticising the readiness of the post-war US army. 'Couldn't fight its way out of a paper bag,' was one of his kinder observations. He'd also been publicly critical of the nuclear option, a stance that put him at odds with Ike.

The director's eyes shifted and focused on Air Force General Hoyt Vandenberg. The handsome flyer with the outgoing personality was everything Bradley was not. Eisenhower had been so irked by Bradley's self-effacement during the war that he'd sent the war correspondent Ernie Piles to write him up as 'The GI's General'. Vandenberg had already graced the cover of *Time* magazine, a fact that led some to consider him a lightweight. The director knew that Vandenberg's chestful of medals had been earned in a cockpit or banging heads together to get things done. Like Bradley, he fretted at the diverting of dollars from the conventional forces to the nuclear programme. And the navy? Navy's Admiral Fechteler had requested a supercarrier and got a nuclear submarine. He could tack either way in the nuclear versus conventional argument.

The new kid on the block sat at the foot of the table. The Marines had been invited late to this particular party. Marine General Shepherd Junior was the first Marine Commandant ever to sit on the Joint Chiefs Board, though the fact that his speaking rights were limited to matters of concern to the Marine Corps might cramp his style. *He's the wild card at the table*, the director judged before switching his attention to Frank Everest; the non-voting Director of the Joint Chiefs was a fair and broad-minded man.

He'd done his homework, it was time to play.

He'd sat beside a retired general once, at one of those interminable functions his position obliged him to attend. The old man confided an interest in Roman war tactics and a particular fascination with the impenetrable infantry phalanx. The director had already tried to anaesthetise the evening with a large shot of bourbon and asked the first question that popped into his head.

'So, how do you open that particular can, General?'

He'd regretted his flippancy as soon as the words left his mouth but the old man looked at him with something like approval.

'That's the only damn question worth answering,' he'd said. 'And here's the answer. When you come face to face with a Roman

Legionnaire, you turn to the man beside him and kick him in the nuts.'

'Pardon?' he'd said feebly, not sure if he'd heard right.

'You hard of hearing?' the old boy had asked tetchily. 'Listen up, son. Roman Legionnaires stabbed their short swords sideways – they protected their partner and held the line by stabbing sideways. You gotta do the same. When the partner goes down, it leaves a hole in the line until the next man steps up. If there's no backup, you got a rout.'

The story had been new to him and he'd remembered it. The brass in the room had probably learned it at their mother's breast. They were army, navy, air force and marines, but faced with a common enemy, and constrained by their respect for the Commander-in-Chief, they stabbed sideways. Incensed by the cuts in their budgets and the rerouting of millions to 'The Bomb', they avoided the real issue and attacked the Central Intelligence Agency.

'Its shadow army employs no conventional weapons and can't come up with hard facts to defend expenditure or hard evidence to prove its effectiveness.'

That was Bradley's sucker punch before the fight turned into a brawl. It was one against four and they lined up to take their shots. One cited the lack of warning provided by the agency before the DDR uprising while another decried the lost opportunity for an intervention by the conventional forces. They widened the front to include Iran and South America. To the clamour of their criticism, troops marched, planes flew and carriers sailed across the polished table as they played the military war games they might have won if they'd been given the money that had been wasted on an ineffective and expensive intelligence service – a service defending the US against an improbable nuclear war.

'The best way to win a nuclear war is to make sure it never starts,' Bradley stated, only for Vandenberg to up the ante.

'We could have gone all the way in Europe and Korea if we had better than a one-shot air force.'

Frank Everest had already taken shelter in some mental bunker. The president had found a spot on the ceiling that required his undivided attention. The director could have countered with the fact that Iran now had a pro-American Shah and the forces would have access to cheap gas to fly the planes and drive the tanks. He could have explained the strategy of financing an uprising in the DDR to strain relations between Ulbricht and Moscow and set a precedent for Hungary and Czechoslovakia. He could have stopped them cold with how the agency had eliminated Stalin and paved the way for détente and a nuclear freeze. He had all of that ammunition and couldn't fire a single round. The brass must never know how the secret war was fought. Theirs was the firepower that threatened, his was the warfare that worked. In the nuclear age, it was the spooks who fought the real war and the grunts who shadow-boxed. He said nothing. He sat and let the barrage blast right over his head. And when they'd exhausted their arsenal, he produced a slip of paper.

'Gentlemen,' he said, unfolding the single page and fixing his spectacles, 'today, August twelfth, the Soviet Union exploded a thermo-nuclear bomb at the Semipalatinsk test site in Kazakh SSR.'

The shockwave of that sentence stole the oxygen from his tormentors.

'The blast was six times more powerful than Hiroshima,' he read, 'the equivalent of four hundred kilotons of TNT.' He folded the message and placed it carefully in his inside pocket before removing his spectacles. 'Good day, gentlemen,' he said and left the meeting.

The president slipped into the Oval Office and sighed into his chair.

'You fight dirty, Mister Director,' he said, mopping his bald head.

'That's what I'm paid for, Mister President.'

'So, maybe you'd be good enough to share some new tricks with an old dog. What should I do now?'

'Find a scapegoat,' the director said. 'Throw him as a sacrificial offering to McCarthy and all the other reds–under–the–bed loons in the congress and senate.'

'Oppy?' Ike asked after a long pause.

'Yes. J. Robert Oppenheimer should have his security clearance stopped – today.'

'Anything more?'

You need to cut a swathe through government employees who are getting too pink for comfort. I'll have Cy send you a detailed list. It runs to thousands, Mister President.'

The president nodded. 'Maybe you can't answer this,' he said slowly, 'but I gotta ask. You got to Khrushchev, didn't you?'

'You're right, Mister President,' the director replied, 'I can't answer that. If I did, you'd know and could never claim you didn't. But there's something I can tell you. Roosevelt knew we had to go into the last war. He also knew there were isolationists all over the country, who'd burn him at the ballot box if he did. The Japanese solved his problem when they attacked Pearl Harbour. You want to stop a nuclear war by building an asrenal of nuclear weapons to confront the Russians and make nuclear war a non-option for us and for them. Mister President, Khrushchev has given you your Pearl Harbour.

Our war never stops, he thought, as he read the material Cy passed across his desk. 'Steiger is a busted flush,' he said. 'Freeze the money and burn the connections. No trace to us.'

'Yes, sir.'

'Where to, sir?' the driver asked when he came through at Idlewild airport. He told him and they crossed the city. She was sitting at the bedside reading a book to their comatose son.

'Why don't you go get a cup of coffee, honey? I'll be here.'

He marked the page and closed the book. For a long time, he sat staring at his boy. He hadn't prayed for a very long time and the psalm came haltingly. 'Though I walk in the valley of shadow,' he whispered, and stopped.

She came through the door as he was bending forward to kiss their son.

'It's what we do, son,' he said.

KARL'S APARTMENT, TRASTEVERE, ROME

Karl turned the page and scribbled notes on a pad as his eye ran down the text.

He'd walked with Paolo along the banks of the Tiber that morning – all the way to the Via della Conciliazione. They'd stepped to the edge of Saint Peter's Square.

'Did … did my parents come here? That time?' the boy had asked.

'I don't know, Karl had said.

'But you came here.'

'Yes, I came to see Cardinal Tisserant, to tell him about the *razzia*. You remember what I told you?'

'Yes, the *razzia* was when the Nazis came to take the Jews. Like my parents,' he'd added in a small voice.

'Yes,' Karl had said, 'like your parents.'

As the days passed, the questions had come more often. It was as if Paolo was filling the spaces inside himself created by the loss of his parents.

'Would you like to go inside the Vatican?' he'd asked.

'No, I would like some ice-cream, please.'

'Some day, when you'd like to,' Karl had said, as they passed the Ponte Sisto, 'I'll take you back to the Vatican to meet my friends.'

'The pope?'

'Perhaps, but Tisserant and Emil have better stories.'

He smiled as he remembered the gelati ring around Paolo's mouth and looked up at the tap on the door.

'Come in, Paolo,' he called, but it was Mama who came inside. He tried to read her face and failed. 'Is something wrong?' he asked.

She shook her head. 'No, my son,' she said. 'There is a letter, for you.' She pressed the letter into his hands and reached up to kiss him before leaving. The picture on the stamp was of a dusky, almond-eyed angel, and his eyes blurred. He laid the envelope on the table, held it steady with his left elbow and used his right thumb to open it. A faint smell of frankincense wafted from the letter. He read the greeting and waited until his eyes cleared before reading it again.

'Karl, my dearest love.'

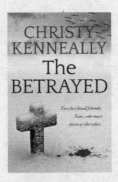

The Betrayed, *the first novel in the Karl Hamner and Max Steiger trilogy is available in all good book shops and as an ebook.*

Reading is so much more than the act of moving from page to page. It's the exploration of new worlds; the pursuit of adventure; the forging of friendships; the breaking of hearts; and the chance to begin to live through a new story each time the first sentence is devoured.

We at Hachette Ireland are very passionate about what we read and what we publish. And we'd love to hear what you think about our books. If you'd like to let us know, or to find out more about us and our titles, please visit www.hachette.ie or our Facebook page www.facebook.com/hachetteireland or follow us on Twitter @HachetteIre